The Dao of Drizzt

R. A. Salvatore

THE DAO OF DRIZZT. Copyright © 2022 by Wizards of the Coast LLC. All rights reserved. Printed in the United States of America. No part of this book may be used or reproduced in any manner whatsoever without written permission except in the case of brief quotations embodied in critical articles and reviews. For information, address HarperCollins Publishers, 195 Broadway, New York, NY 10007.

HarperCollins books may be purchased for educational, business, or sales promotional use. For information, please email the Special Markets Department at SPsales@harpercollins.com.

Harper Voyager and design are trademarks of HarperCollins Publishers LLC.

FIRST EDITION

Designed by Emily Snyder
Cover art by Tyler Walpole
Background image © stock.adobe.com/siam4510

Library of Congress Cataloging-in-Publication Data has been applied for.

ISBN 978-0-06-301128-1

22 23 24 25 26 LSC 10 9 8 7 6 5 4 3 2 1

It is only fitting that I dedicate this book to Drizzt—and, by extension, to all the characters who have become my sounding boards for these last four decades.

These are the guideposts of my trail. Writing is a journey. To look at it any other way is to shortchange the experience. Whether a journal, a piece of fiction, a term paper, a biography (auto- or not), a poem, a song, a tweet, a greeting card—for all of it, writing is, or can be, a journey.

Writing is self-indulgent, in the best sense of the word.

Writing is revelatory if you actually listen to your own words.

Writing is epiphanious (I know—I make up words). Not the Saint, but in the root of the name, for there is nothing more conducive to epiphany than the process of converting that which is in your mind and heart to tangible structure.

Writing is humbling, and not because of outside criticism, but because to go back and look at that which you have recorded is, in itself, revelatory, and a clear reminder to not be so damned sure of yourself, because you'll probably disagree with yourself soon enough!

When you read these books or this collection of Drizzt's essays, you won't know me. What you will see is my journey as I try to make sense of a world that rarely does.

So yes, thank you, Drizzt Do'Urden and all the other sounding boards. You helped me question most of all myself, and so you helped me grow.

—R. A. Salvatore

The Dao of Drizzt

INTRODUCTION BY EVAN WINTER, AUTHOR OF *THE RAGE OF DRAGONS*

Much of what I've learned and love about reading and writing, I took from the pages of books by R. A. Salvatore. For me, his were among the first stories I encountered that resisted being about little more than the conflict between "black and white" moralities.

Indeed, it was while reading his work that I began to understand the complexity that inevitably arises in societies composed of thousands if not millions of individuals, who all have their own interests, hopes, and dreams. In his books, the curtain that is culture was pulled back far enough for me to see how much the things we are taught—both explicitly and implicitly—affect the scope of the choices we are likely to make.

For a young man, it was heady stuff, and to have it woven inextricably with tales of action and adventure in places peopled by folk who felt as real to me as my friends and family was an extraordinary experience and feat. R. A. Salvatore gave me broad, bright, and deep worlds that helped me see my own more clearly, and I don't know how one can properly express appreciation or admiration for a thing like that, but in my own way, I'd like to try.

I've found that a common myth about literature and genre fiction is the belief that the former is more likely to treat the important concerns of the human condition. A value of literature, some might say, is that it reveals transformative significance that could have otherwise remained buried beneath the busy work of simple survival. However, and though I'm unlikely to read even one one-thousandth of the books that I'd want to, what I have read pushes me to resist that framing.

I say this because, more often than seems worthwhile, the findings from the exploration and explication of the human condition in lauded and proudly nongenre works is the subtle suggestion that a life best lived is one in which we mature enough to accept that we are too small to change our imperfect or even broken world. In too many of these stories, the protagonist's triumph comes from learning to find happiness by taking hold of and appreciating the best of what is within easy reach. Success, then—victory even—is finding solace or satisfaction in one's place and role in the world as it is, and from early on, we're taught and told that such stories, along with the lessons they subtly teach, are serious works. After all, they shed the hopeful but senseless dreams of adolescence to see (and show us how to see) things as they actually are.

But, is that really what they do? Are we being shown things as they actually are? Are the hopes we once held for lasting and positive change adolescent or are they revolutionary? Are they idle dreams or necessary ones?

I'm no longer a young man, but I remain unconvinced that victory, triumph, or a life lived best can be found in surrender. I think, largely, it's why I prefer genre fiction—particularly fantasy. In our books, resistance and revolution are almost always found. It's in our books where people like Drizzt Do'Urden refuse to relinquish their dreams for a better world.

Instead, our icons, though they may have been reared, cultured, and suffused by inequity, refuse to accept or thrive in it. And, journeying alongside them, we may begin to wonder how we could ever have been expected to do so either.

Repurposing G. K. Chesterton's well-known quote, let me say

that, in our preferred books, there's no realism or maturity in learning to live with cruel dragons. In the myths we make, we still hope to fight and defeat them.

So, as you travel with Drizzt through the following pages, hearing his thoughts and dreams, my wish for you is that his continual hope for better tomorrows helps you see our world in those terms too.

And to R. A. Salvatore, thank you. Without ever meeting me, you helped me fall in love with reading; you made clear the power and value that stories about other worlds have for our own; and your writing always encouraged me to think more deeply about what it means to be a good person.

Thank you. Thank you for it all.

The Dark Elf Trilogy

Homeland

Never does a star grace this land with a poet's light of twinkling mysteries, nor does the sun send to here its rays of warmth and life. This is the Underdark, the secret world beneath the bustling surface of the Forgotten Realms, whose sky is a ceiling of heartless stone and whose walls show the gray blandness of death in the torchlight of the foolish surface-dwellers that stumble here. This is not their world, not the world of light. Most who come here uninvited do not return.

Those who do escape to the safety of their surface homes return changed. Their eyes have seen the shadows and the gloom, the inevitable doom of the Underdark.

Dark corridors meander throughout the dark realm in winding courses, connecting caverns great and small, with ceilings high and low. Mounds of stone as pointed as the teeth of a sleeping dragon leer down in silent threat or rise up to block the way of intruders.

There is a silence here, profound and foreboding, the crouched hush of a predator at work. Too often the only sound, the only reminder to travelers in the Underdark that they have not lost their sense of hearing altogether, is a distant and echoing drip of water, beating like the heart of a beast, slipping through the silent stones to the deep Underdark pools of chilled water. What lies beneath the still onyx surface of these pools one can only guess. What secrets await the brave, what horrors await the foolish, only the imagination can reveal—until the stillness is disturbed.

This is the Underdark.

There are pockets of life here, cities as great as many of those on the surface. Around any of the countless bends and turns in the gray stone a traveler might stumble suddenly into the perimeter of such a city, a stark contrast to the emptiness of the corridors. These places are not havens, though; only the foolish traveler would assume so. They are the homes of the most evil races in all the Realms, most notably the duergar, the kuo-toa, and the drow.

In one such cavern, two miles wide and a thousand feet high, looms Menzoberranzan, a monument to the otherworldly and—ultimately—deadly grace that marks the race of drow elves. Menzoberranzan is not a large city by drow standards; only twenty thousand dark elves reside there. Where, in ages past, there had been an empty cavern of roughly shaped stalactites and stalagmites now stands artistry, row after row of carved castles thrumming in a quiet glow of magic. The city is perfection of form, where not a stone has been left to its natural shape. This sense of order and control, however, is but a cruel facade, a deception hiding the chaos and vileness that rule the dark elves' hearts. Like their cities, they are a beautiful, slender, and delicate people, with features sharp and haunting.

Yet the drow are the rulers of this unruled world, the deadliest of the deadly, and all other races take cautious note of their passing. Beauty itself pales at the end of a dark elf's sword. The drow are the survivors, and this is the Underdark, the valley of death—the land of nameless nightmares.

Station: In all the world of the drow, there is no more important word. It is the calling of their—of our—religion, the incessant pulling of hungering heartstrings. Ambition overrides good sense and compassion is thrown away in its face, all in the name of Lolth, the Spider Queen. Ascension to power in drow society is a simple process of assassination. The Spider Queen is a deity of chaos, and she and her high priestesses, the true rulers of the drow world, do not look with ill favor upon ambitious individuals wielding poisoned daggers. Of course, there are rules of behavior; every society must boast of these. To openly commit murder or wage war invites the pretense of justice, and penalties exacted in the name of drow justice are merciless. To stick a dagger in the back of a rival during the chaos of a larger battle or in the quiet shadows of an alley, however, is quite acceptable— even applauded. Investigation is not the forte of drow justice. No one cares enough to bother. Station is the way of Lolth, the ambition she bestows to further the chaos, to keep her drow "children" along their appointed course of self-imprisonment. Children? Pawns, more likely, dancing dolls for the Spider Queen, puppets on the imperceptible but impervious strands of her web. All climb the Spider Queen's ladders; all hunt for her pleasure; and all fall to the hunters of her pleasure. Station is the paradox of the world of my people, the limitation of our power within the hunger for power. It is gained through treachery and invites treachery against those who gain it. Those most powerful in Menzoberranzan spend their days watching over their shoulders, defending against the daggers that would find their backs. Their deaths usually come from the front.

Empty hours, empty days. I find that I have few memories of that first period of my life, those first sixteen years when I labored as a servant. Minutes blended into hours, hours into days, and so on, until the whole of it seemed one long and barren moment. Several times I managed to sneak out onto the balcony of House Do'Urden and look out over the magical lights of Menzoberranzan. On all of those secret journeys. I found myself entranced by the growing, and dissipating, heatlight of Narbondel, the timeclock pillar. Looking back on that now, on those long hours watching the glow of the wizard's fire slowly walk its way up and down the pillar, I am amazed at the emptiness of my early days. I clearly remember my excitement, tingling excitement, each time I got out of the house and set myself into position to observe the pillar. Such a simple thing it was, yet so fulfilling compared to the rest of my existence. Whenever I hear the crack of a whip, another memory—more a sensation than a memory actually—sends a shiver through my spine. The shocking jolt and the ensuing numbness from those snake-headed weapons is not something that any person would soon forget. They bite under your skin, sending waves of magical energy through your body, waves that make your muscles snap and pull beyond their limits. Yet I was luckier than most. My sister Vierna was near to becoming a high priestess when she was assigned the task of rearing me and was at a period of her life where she possessed far more energy than such a job required. Perhaps, then, there was more to those first ten years under her care than I now recall. Vierna never showed the intense wickedness of our mother—or, more particularly, of our oldest sister, Briza. Perhaps there were good times in the solitude of the house chapel; it is possible that Vierna allowed a more gentle side of herself to show through to her baby brother. Maybe not. Even though I count Vierna as the kindest of my sisters, her words drip in the venom of Lolth as surely as those of any cleric in Menzoberranzan. It seems unlikely that she would risk her aspirations toward high priestesshood for the sake of a mere child, a mere male child. Whether there were indeed joys in those years, obscured in the unrelenting assault of Menzoberranzan's wickedness, or whether that earliest period of my life was even more painful than the years that followed—so painful that my mind hides the memories—I cannot be certain. For all my efforts, I cannot remember them. I have more insight into the next six years, but the most prominent recollection of the days I spent serving the court of Matron Malice—aside from the secret trips outside the house—is the image of my own feet. A page prince is never allowed to raise his gaze.

The Academy. It is the propagation of the lies that bind drow society together, the ultimate perpetration of falsehoods repeated so many times that they ring true against any contrary evidence. The lessons young drow are taught of truth and justice are so blatantly refuted by everyday life in wicked Menzoberranzan that it is hard to understand how any could believe them. Still they do. Even now, decades removed, the thought of the place frightens me, not for any physical pain or the ever-present sense of possible death—I have trod down many roads equally dangerous in that way. The Academy of Menzoberranzan frightens me when I think of the survivors, the graduates, existing—reveling—within the evil fabrications that shape their world. They live with the belief that anything is acceptable if you can get away with it, that self-gratification is the most important aspect of existence, and that power comes only to she or he who is strong enough and cunning enough to snatch it from the failing hands of those who no longer deserve it. Compassion has no place in Menzoberranzan, and yet it is compassion, not fear, that brings harmony to most races. It is harmony, working toward shared goals, that precedes greatness. Lies engulf the drow in fear and mistrust, refute friendship at the tip of a Lolth-blessed sword. The hatred and ambition fostered by these amoral tenets are the doom of my people, a weakness that they perceive as strength. The result is a paralyzing, paranoid existence that the drow call the edge of readiness. I do not know how I survived the Academy, how I discovered the falsehoods early enough to use them in contrast, and thus strengthen, those ideals I most cherish. It was Zaknafein, I must believe, my teacher. Through the experiences of Zak's long years, which embittered him and cost him so much, I came to hear the screams: the screams of protest against murderous treachery; the screams of rage from the leaders of drow society, the high priestesses of the Spider Queen, echoing down the paths of my mind, ever to hold a place within my mind. The screams of dying children.

What eyes are these that see the pain I know
    in my innermost soul?
What eyes are these that see the twisted
    strides of my kindred,
Led on in the wake of toys unbridled:
    Arrow, bolt, and sword tip?
Yours . . . aye, yours,
Straight run and muscled spring,
Soft on padded paws, sheathed claws,
Weapons rested for their need,
Stained not by frivolous blood or murderous
    deceit.
Face-to-face, my mirror:
Reflection in a still pool by light.
Would that I might keep that image
Upon this face mine own.
Would that I might keep that heart within
    my breast untainted.
Hold tight to the proud honor of your spirit,
Mighty Guenhwyvar, and hold tight to my
    side,
My dearest friend.

Zaknafein Do'Urden: mentor, teacher, friend. I, in the blind agony of my own frustrations, more than once came to recognize Zaknafein as none of these. Did I ask of him more than he could give? Did I expect perfection of a tormented soul; hold Zaknafein up to standards beyond his experiences, or standards impossible in the face of his experiences? I might have been him. I might have lived, trapped within the helpless rage, buried under the daily assault of the wickedness that is Menzoberranzan and the pervading evil that is my own family, never in life to find escape. It seems a logical assumption that we learn from the mistakes of our elders. This, I believe, was my salvation. Without the example of Zaknafein, I, too, would have found no escape—not in life. Is this course I have chosen a better way than the life Zaknafein knew? I think, yes, though I find despair often enough sometimes to long for that other way. It would have been easier. Truth, though, is nothing in the face of self-falsehood, and principles are of no value if the idealist cannot live up to his own standards. This, then, is a better way. I live with many laments, for my people, for myself, but mostly for that weapons master, lost to me now, who showed me how—and why—to use a blade. There is no pain greater than this; not the cut of a jagged-edged dagger nor the fire of a dragon's breath. Nothing burns in your heart like the emptiness of losing something, someone, before you truly have learned of its value. Often now I lift my cup in a futile toast, an apology to ears that cannot hear: to Zak, the one who inspired my courage.

Exile

I remember vividly the day I walked away from the city of my birth, the
city of my people. All the Underdark lay before me, a life of adventure
and excitement, with possibilities that lifted my heart. More than that,
though, I left Menzoberranzan with the belief that I could now live
my life in accordance with my principles. I had Guenhwyvar at my
side and my scimitars belted on my hips. My future was my own to
determine. But that drow, the young Drizzt Do'Urden who walked out
of Menzoberranzan on that fated day, barely into my fourth decade of
life, could not begin to understand the truth of time, of how its passage
seemed to slow when the moments were not shared with others. In
my youthful exuberance, I looked forward to several centuries of life.
How do you measure centuries when a single hour seems a day and a
single day seems a year? Beyond the cities of the Underdark, there is
food for those who know how to find it and safety for those who know
how to hide. More than anything else, though, beyond the teeming
cities of the Underdark, there is solitude. As I became a creature of the
empty tunnels, survival became easier and more difficult all at once.
I gained in the physical skills and experience necessary to live on. I
could defeat almost anything that wandered into my chosen domain,

and those few monsters that I could not defeat, I could surely flee or hide from. It did not take me long, however, to discover one nemesis that I could neither defeat nor flee. It followed me wherever I went—indeed, the farther I ran, the more it closed in around me. My enemy was solitude, the interminable, incessant silence of hushed corridors. Looking back on it these many years later, I find myself amazed and appalled at the changes I endured under such an existence. The very identity of every reasoning being is defined by the language, the communication, between that being and others around it. Without that link, I was lost. When I left Menzoberranzan, I determined that my life would be based on principles, my strength adhering to unbending beliefs. Yet after only a few months alone in the Underdark, the only purpose for my survival was my survival. I had become a creature of instinct, calculating and cunning but not thinking, not using my mind for anything more than directing the newest kill. Guenhwyvar saved me, I believe. The same companion that had pulled me from certain death in the clutches of monsters unnumbered rescued me from a death of emptiness—less dramatic, perhaps, but no less fatal. I found myself living for those moments when the cat could walk by my side, when I had another living creature to hear my words, strained though they had become. In addition to every other value, Guenhwyvar became my timeclock, for I knew that the cat could come forth from the Astral Plane for a half day every other day. Only after my ordeal had ended did I realize how critical that one-quarter of my time actually was. Without Guenhwyvar, I would not have found the resolve to continue. I would never have maintained the strength to survive. Even when Guenhwyvar stood beside me, I found myself growing more and more ambivalent toward the fighting. I was secretly hoping that some denizen of the Underdark would prove stronger than I. Could the pain of tooth or talon be greater than the emptiness and the silence? I think not.

Friendship: The word has come to mean many different things among the various races and cultures of both the Underdark and the surface of the Realms. In Menzoberranzan, friendship is generally born out of mutual profit. While both parties are better off for the union, it remains secure. But loyalty is not a tenet of drow life, and as soon as a friend believes that he will gain more without the other, the union—and likely the other's life—will come to a swift end. I have had few friends in my life, and if I live a thousand years, I suspect that this will remain true. There is little to lament in this fact, though, for those who have called me friend have been persons of great character and have enriched my existence, given it worth. First there was Zaknafein, my father and mentor, who showed me that I was not alone and that I was not incorrect in holding to my beliefs. Zaknafein saved me, from both the blade and the chaotic, evil, fanatic religion that damns my people. Yet I was no less lost when a handless deep gnome came into my life, a svirfneblin that I had rescued from certain death, many years before, at my brother Dinin's merciless blade. My deed was repaid in full, for when the svirfneblin and I again met, this time in the clutches of his people, I would have been killed—truly would have preferred death—were it not for Belwar Dissengulp. My time in Blingdenstone, the city of the deep gnomes, was such a short span in the measure of my years. I remember well Belwar's city and his people, and I always shall. Theirs was the first society I came to know that was based on the strengths of community, not the paranoia of selfish individualism. Together the deep gnomes survive against the perils of the hostile Underdark, labor in their endless toils of mining the stone, and play games that are hardly distinguishable from every other aspect of their rich lives. Greater indeed are pleasures that are shared.

To live or to survive? Until my second time out in the wilds of the Underdark, after my stay in Blingdenstone, I never would have understood the significance of such a simple question. When first I left Menzoberranzan, I thought survival enough; I thought that I could fall within myself, within my principles, and be satisfied that I had followed the only course open to me. The alternative was the grim reality of Menzoberranzan and compliance with the wicked ways that guided my people. If that was life, I believed, simply surviving would be far preferable. And yet, that "simple survival" nearly killed me. Worse, it nearly stole everything that I held dear. The svirfneblin of Blingdenstone showed me a different way. Svirfneblin society, structured and nurtured on communal values and unity, proved to be everything that I had always hoped Menzoberranzan would be. The svirfneblin did much more than merely survive. They lived and laughed and worked, and the gains they made were shared by the whole, as was the pain of the losses they inevitably suffered in the hostile subsurface world. Joy multiplies when it is shared among friends, but grief diminishes with every division. That is life. And so, when I walked back out of Blingdenstone, back into the empty Underdark's lonely chambers, I walked with hope. At my side went Belwar, my new friend, and in my pocket went the magical figurine that could summon Guenhwyvar, my proven friend. In my brief stay with the deep gnomes, I had witnessed life as I always had hoped it would be—I could not return to simply surviving. With my friends beside me, I dared to believe that I would not have to.

There have been many times in my life when I have felt helpless. It is perhaps the most acute pain a person can know, founded in frustration and ventless rage. The nick of a sword upon a battling soldier's arm cannot compare to the anguish a prisoner feels at the crack of a whip. Even if the whip does not strike the helpless prisoner's body, it surely cuts deeply at his soul. We all are prisoners at one time or another in our lives, prisoners to ourselves or to the expectations of those around us. It is a burden that all people endure, that all people despise, and that few people ever learn to escape. I consider myself fortunate in this respect, for my life has traveled along a fairly straight-running path of improvement. Beginning in Menzoberranzan, under the relentless scrutiny of the evil Spider Queen's high priestesses, I suppose that my situation could only have improved. In my stubborn youth, I believed that I could stand alone, that I was strong enough to conquer my enemies with sword and with principles. Arrogance convinced me that by sheer determination, I could conquer helplessness itself. Stubborn and foolish youth, I must admit, for when I look back on those years now, I see quite clearly that rarely did I stand alone and rarely did I have to stand alone. Always there were friends, true and dear, lending me support even when I believed I did not want it, and even when I did not realize they were doing it. Zaknafein, Belwar, Clacker, Mooshie, Bruenor, Regis, Catti-brie, Wulfgar, and, of course, Guenhwyvar, dear Guenhwyvar. These were the companions who justified my principles, who gave me the strength to continue against any foe, real or imagined. These were the companions who fought the helplessness, the rage, and the frustration. These were the friends who gave me my life.

Spirit. It cannot be broken and it cannot be stolen away. A victim in the throes of despair might feel otherwise, and certainly the victim's "master" would like to believe it so. But in truth, the spirit remains, sometimes buried but never fully removed. That is the false assumption of Zin-carla and the danger of such sentient animation. The priestesses, I have come to learn, claim it as the highest gift of the Spider Queen deity who rules the drow. I think not. Better to call Zin-carla Lolth's greatest lie. The physical powers of the body cannot be separated from the rationale of the mind and the emotions of the heart. They are one and the same, a compilation of a singular being. It is in the harmony of these three—body, mind, and heart—that we find spirit. How many tyrants have tried? How many rulers have sought to reduce their subjects to simple, unthinking instruments of profit and gain? They steal the loves, the religions, of their people; they seek to steal the spirit. Ultimately and inevitably, they fail. This I must believe. If the flame of the spirit's candle is extinguished, there is only death, and the tyrant finds no gain in a kingdom littered with corpses. But it is a resilient thing, this flame of spirit, indomitable and ever-striving. In some, at least, it will survive, to the tyrant's demise. Where, then, was Zaknafein, my father, when he set out purposefully to destroy me? Where was I in my years alone in the wilds, when this hunter that I had become blinded my heart and guided my sword hand often against my conscious wishes? We both were there all along, I came to know, buried but never stolen. Spirit. In every language in all the Realms, surface and Underdark, in every time and every place, the word has a ring of strength and determination. It is the hero's strength, the mother's resilience, and the poor man's armor. It cannot be broken, and it cannot be taken away. This I must believe.

Sojourn

It burned at my eyes and pained every part of my body. It destroyed my *piwafwi* and boots, stole the magic from my armor, and weakened my trusted scimitars. Still, every day, without fail, I was there, sitting upon my perch, my judgment seat, to await the arrival of the sunrise. It came to me each day in a paradoxical way. The sting could not be denied, but neither could I deny the beauty of the spectacle. The colors just before the sun's appearance grabbed my soul in a way that no patterns of heat emanations in the Underdark ever could. At first, I thought my entrancement a result of the strangeness of the scene, but even now, many years later, I feel my heart leap at the subtle brightening that heralds the dawn. I know now that my time in the sun—my daily penance—was more than mere desire to adapt to the ways of the surface world. The sun became the symbol of the difference between the Underdark and my new home. The society that I had run away from, a world of secret dealings and treacherous conspiracies, could not exist in the open spaces under the light of day. This sun, for all the anguish it brought me physically, came to represent my denial of that other, darker world. Those rays of revealing light reinforced my principles as surely as they weakened the drow-made magical items. In the sunlight the *piwafwi*, the shielding cloak that defeated probing eyes, the garment of thieves and assassins, became no more than a worthless rag of tattered cloth.

Does anything in all the world force a heavier weight upon one's shoulders than guilt? I have felt the burden often, have carried it over many steps, on long roads. Guilt resembles a sword with two edges. On the one hand it cuts for justice, imposing practical morality upon those who fear it. Guilt, the consequence of conscience, is what separates the goodly persons from the evil. Given a situation that promises gain, most drow can kill another, kin or otherwise, and walk away carrying no emotional burden at all. The drow assassin might fear retribution but will shed no tears for his victim. To humans—and to surface elves, and to all of the other goodly races—the suffering imposed by conscience will usually far outweigh any external threats. Some would conclude that guilt—conscience—is the primary difference between the varied races of the Realms. In this regard, guilt must be considered a positive force. But there is another side to that weighted emotion. Conscience does not always adhere to rational judgment. Guilt is always a self-imposed burden, but is not always rightly imposed. So it was for me along the road from Menzoberranzan to Icewind Dale. I carried out of Menzoberranzan guilt for Zaknafein, my father, sacrificed on my behalf. I carried into Blingdenstone guilt for Belwar Dissengulp, the svirfneblin my brother had maimed. Along the many roads there came many other burdens: Clacker, killed by the monster that hunted for me; the gnolls, slain by my own hand; and the farmers—most painfully—that simple farm family murdered by the barghest whelp. Rationally I knew that I was not to blame, that the actions were beyond my influence, or in some cases, as with the gnolls, that I had acted properly. But rationale is little defense against the weight of guilt. In time, bolstered by the confidence of trusted friends, I came to throw off many of those burdens. Others remain and always shall. I accept this as inevitable, and use the weight to guide my future steps. This, I believe, is the true purpose of conscience.

To all the varied peoples of the world nothing is so out of reach, yet so deeply personal and controlling, as the concept of god. My experience in my homeland showed me little of these supernatural beings beyond the influences of the vile drow deity, the Spider Queen, Lolth. After witnessing the carnage of Lolth's workings, I was not so quick to embrace the concept of any god, of any being, that could so dictate codes of behavior and precepts of an entire society. Is morality not an internal force, and if it is, are principles then to be dictated or felt?

So follows the question of the gods themselves: Are these named entities, in truth, actual beings, or are they manifestations of shared beliefs? Are the dark elves evil because they follow the precepts of the Spider Queen, or is Lolth a culmination of the drow's natural evil conduct? Likewise, when the barbarians of Icewind Dale charge across the tundra to war, shouting the name of Tempus, Lord of Battles, are they following the precepts of Tempus, or is Tempus merely the idealized name they give to their actions? This I cannot answer, nor, I have come to realize, can anyone else, no matter how loudly they— particularly priests of certain gods—might argue otherwise. In the end, to a preacher's ultimate sorrow, the choice of a god is a personal one, and the alignment to a being is in accord with one's internal code of principles. A missionary might coerce and trick would-be disciples, but no rational being can truly follow the determined orders of any god-figure if those orders run contrary to his own tenets.

Neither I, Drizzt Do'Urden, nor my father, Zaknafein, could ever have become disciples of the Spider Queen. And Wulfgar of Icewind Dale, my friend of later years, though he still might yell out to the battle god, does not please this entity called Tempus except on those occasions when he puts his mighty war hammer to use. The gods of the Realms are many and varied—or they are the many and varied names and identities tagged onto the same being. I know not—and care not—which.

I now view my long road as a search for truth—truth in my own heart, in the world around me, and in the larger questions of purpose and of existence. How does one define good and evil? I carried an internal code of morals with me on my trek, though whether I was born with it or it was imparted to me by Zaknafein—or whether it simply developed from my perceptions—I cannot ever know. This code forced me to leave Menzoberranzan, for though I was not certain of what those truths might have been, I knew beyond doubt that they would not be found in the domain of Lolth. After many years in the Underdark outside of Menzoberranzan and after my first awful experiences on the surface, I came to doubt the existence of any universal truth, came to wonder if there was, after all, any purpose to life. In the world of drow, ambition was the only purpose, the seeking of material gains that came with increased rank. Even then, that seemed a little thing to me, hardly a reason to exist. I thank you, Montolio DeBrouchee, for confirming my suspicions. I have learned that the ambition of those who follow selfish precepts is no more than a chaotic waste, a finite gain that must be followed by infinite loss. For there is indeed a harmony in the universe, a concordant singing of common weal. To join that song, one must find inner harmony, must find the notes that ring true. There is one other point to be made about that truth: evil creatures cannot sing.

How different the trail seemed as I departed Mooshie's Grove from the road that had led me there. Again I was alone, except when Guenhwyvar came to my call. On this road, though, I was alone only in body. In my mind I carried a name, the embodiment of my valued principles. Mooshie had called Mielikki a goddess; to me she was a way of life. She walked beside me always along the many surface roads I traversed. She led me out to safety and fought off my despair when I was chased away and hunted by the dwarves of Citadel Adbar, a fortress northeast of Mooshie's Grove. Mielikki, and my belief in my own value, gave me the courage to approach town after town throughout the northland. The receptions were always the same: shock and fear that quickly turned to anger. The more generous of those I encountered told me simply to go away; others chased me with weapons bared. On two occasions I was forced to fight, though I managed to escape without anyone being badly injured. The minor nicks and scratches were a small price to pay. Mooshie had bidden me not to live as he had, and the old ranger's perceptions, as always, proved true. On my journeys throughout the northland I retained something— hope—that I never would have held if I had remained a hermit in the evergreen grove. As each new village showed on the horizon, a tingle of anticipation quickened my steps. One day, I was determined, I would find acceptance and find my home. It would happen suddenly, I imagined. I would approach a gate, speak a formal greeting, then reveal myself as a dark elf. Even my fantasy was tempered by reality, for the gate would not swing wide at my approach. Rather, I would be allowed guarded entry, a trial period much like the one I endured in Blingdenstone, the svirfneblin city. Suspicions would linger about me for many months, but in the end, principles would be seen and accepted for what they were: the character of the person would outweigh the color of his skin and the reputation of his heritage. I replayed that fantasy countless times over the years. Every word of every meeting in my imagined town became a litany against the continued rejections. It would not have been enough, but always there was Guenhwyvar, and now there was Mielikki.

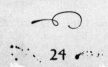

Of all the races in the known Realms, none is more confusing, or more confused, than humans. Mooshie convinced me that gods, rather than being outside entities, are personifications of what lies in our hearts. If this is true, then the many, varied gods of the human sects—deities of vastly different demeanors—reveal much about the race.

If you approach a halfling, or an elf, or a dwarf, or any of the other races, good and bad, you have a fair idea of what to expect. There are exceptions, of course; I name myself as one most fervently! But a dwarf is likely to be gruff, though fair, and I have never met an elf, or even heard of one, who preferred a cave to the open sky. A human's preference, though, is his own to know—if even he can sort it out.

In terms of good and evil, then, the human race must be judged most carefully. I have battled vile human assassins, witnessed human wizards so caught up in their power that they mercilessly destroyed all other beings in their paths, and seen cities where groups of humans preyed upon the unfortunate of their own race, living in kingly palaces while other men and women, and even children, starved and died in the gutters of the muddy streets. But I have met other humans—Catti-brie, Mooshie, Wulfgar, Agorwal of Termalaine—whose honor could not be questioned and whose contributions to the good of the realms in their short life spans will outweigh that of most dwarves and elves who might live half a millennium and more.

They are indeed a confusing race, and the fate of the world comes more and more into their ever-reaching hands. It may prove a delicate balance, but certainly not a dull one. Humans encompass the spectrum of character more fully than any other beings; they are the only "goodly" race that wages war upon itself—with alarming frequency.

The surface elves hold out hope in the end. They who have lived the longest and seen the birth of many centuries take faith that the human race will mature to goodness, that the evil in it will crush itself to nothingness, leaving the world to those who remain.

In the city of my birth I witnessed the limitations of evil, the self-destruction and inability to achieve higher goals, even goals based upon the acquisition of power. For this reason, I, too, will hold out hope for the humans, and for the Realms. As they are the most varied, so too are humans the most malleable, the most able to disagree with that within themselves that they learn to be false.

My very survival has been based upon my belief that there is a higher purpose to this life: that principles are a reward in and of themselves. I cannot, therefore, look forward in despair, but rather with higher hopes for all in mind and with the determination that I might help to reach those heights.

This is my tale, then, told as completely as I can recall and as completely as I choose to divulge. Mine has been a long road filled with ruts and barriers, and only now that I have put so much so far behind me am I able to recount it honestly. I will never look back on those days and laugh; the toll was too great for humor to seep through. I do often remember Zaknafein, though, and Belwar and Mooshie, and all the other friends I have left behind.

I have often wondered, too, of the many enemies I have faced, of the many lives my blades have ended. Mine has been a violent life in a violent world, full of enemies to myself and to all that I hold dear. I have been praised for the perfect cut of my scimitars, for my abilities in battle, and I must admit that I have many times allowed myself to feel pride in those hard-earned skills.

Whenever I remove myself from the excitement and consider the whole more fully, though, I lament that things could not have been different. It pains me to remember Masoj Hun'ett, the only drow I ever killed; it was he who initiated our battle and he certainly would have killed me if I had not proven the stronger. I can justify my actions on that fated day, but never will I be comfortable with their necessity. There should be a better way than the sword.

In a world so filled with danger, where orcs and trolls loom, seemingly, around every bend in the road, he who can fight is most often hailed as the hero and given generous applause. There is more to the mantle of "hero," I say, than strength of arm or prowess in battle. Mooshie was a hero, truly, because he overcame adversity, because he never blinked at unfavorable odds, and mostly because he acted within a code of clearly defined principles. Can less be said of Belwar Dissengulp, the handless deep gnome who befriended a renegade drow? Or of Clacker, who offered his own life rather than bring danger to his friends?

Similarly, I name Wulfgar of Icewind Dale a hero, who adhered to principle above battle lust. Wulfgar overcame the misperceptions of his savage boyhood, learned to see the world as a place of hope rather than a field of potential conquests. And Bruenor, the dwarf who taught Wulfgar that important difference, is as rightful a king as ever there was in all the realms. He embodies those tenets that his people hold most dear, and they will gladly defend Bruenor with their very lives, singing a song to him even with their dying breaths.

In the end, when he found the strength to deny Matron Malice, my father, too, was a hero. Zaknafein, who had lost his battle for principles and identity throughout most of his life, won in the end. None of these warriors, though, outshines a young girl I came to know when I first traveled across Ten Towns. Of all the people I have ever met, none has held themselves to higher standards of honor and decency than Catti-brie. She has seen many battles, yet her eyes sparkle clearly with innocence and her smile shines untainted. Sad will be the day, and let all the world lament, when a discordant tone of cynicism spoils the harmony of her melodic voice. Often those who call me a hero speak solely of my battle prowess and know nothing of the principles that guide my blades. I accept their mantle for what it is worth, for their satisfaction and not my own. When Catti-brie names me so, then will I allow my heart to swell with the satisfaction of knowing that I have been judged for my heart and not my sword arm; then will I dare to believe that the mantle is justified. And so my tale ends—do I dare to say? I sit now in comfort beside my friend, the rightful king of Mithral Hall, and all is quiet and peaceful and prosperous. Indeed this drow has found his home and his place. But I am young, I must remind myself. I may have ten times the years remaining as those that have already passed. And for all my present contentment, the world remains a dangerous place, where a ranger must hold to his principles, but also to his weapons. Do I dare to believe that my story is fully told? I think not.

Icewind Dale Trilogy

The Crystal Shard

Come gather 'round
Hardy men of the steppes
And listen to my tale
Of heroes bold and friendships fast
And the Tyrant of Icewind Dale
Of a band of friends
By trick or by deed
Bred legends for the bard
The baneful pride of one poor wretch
And the horror of the Crystal Shard

If I could choose what life would be mine, it would be this life that I now have, at this time. I am at peace, and yet, the world around me swirls with turmoil, with the ever-present threat of barbarian raids and goblin wars, with tundra yetis and gigantic polar worms. The reality of existence here in Icewind Dale is harsh indeed, an environment unforgiving, where one mistake will cost you your life. That is the joy of the place, the very edge of disaster, and not because of treachery, as I knew in my home of Menzoberranzan. I can accept the risks of Icewind Dale; I can revel in them and use them to keep my warrior instincts finely honed. I can use them to remind me every day of the glory and joy of life. There is no complacency here, in this place where safety cannot be taken for granted, where a turn of the wind can pile snow over your head, where a single misstep on a boat can put you into water that will steal your breath away and render muscles useless in mere seconds, or a simple lapse on the tundra can put you in the belly of a fierce yeti. When you live with death so close, you come to appreciate life all the more. And when you share that life with friends like those whom I have come to know these last years, then you know paradise. Never could I have imagined in my years in Menzoberranzan, or in the wilds of the Underdark, or even when I first came to the surface world, that I would ever surround myself with such friends as these. They are of different races, all three, and all three different from my own, and yet, they are more like what is in my heart than anyone I have ever known, save, perhaps, my father Zaknafein and the ranger, Montolio, who trained me in the ways of Mielikki. I have met many folk up here in Ten Towns, in the savage land of Icewind Dale, who accept me despite my dark elf heritage, and yet, these three, above all others, have become as family to me. Why them? Why Bruenor, Regis, and Catti-brie above all others, three friends whom I treasure as much as Guenhwyvar, my companion for all these years? Everyone knows Bruenor as blunt—that is the trademark of many dwarves, but in Bruenor, the trait runs pure. Or so he wants all to believe. I know better. I know the other side of Bruenor, the hidden side, that soft and warm place. Yes, he has a heart, though he tries hard to bury it! He is blunt, yes, particularly with criticism. He speaks of errors without apology and without judgment, simply telling the honest truth and leaving it up to the offender to correct, or not correct, the situation. Bruenor never allows tact or empathy to get in the way of his telling the world how it can be better! But that is only half of the tale concerning the dwarf; on the other side of the coin, he is far from blunt. Concerning compliments, Bruenor is not dishonest, just quiet. Perhaps that is why I love him. I see in him Icewind Dale itself, cold and harsh and unforgiving, but ultimately honest. He keeps me at my best, all the time, and in doing that, he helps me to survive in this place. There is only one Icewind Dale, and only one Bruenor Battlehammer, and if ever I met a creature and a land created for each other . . . Conversely, Regis stands (or more appropriately, reclines) as a reminder to me of the goals and rewards of a job well done—not that Regis is ever the one who does that job. Regis reminds me, and Bruenor, I would guess, that there is more to life than responsibility, that there are times for personal relaxation and enjoyment of the rewards brought about by good work and vigilance. He is too soft for the tundra, too round in the belly and too slow on his feet. His fighting skills are lacking and he could not track a herd of caribou on fresh snow. Yet he survives, even thrives, up here with wit and attitude, with an understanding, better than Bruenor's surely, and even better than my own, of how to appease and please those around him, of how to anticipate, rather than just react to the moves of others. Regis knows more than just what people do, he knows why they do it, and that ability to understand motivation allowed him to see past the color of my skin and the reputation of my people. If Bruenor is honest in expressing his observations, then Regis is honest in following the course of his heart. And finally there is Catti-brie, wonderful and so full of life. Catti-brie is the opposite side of the same coin to me, a different reasoning to reach the same conclusions. We are soul mates who see and judge different things in the world to arrive at the same place. Perhaps we thus validate each other. Perhaps seeing Catti-brie arriving at the same place as myself, and knowing that she arrived there along a different road, tells me that I followed my heart truly. Is that it? Do I trust her more than I trust myself? That question is neither indictment of my feelings, nor any self-incrimination. We share beliefs about the way of the world and the way the world should be.

She is akin to my heart as is Mielikki, and if I found my goddess by looking honestly into my own heart, then so I have found my dearest friend and ally. They are with me, all three, and Guenhwyvar, dear Guenhwyvar, as well. I am living in a land of stark beauty and stark reality, a place where you have to be wary and alert and at your very best at all times. I call this paradise.

Tradition.

The very sound of the word invokes a sense of gravity and solemnity. Tradition. "Suuz'chok" in the drow language, and there, too, as in every language that I have heard, the word rolls off of one's tongue with tremendous weight and power. Tradition. It is the root of who we are, the link to our heritage, the reminder that we as a people, if not individually, will span the ages. To many people and many societies, tradition is the source of structure and of law, the abiding fact of identity that denies the contrary claims of the outlaw or the misbehavior of the rogue. It is that echoing sound deep in our hearts and our minds and our souls that reminds us of who we are by reinforcing who we were. To many it is even more than the law; it is the religion, guiding faith as it guides morality and society. To many, tradition is a god itself, the ancient rituals and holy texts, scribbled on unreadable parchments yellowed with age or chiseled into eternal rocks. To many, tradition is all. Personally, I view it as a double-edged sword, and one that can cut even more deeply in the way of error.

I saw the workings of tradition in Menzoberranzan, the ritualistic sacrifice of the third male child (which was almost my own fate), the workings of the three drow schools. Tradition justified my sister's advances toward me in the graduation of Melee-Magthere, and denied me any claims against that wretched ceremony. Tradition holds the matrons in power, limiting the ascent of any males. Even the vicious wars of Menzoberranzan, house against house, are rooted in tradition.

are justified because that is the way it has always been. Such failings are not exclusive to the drow. Often I sit on the northern face of Kelvin's Cairn looking out over the empty tundra and the twinkling lights of the campfires in the vast barbarian encampments. There, too, is a people wholly consumed by tradition, a people clinging to ancient codes and ways that once allowed them to survive as a society in an inhospitable land but that now hinder them as much as, or more than, help them. The barbarians of Icewind Dale follow the caribou herd from one end of the dale to the other. In days long past that was the only way they could have survived up here, but how much easier might their existence be now if they only traded with the folk of Ten Towns, offering pelts and good meat in exchange for stronger materials brought up from the south so they might construct more permanent homes for themselves? In days long past, before any real civilization crept this far to the north, the barbarians refused to speak with, or even to accept, anyone else within Icewind Dale, the various tribes often joining for the sole purpose of driving out any intruders. In those past times, any newcomers would inevitably become rivals for the meager food and other scarce supplies, and so such xenophobia was necessary for basic survival. The folk of Ten Towns, with their advanced fishing techniques, and their rich trade with Luskan, are not rivals of the barbarians—most have never even eaten venison, I would guess. And yet, tradition demands of the barbarians that they do not make friends with those folk, and indeed, often war upon them. Tradition. What gravity indeed does that word impart! What power it wields! As it roots us and grounds us and gives us hope for who we are because of who we were, so it also wreaks destruction and denies change. I would never pretend to understand another people well enough to demand that they change their traditions, yet how foolish it seems to me to hold fast and unyieldingly to those mores and ways without regard for any changes that have taken place in the world about us. For that world is a changing place, moved by advancements in technology and magic, by the rise and fall of populations, even by the blending of races, as in the half-elf communities. The world is not static, and if the roots of our perceptions, traditions, hold static, then we are doomed, I say, into destructive dogma. Then we fall upon the darker blade of that double-edged sword.

What does Wulfgar see when he looks out over the tundra—when his crystal blue eyes stare across the dark plain to the points of light that mark the fires of his people's encampment? Does he view the past, perhaps, with a longing to return to that place and those ways? Does he view the present, comparing that which he has learned with me and Bruenor with those harsh lessons of life among his nomadic tribesmen? Or does Wulfgar see the future, the potential for change, for bringing new and better ways to his people? A bit of all three, I would guess. That is the turmoil within Wulfgar, I suspect, the simmering fire behind those blue eyes. He fights with such passion! Some of that comes from his upbringing among the fierce tribesmen, the war games of the barbarian boys, often bloody, sometimes even fatal. Part of that passion for battle stems from Wulfgar's inner turmoil, the frustration he must feel when he contrasts his lessons at my hands and at Bruenor's hands with those gained in his years among his own people. Wulfgar's people invaded Ten Towns, entered with merciless rage ready to slaughter anyone who stood in their path without regard. How does Wulfgar reconcile that truth with the fact that Bruenor Battlehammer did not let him die on the field, that the dwarf saved him, though he tried to kill Bruenor in battle (though the foolish young lad made the mistake of swatting Bruenor on the head!)? How does Wulfgar reconcile the love Bruenor has shown him against his previous notions of dwarves as hateful, merciless enemies? For that is how the barbarians of Icewind Dale surely view dwarves, a lie that they perpetuate among themselves so they may justify their murderous raiding ways. It is not so different than the lies that the drow tell themselves to justify their hatred of anyone who is not drow. But now Wulfgar has been faced with the truth of Bruenor and the dwarves. Irrevocably. He must weigh that personal revelation against every "truth" he spent his years of childhood learning. He must come to accept that what his parents and all the elders of the tribe told him were lies. I know from personal experience that this is no easy thing to reconcile. For to do so is to admit that a great part of your own life was no more than a lie, that a great part of that which makes you who you are is wrong. I recognized the ills of Menzoberranzan early on, because its teachings went against logic and went against that which was in my heart. Yet even though those wrongs were painfully obvious, those first steps that carried me out of my homeland were not easy ones. The errors of the barbarians of Icewind Dale pale compared to those of the drow, and so the steps that Wulfgar must take emotionally away from his people will be even more difficult, I fear. There is far more truth in the ways of the barbarians, more justification for their actions, warlike though they may be, yet it falls upon Wulfgar's strong, but painfully young, shoulders to differentiate between the ways of his people and those of his new friends, to accept compassion and acceptance above the solid walls of prejudice that have so encapsulated his entire youth. I do not envy him the task before him, the confusion, the frustration. It is good that he fights every day—I only pray that in a blind fit while playing out that frustration, my sparring companion does not tear the head from my shoulders.

Streams of Silver

I pray that the world never runs out of dragons. I say that in all sincerity, though I have played a part in the death of one great wyrm. For the dragon is the quintessential enemy, the greatest foe, the unconquerable epitome of devastation. The dragon, above all other creatures, even the demons and the devils, evokes images of dark grandeur, of the greatest beast curled asleep on the greatest treasure hoard. They are the ultimate test of the hero and the ultimate fright of the child. They are older than the elves and more akin to the earth than the dwarves. The great dragons are the preternatural beast, the basic element of the beast, that darkest part of our imagination. The wizards cannot tell you of their origin, though they believe that a great wizard, a god of wizards, must have played some role in the first spawning of the beast. The elves, with their long fables explaining the creation of every aspect of the world, have many ancient tales concerning the origin of the dragons, but they admit, privately, that they really have no idea of how the dragons came to be.

My own belief is more simple, and yet more complicated, by far. I believe that dragons appeared in the world immediately after the spawning of the first reasoning race. I do not credit any god of wizards with their creation, but rather, the most basic imagination, wrought of unseen fears, of those first reasoning mortals. We make the dragons as we make the gods, because we need them, because, somewhere deep in our hearts, we recognize that a world without them is a world not worth living in. There are so many people in the land who want an answer, a definitive answer, for everything in life, and even for everything after life. They study and they test, and because those few find the answers for some simple questions, they assume that there are answers to be had for every question. What was the world like before there were people? Was there nothing but darkness before the sun and the stars? Was there anything at all? What were we, each of us, before we were born? And what, most importantly of all, shall we be after we die? Out of compassion, I hope that those questioners never find that which they seek. One self-proclaimed prophet came through Ten Towns denying the possibility of an afterlife, claiming that those people who had died and were raised by priests, had, in fact, never died, and that their claims of experiences beyond the grave were an elaborate trick played on them by their own hearts, a ruse to ease the path to nothingness. For that is all there was, he said, an emptiness, a nothingness. Never in my life have I ever heard one begging so desperately for someone to prove him wrong. For what are we left with if there remains no mystery? What hope might we find if we know all of the answers? What is it within us, then, that so desperately wants to deny magic and to unravel mystery?

Fear, I presume, based on the many uncertainties of life and the greatest uncertainty of death. Put those fears aside, I say, and live free of them, for if we just step back and watch the truth of the world, we will find that there is indeed magic all about us, unexplainable by numbers and formulas. What is the passion evoked by the stirring speech of the commander before the desperate battle, if not magic? What is the peace that an infant might know in its mother's arms, if not magic? What is love, if not magic? No, I would not want to live in a world without dragons, as I would not want to live in a world without magic, for that is a world without mystery, and that is a world without faith. And that, I fear, for any reasoning, conscious being, would be the cruelest trick of all.

He wants to go home. He wants to find a world he once knew. I know not if it is the promise of riches or of simplicity that now drives Bruenor. He wants to go and find Mithral Hall, to clear it of whatever monsters might now inhabit the place, to reclaim it for Clan Battlehammer. On the surface that desire seems a reasonable, even noble, thing. We all quest for adventure, and for those whose families have lived in noble tradition, the desire to avenge a wrong and restore family name and position cannot be underestimated.

Our road to Mithral Hall will not likely be an easy one. Many dangerous, uncivilized lands lay between Icewind Dale and the region far to the east of Luskan, and certainly that road promises to become even darker if we do find the entrance to those lost dwarven mines. But I am surrounded by capable and powerful friends, and so I fear no monsters—none that we can fight with sword, at least. No, my one fear concerning this journey we undertake is a fear for Bruenor Battlehammer. He wants to go home, and there are many good reasons why he should. There remains one good reason why he should not, and if that reason, nostalgia, is the source of his desire, then I fear he will be bitterly disappointed. Nostalgia is possibly the greatest of the lies that we all tell ourselves. It is the glossing of the past to fit the sensibilities of the present. For some, it brings a measure of comfort, a sense of self and of source, but others, I fear, take these altered memories too far, and because of that, paralyze themselves to the realities about them.

How many people long for that "past, simpler, and better world," I wonder, without ever recognizing the truth that perhaps it was they who were simpler and better, and not the world about them? As a drow elf, I expect to live several centuries, but those first few decades of life for a drow, and for a surface elf, are not so different in terms of emotional development from those of a human, or a halfling or a dwarf. I, too, remember that idealism and energy of my more youthful days, when the world seemed an uncomplicated place, when right and wrong were plainly written on the path before my every stride. Perhaps, in a strange sort of way, because of the fact that my early years were so full of terrible experiences, were so full of an environment and an experience that I simply could not tolerate, I am better off now. For unlike so many of those I have met on the surface, my existence has steadily improved. Has that contributed to my optimism, for my own existence and for all the world around me? So many people, particularly humans who have passed the middle of their expected lives, continue to look back for their paradise, continue to claim that the world was a far better place when they were young. I cannot believe that. There may be specific instances where that is true—a tyrant king replaces a compassionate ruler, a plague engulfs the land after an era of health—but I believe, I must believe, that the people of the world are an improving lot, that the natural evolution of civilizations, though not necessarily a straight-line progression, moves toward the betterment of the world. For every time a better way is found, the people will naturally gravitate in that direction while failed experiments will be abandoned. I have listened to Wulfgar's renderings of the history of his people, the barbarian tribes of Icewind Dale, for example, and I am amazed and horrified by the brutality of their past, the constant fighting of tribe against tribe, the wholesale rape of captured women and the torture of captured men. The tribesmen of Icewind Dale are still a brutal lot, no doubt, but not, if the oral traditions are to be believed, on a par with their predecessors. And that makes perfect sense to me, and thus, I have hopes that the trend will continue. Perhaps one day, a great barbarian leader will emerge who truly finds love with a woman, who finds a wife who forces from him a measure of respect practically unknown among the barbarians. Will that leader somewhat elevate the status of women among the tribes? If that happens, the barbarian tribes of

Icewind Dale will find a strength that they simply do not understand within half of their population. If that happens, if the barbarian women find an elevation of status, then the tribesmen will never, ever, force them back into their current roles that can only be described as slavery. And all of them, man and woman, will be better for the change. Because for change to be lasting among reasoning creatures, that change must be for the better. And so civilizations, peoples, evolve to a better understanding and a better place. For the Matron Mothers of Menzoberranzan, as with many generations of tyrant families, as with many rich landowners, change can be seen as a definite threat to their power base, and so their resistance to it seems logical, even expected. How, then, can we find explanation in the fact that so many, many people, even people who live in squalor, as did their parents and their parents' parents, and back for generation after generation, view any change with an equal fear and revulsion? Why would not the lowliest peasant desire evolution of civilization if that evolution might lead to a better life for his children? That would seem logical, but I have seen that it is not the case, for many if not most of the short-lived humans who have passed their strongest and healthiest years, who have put their own better days behind them, accepting any change seems no easy thing. No, so many of them clutch at the past, when the world was "simpler and better." They rue change on a personal level, as if any improvements those coming behind them might make will shine a bright and revealing light on their own failings. Perhaps that is it. Perhaps it is one of our most basic fears, and one wrought of foolish pride, that our children will know better than we do. At the same time that so many people tout the virtues of their children, is there some deep fear within them that those children will see the errors of their parents? I have no answers to this seeming paradox, but for Bruenor's sake, I pray that he seeks Mithral Hall for the right reasons, for the adventure and the challenge, for the sake of his heritage and the restoration of his family name, and not for any desire he might have to make the world as it once was. Nostalgia is a necessary thing, I believe, and a way for all of us to find peace in that which we have accomplished, or even failed to accomplish. At the same time, if nostalgia precipitates actions to return to that fabled, rosy-painted time, particularly in one who believes his life to be a failure, then it is an empty thing, doomed to produce nothing but frustration and an even greater sense of failure. Even worse, if nostalgia throws barriers in the path toward evolution, then it is a limiting thing indeed.

In my travels on the surface, I once met a man who wore his religious beliefs like a badge of honor upon the sleeves of his tunic. "I am a Gondsman!" he proudly told me as we sat beside each other at a tavern bar, I sipping my wine, and he, I fear, partaking a bit too much of his more potent drink. He went on to explain the premise of his religion, his very reason for being, that all things were based in science, in mechanics, and in discovery. He even asked if he could take a piece of my flesh, that he might study it to determine why the skin of the drow elf is black. "What element is missing," he wondered, "that makes your race different from your surface kin?" I think that the Gondsman honestly believed his claim that if he could merely find the various elements that comprised the drow skin, he might effect a change in that pigmentation to make the dark elves become more akin to their surface relatives, and given his devotion, almost fanaticism, it seemed to me as if he felt he could effect a change in more than physical appearance. Because, in his view of the world, all things could be so explained and corrected. How could I even begin to enlighten him to the complexity? How could I show him the variations between drow and surface elf in the very view of the world resulting from eons of walking widely disparate roads? To a Gondsman fanatic, everything can be broken down, taken apart, and put back together. Even a wizard's magic might be no more than a way of conveying universal energies—and that, too, might one day be replicated. My Gondsman companion promised me that he and his fellow inventor priests would one day replicate every spell in any wizard's repertoire, using natural elements in the proper combinations. But there was no mention of the discipline any wizard must attain as he perfects his craft. There was no mention of the fact that powerful wizardly magic is not given to anyone, but rather, is earned, day by day, year by year, and decade by decade. It is a lifelong pursuit with a gradual increase in power, as mystical as it is secular. So it is with the warrior. The Gondsman spoke of some weapon called an arquebus, a tubular missile thrower with many times the power of the strongest crossbow. Such a weapon strikes terror into the heart of the true warrior, and not because he fears that he will fall victim to it, or even that he fears that it will one day replace him. Such weapons offend because the true warrior understands that while one is learning how to use a sword, one should also be learning why and when to use a sword. To grant the power of a weapon master to anyone at all, without effort, without training and proof that the lessons have taken hold, is to deny the responsibility that comes with such power. Of course, there are wizards and warriors who perfect their craft without learning the level of emotional discipline to accompany it, and certainly there are those who attain great prowess in either profession to the detriment of all the world—Artemis Entreri seems a perfect example—but these individuals are, thankfully, rare, and mostly because their emotional lacking will be revealed early in their careers, and it often brings about a fairly abrupt downfall. But if the Gondsman has his way, if his errant view of paradise should come to fruition, then all the years of training will mean little. Any fool could pick up an arquebus or some other powerful weapon and summarily destroy a skilled warrior. Or any child could utilize a Gondsman's magic machine and replicate a fireball, perhaps, and burn down half a city. When I pointed out some of my fears to the Gondsman, he seemed shocked—not at the devastating possibilities, but rather, at my, as he put it, arrogance. "The inventions of the priests of Gond will make all equal!" he declared. "We will lift up the lowly peasant." Hardly. All that the Gondsman and his cronies would do is ensure death and destruction at a level heretofore unknown across the Realms. There was nothing more to be said, for I knew that the man would never hear my words. He thought me, or, for that matter, anyone who achieved a level of skill in the fighting or magic arts, arrogant, because he could not appreciate the sacrifice and dedication necessary for such achievement.

Arrogant? If the Gondsman's so-called lowly peasant came to me with a desire to learn the fighting arts, I would gladly teach him. I would revel in his successes as much as in my own, but I would demand, always I would demand, a sense of humility, dedication, and an understanding of this power I was teaching, an appreciation of the potential for destruction. I would teach no one who did not continue to display an appropriate level of compassion and community. To learn how to use a sword, one must first master when to use a sword. There is one other error in the Gondsman's line of reasoning, I believe, on a purely emotional level. If machines replace achievement, then to what will people aspire? And who are we, truly, without such goals? Beware the engineers of society, I say, who would make everyone in all the world equal. Opportunity should be equal, must be equal, but achievement must remain individual.

The Halfling's Gem

I am dying. Every day, with every breath I draw, I am closer to the
end of my life. For we are born with a finite number of breaths, and
each one I take edges the sunlight that is my life toward the inevitable
dusk. It is a difficult thing to remember, especially while we are in the
health and strength of our youth, and yet, I have come to know that
it is an important thing to keep in mind—not to complain or to make
melancholy, but simply because only with the honest knowledge that
one day I will die can I ever truly begin to live. Certainly I do not
dwell on the reality of my own mortality, but I believe that a person
cannot help but dwell, at least subconsciously, on that most imposing
specter until he has come to understand, to truly understand and
appreciate, that he will one day die. That he will one day be gone from
this place, this life, this consciousness and existence, to whatever it
is that awaits. For only when a person completely and honestly accepts
the inevitability of death is he free of the fear of it. So many people,
it seems, stick themselves into the same routines, going through each
day's rituals with almost religious precision. They become creatures of
simple habit. Part of that is the comfort afforded by familiarity, but there
is another aspect to it, a deep-rooted belief that as long as they keep

everything the same, everything will remain the same. Such rituals are a way to control the world about them, but in truth, they cannot. For even if they follow the exact routine day after day after day, death will surely find them.

I have seen other people paralyze their entire existence around that greatest of mysteries, shaping their every movement, their every word, in a desperate attempt to find the answers to the unanswerable. They fool themselves, either through their interpretations of ancient texts or through some obscure sign from a natural event, into believing that they have found the ultimate truth, and thus, if they behave accordingly concerning that truth, they will surely be rewarded in the afterlife. This must be the greatest manifestation of that fear of death, the errant belief that we can somehow shape and decorate eternity itself, that we can curtain its windows and place its furniture in accordance with our own desperate desires. Along the road that led me to Icewind Dale, I came upon a group of followers of Ilmater, the god of suffering, who were so fanatical in their beliefs that they would beat each other senseless, and welcomed torment, even death itself, in some foolish belief that by doing so they would pay the highest tribute to their god. I believe them to be wrong, though in truth, I cannot know anything for certain concerning what mystery lies beyond this mortal coil. And so I, too, am but a creature of faith and hope. I hope that Zaknafein has found eternal peace and joy, and pray with all my heart that when I cross over the threshold into the next existence, I will see him again. Perhaps the greatest evil I see in this existence is when supposedly holy men prey upon the basic fears of death of the common folk to take from them. "Give to the church!" they cry. "Only then will you find salvation!" Even more subtle are the many religions that do not directly ask for a person's coin, but insist that anyone of goodly and godly heart who is destined for their particular description of heaven would willingly give that coin over. And of course, Toril is ripe with "doomsdayers," people who claim that the end of the world is at hand, and cry for repentance and for almost slavish dedication. I can only look at it all and sigh, for as death is the greatest mystery, so it is the most personal of revelations. We will not know, none of us, until the moment it is upon us, and we cannot truly and in good conscience convince another of our beliefs.

It is a road we travel alone, but a road that I no longer fear, for in accepting the inevitable, I have freed myself from it. In coming to recognize my mortality, I have found the secret to enjoying those centuries, years, months, days, or even hours, that I have left to draw breath. This is the existence I can control, and to throw away the precious hours over fear of the inevitable is a foolish thing indeed. And to subconsciously think ourselves immortal, and thus not appreciate those precious few hours that we all have, is equally foolish. I cannot control the truth of death, whatever my desperation. I can only make certain that those moments of my life I have remaining are as rich as they can be.

⌒

The world is full of ruffians. The world is full of people of good character. Both of these statements are true, I believe, because within most of the people I have known lie the beginning points of both seemingly disparate paths.

Some people are too timid to ever be ruffians, of course, and others too kindhearted, and similarly, some folk are too hard-tempered to ever let their good qualities show. But the emotional makeup of most people lies somewhere in the middle, a shade of gray that can be easily darkened or lightened by simple interaction. Race can certainly alter the shade—how well I have seen that since my road led me to the surface! An elf might noticeably flinch at the approach of a dwarf, while a dwarf might do likewise, or even spit upon the ground, if the situation is reversed. Those initial impressions are sometimes difficult to overcome, and sometimes become lasting, but beyond race and appearance and other things that we cannot control, I have learned that there are definite decisions that I can make concerning which reaction I will edge someone else toward. The key to it all, I believe, is respect. When I was in Luskan with Wulfgar, we crossed through a tavern full of ruffians, men who used their fists and weapons on an almost daily basis. Yet, another friend of mine, Captain Deudermont of the *Sea Sprite*, often frequents such taverns, and rarely, very rarely, ever gets into so much as a verbal argument. Why is this? Why would a man such as Deudermont, obviously (as is shown by his dress and manner) a man of some wealth, and a man of respectable society, as well, not find himself immersed in brawls as regularly as the others? He often goes in alone, and stands quietly at the bar, but though he hardly says a word, he surely stands out among the more common patrons.

Is it fear that holds the ruffians from the man? Are they afraid that if they tangle with Deudermont, they will find retribution at the hands of his crew? Or has Deudermont simply brought with him such a reputation for ferocity as to scare off any potential challengers? Neither, I say. Certainly the captain of the *Sea Sprite* must be a fine warrior, but that is no deterrent to the thugs of the taverns; indeed, the greatest fighting reputation only invites challenges among those folk. And though Deudermont's crew is formidable, by all accounts, more powerful and connected men than he have been found dead in the gutters of Luskan. No, what keeps Captain Deudermont safe is his ability to show respect for anyone he meets. He is a man of charm, who holds well his personal pride. He grants respect at the outset of a meeting and continues that respect until the person forfeits it. This is very different from the way most people view the world. Most people insist that respect has to be earned, and with many, I have come to observe, earning it is no easy task! Many, and I include Bruenor and Wulfgar in this group, demand that anyone desiring their friendship first earn their respect, and I can understand their point of view, and once believed that I held one similar.

On my journey south on the *Sea Sprite*, Captain Deudermont taught me better, made me realize, without ever uttering a word on the subject, that demanding of another that he earns your respect is, in and of itself, an act of arrogance, a way of self-elevation, implying by its very nature that your respect is worth earning. Deudermont takes the opposite approach, one of acceptance and one lacking initial judgment. This may seem a subtle alternative, but it most certainly is not. Would that the man be anointed a king, I say, for he has learned the secret of peace. When Captain Deudermont, dressed in his finery, enters a tavern of common peasant thugs, most within the place, and society at large, would view him as superior. And yet, in his interactions with these people, there is no air of superiority about the man at all. In his eyes and in his heart, he is among peers, among other intelligent creatures whose paths have led them to a different—and not better or worse—place than his own. And when Deudermont grants respect to men who would think nothing of cutting his heart out, he disarms them, he takes away whatever reason they might have found to fight with him. There is much more to it than that. Captain Deudermont is able to do this because he can honestly attempt to see the world through the eyes of another. He is a man of empathy, a man who revels in the differences of people rather than fearing those differences. How rich is his life! How full of wonder and how wide of experience! Captain Deudermont taught these things to me, by example. Respect is one of the most basic needs of reasoning creatures, particularly among men. An insult is just that because it is an assault upon respect, upon esteem, and upon that most dangerous of qualities: pride. So when I meet people now, they do not have to earn my respect. I grant it, willingly and happily, expecting that in doing so I will come to learn even more about this beautiful world around me, that my experiences will widen. Certainly some people will see this as weakness or cowardice, will misconstrue my intentions as sublimation, rather than an acceptance of equal worth. But it is not fear that guides my actions—I have seen far too much of battle to fear it any longer—it is hope. The hope that I will find another Bruenor, or another Catti-brie, for I have come to know that I can never have too many friends. So I offer you respect, and it will take much for you to lose it. But if you do, if you choose to see it as weakness and seize upon your perceived advantage, well . . . Perhaps I'll then let you talk with Guenhwyvar.

⌒ↄ⌒

It is like looking into a mirror that paints the world with opposing colors: white hair to black; black skin to white, light eyes to dark. What an intricate mirror it is to replace a smile with a frown, and an expression of friendship with a seemingly perpetual scowl.

For that is how I view Artemis Entreri, this warrior who can complement every movement I make with similar precision and grace, the warrior who, in every way but one, I would regard as my equal. How difficult it was for me to stand with him in the depths of Mithral Hall, fighting side by side for both our lives! Strangely, it was not any moral imperative that bothered me about fighting in that situation. It was no belief that Entreri should die, had to die, and that I, if I was not such a coward, would have killed him then and there, even if the action cost me my own life as I tried to escape the inhospitable depths. No, nothing like that. What made it all so difficult for me was watching that man, that human assassin, and knowing, without the slightest shred of doubt, that I very well might have been looking at myself. Is that who I would have become had I not found Zaknafein in those early years in Menzoberranzan? Had I not discovered the example of one who so validated my own beliefs that the ways of the drow were not right, morally and practically? Is that cold-hearted killer who I would have become had it been my vicious sister Briza training me instead of the more gentle Vierna?

I fear that it is, that I, despite all that I know to be true within the depths of my very heart, would have been overwhelmed by the situation about me, would have succumbed to the despair to a point where there remained little of compassion and justice. I would have become an assassin, holding strong within my own code of ethics, but with that code so horribly warped that I could no longer understand the truth of my actions, that I could justify them with the sheerest cynicism. I saw all of that when I looked upon Entreri, and thanked Mielikki profoundly for those in my life, for Zaknafein, for Belwar Dissengulp, and for Montolio, who helped me to steer the correct course. And if I saw a potential for myself within Entreri, then I must admit that there once was a potential for Entreri to become as I have become, to know compassion and community, to know friends, good friends, and to know love. I think about him a lot, as he, no doubt, thinks about me. While his obsession is based in pride, in the challenge of overcoming me in battle, mine own is wrought of curiosity, of seeking answers within myself by observing the actions of who I might have become. Do I hate him? Strangely, I do not. That lack of hatred is not based on the respect that I give the man for his fighting prowess, for that measure of respect ends right there, at the edge of the battlefield. No, I do not hate Artemis Entreri because I pity him, the events that led to the wrong decisions he has made. There is true strength within him, and there is, or once was, a substantial potential to do good in a world so in need of heroes. For, despite his actions, I have come to understand that Entreri operates within a very strict code.

In his own warped view of the world, I believe that Entreri honestly believes that he never killed anyone who did not deserve it. He held Catti-brie captive but did not rape her. As for his actions concerning Regis . . . well, Regis was, in reality, a thief, and though he stole from another thief that does not excuse that crime. In Luskan, as in most cities in the Realms, thieves lose their hands, or worse, and certainly a bounty hunter sent to retrieve a stolen item, and the person who stole it, is well within the law to kill that person, and anyone else who hinders his task. In Calimport, Artemis Entreri operates among thieves and thugs, among the very edge of civilization. In that capacity, he deals death, as did Zaknafein in the alleys of Menzoberranzan. There is a difference—certainly!—between the two, and I do not in any way mean to excuse Entreri from his crimes. Neither will I consider him the simple killing monster that was, say, Errtu. No, there was once potential there, I know, though I fear he is far gone from that road, for when I look upon Artemis Entreri, I see myself, I see the capacity to love, and also the capacity to lose all of that and become cold. So very cold.

Perhaps we will meet again and do battle, and if I kill him, I will shed no tears for him. Not for who he is, at least, but quite possibly, I will cry for who this marvelous warrior might have become. If I kill him, I will be crying for myself.

Legacy of the Drow Quartet

The Legacy

Nearly three decades have passed since I left my homeland, a small measure of time by the reckoning of a drow elf, but a period that seems a lifetime to me. All that I desired, or believed that I desired, when I walked out of Menzoberranzan's dark cavern was a true home, a place of friendship and peace where I might hang my scimitars above the mantel of a warm hearth and share stories with trusted companions. I have found all that now, beside Bruenor in the hallowed halls of his youth. We prosper. We have peace. I wear my weapons only on my five-day journeys between Mithral Hall and Silverymoon.

Was I wrong? I do not doubt, nor do I ever lament, my decision to leave the vile world of Menzoberranzan, but I am beginning to believe now, in the (endless) quiet and peace, that my desires at that critical time were founded in the inevitable longing of inexperience. I had never known that calm existence I so badly wanted. I cannot deny that my life is better, a thousand times better, than anything I ever knew in the Underdark. And yet, I cannot remember the last time I felt the anxiety, the inspiring fear, of impending battle, the tingling that can come only when an enemy is near or a challenge must be met.

Oh, I do remember the specific instance—just a year ago, when

Wulfgar, Guenhwyvar, and I worked the lower tunnels in the cleansing of Mithral Hall—but that feeling, that tingle of fear, has long since faded from memory. Are we then creatures of action? Do we say that we desire those accepted cliches of comfort when, in fact, it is the challenge and the adventure that truly give us life?

I must admit, to myself at least, that I do not know. There is one point that I cannot dispute, though, one truth that will inevitably help me resolve these questions and which places me in a fortunate position. For now, beside Bruenor and his kin, beside Wulfgar and Catti-brie and Guenhwyvar, dear Guenhwyvar, my destiny is my own to choose. I am safer now than ever before in my sixty years of life. The prospects have never looked better for the future, for continued peace and continued security. And yet, I feel mortal. For the first time, I look to what has passed rather than to what is still to come. There is no other way to explain it. I feel that I am dying, that those stories I so desired to share with friends will soon grow stale, with nothing to replace them.

But, I remind myself again, the choice is mine to make.

There is no word in the drow language for love. The closest word I can think of is "ssinssrigg," but that is a term better equated with physical lust or selfish greed. The concept of love exists in the hearts of some drow, of course, but true love, a selfless desire often requiring personal sacrifice, has no place in a world of such bitter and dangerous rivalries.

The only sacrifices in drow culture are gifts to Lolth, and those are surely not selfless, since the giver hopes, prays, for something greater in return. Still, the concept of love was not new to me when I left the Underdark. I loved Zaknafein. I loved both Belwar and Clacker. Indeed, it was the capacity, the need, for love that ultimately drove me from Menzoberranzan.

Is there in all the wide world a concept more fleeting, more elusive? Many people of all the races seem simply not to understand love, burden its beauteous simplicity with preconceived notions and unrealistic expectations. How ironic that I, walking from the darkness of loveless Menzoberranzan, can better grasp the concept than many of those who have lived with it, or at least with the very real possibility of it, for all of their lives.

Some things a renegade drow will not take for granted. My few journeys to Silverymoon in these past tendays have invited good-hearted jests from my friends. "Suren the elf has his eyes fixed on another wedding!" Bruenor has often crooned, regarding my relationship with Alustriel, the Lady of Silverymoon. I accept the taunts in light of the sincere warmth and hopes behind them, and have not dashed those hopes by explaining to my dear friends that their notions are misguided.

I appreciate Alustriel and the goodness she has shown me. I appreciate that she, a ruler in a too often unforgiving world, has taken such a chance as to allow a dark elf to walk freely down her city's wondrous avenues. Alustriel's acceptance of me as a friend has allowed me to draw my desires from my true wishes, not from expected limitations. But do I love her? No more than she loves me. I will admit, though, I do love the notion that I could love Alustriel, and she could love me, and that, if the attraction were present, the color of my skin and the reputation of my heritage would not deter the noble Lady of Silverymoon. I know now, though, that love has become the most prominent part of my existence, that my bond of friendship with Bruenor and Wulfgar and Regis is of utmost importance to any happiness that this drow will ever know.

My bond with Catti-brie runs deeper still. Honest love is a selfless concept, that I have already said, and my own selflessness has been put to a severe test this spring. I fear now for the future, for Catti-brie and Wulfgar and the barriers they must, together, overcome. Wulfgar loves her, I do not doubt, but he burdens his love with a possessiveness that borders on disrespect. He should understand the spirit that is Catti-brie, should see clearly the fuel that stokes the fires in her marvelous blue eyes. It is that very spirit that Wulfgar loves, and yet he will undoubtedly smother it under the notions of a woman's place as her husband's possession.

My barbarian friend has come far from his youthful days roaming the tundra. Farther still must he come to hold the heart of Bruenor's fiery daughter, to hold Catti-brie's love. Is there in all the world a concept more fleeting, more elusive?

∽

What dangerous paths I have trod in my life; what crooked ways these feet have walked, in my homeland, in the tunnels of the Underdark, across the surface northland, and even in the course of following my friends. I shake my head in wonderment—is every corner of the wide world possessed of people so self-absorbed that they cannot let others cross the paths of their lives? People so filled with hatred that they must take up chase and vindicate themselves against perceived wrongs, even if those wrongs were no more than an honest defense against their own encroaching evils? I left Artemis Entreri in Calimport, left him there in body and with my taste for vengeance rightfully sated. Our paths had crossed and separated, to the betterment of us both. Entreri had no practical reason to pursue me, had nothing to gain in finding me but the possible redemption of his injured pride.

What a fool he is. He has found perfection of the body, has honed his fighting skills as perfectly as any I have known. But his need to pursue reveals his weakness. As we uncover the mysteries of the body, so too must we unravel the harmonies of the soul. But Artemis Entreri, for all his physical prowess, will never know what songs his spirit might sing. Always will he listen jealously for the harmonies of others, absorbed with bringing down anything that threatens his craven superiority.

So much like my people is he, and so much like many others I have met, of varied races: barbarian warlords whose positions of power hinge

60

on their ability to wage war on enemies who are not enemies; dwarf kings who hoard riches beyond imagination, while when sharing but a pittance of their treasures could better the lives of all those around them and in turn allow them to take down their ever-present military defenses and throw away their consuming paranoia; haughty elves who avert their eyes to the sufferings of any who are not elven, feeling that the "lesser races" somehow brought their pains unto themselves.

I have run from these people, passed these people by, and heard countless stories of them from travelers of every known land. And I know now that I must battle them, not with blade or army, but by remaining true to what I know in my heart is the rightful course of harmony. By the grace of the gods, I am not alone. Since Bruenor regained his throne, the neighboring peoples take hope in his promises that the dwarven treasures of Mithral Hall will better all the region. Catti-brie's devotion to her principles is no less than my own, and Wulfgar has shown his warrior people the better way of friendship, the way of harmony. They are my armor, my hope in what is to come for me and for all the world. And as the lost chasers such as Entreri inevitably find their paths linked once more with my own, I remember Zaknafein, kindred of blood and soul. I remember Montolio and take heart that there are others who know the truth, that if I am destroyed, my ideals will not die with me. Because of the friends I have known, the honorable people I have met, I know I am no solitary hero of unique causes. I know that when I die, that which is important will live on.

This is my legacy; by the grace of the gods, I am not alone.

What turmoil I felt when first I broke my most solemn, principle-intentioned vow: that I would never again take the life of one of my people. The pain, a sense of failure, a sense of loss, was acute when I realized what wicked work my scimitars had done. The guilt faded quickly, though—not because I came to excuse myself for any failure, but because I came to realize that my true failure was in making the vow, not in breaking it. When I walked out of my homeland, I spoke the words out of innocence, the naivete of unworldly youth, and I meant them when I said them, truly. I came to know, though, that such a vow was unrealistic, that if I pursued a course in life as defender of those ideals I so cherished, I could not excuse myself from actions dictated by that course if ever the enemies showed themselves to be drow elves.

Quite simply, adherence to my vow depended on situations completely beyond my control. If, after leaving Menzoberranzan, I had never again met a dark elf in battle, I never would have broken my vow. But that, in the end, would not have made me any more honorable. Fortunate circumstances do not equate to high principles.

When the situation arose, however, that dark elves threatened my dearest friends, precipitated a state of warfare against people who had done them no wrong, how could I, in good conscience, have kept my scimitars tucked away? What was my vow worth when weighed against the lives of Bruenor, Wulfgar, and Catti-brie, or when weighed against the lives of any innocents, for that matter? If, in my travels, I happened upon a drow raid against surface elves, or against a small village, I know beyond any doubts that I would have joined in the fighting, battling the unlawful aggressors with all my strength. In that event, no doubt, I would have felt the acute pangs of failure and soon would have dismissed them, as I do now. I do not, therefore, lament breaking my vow—though it pains me, as it always does, that I have had to kill. Nor do I regret making the vow, for the declaration of my youthful folly caused no subsequent pain. If I had attempted to adhere to the unconditional words of that declaration, though, if I had held my blades in check for a sense of false pride, and if that inaction had subsequently resulted in injury to an innocent person, then the pain in Drizzt Do'Urden would have been more acute, never to leave.

There is one more point I have come to know concerning my declaration, one more truth that I believe leads me farther along my chosen road in life. I said I would never again kill a drow elf. I made the assertion with little knowledge of the many other races of the wide world, surface and Underdark, with little understanding that many of these myriad peoples even existed. I would never kill a drow, so I said, but what of the svirfneblin, the deep gnomes? Or the halflings, elves, or dwarves? And what of the humans? I have had occasion to kill men, when Wulfgar's barbarian kin invaded Ten Towns. To defend those innocents meant to battle, perhaps to kill, the aggressor humans. Yet that act, unpleasant as it may have been, did not in any way affect my most solemn vow, despite the fact that the reputation of humankind far outshines that of the dark elves. To say, then, that I would never again slay a drow, purely because they and I are of the same physical heritage, strikes me now as wrong, as simply racist. To place the measure of a living being's worth above that of another simply because that being wears the same color skin as I belittles my principles. The false values embodied in that long-ago vow have no place in my world, in the wide world of countless physical and cultural differences. It is these very differences that make my journeys exciting, these very differences that put new colors and shapes on the universal concept of beauty.

I now make a new vow, one weighed in experience and proclaimed with my eyes open: I will not raise my scimitars except in defense—in defense of my principles, of my life, or of others who cannot defend themselves. I will not do battle to further the causes of false prophets, to further the treasures of kings, or to avenge my own injured pride. And to the many gold-wealthy mercenaries, religious and secular, who would look upon such a vow as unrealistic, impractical, even ridiculous, I cross my arms over my chest and declare with conviction: I am the richer by far!

When I die . . .

I have lost friends, lost my father, my mentor, to that greatest of mysteries called death. I have known grief since the day I left my homeland, since the day wicked Malice informed me that Zaknafein had been given to the Spider Queen. It is a strange emotion, grief, its focus shifting. Do I grieve for Zaknafein, for Montolio, for Wulfgar? Or do I grieve for myself, for the loss I must forever endure?

It is perhaps the most basic question of mortal existence, and yet it is one for which there can be no answer. . . . Unless the answer is one of faith. I am sad still when I think of the sparring games against my father, when I remember the walks beside Montolio through the mountains, and when those memories of Wulfgar, most intense of all, flash through my mind like a summary of the last several years of my life. I remember a day on Kelvin's Cairn, looking out over the tundra of Icewind Dale, when young Wulfgar and I spotted the campfires of his nomadic people. That was the moment when Wulfgar and I truly became friends, the moment when we came to learn that, for all the other uncertainties in both our lives, we would have each other. I remember the white dragon, Icingdeath, and the giant-kin, Biggrin, and how, without heroic Wulfgar at my side, I would have perished in either of those fights. I remember, too, sharing the victories with my friend, our bond of trust and love tightening—close, but never uncomfortable. I was not there when he fell, could not lend him the support he certainly would have lent me. I could not say "Farewell!" When I die, will I be alone? If not for the weapons of monsters or the clutch of disease, I surely will outlive Catti-brie and Regis, even Bruenor. At this time in my life I do firmly believe that, no matter who else might be beside me, if those three were not, I would indeed die alone. These thoughts are not so dark. I have said farewell to Wulfgar a thousand times. I have said it every time I let him know how dear he was to me, every time my words or actions affirmed our love. Farewell is said by the living, in life, every day. It is said with love and friendship, with the affirmation that the memories are lasting if the flesh is not.

Wulfgar has found another place, another life—I have to believe that, else what is the point of existence? My very real grief is for me, for the loss I know I will feel to the end of my days, however many centuries have passed. But within that loss is a serenity, a divine calm. Better to have known Wulfgar and shared those very events that now fuel my grief, than never to have walked beside him, fought beside him, looked at the world through his crystal-blue eyes.

When I die . . . may there be friends who will grieve for me, who will carry our shared joys and pains, who will carry my memory. This is the immortality of the spirit, the ever-lingering legacy, the fuel of grief. But so, too, the fuel of faith.

Starless Night

No race in all the Realms better understands the word "vengeance"
than the drow. Vengeance is their dessert at their daily table, the
sweetness they taste upon their smirking lips as though it was the
ultimate delicious pleasure. And so hungering did the drow come
for me. I cannot escape the anger and the guilt I feel for the loss of
Wulfgar, for the pains the enemies of my dark past have brought to the
friends I hold so dear. Whenever I look into Catti-brie's fair face, I see
a profound and everlasting sadness that should not be there, a burden
that has no place in the sparkling eyes of a child. Similarly wounded,
I have no words to comfort her and doubt that there are any words
that might bring solace. It is my course, then, that I must continue to
protect my friends. I have come to realize that I must look beyond my
own sense of loss for Wulfgar, beyond the immediate sadness that
has taken hold of the dwarves of Mithral Hall and the hardy men of
Settlestone. By Catti-brie's account of that fateful fight, the creature
Wulfgar battled was a yochlol, a handmaiden of Lolth. With that grim
information, I must look beyond the immediate sorrow and consider
that the sadness I fear is still to come.

I do not understand all the chaotic games of the Spider Queen—I doubt that even the evil high priestesses know the foul creature's true designs—but there lies in a yochlol's presence a significance that even I, the worst of the drow religious students, cannot miss. The handmaiden's appearance revealed that the hunt was sanctified by the Spider Queen. And the fact that the yochlol intervened in the fighting does not bode well for the future of Mithral Hall.

It is all supposition, of course. I know not that my sister Vierna acted in concert with any of Menzoberranzan's other dark powers, or that, with Vierna's death, the death of my last relative, my link to the city of drow would ever again be explored. When I look into Catti-brie's eyes, when I look upon Bruenor's horrid scars, I am reminded that hopeful supposition is a feeble and dangerous thing.

My evil kin have taken one friend from me. They will take no more. I can find no answers in Mithral Hall, will never know for certain if the dark elves hunger still for vengeance, unless another force from Menzoberranzan comes to the surface to claim the bounty on my head. With this truth bending low my shoulders, how could I ever travel to Silverymoon, or to any other nearby town, resuming my normal lifestyle? How could I sleep in peace while holding within my heart the very real fear that the dark elves might soon return and once more imperil my friends?

The apparent serenity of Mithral Hall, the brooding quiet, will show me nothing of the future designs of the drow. Yet, for the sake of my friends, I must know those dark intentions. I fear that there remains only one place for me to look. Wulfgar gave his life so that his friends might live. In good conscience, could my own sacrifice be any less?

Not since the day I walked out of Menzoberranzan have I been so torn about a pending decision. I sat near the entrance of a cave, looking out at the mountains before me, with the tunnel leading to the Underdark at my back. This was the moment in which I had believed my adventure would begin. When I had set out from Mithral Hall, I had given little thought to the part of my journey that would take me to this cave, taking for granted that the trip would be uneventful. Then I had glimpsed Ellifain, the maiden I had saved more than three decades before, when she had been just a frightened child. I wanted to go to her again, to speak with her and help her overcome the trauma of that terrible drow raid. I wanted to run out of that cave and catch up with Tarathiel, and ride beside the elf back to the Moonwood. But I could not ignore the issues that had brought me to this place. I had known from the outset that visiting Montolio's grove, the place of so many fond memories, would prove an emotional, even spiritual, experience. He had been my first surface friend, my mentor, the one who had guided me to Mielikki. I can never express the joy I felt in learning that Montolio's grove was under the protective eye of a unicorn. A unicorn! I have seen a unicorn, the symbol of my goddess, the pinnacle of natural perfection!

I might well be the first of my race to have ever touched the soft mane and muscled neck of such a beast, the first to encounter a unicorn in friendship. It is a rare pleasure to glimpse the signs that a unicorn has been about, and rarer still to ever gaze at one. Few in the Realms can say that they have ever been near a unicorn; fewer still have ever touched one. I have. Was it a sign from my goddess? In good faith, I had to believe that it was, that Mielikki had reached out to me in a tangible and thrilling way. But what did it mean?

I rarely pray. I prefer to speak to my goddess through my daily actions, and through my honest emotions. I need not gloss over what has occurred with pretty words, twisting them to show myself most favorably. If Mielikki is with me, then she knows the truth, knows how I act and how I feel.

I prayed that night in the cave entrance, though. I prayed for guidance, for something that would indicate the significance of the unicorn's appearance. The unicorn allowed me to touch it; it accepted me, and that is the highest honor a ranger can ask. But what was the implication of that honor?

Was Mielikki telling me that here, on the surface, I was, and would continue to be, accepted, and that I should not leave this place? Or was the unicorn's appearance to show me the goddess's approval of my choice to return to Menzoberranzan? Or was the unicorn Mielikki's special way of saying farewell? That last thought haunted me all through the night. For the first time since I had set out from Mithral Hall, I began to consider what I, Drizzt Do'Urden, had to lose. I thought of my friends, Montolio and Wulfgar, who had passed on from this world, and thought of those others I would likely never see again. A host of questions assailed me. Would Bruenor ever get over the loss of his adopted son? And would Catti-brie overcome her own grief? Would the enchanted sparkle, the sheer love of life, ever return to her blue eyes? Would I ever again prop my weary head against Guenhwyvar's muscled flank? More than ever, I wanted to run from the cave, home to Mithral Hall, and stand beside my friends, to see them through their grief, to guide them and listen to them and simply embrace them. Again I could not ignore the issues that had brought me to this cave. I could go back to Mithral Hall, but so could my dark kin. I did not blame myself for Wulfgar's death—I could not have known that the dark elves would come. And now I could not deny my understanding of the awful ways and continuing hunger of Lolth. If the drow returned and extinguished that—cherished!—light in Catti-brie's eyes, then Drizzt Do'Urden would die a thousand horrible deaths. I prayed all that night, but found no divine guidance. In the end, as always, I came to realize that I had to follow what I knew in my heart was the right course, had to trust that what was in my heart was in accord with Mielikki's will. I left the fire blazing at the entrance of that cave. I needed to see its light, to gain courage from it, for as many steps as possible as I walked into the tunnel. As I walked into darkness.

⟡

There are no shadows in the Underdark. Only after years on the surface have I come to understand the significance of that seemingly minute fact, the significance of the contrast between lightness and darkness. There are no shadows in the Underdark, no areas of mystery where only the imagination can go. What a marvelous thing is a shadow! I have seen my own silhouette walk under me as the sun rode high; I have seen a gopher grow to the size of a large bear, the light low behind him, spreading his ominous silhouette far across the ground. I have walked through the woods at twilight, my gaze alternating between the lighter areas catching the last rays of day, leafy green slipping to gray, and those darkening patches, those areas where only my mind's eye could go. Might a monster be there? An orc or a goblin? Or might a hidden treasure, as magnificent as a lost, enchanted sword or as simple as a fox's den, lay within the sheltering gloom?

When I walk the woods at twilight, my imagination walks beside me, heightens my senses, opens my mind to any possibilities. But there are no shadows in the Underdark, and there is no room for fanciful imagining. All, everywhere, is gripped in a brooding, continual, predatory hush and a very real, ever present danger. To imagine a crouched enemy, or a hidden treasure, is an exercise in enjoyment, a conjured state of alertness, of aliveness. But when that enemy is too often real and not imagined, when every jag in the stone, every potential hiding place, becomes a source of tension, then the game is not so much fun. One cannot walk the corridors of the Underdark with his imagination beside him. To imagine an enemy behind one stone might well blind a person to the very real enemy behind another. To slip into a daydream is to lose that edge of readiness, and in the Underdark, to be unwary is to die.

This proved the most difficult transition for me when I went back into those lightless corridors. I had to again become the primal hunter, had to survive, every moment, on that instinctual edge, a state of nervous energy that kept my muscles always taut, always ready to spring. Every step of the way, the present was all that mattered, the search for potential hiding places of potential enemies. I could not afford to imagine those enemies. I had to wait for them and watch for them, react to any movements. There are no shadows in the Underdark.

There is no room for imagination in the Underdark. It is a place for alertness, but not aliveness, a place with no room for hopes and dreams.

⌘

One of the sects of Faerun names the sins of humanity as seven, and foremost among them is pride. My interpretation of this had always been to think of the arrogance of kings, who proclaimed themselves gods, or at least convinced their subjects that they spoke with some divine beings, thus conveying the image that their power was god-given. That is only one manifestation of this most deadly of sins. One does not have to be a king to be taken down by false pride. Montolio DeBrouchee, my ranger mentor, warned me about this, but his lessons concerned a personal aspect of pride. "A ranger often walks alone, but never walks without friends nearby," the wise man explained. "A ranger knows his surroundings and knows where allies might be found."

To Montolio's way of thinking, pride was blindness, a blurring of insight and wisdom, and the defeat of trust. A too-proud man walked alone and cared not where allies might be found. When I discovered the web of Menzoberranzan growing thick about me, I understood my error, my arrogance. Had I come to think so much of myself and my abilities that I forgot those allies who had, to this point, allowed me to survive? In my anger over the death of Wulfgar and my fears for Catti-brie, Bruenor, and Regis, I never considered that those living friends could help to take care of themselves. The problem that had befallen us all was my own fault, I had decided, and, thus, was my duty to correct, however impossible that might be for a single person.

I would go to Menzoberranzan, discover the truth, and end the conflict, even if that end meant the sacrifice of my own life. What a fool I had been. Pride told me that I was the cause of Wulfgar's death; pride told me that I could be the one to right the wrong. Sheer arrogance prevented me from dealing openly with my friend, the dwarven king, who could muster the forces necessary to combat any forthcoming drow attacks. On that ledge on the Isle of Rothé, I realized that I would pay for my arrogance; later, I would learn that others dear to me might pay as well. It is a defeat of the spirit to learn that one's arrogance causes such loss and pain. Pride invites you to soar to heights of personal triumph, but the wind is stronger at those heights and the footing, tentative. Farther, then, is the fall.

Courage.

In any language, the word has a special ring to it, as much, I suspect, from the reverent way in which it is spoken as from the actual sounds of the letters. Courage. The word evokes images of great deeds and great character: the grim set of the faces of men defending their town's walls from raiding goblins; the resilience of a mother caring for young children when all the world has seemingly turned hostile. In many of the larger cities of the Realms, young waifs stalk the streets, without parents, without homes. Theirs is a unique courage, a braving of hardships both physical and emotional. I suspect that Artemis Entreri fought such a battle in the mud-filled lanes of Calimport. On one level, he certainly won, certainly overcame any physical obstacles and rose to a rank of incredible power and respect.

On another level, Artemis Entreri surely lost. What might he have been, I often wonder, if his heart had not been so tainted? But I do not mistake my curiosity for pity. Entreri's odds were no greater than my own. He could have won out over his struggles, in body and in heart. I thought myself courageous, altruistic, when I left Mithral Hall determined to end the threat to my friends. I thought I was offering the supreme sacrifice for the good of those dear to me. When Catti-brie entered my cell in House Baenre, when, through half-closed eyes, I glimpsed her fair and deceivingly delicate features, I learned the truth. I did not understand my own motivations when I walked from Mithral Hall. I was too full of unknown grief to recognize my own resignation.

I was not courageous when I walked into the Underdark, because, in the deepest corner of my heart, I felt as if I had nothing to lose. I had not allowed myself to grieve for Wulfgar, and that emptiness stole my will and my trust that things could be put aright.

Courageous people do not surrender hope. Similarly, Artemis Entreri was not courageous when he came with Catti-brie to rescue me. His actions were wrought of sheer desperation, for if he remained in Menzoberranzan, he was surely doomed. Entreri's goals, as always, were purely selfish. By his rescue attempt he made a conscious choice that coming after me was his best chance for survival. The rescue was an act of calculation, not of courage. By the time Catti-brie had run out of Mithral Hall in pursuit of her foolish drow friend, she had honestly overcome her grief for Wulfgar. The grieving process had come full circle for Catti-brie, and her actions were motivated only by loyalty. She had everything to lose, yet had gone alone into the savage Underdark for the sake of a friend. I came to understand this when first I looked into her eyes in the dungeons of House Baenre. I came to understand fully the meaning of the word "courage." And I came, for the first time since Wulfgar fell, to know inspiration. I had fought as the hunter, savagely, mercilessly, but it wasn't until I looked again upon my loyal friend that I regained the eyes of the warrior. Gone was my resignation and acceptance of fate; gone was my belief that all would be right if House Baenre got its sacrifice—if I gave my heart to Lolth.

In that dungeon, the healing potions returned strength to my battered limbs; the sight of grim, determined Catti-brie returned strength to my heart. I vowed then that I would resist, that I would fight the overwhelming events, and would fight to win. When I saw Catti-brie, I remembered all that I had to lose.

Siege of Darkness

I watched the preparations unfolding at Mithral Hall, preparations for war, for, though we, especially Catti-brie, had dealt House Baenre a stinging defeat back in Menzoberranzan, none of us doubted that the dark elves might come our way once more.

Above all else, Matron Mother Baenre was likely angry, and having spent my youth in Menzoberranzan, I knew it was not a good thing to make an enemy of the Matron Mother. Still, I liked what I was seeing here in the dwarven stronghold. Most of all, I enjoyed the spectacle of Bruenor Battlehammer. Bruenor! My dearest friend. The dwarf I had fought beside since my days in Icewind Dale—days that seemed very long ago indeed! I had feared Bruenor's spirit forever broken when Wulfgar fell, that the fire that had guided this most stubborn of dwarves through seemingly insurmountable obstacles in his quest to reclaim his lost homeland had been forever doused. Not so, I learned in those days of preparation. Bruenor's physical scars were deeper now— his left eye was lost, and a bluish line ran diagonally across his face, from forehead to jawbone—but the flames of spirit had been rekindled, burning bright behind his good eye. Bruenor directed the preparations, from agreeing to the fortification designs being constructed in the lowest tunnels to sending out emissaries to the neighboring settlements in search of allies. He asked for no help in the decision-making, and needed none, for this was Bruenor, Eighth King of Mithral Hall, a veteran of so many adventures, a dwarf who had earned his title.

His grief was gone, and he was king again, to the joy of his friends and subjects. "Let the damned drow come!" Bruenor growled quite often, and always he nodded in my direction if I was about, as if to remind me that he meant no personal insult.

In truth, that determined war cry from Bruenor Battlehammer was among the sweetest things I had ever heard. What was it, I wondered, that had brought the grieving dwarf from his despair? And it wasn't just Bruenor. All around me I saw an excitement, in the dwarves, in Catti-brie, even in Regis, the halfling known more for preparing for lunch and nap than for war. I felt it, too. That tingling anticipation, that camaraderie that had me and all the others patting each other on the back, offering praises for the simplest of additions to the common defense, and raising our voices together in cheer whenever good news was announced. What was it? It was more than shared fear, more than giving thanks for what we had while realizing that it might soon be stolen away. I didn't understand it then, in that time of frenzy, in that euphoria of frantic preparations. Now, looking back, it is an easy thing to recognize. It was hope. To any intelligent being, there is no emotion more important than hope. Individually or collectively, we must hope that the future will be better than the past, that our offspring, and theirs after them, will be a bit closer to an ideal society, whatever our perception of that might be. Certainly a warrior barbarian's hope for the future might differ from the ideal fostered in the imagination of a peaceful farmer. And a dwarf would not strive to live in a world that resembled an elf's ideal! But the hope itself is not so different. It is at those times when we feel we are contributing to that ultimate end, as it was in Mithral Hall when we believed the battle with Menzoberranzan would soon come—that we would defeat the dark elves and end, once and for all, the threat from the Underdark city—we feel true elation.

Hope is the key. The future will be better than the past, or the present. Without this belief, there is only the self-indulgent, ultimately empty striving of the present, as in drow society, or simple despair, the time of life wasted in waiting for death. Bruenor had found a cause— we all had—and never have I been more alive than in those days of preparation in Mithral Hall.

Forever after, the bards of the Realms called it the Time of Troubles, the time when the gods were kicked out of the heavens, their avatars walking among the mortals. The time when the Tablets of Fate were stolen, invoking the wrath of Ao, Overlord of the Gods, when magic went awry, and when, as a consequence, social and religious hierarchies, so often based on magical strength, fell into chaos. I have heard many tales from fanatical priests of their encounters with their particular avatars, frenzied stories from men and women who claim to have looked upon their deities. So many others came to convert to a religion during this troubled time, likewise claiming they had seen the light and the truth, however convoluted it might be. I do not disagree with the claims, and would not openly attack the premise of their encounters. I am glad for those who have found enrichment amid the chaos; I am glad whenever another person finds the contentment of spiritual guidance.

But what of faith? What of fidelity and loyalty? Complete trust? Faith is not granted by tangible proof. It comes from the heart and the soul. If a person needs proof of a god's existence, then the very notion of spirituality is diminished into sensuality and we have reduced what is holy into what is logical. I have touched the unicorn, so rare and so precious, the symbol of the goddess Mielikki, who holds my heart and soul. This was before the onset of the Time of Troubles, yet were I of a like mind to those who make the claims of viewing avatars, I could say the same. I could say that I have touched Mielikki, that she came to me in a magical glade in the mountains near Dead Orc Pass. The unicorn was not Mielikki, and yet it was, as is the sunrise and the seasons, as are the birds and the squirrels, and the strength of a tree that has lived through the dawn and death of centuries. As are the leaves, blowing on autumn winds and the snow piling deep in cold mountain vales. As are the smell of a crisp night, the twinkle of the starry canopy, and the howl of a distant wolf. No, I'll not argue openly against one who has claimed to have seen an avatar, because that person will not understand that the mere presence of such a being undermines the very purpose of, and value of, faith. Because if the true gods were so tangible and so accessible, then we would no longer be independent creatures set on a journey to find the truth, but merely a herd of sheep needing the guidance of a shepherd and his dogs, unthinking and without the essence of faith.

The guidance is there, I know. Not in such a tangible form, but in what we know to be good and just. It is our own reactions to the acts of others that show us the value of our own actions, and if we have fallen so far as to need an avatar, an undeniable manifestation of a god, to show us our way, then we are pitiful creatures indeed. The Time of Troubles? Yes. And even more so if we are to believe the suggestion of avatars, because truth is singular and cannot, by definition, support so many varied, even opposing, manifestations. The unicorn was not Mielikki, and yet it was, for I have touched Mielikki. Not as an avatar, or as a unicorn, but as a way of viewing my place in the world. Mielikki is my heart. I follow her precepts because, were I to write precepts based on my own conscience, they would be the same. I follow Mielikki because she represents what I call truth.

Such is the case for most of the followers of most of the various gods, and if we looked more closely at the pantheon of the Realms, we would realize that the precepts of the "goodly" gods are not so different. It is the worldly interpretations of those precepts that vary from faith to faith. As for the other gods, the gods of strife and chaos, such as Lolth, the Spider Queen, who possesses the hearts of those priestesses who rule Menzoberranzan . . . they are not worth mentioning. There is no truth, only worldly gain, and any religion based on such principles is, in fact, no more than a practice of self-indulgence and in no way a measure of spirituality. In worldly terms, the priestesses of the Spider Queen are quite formidable; in spiritual terms, they are empty. Thus, their lives are without love and without joy.

So tell me not of avatars. Show me not your proof that yours is the true god. I grant you your beliefs without question and without judgment, but if you grant me what is in my heart, then such tangible evidence is irrelevant.

How I wanted to go to Catti-brie after I realized the dangers of her sword! How I wanted to stand by her and protect her! The item had possessed her, after all, and was imbued with a powerful and obviously sentient magic.

Catti-brie wanted me by her side—who wouldn't want the supportive shoulder of a friend with such a struggle looming?—and yet she did not want me there, could not have me there, for she knew this battle was hers to fight alone. I had to respect her conclusion, and in those days when the Time of Troubles began to end and the magics of the world sorted themselves out once more, I came to learn that sometimes the most difficult battles are the ones we are forced not to fight. I came to learn then why mothers and fathers seldom have fingernails and often carry an expression of forlorn resignation. What agony it must be for a parent in Silverymoon to be told by her offspring, no longer a child, that he or she has decided to head out to the west, to Waterdeep, to sail for adventure along the Sword Coast. Everything within that parent wants to yell out "Stay!" Every instinct within that parent wants to hug the child close, to protect that child forever. And yet, ultimately, those instincts are wrong. In the heart, there is no sting greater than watching the struggles of one you love, knowing that only through such strife will that person grow and recognize the potential of his or her existence. Too many thieves in the Realms believe the formula for happiness lies in an unguarded treasure trove. Too many wizards seek to circumvent the years of study required for true power. They find a spell on a scroll or an enchanted item that is far beyond their understanding, yet they try it anyway, only to be consumed by the powerful magic. Too many priests in the Realms, and too many religious sects in general, ask of themselves and of their congregations only humble servitude. All of them are doomed to fail in the true test of happiness. There is one ingredient missing in stumbling upon an unguarded treasure hoard; there is one element absent when a minor wizard lays his hands on an archmage's staff; there is one item unaccounted for in humble, unquestioning, and unambitious servitude.

A sense of accomplishment. It is the most important ingredient in any rational being's formula of happiness. It is the element that builds confidence and allows us to go on to other, greater tasks. It is the item that promotes a sense of self-worth, that allows any person to believe there is value in life itself, that gives a sense of purpose to bolster us as we face life's unanswerable questions. So it was with Catti-brie and her sword. This battle had found her, and she had determined to fight it. Had I followed my protective instincts, I would have refused to aid her in taking on this quest.

My protective instincts told me to go to Bruenor, who would have surely ordered the sentient sword destroyed. By doing that, or taking any other course to prevent Catti-brie's battle, I would have, in effect, failed to trust in her, failed to respect her individual needs and her chosen destiny, and thus, I would have stolen a bit of her freedom. That had been Wulfgar's single failure. In his fears for the woman he so dearly loved, the brave and proud barbarian had tried to smother her in his protective hug.

I think he saw the truth of his error in the moments before his death. I think he remembered then the reasons he loved Catti-brie: her strength and independence. How ironic it is that our instincts often run exactly opposite from what we truly desire for those we love. In the situation I earlier named, the parents would have to let their child go to Waterdeep and the Sword Coast. And so it was with Catti-brie. She chose to take her sword, chose to explore its sentient side, perhaps at great personal risk. The decision was hers to make, and once she had made it, I had to respect it, had to respect her. I didn't see her much over the next couple of tendays, as she waged her private battle. But I thought of her and worried for her every waking moment, and even in my dreams.

∽

I noticed something truly amazing, and truly heartwarming, as we, all the defenders of Mithral Hall and the immediate region, neared the end of preparations, neared the time when the drow would come. I am drow. My skin proves that I am different. The ebony hue shows my heritage clearly and undeniably. And yet, not a glare was aimed my way, not a look of consternation from the Harpells and the Longriders, not an angry word from volatile Berkthgar and his warrior people. And no dwarf, not even General Dagna, who did not like anyone who was not a dwarf, pointed an accusing finger at me. We did not know why the drow had come, be it for me or for the promise of treasure from the rich dwarven complex. Whatever the cause, to the defenders, I was without blame. How wonderful that felt to me, who had worn the burden of self-imposed guilt for many months, guilt for the previous raid, guilt for Wulfgar, guilt that Catti-brie had been forced by friendship to chase me all the way to Menzoberranzan. I had worn this heavy collar, and yet those around me who had as much to lose as I placed no burden on me. You cannot understand how special that realization was to one of my past. It was a gesture of sincere friendship, and what made it all the more important is that it was an unintentional gesture, offered without thought or purpose. Too often in the past, my "friends" would make such gestures as if to prove something, more to themselves than to me. They could feel better about themselves because they could look beyond the obvious differences, such as the color of my skin. Guenhwyvar never did that. Bruenor never did that. Neither did Catti-brie or Regis. Wulfgar at first despised me, openly and without excuse, simply because I was drow. They were honest, and thus, they were always my friends. But in the days of preparation for war, I saw that sphere of friendship expand many times over. I came to know that the dwarves of Mithral Hall, the men and women of Settlestone, and many, many more, truly accepted me.

That is the honest nature of friendship. That is when it becomes sincere, and not self-serving. So in those days, Drizzt Do'Urden came to understand, once and for all, that he was not of Menzoberranzan. I threw off the collar of guilt. I smiled.

They came as an army, but not so. Eight thousand dark elves and a larger number of humanoid slaves, a mighty and massive force, swarmed toward Mithral Hall. The descriptions are fitting in terms of sheer numbers and strength, and yet "army" and "force" imply something more, a sense of cohesion and collective purpose. Certainly the drow are among the finest warriors in the Realms, trained to fight from the youngest age, alone or in groups, and certainly the purpose seems clear when the war is racial, when it is drow battling dwarves. Yet, though their tactics are perfect, groups working in unison to support each other, that cohesion among drow ranks remains superficial. Few, if any, dark elves of Lolth's army would give her or his life to save another, unless she or he was confident that the sacrifice would guarantee a place of honor in the afterlife at the Spider Queen's side. Only a fanatic among the dark elves would take a hit, however minor, to spare another's life, and only because that fanatic thought the act in her own best interest. The drow came crying for the glory of the Spider Queen, but in reality, they each were looking for a piece of her glory.

Personal gain was always the dark elves' primary precept. That was the difference between the defenders of Mithral Hall and those who came to conquer. That was the one hope of our side when faced with such horrendous odds, outnumbered by skilled drow warriors! If a single dwarf came to a battle in which his comrades were being overrun, he would roar in defiance and charge in headlong, however terrible the odds. Yet if we could catch a group of drow, a patrol, perhaps, in an ambush, those supporting groups flanking their unfortunate comrades would not join in unless they could be assured of victory. We, not they, had true collective purpose. We, not they, understood cohesion, fought for a shared higher principle, and understood and accepted that any sacrifice we might make would be toward the greater good.

There is a chamber—many chambers, actually—in Mithral Hall, where the heroes of wars and past struggles are honored. Wulfgar's hammer is there; so was the bow—the bow of an elf—that Catti-brie put into service once more. Though she has used the bow for years, and has added considerably to its legend, Catti-brie refers to it still as "the bow of Anariel," that long-dead elf. If the bow is put into service again by a friend of Clan Battlehammer centuries hence, it will be called "the bow of Catti-brie, passed from Anariel." There is in Mithral Hall another place, the Hall of Kings, where the busts of Clan Battlehammer's patrons, the eight kings, have been carved, gigantic and everlasting.

The drow have no such monuments. My mother, Malice, never spoke of the previous matron mother of House Do'Urden, likely because Malice played a hand in her mother's death. In the Academy, there are no plaques of former mistresses and masters. Indeed, as I consider it now, the only monuments in Menzoberranzan are the statues of those punished by Baenre, of those struck by Vendes and her wicked whip, their skin turned to ebony, that they might then be placed on display as testaments of disobedience on the plateau of Tier Breche outside the Academy. That was the difference between the defenders of Mithral Hall and those who came to conquer. That was the one hope.

Passage to Dawn

Six years. Not so long in the life span of a drow, and yet, in counting the months, the tendays, the days, the hours, it seemed to me as if I had been away from Mithral Hall a hundred times that number. The place was removed, another lifetime, another way of life, a mere stepping-stone to . . . To what? To where?

My most vivid memory of Mithral Hall is of riding away from the place with Catti-brie at my side, is the view in looking back over the plumes of smoke rising from Settlestone to the mountain called Fourthpeak. Mithral Hall was Bruenor's kingdom, Bruenor's home, and Bruenor was among the most dear of friends to me. But it was not my home, had never been so. I couldn't explain it then, and still cannot. All should have been well there after the defeat of the invading drow army. Mithral Hall shared prosperity and friendship with all of the neighboring communities, was part of an assortment of kingdoms with the power to protect their borders and feed their poor. All of that, but still Mithral Hall was not home. Not for me, and not for Catti-brie. Thus had we taken to the road, riding west to the coast, to Waterdeep. I never argued with Catti-brie—though she had certainly expected me to—concerning her decision to leave Mithral Hall. We were of like minds. We had never really set down our hearts in the place; we had been too busy, in defeating the enemies who ruled there, in reopening the dwarven mines, in traveling to Menzoberranzan and in battling the dark elves who had come to Mithral Hall. All that completed, it seemed time to settle, to rest, to tell and to lengthen tales of our adventures. If Mithral Hall had been our home before the battles, we would have remained. After the battles, after the losses . . . for both Catti-brie and Drizzt Do'Urden, it was too late. Mithral Hall was Bruenor's place, not ours. It was the war-scarred place where I had to again face the legacy of my dark heritage. It was the beginning of the road that had led me back to Menzoberranzan.

It was the place where Wulfgar had died. Catti-brie and I vowed that we would return there one day, and so we would, for Bruenor was there, and Regis. But Catti-brie had seen the truth. You can never get the smell of blood out of the stones. If you were there when that blood was spilled, the continuing aroma evokes images too painful to live beside. Six years, and I have missed Bruenor and Regis, Stumpet Rakingclaw, and even Berkthgar the Bold, who rules Settlestone. I have missed my journeys to wondrous Silverymoon, and watching the dawn from one of Fourthpeak's many rocky perches. I ride the waves along the Sword Coast now, the wind and spray in my face. My ceiling is the rush of clouds and the canopy of stars; my floor is the creaking boards of a swift, well-weathered ship, and beyond that, the azure blanket, flat and still, heaving and rolling, hissing in the rain and exploding under the fall of a breaching whale. Is this my home? I know not. Another stepping-stone, I would guess, but whether there really is a road that would lead me to a place called home, I do not know. Nor do I think about it often, because I've come to realize that I do not care. If this road, this series of stepping-stones, leads nowhere, then so be it. I walk the road with friends, and so I have my home.

We are the center. In each of our minds—some may call it arrogance, or selfishness—we are the center, and all the world moves about us, and for us, and because of us. This is the paradox of community, the one and the whole, the desires of the one often in direct conflict with the needs of the whole. Who among us has not wondered if all the world is no more than a personal dream? I do not believe that such thoughts are arrogant or selfish. It is simply a matter of perception; we can empathize with someone else, but we cannot truly see the world as another person sees it, or judge events as they affect the mind and the heart of another, even a friend. But we must try. For the sake of all the world, we must try. This is the test of altruism, the most basic and undeniable ingredient for society. Therein lies the paradox, for ultimately, logically, we each must care more about ourselves than about others, and yet, if, as rational beings we follow that logical course, we place our needs and desires above the needs of our society, and then there is no community. I come from Menzoberranzan, city of drow, city of self. I have seen that way of selfishness. I have seen it fail miserably. When self-indulgence rules, then all the community loses, and in the end, those striving for personal gains are left with nothing of any real value.

Because everything of value that we will know in this life comes from our relationships with those around us. Because there is nothing material that measures against the intangibles of love and friendship.

Thus, we must overcome that selfishness and we must try; we must care. I saw this truth plainly following the attack on Captain Deudermont in Waterdeep. My first inclination was to believe that my past had precipitated the trouble, that my life course had again brought pain to a friend. I could not bear this thought. I felt old and I felt tired. Subsequently learning that the trouble was possibly brought on by Deudermont's old enemies, not my own, gave me more heart for the fight. Why is that? The danger to me was no less, nor was the danger to Deudermont, or to Catti-brie, or any of the others about us. Yet my emotions were real, very real, and I recognized and understood them, if not their source. Now, in reflection, I recognize that source, and take pride in it. I have seen the failure of self-indulgence, and I have run from such a world. I would rather die because of Deudermont's past than have him die because of my own. I would suffer the physical pains, even the end of my life. Better that than watch one I love suffer and die because of me. I would rather have my physical heart torn from my chest than have my heart of hearts, the essence of love, the empathy and the need to belong to something bigger than my corporeal form, destroyed.

They are a curious thing, these emotions. How they fly in the face of logic, how they overrule the most basic instincts. Because, in the measure of time, in the measure of humanity, we sense those self-indulgent instincts to be a weakness, we sense that the needs of the community must outweigh the desires of the one. Only when we admit to our failures and recognize our weaknesses can we rise above them. Together.

They are the absolutes, the pantheon of ideals, the goodly gods and the evil fiends, forever locked in the struggle for the souls of the mortals. The concept that is Lolth is purely evil; that of Mielikki, purely good. As opposite as black and white, with no shades of gray in between. Thus are the concepts, good and evil. Absolute, rigid. There can be no justification for a truly evil act. There are no shades of gray. While an act of good often brings personal gain, the act itself is absolute as its measure is based on intent. This is epitomized by our beliefs in the pantheon, but what of the mortal races, the rational beings—the humans and the races of elvenkind and dwarvenkind, the gnomes and the halflings, the goblinoids and giantkin? Here the question muddles, the absolutes blend. To many, the equation is simple: I am drow, drow are evil, thus I am evil.

They are wrong. For what is a rational being if not a choice? And there can be no evil, nor any good, without intent. It is true that in the Realms there are races and cultures, particularly the goblinoids, which show a general weal of evil. and those. such as the surface elves. which lean toward the concept of good. But even in these. which many consider personifications of an absolute. it is the individual's intents and actions that ultimately decide. I have known a goblin who was not evil. and I am a drow who has not succumbed to the ways of his culture. Still. few drow and fewer goblins can make such claims. and so the generalities hold. Most curious and most diverse among the races are the humans. Here the equation and the expectations muddle most of all. Here perception reigns supreme. Here intent is oft hidden. secret. No race is more adept than humans at weaving a mask of justification. No race is more adept than humans at weaving a mask of excuses. at ultimately claiming good intent. And no race is more adept at believing its own claims. How many wars have been fought. man against man. with both armies espousing that god. a goodly god. was on their side and in their hearts? But good is not a thing of perception. What is "good" in one culture cannot be "evil" in another. This might be true of mores and minor practices. but not of virtue. Virtue is absolute. It must be. Virtue is the celebration of life and of love. the acceptance of others and the desire to grow toward goodness. toward a better place. It is the absence of pride and envy. the willingness to share our joys and to bask in the accomplishments of others. It is above justification because it is what truly lies in each and every heart. If a person does an evil act. then let him weave his mask. but it will not hide the truth. the absolute. from what is naked within his own heart.

There is a place within each of us where we cannot hide from the truth. where virtue sits as judge. To admit the truth of our actions is to go before that court. where process is irrelevant. Good and evil are intents. and intent is without excuse. Cadderly Bonaduce went to that place as willingly and completely as any man I have known. I recognize that growth within him. and see the result. the Spirit Soaring. most majestic and yet most humble of human accomplishments. Artemis Entreri will go to that place. Perhaps not until the moment of his death. but he will go. as we all must eventually go. and what agony he will

realize when the truth of his evil existence is laid bare before him. I
pray that he goes soon, and my hope is not born of vengeance, for
vengeance is an empty prayer. May Entreri go of his own volition to
that most private place within his heart to see the truth and thus, to
correct his ways. He will find joy in his penance, true harmony that
he can never know along his present course.

I go to that place within my heart as often as I am able in order to
escape the trap of easy justification. It is a painful place, a naked place,
but only there might we grow toward goodness. Only there, where no
mask can justify, might we recognize the truth of our intents, and thus,
the truth of our actions. Only there, where virtue sits as judge, are
heroes born.

I remember well that occasion when I returned to Menzoberranzan,
the city of my birth, the city of my childhood. I was floating on a raft
across the lake of Donigarten when the city came into view, a sight
I had feared and longed for at the same time. I did not ever want
to return to Menzoberranzan, and yet, I had to wonder what going
there would feel like. Was the place as bad as my memories told me? I
remember well that moment when we drifted past the cavern's curving
wall, the sculpted stalagmites coming into view. It was a disappointment.
I did not feel any anger, nor any awe. No warmth of nostalgia, true
or false, washed over me. I did not dwell in the memories of my
childhood, not even in the memories of my good times with Zaknafein.
All that I thought of in that critical moment was the fact that there
were lights burning in the city, an unusual and perhaps significant
event. All that I thought of was my critical mission, and how I must
move fast to get the job done. My fears, for indeed they remained, were
of a rational nature. Not the impulsive and unreasonable fears wrought
of childhood memories, but the very real trepidations that I was
walking into the lair of a powerful enemy. Later, when the situation

allowed. I reflected on that moment, confused as to why it had been
so disappointing, so insignificant. Why hadn't I been overwhelmed
by the sight of the city that had been my home for the first three
decades of my life? Only when I turned around the northwestern
corner of the Spine of the World mountain range, back into Icewind
Dale, did I realize the truth. Menzoberranzan had been a place along
my journey, but not a home, never a home. As the blind seer's riddle
had inferred, Icewind Dale had been my home that was first. All that
had come before, all that had led to that windswept and inhospitable
place—from Menzoberranzan to Blingdenstone, to the surface, even
to the enchanted grove of my ranger mentor, Montolio DeBrouchee—
had been but a road, a path to follow. These truths came clear to me
when I turned that corner, facing the dale for the first time in a
decade, feeling the endless wind upon my face, the same wind that had
always been there and that gave the place its name. It is a complicated
word: "home." It carries varied definitions to nearly every person. To
me, home is not just a place, but a feeling, a warm and comfortable
sensation of control. Home is where I need make no excuses for my
actions or the color of my skin, where I must be accepted because
this is my place. It is both a personal and a shared domain, for it is
the place a person most truly belongs, and yet it is so only because of
those friends around him. Unlike my first glimpse of Menzoberranzan,
when I looked upon Icewind Dale I was filled with thoughts of what
had been. There were thoughts of sitting on the side of Kelvin's
Cairn, watching the stars and the fires of the roaming barbarian
tribes, thoughts of battling tundra yeti beside Bruenor. I remembered
the dwarf's sour expression when he licked his axe and first learned
that the brains of a tundra yeti tasted terrible! I remembered my first
meeting with Catti-brie, my companion still. She was but a girl then,
a trusting and beautiful spirit, wild in nature yet always sensitive. I
remembered so very much, a veritable flood of images, and though my
mission on that occasion was no less vital and pressing than the one
that had taken me to Menzoberranzan, I thought nothing of it, didn't

consider my course at all. At that moment, it simply didn't matter. All that I cared about was that I had come home.

Berkthgar was right. He was right in returning his people to Icewind Dale, and even more so in returning to the ancient ways of their heritage. Life may have been easier in Settlestone for the barbarians, their material wealth greater by far. In Settlestone, they had more food and better shelter, and the security of allies all around them. But out here on the open tundra, running with the reindeer herd, was their god. Out here on the tundra, in the soil that held the bones of their ancestors, was their spirit. In Settlestone, the barbarians had been far richer in material terms. Out here they were immortal, and thus, richer by far. So Berkthgar was right in returning to Icewind Dale, and to the old ways. And yet, Wulfgar had been right in uniting the tribes, and in forging alliances with the folk of Ten Towns, especially with the dwarves. And Wulfgar, in inadvertently leading his people from the dale, was right in trying to better the lot of the barbarians, though perhaps they had gone too far from the old ways, the ways of the barbarian spirit. Barbarian leaders come to power in open challenge, "by blood or by deed," and that, too, is how they lead. By blood, by the wisdom of the ages, by the kinship evoked in following the course of best intent. Or by deed, by strength, and by sheer physical prowess. Both Wulfgar and Berkthgar claimed leadership by deed—Wulfgar by slaying Dracos Icingdeath, and Berkthgar by assuming the leadership of Settlestone after Wulfgar's death. There the resemblance ends, though, for Wulfgar had subsequently led by blood, while Berkthgar continues to lead by deed. Wulfgar always sought what was best for his people, trusting in them to follow his wise course, or trusting in them to disapprove and deny that course, showing him the folly of his way.

Berkthgar is possessed of no such trust, in his people or in himself. He leads by deed only, by strength and by intimidation. He was right in returning to the dale, and his people would have recognized that truth and approved of his course, yet never did he give them the chance. Thus Berkthgar errs: he has no guidance for the folly of his way. A return to the old does not have to be complete, does not have to abandon that which was better with the new. As is often the case, the truth sits somewhere in the middle. Revjak knows this, as do many others, particularly the older members of the tribe. These dissenters can do nothing, though, when Berkthgar rules by deed, when his strength has no confidence and thus, no trust. Many others of the tribe, the young and strongmen mostly, are impressed by powerful Berkthgar and his decisive ways; their blood is high, their spirits soar. Off the cliff, I fear.

The better way, within the context of the old, is to hold fast the alliances forged by Wulfgar. That is the way of blood, of wisdom. Berkthgar leads by deed, not by blood. He will take his people to the ancient ways and ancient enemies. His is a road of sorrow.

Paths of Darkness

The Silent Blade

Often I sit and ponder the turmoil I feel when my blades are at rest, when all the world around me seems at peace. This is the supposed ideal for which I strive, the calm that we all hope will eventually return to us when we are at war, and yet, in these peaceful times—and they have been rare occurrences indeed in the more than seven decades of my life—I do not feel as if I have found perfection, but, rather, as if something is missing from my life.

It seems such an incongruous notion, and yet I have come to know that I am a warrior, a creature of action. In those times when there is no pressing need for action, I am not at ease. Not at all. When the road is not filled with adventure, when there are no monsters to battle and no mountains to climb, boredom finds me. I have come to accept this truth of my life, this truth about who I am, and so, on those rare, empty occasions I can find a way to defeat the boredom. I can find a mountain peak higher than the last I climbed.

I see many of the same symptoms now in Wulfgar, returned to us from the grave, from the swirling darkness that was Errtu's corner of the Abyss. But I fear that Wulfgar's state has transcended simple boredom, spilling into the realm of apathy. Wulfgar, too, was a creature of action, but that doesn't seem to be the cure for his lethargy or his apathy. His own people now call out to him, begging action. They have asked him to assume leadership of the tribes. Even stubborn Berkthgar, who would have to give up that coveted position of rulership, supports Wulfgar. He and all the rest of them know, at this tenuous time, that above all others Wulfgar, son of Beornegar, could bring great gains to the nomadic barbarians of Icewind Dale.

Wulfgar will not heed that call. It is neither humility nor weariness stopping him. I recognize, nor any fears that he cannot handle the position or live up to the expectations of those begging him. Any of those problems could be overcome, could be reasoned through or supported by Wulfgar's friends, myself included. But, no, it is none of those rectifiable things. It is simply that he does not care. Could it be that his own agonies at the clawed hands of Errtu were so great and so enduring that he has lost his ability to empathize with the pain of others? Has he seen too much horror, too much agony, to hear their cries? I fear this above all else, for it is a loss that knows no precise cure. And yet, to be honest, I see it clearly etched in Wulfgar's features, a state of self-absorption where too many memories of his own recent horrors cloud his vision.

Perhaps he does not even recognize someone else's pain. Or perhaps, if he does see it, he dismisses it as trivial next to the monumental trials he suffered for those six years as Errtu's prisoner. Loss of empathy might well be the most enduring and deep-cutting scar of all, the silent blade of an unseen enemy, tearing at our hearts and stealing more than our strength.

Stealing our will, for what are we without empathy? What manner of joy might we find in our lives if we cannot understand the joys and pains of those around us, if we cannot share in a greater community? I remember my years in the Underdark after I ran out of Menzoberranzan. Alone, save the occasional visits from Guenhwyvar, I survived those long years through my own imagination. I am not certain that Wulfgar even has that capacity left to him, for imagination requires introspection, a reaching within one's thoughts, and I fear that every time my friend so looks inward, all he sees are the minions of Errtu, the sludge and horrors of the Abyss.

He is surrounded by friends, who love him and will try with all their hearts to support him and help him climb out of Errtu's emotional dungeon. Perhaps Catti-brie, the woman he once loved—and perhaps still does love—so deeply, will prove pivotal to his recovery. It pains me to watch them together, I admit. She treats Wulfgar with such tenderness and compassion, but I know that he feels not her gentle touch. Better that she slap his face, eye him sternly, and show him the truth of his lethargy. I know this and yet I cannot tell her to do so, for their relationship is much more complicated than that. I have nothing but Wulfgar's best interests in my mind and my heart now, and yet, if I showed Catti-brie a way that seemed less than compassionate, it could be, and would be—by Wulfgar at least, in his present state of mind— construed as the interference of a jealous suitor.

Not true. For though I do not know Catti-brie's honest feelings toward this man who once was to be her husband—for she has become quite guarded with her feelings of late—I do recognize that Wulfgar is not capable of love at this time. Not capable of love . . . are there any sadder words to describe a man? I think not, and wish that I could now assess Wulfgar's state of mind differently. But love, honest love, requires empathy. It is a sharing—of joy, of pain, of laughter, and of tears. Honest love makes one's soul a reflection of the partner's moods. And as a room seems larger when it is lined with mirrors, so do the joys become amplified. And as the individual items within the mirrored room seem less acute, so does pain diminish and fade, stretched thin by the sharing.

That is the beauty of love, whether in passion or friendship. A sharing that multiplies the joys and thins the pains. Wulfgar is surrounded now by friends, all willing to engage in such sharing, as it once was between us. Yet he cannot so engage us, cannot let loose those guards that he necessarily put in place when surrounded by the likes of Errtu. He has lost his empathy. I can only pray that he will find it again, that time will allow him to open his heart and soul to those deserving, for without empathy he will find no purpose. Without purpose, he will find no satisfaction. Without satisfaction, he will find no contentment, and without contentment, he will find no joy.

And we, all of us, will have no way to help him.

We each have our own path to tread. That seems such a simple and obvious thought, but in a world of relationships where so many people sublimate their own true feelings and desires in consideration of others, we take many steps off that true path.

In the end, though, if we are to be truly happy, we must follow our hearts and find our way alone. I learned that truth when I walked out of Menzoberranzan and confirmed my path when I arrived in Icewind Dale and found these wonderful friends. After the last brutal fight in Mithral Hall, when half of Menzoberranzan, it seemed, marched to destroy the dwarves, I knew that my path lay elsewhere, that I needed to journey, to find a new horizon on which to set my gaze. Catti-brie knew it, too, and because I understood that her desire to go along was not in sympathy to my desires but true to her own heart, I welcomed the company.

We each have our own path to tread, and so I learned, painfully, that fateful morning in the mountains, that Wulfgar had found one that diverged from my own. How I wanted to stop him! How I wanted to plead with him or, if that failed, to beat him into unconsciousness and drag him back to the camp. When we parted, I felt a hole in my heart nearly as profound as that which I had felt when I first learned of his apparent death in the fight against the yochlol.

And then, after I walked away, pangs of guilt layered above the pain of loss. Had I let Wulfgar go so easily because of his relationship with Catti-brie? Was there some place within me that saw my barbarian friend's return as a hindrance to a relationship that I had been building with the woman since we had ridden from Mithral Hall together?

The guilt could find no true hold and was gone by the time I rejoined my companions. As I had my road to walk, and now Wulfgar his, so too would Catti-brie find hers. With me? With Wulfgar? Who could know? But whatever her road, I would not try to alter it in such a manner. I did not let Wulfgar go easily for any sense of personal gain. Not at all, for indeed my heart weighed heavy. No, I let Wulfgar go without much of an argument because I knew that there was nothing I, or our other friends, could do to heal the wounds within him. Nothing I could say to him could bring him solace, and if Catti-brie had begun to make any progress, then surely it had been destroyed in the flick of Wulfgar's fist slamming into her face.

Partly it was fear that drove Wulfgar from us. He believed that he could not control the demons within him and that, in the grasp of those painful recollections, he might truly hurt one of us. Mostly, though, Wulfgar left us because of shame. How could he face Bruenor again after striking Catti-brie? How could he face Catti-brie? What words might he say in apology when in truth, and he knew it, it very well might happen again? And beyond that one act, Wulfgar perceived himself as weak because the images of Errtu's legacy were so overwhelming him. Logically, they were but memories and nothing tangible to attack the strong man. To Wulfgar's pragmatic view of the world, being defeated by mere memories equated to great weakness.

In his culture, being defeated in battle is no cause for shame, but running from battle is the highest dishonor. Along that same line of reasoning, being unable to defeat a great monster is acceptable, but being defeated by an intangible thing such as a memory equates with cowardice.

He will learn better, I believe. He will come to understand that he should feel no shame for his inability to cope with the persistent horrors and temptations of Errtu and the Abyss. And then, when he relieves himself from the burden of shame, he will find a way to truly overcome those horrors and dismiss his guilt over the temptations. Only then will he return to Icewind Dale, to those who love him and who will welcome him back eagerly. Only then.

That is my hope, not my expectation. Wulfgar ran off into the wilds, into the Spine of the World, where yetis, giants, and goblin tribes make their homes, where wolves will take their food as they find it, whether hunting a deer or a man. I do not honestly know if he means to come out of the mountains back to the tundra he knows well, or to the more civilized southland, or if he will wander the high and dangerous trails, daring death in an attempt to restore some of the courage he believes he has lost. Or perhaps he will tempt death too greatly, so that it will finally win out and put an end to his pain.

That is my fear. I do not know. We each have our own roads to tread, and Wulfgar has found his, and it is a path, I understand, that is not wide enough for a companion.

I watched the miles roll out behind me, whether walking down a road or sailing fast out of Waterdeep for the southlands, putting distance between us and the friend we four had left behind.

The friend? Many times during those long and arduous days, each of us in our own little space came to wonder about that word "friend" and the responsibilities such a label might carry. We had left Wulfgar behind in the wilds of the Spine of the World no less and had no idea if he was well, if he was even still alive. Could a true friend so desert another?

Would a true friend allow a man to walk alone along troubled and dangerous paths? Often I ponder the meaning of that word. "Friend." It seems such an obvious thing, friendship, and yet often it becomes so very complicated. Should I have stopped Wulfgar, even knowing and admitting that he had his own road to walk? Or should I have gone with him? Or should we all four have shadowed him, watching over him? I think not, though I admit that I know not for certain. There is a fine line between friendship and parenting, and when that line is crossed, the result is often disastrous. A parent who strives to make a true friend of his or her child may well sacrifice authority, and though that parent may be comfortable with surrendering the dominant position, the unintentional result will be to steal from that child the necessary guidance and, more importantly, the sense of security the parent is supposed to impart. On the opposite side, a friend who takes a role as parent forgets the most important ingredient of friendship: respect.

For respect is the guiding principle of friendship, the lighthouse beacon that directs the course of any true friendship. And respect demands trust. Thus, the four of us pray for Wulfgar and intend that our paths will indeed cross again.

Though we'll often look back over our shoulders and wonder, we hold fast to our understanding of friendship, of trust, and of respect. We accept, grudgingly but resolutely, our divergent paths. Surely Wulfgar's trials have become my trials in many ways, but I see now that the friendship of mine most in flux is not the one with the barbarian— not from my perspective, anyway, since I understand that Wulfgar alone must decide the depth and course of our bond—but my relationship with Catti-brie. Our love for each other is no secret between us, or to anyone else watching us—and I fear that perhaps the bond that has grown between us might have had some influence in Wulfgar's painful decisions. But the nature of that love remains a mystery to me and to Catti-brie. We have in many ways become as brother and sister, and surely I am closer to her than I could ever have been to any of my natural siblings! For several years we had only each other to count on and both learned beyond any doubt that the other would always be there. I would die for her, and she for me. Without hesitation, without doubt. Truly in all the world there is no one, not even Bruenor, Wulfgar, or Regis—or even Zaknafein—with whom I would rather spend my time.

There is no one who can view a sunrise beside me and better understand the emotions that sight always stirs within me. There is no one who can fight beside me and better complement my movements. There is no one who better knows all that is in my heart and thoughts, though I had not yet spoken a word. But what does that mean? Surely I feel a physical attraction to Catti-brie as well. She is possessed of a combination of innocence and a playful wickedness. For all her sympathy and empathy and compassion, there is an edge to Catti-brie that makes potential enemies tremble in fear and potential lovers tremble in anticipation. I believe that she feels similarly toward me, and yet we both understand the dangers of this uncharted territory, dangers more frightening than any physical enemy we have ever known. I am drow, and young, and with the dawn and twilight of several centuries ahead of me. She is human and, though young, with merely decades of life ahead of her. Of course, Catti-brie's life is complicated enough merely having a drow elf as a traveling companion and friend. What troubles might she find if she and I were more than that?

And what might the world think of our children, if ever that path we walked? Would any society in all the world accept them? I know how I feel when I look upon her, though, and believe that I understand her feelings as well. On that level, it seems such an obvious thing, and yet, alas, it becomes so very complicated.

Whether a king's palace, a warrior's bastion, a wizard's tower, an encampment for nomadic barbarians, a farmhouse with stone-lined or hedge-lined fields, or even a tiny and unremarkable room up the back staircase of a ramshackle inn, we each of us spend great energy in carving out our own little kingdoms. From the grandest castle to the smallest nook, from the arrogance of nobility to the unpretentious desires of the lowliest peasant, there is a basic need within the majority of us for ownership, or at least for stewardship.

We want to—need to—find our realm, our place in a world often too confusing and too overwhelming, our sense of order in one little corner of a world that oft looms too big and too uncontrollable. And so we carve and line, fence and lock, then protect our space fiercely with sword or pitchfork.

The hope is that this will be the end of that road we chose to walk, the peaceful and secure rewards for a life of trials. Yet, it never comes to that, for peace is not a place, whether lined by hedges or by high walls. The greatest king with the largest army in the most invulnerable fortress is not necessarily a man at peace. Far from it, for the irony of it all is that the acquisition of such material wealth can work against any hope of true serenity. But beyond any physical securities there lies yet another form of unrest, one that neither the king nor the peasant will escape. Even that great king, even the simplest beggar will, at times, be full of the unspeakable anger we all sometimes feel. And I do not mean a rage so great that it cannot be verbalized but rather a frustration so elusive and permeating that one can find no words for it. It is the quiet source of irrational outbursts against friends and family, the perpetrator of temper. True freedom from it cannot be found in any place outside one's own mind and soul.

Bruenor carved out his kingdom in Mithral Hall, yet found no peace there. He preferred to return to Icewind Dale, a place he had named home not out of desire for wealth, nor out of any inherited kingdom, but because there, in the frozen northland, Bruenor had come to know his greatest measure of inner peace. There he surrounded himself with friends, myself among them, and though he will not admit this—I am not certain he even recognizes it—his return to Icewind Dale was, in fact, precipitated by his desire to return to that emotional place and time when he and I, Regis, Catti-brie, and yes, even Wulfgar, were together. Bruenor went back in search of a memory.

I suspect that Wulfgar now has found a place along or at the end of his chosen road, a niche, be it a tavern in Luskan or Waterdeep, a borrowed barn in a farming village, or even a cave in the Spine of the World. Because what Wulfgar does not now have is a clear picture of where he emotionally wishes to be, a safe haven to which he can escape. If he finds it again, if he can get past the turmoil of his most jarring memories, then likely he, too, will return to Icewind Dale in search of his soul's true home. In Menzoberranzan I witnessed many of the little kingdoms we foolishly cherish, houses strong and powerful and barricaded from enemies in a futile attempt at security. And when I walked out of Menzoberranzan into the wild Underdark, I, too, sought to carve out my niche. I spent time in a cave talking only to Guenhwyvar and sharing space with mushroomlike creatures that I hardly understood and who hardly understood me. I ventured to Blingdenstone, city of the deep gnomes, and could have made that my home, perhaps, except that staying there, so close to the city of drow, would have surely brought ruin upon those folk. And so I came to the surface and found a home with Montolio DeBrouchee in his wondrous mountain grove, perhaps the first place I ever came to know any real measure of inner peace. And yet I came to learn that the grove was not my home, for when Montolio died I found to my surprise that I could not remain there. Eventually I found my place and found that the place was within me, not about me. It happened when I came to Icewind Dale, when I met Catti-brie and Regis and Bruenor. Only then did I learn to defeat the unspeakable anger within. Only there did I learn true peace and serenity.

Now I take that calm with me, whether my friends accompany me or not. Mine is a kingdom of the heart and soul, defended by the security of honest love and friendship and the warmth of memories. Better than any land-based kingdom, stronger than any castle wall, and most importantly of all, portable. I can only hope and pray that Wulfgar will eventually walk out of his darkness and come to this same emotional place.

Spine of the World

In my homeland of Menzoberranzan, where demons play and drow revel at the horrible demise of rivals, there remains a state of necessary alertness and wariness. A drow off guard is a drow murdered in Menzoberranzan, and thus few are the times when dark elves engage in exotic weeds or drinks that dull the senses. Few, but there are exceptions. At the final ceremony of Melee-Magthere, the school of fighters that I attended, graduated students engage in an orgy of mind-blurring herbs and sensual pleasures with the females of Arach-Tinilith, a moment of the purest hedonism, a party of the purest pleasures without regard to future implications.

I rejected that orgy, though I knew not why at the time. It assaulted my sense of morality, I believed—and still do—and it cheapened so many things that I hold precious. Now, in retrospect, I have come to understand another truth about myself that forced rejection of that orgy. Aside from the moral implications, and there were many, the mere notion of the mind-blurring herbs frightened and repulsed me. I knew that all along, of course—as soon as I felt the intoxication at that ceremony, I instinctively rebelled against it—but it wasn't until very recently that I came to understand the truth of that rejection, the real reason why such influences have no place in my life.

These herbs attack the body in various ways, of course, from slowing reflexes to destroying coordination altogether, but more importantly, they attack the spirit in two different ways. First, they blur the past, erasing memories pleasant and unpleasant, and second, they eliminate any thoughts of the future. Intoxicants lock the imbiber in the present, the here and now, without regard for the future, without consideration of the past. That is the trap, a defeatist perspective that allows for attempted satiation of physical pleasures wantonly, recklessly. An intoxicated person will attempt even foolhardy dares because that inner guidance, even to the point of survival instinct itself, can be so impaired. How many young warriors foolishly throw themselves against greater enemies, only to be slain? How many young women find themselves with child, conceived with lovers they would not even consider as future husbands? That is the trap, the defeatist perspective, that I cannot tolerate. I live my life with hope, always hope, that the future will be better than the present, but only as long as I work to make it so. Thus, with that toil, comes the satisfaction in life, the sense of accomplishment we all truly need for real joy. How could I remain honest to that hope if I allowed myself a moment of weakness that could well destroy all I have worked to achieve and all I hope to achieve? How might I have reacted to so many unexpected crises if, at the time of occurrence, I was influenced by a mind-altering substance, one that impaired my judgment or altered my perspective?

Also, the dangers of where such substances might lead cannot be underestimated. Had I allowed myself to be carried away with the mood of the graduation ceremony of Melee-Magthere, had I allowed myself the sensual pleasures offered by the priestesses, how cheapened might any honest encounter of love have been?

Greatly, to my way of thinking. Sensual pleasures are, or should be, the culmination of physical desires combined with an intellectual and emotional decision, a giving of oneself, body and spirit, in a bond of trust and respect. In such a manner as that graduation ceremony, no such sharing could have occurred; it would have been a giving of body only, and more so than that, a taking of another's offered wares.

There would have been no higher joining, no spiritual experience, and thus, no true joy. I cannot live in such a hopeless basking as that, for that is what it is: a pitiful basking in the lower, base levels of existence brought on, I believe, by the lack of hope for a higher level of existence. And so I reject all but the most moderate use of such intoxicants, and while I'll not openly judge those who so indulge, I will pity them their empty souls. What is it that drives a person to such depths? Pain, I believe, and memories too wretched to be openly faced and handled. Intoxicants can, indeed, blur the pains of the past at the expense of the future. But it is not an even trade. With that in mind, I fear for Wulfgar, my lost friend. Where will he find escape from the torments of his enslavement?

I have lived in many societies, from Menzoberranzan of the drow to Blingdenstone of the deep gnomes, to Ten Towns ruled as the most common human settlements, to the barbarian tribes and their own curious ways, to Mithral Hall of the Clan Battlehammer dwarves. I have lived aboard ship, another type of society altogether. All of these places have different customs and mores, all of them have varied government structures, social forces, churches, and societies. Which is the superior system? You would hear many arguments concerning this, mostly based on prosperity, or god-given right, or simple destiny. For the drow, it is simply a religious matter—they structure their society to the desires of the chaotic Spider Queen, then wage war constantly to change the particulars of that structure, though not the structure itself. For the deep gnomes, it is a matter of paying homage and due respect to the elders of their race, accepting the wisdom of those who have lived for so many years. In the human settlement of Ten Towns, leadership comes from popularity, while the barbarians choose their chieftains purely on physical prowess. For the dwarves, rulership is a matter of bloodline. Bruenor became king because his father was king, and his father's father before him, and his father's father's father before him.

I measure the superiority of any society in a different manner, based completely on individual freedom. Of all the places I have lived, I favor Mithral Hall, but that, I understand, is a matter of Bruenor's wisdom in allowing his flock their freedom, and not because of the dwarven political structure. Bruenor is not an active king. He serves as spokesman for the clan in matters politic, as commander in matters martial, and as mediator in disputes among his subjects, but only when so asked. Bruenor remains fiercely independent and grants that joy to those of Clan Battlehammer. I have heard of many queens and kings, matron mothers and clerics, who justify rulership and absolve themselves of any ills by claiming that the commoners who serve them are in need of guidance. This might be true in many long-standing societies, but if it is, that is only because so many generations of conditioning have stolen something essential from the heart and soul of the subjects, because many generations of subordination have robbed the common folk of confidence in determining their own way. All of the governing systems share the trait of stealing freedom from the individual, of forcing certain conditions upon the lives of each citizen in the name of "community."

That concept, "community," is one that I hold dear, and surely, the individuals within any such grouping must sacrifice and accept certain displeasures in the name of the common good to make any community thrive. How much stronger might that community be if those sacrifices came from the heart of each citizen and not from the edicts of the elders, matron mothers, kings, or queens? Freedom is the key to it all. The freedom to stay or to leave, to work in harmony with others or to choose a more individual course. The freedom to help in the larger issues or to abstain. The freedom to build a good life or to live in squalor. The freedom to try anything, or merely to do nothing. Few would dispute the desire for freedom. Everyone I have ever met desires free will, or thinks he does. How curious then, that so many refuse to accept the inverse cost of freedom: responsibility.

An ideal community would work well because the individual members would accept their responsibility toward the welfare of each other and to the community as a whole, not because they are commanded to do so, but because they understand and accept the benefits to such choices. For there are, indeed, consequences to every choice we make, to everything we do or choose not to do. Those consequences are not so obvious, I fear. The selfish man might think himself gaining, but in times when that person most needs his friends, they likely will not be there, and in the end, in the legacy the selfish person leaves behind, he will not be remembered fondly if at all. The selfish person's greed might bring material luxuries, but cannot bring the true joys, the intangible pleasures of love. So it is with the hateful person, the slothful person, the envious person, the thief and the thug, the drunkard and the gossip. Freedom allows each the right to choose the life before him, but freedom demands that the person accept the responsibility for those choices, good and bad.

I have often heard tales of those who believed they were about to die replaying the events of their lives, even long-past occurrences buried deep within their memories. In the end, I believe, in those last moments of this existence, before the mysteries of what may come next, we are given the blessing, or curse, to review our choices, to see them bared before our consciousness, without the confusion of the trappings of day-to-day living, without blurring justifications or the potential for empty promises to make amends.

How many priests, I wonder, would include this most naked moment in their descriptions of heaven and hell?

ᗡ

The course of events in my life have often made me examine the nature of good and evil. I have witnessed the purest forms of both repeatedly, particularly evil. The totality of my early life was spent living among it, a wickedness so thick in the air that it choked me and forced me away.

Only recently, as my reputation has begun to gain me some acceptance among the human populations—a tolerance, at least, if not a welcome—have I come to witness a more complex version of what I observed in Menzoberranzan, a shade of gray varying in lightness and darkness. So many humans, it seems, a vast majority, have within their makeup a dark side, a hunger for the macabre, and the ability to dispassionately dismiss the agony of another in the pursuit of the self.

Nowhere is this more evident than in the Prisoner's Carnival at Luskan and other such pretenses of justice. Prisoners, sometimes guilty, sometimes not—it hardly matters—are paraded before the blood-hungry mob, then beaten, tortured, and finally executed in grand fashion. The presiding magistrate works very hard to exact the most exquisite screams of the purest agony. His job is to twist the expressions of those prisoners into the epitome of terror, the ultimate horror reflected in their eyes.

Once, when in Luskan with Captain Deudermont of the *Sea Sprite*, I ventured to the carnival to witness the "trials" of several pirates we had fished from the sea after sinking their ship. Witnessing the spectacle of a thousand people crammed around a grand stage, yelling and squealing with delight as these miserable pirates were literally cut into pieces, almost made me walk away from Deudermont's ship, almost made me forgo a life as a pirate hunter and retreat to the solitude of the forest or the mountains. Of course, Catti-brie was there to remind me of the truth of it, to point out that these same pirates often exacted equal tortures upon innocent prisoners. While she admitted that such a truth did not justify the Prisoner's Carnival—Catti-brie was so horrified by the mere thought of the place that she would not go anywhere near it—she argued that such treatment of pirates was preferable to allowing them free run of the high seas. But why? Why any of it? The question has bothered me for all these years, and in seeking its answer I have come to explore yet another facet of these incredibly complex creatures called humans. Why would common, otherwise decent folk descend to such a level as the spectacle of Prisoner's Carnival? Why would some of the *Sea Sprite's* own crew, men and women I knew to be honorable and decent, take pleasure in viewing such a macabre display of torture? The answer, perhaps—if there is a more complicated answer than the nature of evil itself—lies in an examination of the attitudes of other races. Among the goodly races, humans alone "celebrate" the executions and torments of prisoners. Halfling societies would have no part of such a display—halfling prisoners have been known to die of overeating. Nor would dwarves, as aggressive as they can be. In dwarven society, prisoners are dealt with efficiently and tidily, without spectacle and out of public view. A murderer among dwarves would be dealt a single blow to the neck. Never did I see any elves at Prisoner's Carnival, except on one occasion when a pair ventured by, then quickly left, obviously disgusted.

My understanding is that in gnome society there are no executions, just a lifetime of imprisonment in an elaborate cell. So why humans? What is it about the emotional construct of the human being that brings about such a spectacle as Prisoner's Carnival? Evil? I think that too simple an answer. Dark elves relish torture—how well I know!—and their actions are, indeed, based on sadism and evil, and an insatiable desire to satisfy the demonic hunger of the Spider Queen, but with humans, as with everything about humans, the answer becomes a bit more complex. Surely there is a measure of sadism involved, particularly on the part of the presiding magistrate and his torturer assistants, but for the common folk, the powerless paupers cheering in the audience, I believe their joy stems from three sources.

First, peasants in Faerun are a powerless lot, subjected to the whims of unscrupulous lords and landowners, and with the ever-present threat of some invasion or another by goblins, giants, or fellow humans, stomping flat the lives they have carved. Prisoner's Carnival affords these unfortunate folk a taste of power, the power over life and death. At long last they feel some sense of control over their own lives. Second, humans are not long-lived like elves and dwarves. Even halflings will usually outlast them. Peasants face the possibility of death daily. A mother fortunate enough to survive two or three births will likely witness the death of at least one of her children. Living so intimately with death obviously breeds a curiosity and fear, even terror. At Prisoner's Carnival these folk witness death at its most horrible, the worst that death can give, and take solace in the fact that their own deaths, unless they become the accused brought before the magistrates, will not likely be nearly as terrible. I have witnessed your worst, grim Death, and I fear you not. The third explanation for the appeal of Prisoner's Carnival lies in the necessity of justice and punishment in order to maintain order in a society. This was the side of the debate held up by Robillard the wizard upon my return to the *Sea Sprite* after witnessing the horror.

While he took no pleasure in viewing the carnival and rarely attended, Robillard defended it as vigorously as I might expect from the magistrate himself. The public humiliation of these men, the public display of their agony, would keep other folk on an honest course, he believed. Thus, the cheers of the peasant mob were no more than a rousing affirmation of their belief in the law and order of their society.

It is a difficult argument to defeat, particularly concerning the effectiveness of such displays in dissuading future criminals, but is it truly justice?

Armed with Robillard's arguments, I went to some minor magistrates in Luskan on the pretense of deciding better protocol for the *Sea Sprite* to hand over captured pirates, but in truth to get them talking about Prisoner's Carnival. It became obvious to me, and very quickly, that the carnival itself had little to do with justice. Many innocent men and women had found their way to the stage in Luskan, forced into false confession by sheer brutality, then punished publicly for those crimes. The magistrates knew this and readily admitted it by citing their relief that at least the prisoners we brought to them were assuredly guilty!

For that reason alone I can never come to terms with the Prisoner's Carnival. One measure of any society is the way it deals with those who have walked away from the course of community and decency, and an indecent treatment of these criminals decreases the standards of morality to the level of the tortured. Yet the practice continues to thrive in many cities in Faerun and in many, many rural communities, where justice, as a matter of survival, must be even more harsh and definitive. Perhaps there is a fourth explanation for the carnival. Perhaps the crowds gather around eagerly merely for the excitement of the show. Perhaps there is no underlying cause or explanation other than the fun of it. I do not like to consider this a possibility, for if humans on as large a scale are capable of eliminating empathy and sympathy so completely as to actually enjoy the spectacle of watching another suffer horribly, then that, I fear, is the truest definition of evil.

After all of the hours of investigation, debate, and interrogation, and many, many hours of contemplation on the nature of these humans among whom I live, I am left without simple answers to travesties such as the Prisoner's Carnival. I am hardly surprised. Rarely do I find a simple answer to anything concerning humans. That, perhaps, is the reason I find little tedium in my day-to-day travels and encounters. That, perhaps, is the reason I have come to love them.

We think we understand those around us. The people we have come to know reveal patterns of behavior, and as our expectations of that behavior are fulfilled time and again we begin to believe that we know the person's heart and soul. I consider that to be an arrogant perception, for one cannot truly understand the heart and soul of another, one cannot truly appreciate the perceptions another might hold toward similar or recounted experiences.

We all search for truth, particularly within our own sphere of existence, the home we have carved and those friends with whom we choose to share it. But truth, I fear, is not always evident where individuals, so complex and changing, are concerned. If ever I believe that the foundations of my world are rooted in stone, I think of Jarlaxle and I am humbled. I have always recognized that there is more to the mercenary than a simple quest for personal gain—he let me and Catti-brie walk away from Menzoberranzan, after all, and at a time when our heads would have brought him a fine price, indeed. When Catti-brie was his prisoner and completely under his power, he did not take advantage of her, though he has admitted, through actions if not words, that he thinks her quite attractive. So always have I seen a level of character beneath the cold mercenary clothing, but despite that knowledge my last encounter with Jarlaxle has shown me that he is far more complex, and certainly more compassionate, than ever I could have guessed. Beyond that, he called himself a friend of Zaknafein, and though I initially recoiled at such a notion, now I consider it to be not only believable, but likely. Do I now understand the truth of Jarlaxle? And is it the same truth that those around him, within Bregan D'aerthe, perceive? Certainly not, and though I believe my current assessment to be correct, I'll not be as arrogant as to claim certainty, nor do I even begin to believe that I know more of him than my surface reasoning. What about Wulfgar, then? Which Wulfgar is the true Wulfgar? Is he the proud and honorable man Bruenor raised, the man who fought beside me against Biggrin and in so many subsequent battles? The man who saved the barbarian tribes from certain extermination and the folk of Ten Towns from future disasters by uniting the groups diplomatically? The man who ran across Faerun for the sake of his imprisoned friend? The man who helped Bruenor reclaim his lost kingdom? Or is Wulfgar the man who harmed Catti-brie, the haunted man who seems destined, in the end, to fail utterly? He is both, I believe, a compilation of his experiences, feelings, and perceptions, as are we all. It is the second of that composite trio, feelings, brought on by experiences beyond his ability to cope, that control Wulfgar now. The raw emotion of those feelings alter his perceptions to the negative.

Given that reality, who is Wulfgar now, and more importantly, if he survives this troubled time, who will he become? How I long to know. How I wish that I could walk beside him on this perilous journey, could speak with him and influence him, perhaps. That I could remind him of who he was, or at least, who we perceived him to be. But I cannot, for it is the heart and soul of Wulfgar, ultimately, and not his particular daily actions, that will surface in the end. And I, and anyone else, could no more influence that heart and soul than I could influence the sun itself.

Curiously, it is in the daily rising of that celestial body that I take my comfort now when thinking about Wulfgar. Why watch the dawn? Why then, why that particular time, instead of any other hour of daylight? Because at dawn the sun is more brilliant by far. Because at dawn, we see the resurgence after the darkness. There is my hope, for as with the sun, so it can be true of people. Those who fall can climb back up, then brighter will they shine in the eyes of those around them. I watch the dawn and think of the man I thought I knew, and pray that my perceptions were correct.

Sea of Swords

It is good to be home. It is good to hear the wind of Icewind Dale, to feel its invigorating bite, like some reminder that I am alive. That seems such a self-evident thing—that I, that we, are alive—and yet, too often, I fear, we easily forget the importance of that simple fact. It is so easy to forget that you are truly alive, or at least, to appreciate that you are truly alive, that every sunrise is yours to view and every sunset is yours to enjoy. And all those hours in between, and all those hours after dusk, are yours to make of what you will.

It is easy to miss the possibility that every person who crosses your path can become an event and a memory, good or bad, to fill in the hours with experience instead of tedium, to break the monotony of the passing moments.

Those wasted moments, those hours of sameness, of routine, are the enemy, I say, are little stretches of death within the moments of life. Yes, it is good to be home, in the wild land of Icewind Dale, where monsters roam aplenty and rogues threaten the roads at every turn. I am more alive and more content than in many years. For too long, I struggled with the legacy of my dark past. For too long, I struggled with the reality of my longevity, that I would likely die long after Bruenor, Wulfgar, and Regis. And Catti-brie.

What a fool I am to rue the end of her days without enjoying the days that she, that we, now have! What a fool I am to let the present slip into the past, while lamenting a potential—and only potential—future!

We are all dying, every moment that passes of every day. That is the inescapable truth of this existence. It is a truth that can paralyze us with fear, or one that can energize us with impatience, with the desire to explore and experience, with the hope—nay, the iron will!—to find a memory in every action. To be alive, under sunshine or under starlight, in weather fair or stormy. To dance every step, be they through gardens of bright flowers or through deep snows.

The young know this truth so many of the old, or even middle-aged, have forgotten. Such is the source of the anger, the jealousy, that so many exhibit toward the young. So many times have I heard the common lament, "If only I could go back to that age, knowing what I now know!" Those words amuse me profoundly, for in truth, the lament should be, "If only I could reclaim the lust and the joy I knew then!" That is the meaning of life, I have come at last to understand, and in that understanding, I have indeed found that lust and that joy. A life of twenty years where that lust and joy, where that truth is understood, might be more full than a life of centuries with head bowed and shoulders slumped.

I remember my first battle beside Wulfgar, when I led him in, against tremendous odds and mighty giants, with a huge grin and a lust for life. How strange that as I gained more to lose, I allowed that lust to diminish! It took me this long, through some bitter losses, to recognize the folly of that reasoning. It took me this long, returned to Icewind Dale after unwittingly surrendering the Crystal Shard to Jarlaxle and completing at last—and forever, I pray—my relationship with Artemis Entreri, to wake up to the life that is mine, to appreciate the beauty around me, to seek out and not shy away from the excitement that is there to be lived.

There remain worries and fears, of course. Wulfgar is gone from us—I know not where—and I fear for his head, his heart, and his body. But I have accepted that his path was his own to choose, and that he, for the sake of all three—head, heart, and body—had to step away from us. I pray that our paths will cross again, that he will find his way home. I pray that some news of him will come to us, either calming our fears or setting us into action to recover him. But I can be patient and convince myself of the best. For to brood upon my fears for him, I am defeating the entire purpose of my own life. That I will not do.

There is too much beauty. There are too many monsters and too many rogues.

There is too much fun.

It has often struck me how reckless human beings tend to be. In comparison to the other goodly reasoning beings, I mean, for comparisons of humans to dark elves and goblins and other creatures of selfish and vicious ends make no sense. Menzoberranzan is no safe place, to be sure, and most dark elves die long before the natural expiration of their corporeal bodies, but that, I believe, is more a matter of ambition and religious zeal, and also a measure of hubris. Every dark elf, in his ultimate confidence, rarely envisions the possibility of his own death, and when he does, he often deludes himself into thinking that any death in the chaotic service of Lolth can only bring him eternal glory and paradise beside the Spider Queen.

The same can be said of the goblinkin, creatures who, for whatever misguided reasons, often rush headlong to their deaths. Many races, humans included, often use the reasoning of godly service to justify dangerous actions, even warfare, and there is a good deal of truth to the belief that dying in the cause of a greater good must be an ennobling thing. But aside from the fanaticism and the various cultures of warfare, I find that humans are often the most reckless of the goodly reasoning beings. I have witnessed many wealthy humans venturing to Ten Towns for holiday, to sail on the cold and deadly waters of Maer Dualdon, or to climb rugged Kelvin's Cairn, a dangerous prospect. They risk everything for the sake of minor accomplishment.

I admire their determination and trust in themselves. I suspect that this willingness to risk is in part due to the short expected life span of the humans. A human of four decades risking his life could lose a score of years, perhaps two, perhaps three in extraordinary circumstances, but an elf of four decades would be risking several centuries of life! There is, then, an immediacy and urgency in being human that elves, light or dark, and dwarves will never understand. And with that immediacy comes a zest for life beyond anything an elf or a dwarf might know. I see it, every day, in Catti-brie's fair face—this love of life, this urgency, this need to fill the hours and the days with experience and joy. In a strange paradox, I saw that urgency only increase when we thought that Wulfgar had died, and in speaking to Catti-brie about this, I came to know that such eagerness to experience, even at great personal risk, is often experienced by humans who have lost a loved one, as if the reminder of their own impending mortality serves to enhance the need to squeeze as much living as possible into the days and years remaining.

What a wonderful way to view the world, and sad, it seems, that it takes a loss to correct the often mundane path. What course for me, then, who might know seven centuries of life, even eight, perhaps? Am I to take the easy trail of contemplation and sedentary existence, so common to the elves of Toril? Am I to dance beneath the stars every night, and spend the days in reverie, turning inward to better see the world about me? Both worthy pursuits, indeed, and dancing under the nighttime sky is a joy I would never forsake. But there must be more for me, I know. There must be the pursuit of adventure and experience. I take my cue from Catti-brie and the other humans on this, and remind myself of the fuller road with every beautiful sunrise.

The fewer the lost hours, the fuller the life, and a life of a few decades can surely, in some measures, be longer than a life of several centuries. How else to explain the accomplishments of a warrior such as Artemis Entreri, who could outfight many drow veterans ten times his age? How else to explain the truth that the most accomplished wizards in the world are not elves but humans, who spend decades, not centuries, pondering the complexities of the magical Weave?

I have been blessed indeed in coming to the surface, in finding a companion such as Catti-brie. For this, I believe, is the mission of my existence, not just the purpose, but the point of life itself. What opportunities might I find if I can combine the life span of my heritage with the intensity of humanity? And what joys might I miss if I follow the more patient and sedate road, the winding road dotted with signposts reminding me that I have too much to lose, the road that avoids mountain and valley alike, traversing the plain, sacrificing the heights for fear of the depths?

Often elves forsake intimate relationships with humans, denying love, because they know, logically, that it cannot be, in the frame of elven time, a long-lasting partnership.

Alas, a philosophy doomed to mediocrity. We need to be reminded sometimes that a sunrise lasts but a few minutes. But its beauty can burn in our hearts eternally.

Once again Catti-brie shows me that she knows me better than I know myself. As we came to understand that Wulfgar was climbing out of his dark hole, was truly resurfacing into the warrior he had once been, I have to admit a bit of fear, a bit of jealousy. Would he come back as the man who once stole Catti-brie's heart? Or had he, in fact, ever really done that? Was their planned marriage more a matter of convenience on both parts, a logical joining of the only two humans, matched in age and beauty, among our little band? I think it was a little of both, and hence my jealousy. For though I understand that I have become special to Catti-brie in ways I had never before imagined, there is a part of me that wishes no one else ever had. For though I am certain that we two share many feelings that are new and exciting to both of us, I do not like to consider the possibility that she ever shared such emotions with another, even one who is so dear a friend.

Perhaps especially one who is so dear a friend! But even as I admit all this, I know that I must take a deep breath and blow all of my fears and jealousies away. I must remind myself that I love this woman, Catti-brie, and that this woman is who she is because of a combination of all the experiences that brought her to this point. Would I prefer that her human parents had never died? On the one hand, of course! But if they hadn't, Catti-brie would not have wound up as Bruenor's adopted daughter, would likely not have come to reside in Icewind Dale at all. Given that, it is unlikely that we would have ever met. Beyond that, if she had been raised in a traditional human manner, she never would have become the warrior that she now is, the person who can best share my sense of adventure, who can accept the hardships of the road with good humor and risk, and allow me to risk—everything!—when going against the elements and the monsters of the world. Hindsight, I think, is a useless tool. We, each of us, are at a place in our lives because of innumerable circumstances, and we, each of us, have a responsibility, if we do not like where we are, to move along life's road, to find a better path if this one does not suit, or to walk happily along this one if it is indeed our life's way. Changing even the bad things that have gone before would fundamentally change who we now are, and whether or not that would be a good thing, I believe, is impossible to predict. So I take my past experiences and let Catti-brie take hers and try to regret nothing for either. I just try to blend our current existence into something grander and more beautiful together.

What of Wulfgar, then? He has a new bride and a child who is neither his nor hers naturally. And yet, it was obvious from Delly Curtie's face, and from her willingness to give of herself if only the child would be unharmed that she loves the babe as if it was her own. I think the same must be true for Wulfgar because, despite the trials, despite the more recent behaviors, I know who he is, deep down, beneath the crusted, emotionally hardened exterior.

I know from her words that he loves this woman, Delly Curtie, and yet I know that he once loved Catti-brie as well. What of this mystery, love? What is it that brings about this most elusive of magic? So many times I have heard people proclaim that their partner is their only love, the only possible completion to their soul, and surely I feel that way about Catti-brie, and I expect that she feels the same about me. But logically, is that possible? Is there one other person out there who can complete the soul of another? Is it really one for one, or is it rather a matter of circumstance?

Or do reasoning beings have the capacity to love many, and situation instead of fate brings them together? Logically, I know the answer to be the latter. I know that if Wulfgar, or Catti-brie, or myself resided in another part of the world, we would all likely find that special completion to our soul, and with another. Logically, in a world of varying races and huge populations, that must be the case, or how, then, would true lovers ever meet? I am a thinking creature, a rational being, and so I know this to be the truth. Why is it, then, that when I look at Catti-brie, all of those logical arguments make little sense?

I remember our first meeting, when she was barely a young woman— more a girl, actually—and I saw her on the side of Kelvin's Cairn. I remember looking into her blue eyes on that occasion, feeling the warmth of her smile and the openness of her heart—something I had not much encountered since coming to the surface world—and feeling a definite bond there, a magic I could not explain. And as I watched her grow, that bond only strengthened. So was it situation or fate? I know what logic says. But I know, too, what my heart tells me. It was fate. She is the one. Perhaps situation allows for some, even most, people to find a suitable partner, but there is much more to it than finding just that.

Perhaps some people are just more fortunate than others. When I look into Catti-brie's blue eyes, when I feel the warmth of her smile and the openness of her heart, I know that I am.

The weather was terrible, the cold biting at my fingers, the ice crusting my eyes until it pained me to see. Every pass was fraught with danger—an avalanche waiting to happen, a monster ready to spring. Every night was spent in the knowledge that we might get buried within whatever shelter we found—if we were even lucky enough to find shelter—unable to claw our way out, certain to die. Not only was I in mortal danger, but so were my dearest friends. Never in my life have I been more filled with joy.

For a purpose guided our steps, every one through the deep and driving snow. Our goal was clear, our course correct. In traversing the snowy mountains in pursuit of the pirate Kree and the warhammer Aegis-fang, we were standing for what we believed in, were following our hearts and our spirits.

Though many would seek shortcuts to the truth, there is no way around the simplest of tenets: hardship begets achievement and achievement begets joy—true joy, and the sense of accomplishment that defines who we are as thinking beings. Often have I heard people lament that if only they had the wealth of the king, then they could be truly happy, and I take care not to argue the point, though I know they are surely wrong. There is a truth I will grant that, for the poorest, some measure of wealth can allow for some measure of happiness, but beyond filling the basic needs, the path to joy is not paved in gold, particularly in gold unearned. Hardly that! The path to joy is paved in a sense of confidence and self-worth, a feeling that we have made the world a little bit better, perhaps, or that we fought on for our beliefs despite adversity. In my travels with Captain Deudermont, I dined with many of the wealthiest families of Waterdeep. I broke bread with many of the children of the very rich. Deudermont himself was among that group, his father being a prominent landowner in Waterdeep's southern district. Many of the current crop of young aristocrats would do well to hold Captain Deudermont up as an example, for he was unwilling to rest on the laurels of the previous generation. He spotted, very young, the entrapment of wealth without earning. And so the good captain decided at a young age the course of his own life, an existence following his heart and trying very hard to make the waters of the Sword Coast a better place for decent and honest sailors.

Captain Deudermont might die young because of that choice to serve, as I might because of my own, as Catti-brie might beside me. But the simple truth of it is that, had I remained in Menzoberranzan those decades ago, or had I chosen to remain safe and sound in Ten Towns or Mithral Hall at this time, I would already, in so many ways, be dead.

No, give me the road and the dangers, give me the hope that I am striding purposefully for that which is right, give me the sense of accomplishment, and I will know joy.

So deep has my conviction become that I can say with confidence that even if Catti-brie were to die on the road beside me, I would not backtrack to that safer place. For I know that her heart is much as my own on this matter. I know that she will—that she must—pursue those endeavors, however dangerous, that point her in the direction of her heart and her conscience.

Perhaps that is the result of being raised by dwarves, for no race on all of Toril better understands this simple truth of happiness better than the growling, grumbling, bearded folk. Dwarven kings are almost always among the most active of the clan, the first to fight and the first to work. The first to envision a mighty underground fortress and the first to clear away the clay that blocks the cavern in which it will stand. The tough, hard-working dwarves long ago learned the value of accomplishment versus luxury, long ago came to understand that there are riches of spirit more valuable by far than gold—though they do love their gold!

So I find myself in the cold, windblown snow, and the treacherous passes surrounded by enemies, on our way to do battle with an undeniably formidable foe.

Could the sun shine any brighter?

Sellswords

Servant of the Shard

I live in a world where there truly exists the embodiment of evil. I speak not of wicked men, nor of goblins—often of evil weal—nor even of my own people, the dark elves, wickeder still than the goblins. These are creatures—all of them—capable of great cruelty, but they are not, even in the very worst of cases, the true embodiment of evil. No, that title belongs to others, to the demons and devils often summoned by priests and mages. These creatures of the lower planes are the purest of evil, untainted vileness running unchecked. They are without possibility of redemption, without hope of accomplishing anything in their unfortunately nearly eternal existence that even borders on goodness.

I have wondered if these creatures could exist without the darkness that lies within the hearts of the reasoning races. Are they a source of evil, as are many wicked men or drow, or are they the result, a physical manifestation of the rot that permeates the hearts of far too many? The latter, I believe. It is not coincidental that demons and devils cannot walk the Material Plane of existence without being brought here by the actions of one of the reasoning beings. They are no more than a tool, I know, an instrument to carry out the wicked deeds in service to the truer source of that evil.

What then of Crenshinibon? It is an item, an artifact—albeit a sentient one—but it does not exist in the same state of intelligence as does a reasoning being. For the Crystal Shard cannot grow, cannot change, cannot mend its ways. The only errors it can learn to correct are those of errant attempts at manipulation, as it seeks to better grab at the hearts of those around it. It cannot even consider, or reconsider, the end it desperately tries to achieve—no, its purpose is forever singular.

Is it truly evil, then? No.

I would have thought differently not too long ago, even when I carried the dangerous artifact and came better to understand it. Only recently, upon reading a long and detailed message sent to me from High Priest Cadderly Bonaduce of the Spirit Soaring, have I come to see the truth of the Crystal Shard, have I come to understand that the item itself is an anomaly, a mistake, and that its never-ending hunger for power and glory, at whatever cost, is merely a perversion of the intent of its second maker, the eighth spirit that found its way into the very essence of the artifact.

The Crystal Shard was created originally by seven liches, so Cadderly has learned, who designed to fashion an item of the very greatest power. As a further insult to the races these undead kings intended to conquer, they made the artifact a draw against the sun itself, the giver of life. The liches were consumed at the completion of their joining magic. Despite what some sages believe, Cadderly insists that the conscious aspects of those vile creatures were not drawn into the power of the item, but were, rather, obliterated by its sunlike properties. Thus, their intended insult turned against them and left them as no more than ashes and absorbed pieces of their shattered spirits. That much of the earliest history of the Crystal Shard is known by many, including the demons that so desperately crave the item. The second story, though, the one Cadderly uncovered, tells a more complicated tale, and shows the truth of Crenshinibon, the ultimate failure of the artifact as a perversion of goodly intentions.

Crenshinibon first came to the material world centuries ago in the far-off land of Zakhara. At the time, it was merely a wizard's tool, though a great and powerful one, an artifact that could throw fireballs and create great blazing walls of light so intense they could burn flesh from bone. Little was known of Crenshinibon's dark past until it fell to the hands of a sultan. This great leader, whose name has been lost to the ages, learned the truth of the Crystal Shard, and with the help of his many court wizards, decided that the work of the liches was incomplete.

Thus came the "second creation" of Crenshinibon, the heightening of its power and its limited consciousness. This sultan had no dreams of domination, only of peaceful existence with his many warlike neighbors. Thus, using the newest power of the artifact, he envisioned, then created, a line of crystalline towers. The towers stretched from his capital across the empty desert to his kingdom's second city, an oft-raided frontier city, in intervals equating to a single day's travel. He strung as many as a hundred of the crystalline towers, and nearly completed the mighty defensive line. But alas, the sultan overreached the powers of Crenshinibon, and though he believed that the creation of each tower strengthened the artifact, he was, in fact, pulling the Crystal Shard and its manifestations too thin. Soon after, a great sandstorm came up, sweeping across the desert. It was a natural disaster that served as a prelude to an invasion by a neighboring sheikdom. So thin were the walls of those crystalline towers that they shattered under the force of the sand, taking with them the sultan's dream of security.

The hordes overran the kingdom and murdered the sultan's family while he helplessly looked on. Their merciless sheik would not kill the sultan, though—he wanted the painful memories to burn at the man— but Crenshinibon took the sultan, took a piece of his spirit, at least.

Little more of those early days is known, even to Cadderly, who counts demigods among his sources, but the young high priest of Deneir is convinced that this "second creation" of Crenshinibon is the one that remains key to the present hunger of the artifact. If only Crenshinibon could have held its highest level of power. If only the crystalline towers had remained strong. The hordes would have been turned away, and the sultan's family, his dear wife and beautiful children, would not have been murdered.

Now the artifact, imbued with the twisted aspects of seven dead liches and with the wounded and tormented spirit of the sultan, continues its desperate quest to attain and maintain its greatest level of power, whatever the cost.

There are many implications to the story. Cadderly hinted in his note to me, though he drew no definitive conclusions, that the creation of the crystalline towers actually served as the catalyst for the invasion, with the leaders of the neighboring sheikdom fearful that their borderlands would soon be overrun. Is the Crystal Shard, then, a great lesson to us?

Does it show clearly the folly of overblown ambition, even though that particular ambition was rooted in good intentions? The sultan wanted strength for the defense of his peaceable kingdom, and yet he reached for too much power.

That was what consumed him, his family, and his kingdom. What of Jarlaxle, then, who now holds the Crystal Shard? Should I go after him and try to take back the artifact, then deliver it to Cadderly for destruction? Surely the world would be a better place without this mighty and dangerous artifact.

Then again, there will always be another tool for those of evil weal, another embodiment of their evil, be it a demon, a devil, or a monstrous creation similar to Crenshinibon. No, the embodiments are not the problem, for they cannot exist and prosper without the evil that is within the hearts of reasoning beings. Beware, Jarlaxle. Beware.

Entreri again teamed with Jarlaxle? What an odd pairing that seems, and to some (and initially to me, as well) a vision of the most unsettling nightmare imaginable. There is no one in all the world, I believe, more crafty and ingenious than Jarlaxle of Bregan D'aerthe, the consummate opportunist, a wily leader who can craft a kingdom out of the dung of rothé. Jarlaxle, who thrived in the matriarchal society of Menzoberranzan as completely as any matron mother.

Jarlaxle of mystery, who knew my father, who claims a past friendship with Zaknafein.

How could a drow who befriended Zaknafein ally with Artemis Entreri? At quick glance, the notion seems incongruous, even preposterous. And yet, I do believe Jarlaxle's claims of the former and know the latter to be true—for the second time.

Professionally, I see no mystery in the union. Entreri has ever preferred a position of the shadows, serving as the weapon of a high-paying master—no, not master. I doubt that Artemis Entreri has ever known a master. Rather, even in the service of the guilds, he worked as a sword for hire. Certainly such a skilled mercenary could find a place within Bregan D'aerthe, especially since they've come to the surface and likely need humans to front and cover their true identity. For Jarlaxle, therefore, the alliance with Entreri is certainly a convenient thing.

But there is something else, something more, between them. I know this from the way Jarlaxle spoke of the man, and from the simple fact that the mercenary leader went so far out of his way to arrange the last fight between me and Entreri. It was for the sake of Entreri's state of mind, no less, and certainly as no favor to me, and as no mere source of entertainment for Jarlaxle. He cares for Entreri as a friend might, even as he values the assassin's multitude of skills.

There lies the incongruity.

For though Entreri and Jarlaxle have complementary professional skills, they do not seem well matched in temperament or in moral standards—two essentials, it would seem, for any successful friendship.

Or perhaps not.

Jarlaxle's heart is far more generous than that of Artemis Entreri. The mercenary can be brutal, of course, but not randomly so. Practicality guides his moves, for his eye is ever on the potential gain, but even in that light of efficient pragmatism, Jarlaxle's heart often overrules his lust for profit. Many times has he allowed my escape, for example, when bringing my head to Matron Malice or Matron Mother Baenre would have brought him great gain. Is Artemis Entreri similarly possessed of such generosity?

Not at all.

In fact, I suspect that if Entreri knew that Jarlaxle had saved me from my apparent death in the tower, he would have first tried to kill me and turned his anger upon Jarlaxle. Such a battle might well yet occur, and if it does, I believe that Artemis Entreri will learn that he is badly overmatched. Not by Jarlaxle individually, though the mercenary leader is crafty and reputedly a fine warrior in his own right, but by the pragmatic Jarlaxle's many, many deadly allies.

Therein lies the essence of the mercenary leader's interest in, and control of, Artemis Entreri. Jarlaxle sees the man's value and does not fear him, because what Jarlaxle has perfected, and what Entreri is sorely lacking in, is the ability to build an interdependent organization. Entreri won't attempt to kill Jarlaxle because Entreri will need Jarlaxle. Jarlaxle will make certain of that. He weaves his web all around him. It is a network that is always mutually beneficial, a network in which all security—against Bregan D'aerthe's many dangerous rivals—inevitably depends upon the controlling and calming influence that is Jarlaxle. He is the ultimate consensus builder, the purest of diplomats, while Entreri is a loner, a man who must dominate all around him. Jarlaxle coerces. Entreri controls.

But with Jarlaxle, Entreri will never find any level of control. The mercenary leader is too entrenched and too intelligent for that. And yet, I believe that their alliance will hold, and their friendship will grow. Certainly there will be conflicts and perhaps very dangerous ones for both parties. Perhaps Entreri has already learned the truth of my departure and has killed Jarlaxle or died trying. But the longer the alliance holds, the stronger it will become, the more entrenched in friendship.

I say this because I believe that, in the end, Jarlaxle's philosophy will win out. Artemis Entreri is the one of this duo who is limited by fault. His desire for absolute control is fueled by his inability to trust. While that desire has led him to become as fine a fighter as I have ever known, it has also led him to an existence that even he is beginning to recognize as empty.

Professionally, Jarlaxle offers Artemis Entreri security, a base for his efforts, while Entreri gives Jarlaxle and all of Bregan D'aerthe a clear connection to the surface world. But personally, Jarlaxle offers even more to Entreri, offers him a chance to finally break out of the role that he has assumed as a solitary creature. I remember Entreri upon our departure from Menzoberranzan, where we were both imprisoned, each in his own way. He was with Bregan D'aerthe then as well, but down in that city, Artemis Entreri looked into a dark and empty mirror that he did not like. Why, then, is he now returned to Jarlaxle's side?

It is a testament to the charm that is Jarlaxle, the intuitive understanding that that most clever of dark elves holds for creating desire and alliance. The mere fact that Entreri is apparently with Jarlaxle once again tells me that the mercenary leader is already winning the inevitable clash between their basic philosophies, their temperament and moral standards. Though Entreri does not yet understand it, I am sure, Jarlaxle will strengthen him more by example than by alliance.

Perhaps with Jarlaxle's help, Artemis Entreri will find his way out of his current empty existence. Or perhaps Jarlaxle will eventually kill him. Either way, the world will be a better place, I think.

There is a simple beauty in the absolute ugliness of demons. There is no ambiguity there, no hesitation, no misconception, about how one must deal with such creatures. You do not parley with demons. You do not hear their lies. You cast them out, destroy them, rid the world of them—even if the temptation is present to utilize their powers to save what you perceive to be a little corner of goodness.

This is a difficult concept for many to grasp and has been the downfall of many wizards and priests who have errantly summoned demons and allowed the creatures to move beyond their initial purpose—the answering of a question, perhaps—because they were tempted by the power offered by the creature. Many of these doomed spellcasters thought they would be doing good by forcing the demons to their side, by bolstering their cause, their army, with demonic soldiers.

What ill, they supposed, if the end result proved to the greater good? Would not a goodly king be well advised to add "controlled" demons to his cause if goblins threatened his lands? I think not, because if the preservation of goodness relies upon the use of such obvious and irredeemable evil to defeat evil, then there is nothing, truly, worth saving.

The sole use of demons, then, is to bring them forth only in times when they must betray the cause of evil, and only in a setting so controlled that there is no hope of their escape. Cadderly has done this within the secure summoning chamber of the Spirit Soaring, as have, I am sure, countless priests and wizards. Such a summoning is not without peril, though, even if the circle of protection is perfectly formed, for there is always a temptation that goes with the manipulation of powers such as a balor or a nalfeshnee.

Within that temptation must always lie the realization of irredeemable evil. Irredeemable. Without hope. That concept, redemption, must be the crucial determinant in any such dealings. Temper your blade when redemption is possible, hold it when redemption is at hand, and strike hard and without remorse when your opponent is beyond any hope of redemption.

Where on that scale does Artemis Entreri lie, I wonder? Is the man truly beyond help and hope? Yes, to the former, I believe, and no to the latter. There is no help for Artemis Entreri because the man would never accept any. His greatest flaw is his pride—not the boasting pride of so many lesser warriors, but the pride of absolute independence and unbending self-reliance. I could tell him his errors, as could anyone who has come to know him in any way, but he would not hear my words.

Yet perhaps there may be hope of some redemption for the man. I know not the source of his anger, though it must have been great. And yet I will not allow that the source, however difficult and terrible it might have been, in any way excuses the man from his actions. The blood on Entreri's sword and trademark dagger is his own to wear. He does not wear it well, I believe. It burns at his skin as might the breath of a black dragon and gnaws at all that is within him. I saw that during our last encounter, a quiet and dull ache at the sides of his dark eyes. I had him beaten, could have killed him, and I believe that in many ways he hoped I would finish the task and be done with it, and end his mostly self-imposed suffering.

That ache is what held my blade, that hope within me that somewhere deep inside Artemis Entreri there is the understanding that his path needs to change, that the road he currently walks is one of emptiness and ultimate despair. Many thoughts coursed my mind as I stood there, weapons in hand, with him defenseless before me. How could I strike when I saw that pain in his eyes and knew that such pain might well be the precursor to redemption? And yet how could I not, when I was well aware that letting Artemis Entreri walk out of that crystalline tower might spell the doom of others? Truly it was a dilemma, a crisis of conscience and of balance. I found my answer in that critical moment in the memory of my father, Zaknafein. To Entreri's thinking, I know, he and Zaknafein are not so different, and there are indeed similarities. Both existed in an environment hostile and to their respective perceptions evil. Neither, to their perceptions, did either go out of his way to kill anyone who did not deserve it. Are the warriors and assassins who fight for the wretched pashas of Calimport any better than the soldiers of the drow houses? Thus, in many ways, the actions of Zaknafein and those of Artemis Entreri are quite similar. Both existed in a world of intrigue, danger, and evil. Both survived their imprisonment through ruthless means. If Entreri views his world, his prison, as full of wretchedness as Zaknafein viewed Menzoberranzan, then is not Entreri as entitled to his manner as was Zaknafein, the weapons master who killed many, many dark elves in his tenure as patron of House Do'Urden?

It is a comparison I realized when first I went to Calimport, in pursuit of Entreri, who had taken Regis as prisoner (and even that act had justification, I must admit), and a comparison that truly troubled me. How close are they, given their abilities with the blade and their apparent willingness to kill? Was it, then, some inner feelings for Zaknafein that stayed my blade when I could have cut Entreri down?

No, I say, and I must believe, for Zaknafein was far more discerning in whom he would kill or would not kill. I know the truth of Zaknafein's heart. I know that Zaknafein was possessed of the ability to love, and the reality of Artemis Entreri simply cannot hold up against that. Not in his present incarnation, at least, but is there hope that the man will find a light beneath the murderous form of the assassin? Perhaps, and I would be glad indeed to hear that the man so embraced that light. In truth, though, I doubt that anyone or anything will ever be able to pull that lost flame of compassion through the thick and seemingly impenetrable armor of dispassion that Artemis Entreri now wears.

Promise of the Witch-King

When Gareth's holy sword did flash on high
When Zhengyi's form was shattered.
A blackened flame of detritus
His corporeal form a'tattered.
When did victory's claim ring loudly
When did hearts of hope swollen pride
Rejoice brave men, at Gareth's blow
The pieces of Zhengyi flung wide.
But you cannot kill what is not alive
You cannot strike a notion
You cannot smite with force of arm
The magic of dark devotion.
Thus Gareth's sword did undo
The physical, the corporeal shattered.
The Witch-King focus was denied
The magical essence scattered.
So harken you children to Mother's words
Walk straight to Father, follow.
For a piece of Zhengyi watches you
In dark Wilderness's hollow.

Road of the Patriarch

Are they still together, walking side by side, hands ever near the hilts of their weapons—to defend against each other, I would guess, as much as from other enemies?

Many times I think of them, Artemis Entreri and Jarlaxle. Even with the coming of King Obould and his orc hordes, even amid the war and the threat to Mithral Hall, I find my thoughts often wandering the miles of distance and time to find in my mind's eye a reckoning of the unlikely pair.

Why do I care? For Jarlaxle, there is the ever-present notion that he once knew my father, that he once wandered the ways of Menzoberranzan beside Zaknafein, perhaps much as he now wanders the ways of the World Above beside Artemis Entreri. I have always known that there was a complexity to this strange creature that defied the easy expectations one might have of a drow—even that one drow might have for another. I find comfort in the complexity of Jarlaxle, for it serves as a reminder of individualism. Given my dark heritage, oftentimes it is only the belief in individualism that allows me to retain my sanity. I am not trapped by my heritage, by my elf's ears and my coal-colored skin. While I often find myself a victim of the expectations of others, they cannot define me, limit me, or control me as long as I understand that there is no racial truth, that their perceptions of who I must be are irrelevant to the truth of who I am.

Jarlaxle reinforces that reality, as blunt a reminder as anyone could ever be that there resides in each of us a personality that defies external limitations. He is a unique one, to be sure, and a good thing that is, I believe, for the world could not survive too many of his ilk. I would be a liar indeed if I pretended that my interest in Artemis Entreri only went so far as his connection to the affirmation that is Jarlaxle. Even if Jarlaxle had returned to the Underdark, abandoning the assassin to his lonely existence, I admit that I would regularly turn my thoughts to him. I do not pity him, and I would not befriend him. I do not expect his redemption or salvation, or repentance for, or alteration of, the extreme selfishness that defines his existence. In the past I have considered that Jarlaxle will affect him in positive ways, at least to the extent that he will likely show Entreri the emptiness of his existence.

But that is not the impetus of my thoughts for the assassin. It is not in hope that I so often turn my thoughts to him, but in dread. I do not fear that he will seek me out that we might do battle yet again. Will that happen? Perhaps, but it is nothing I fear, from which I shy, or of which I worry. If he seeks me, if he finds me, if he draws a weapon upon me, then so be it. It will be another fight in a life of battle—for us both, it seems.

But no, the reason Artemis Entreri became a staple in my thoughts, and with dread, is that he serves as a reminder to me of who I might have been. I walked a line in the darkness of Menzoberranzan, a tightrope of optimism and despair, a path that bordered hope even as it bordered nihilism. Had I succumbed to the latter, had I become yet another helpless victim of crushing drow society, I would have loosed my blades in fury instead of in the cause of righteousness—or so I hope and pray that such is indeed the purpose of my fight—in those times of greatest stress, as when I believed my friends lost to me,

I find that rage of despair. I abandon my heart. I lose my soul. Artemis Entreri abandoned his heart many years ago. He succumbed to his despair, 'tis obvious. How different is he from Zaknafein. I have to ask—though doing so is surely painful. It almost seems to me as if I am being disrespectful of my beloved father by offering such a comparison.

Both Entreri and Zaknafein loose the fury of their blades without remorse, because both believe that they are surrounded by a world not worthy of any element of their mercy. I make the case in differentiating between the two that Zaknafein's antipathy was rightly placed, where Entreri is blind to aspects of his world deserving of empathy and undeserving of the harsh and final judgment of steel. But Entreri does not differentiate. He sees his environs as Zaknafein viewed Menzoberranzan, with the same bitter distaste, the same sense of hopelessness, and thus, the same lack of remorse for waging battle against that world.

He is wrong, I know, but it is not hard for me to recognize the source of his ruthlessness. I have seen it before, and in a man I hold in the highest esteem. Indeed, in a man to whom I owe my very life. We are all creatures of ambition, even if that ambition is to free ourselves of responsibility. The desire to escape ambition is, in and of itself, ambition, and thus ambition is an inescapable truth of rational existence.

Like Zaknafein, Artemis Entreri has internalized his goals. His ambition is based in the improvement of the self. He seeks perfection of the body and the arts martial, not for any desire to use that perfection toward a greater goal, but rather to use it for survival. He seeks to swim above the muck and mire for the sake of his own clean breath.

Jarlaxle's ambition is quite the opposite, as is my own—though our purposes, I fear, are not of the same ilk. Jarlaxle seeks to control not himself, but his environment. Where Entreri may spend hours building the muscle memory for a single maneuver, Jarlaxle spends his time in coercing and manipulating those around him to create an environment that fulfills his needs. I do not pretend to understand those needs where Jarlaxle is concerned. They are internal ambitions,

I believe, and not to do with the greater needs of society or any sense of the common good. If I were to wager a guess based on my limited experience with that most unusual drow, I would say that Jarlaxle creates tension and conflict for the sake of entertainment. He finds personal gain in his machinations—no doubt orchestrating the fight between myself and Artemis Entreri in the replica of Crenshinibon was a maneuver designed to bring the valuable asset of Entreri more fully into his fold. But I expect that Jarlaxle would cause trouble even without the lure of treasure or personal gain.

Perhaps he is bored with too many centuries of existence, where the mundane has become to him representative of death itself. He creates excitement for the sake of excitement. That he does so with callous disregard to those who become unwitting principals in his often deadly game is a testament to the same sort of negative resignation that long ago infected Artemis Entreri, and Zaknafein. When I think of Jarlaxle and Zaknafein side by side in Menzoberranzan, I have to wonder if they did not sweep through the streets like some terrible monsoon, leaving a wake of destruction along with a multitude of confused dark elves scratching their heads at the receding laughter of the wild pair. Perhaps in Entreri, Jarlaxle has found another partner in his private storm.

But Artemis Entreri, for all their similarities, is no Zaknafein. The variance of method, and more importantly, of purpose, between Entreri and Jarlaxle will prove a constant tug between them, I expect—if it has not already torn them asunder and left one or both dead in the gutter. Zaknafein, as Entreri, might have found despair, but he never lost his soul within it. He never surrendered to it.

That is a white flag Artemis Entreri long ago raised, and it is one not easily torn down.

I am not a king. Not in temperament, nor by desire, nor heritage, nor popular demand. I am a small player in the events of a small region in a large world. When my day is past, I will be remembered, I hope, by those whose lives I've touched. When my day is past, I will be remembered, I hope, fondly.

Perhaps those who have known me, or who have been affected by the battles I've waged and the work I've done, will tell the tales of Drizzt Do'Urden to their children. Perhaps not. But likely, beyond that possible second generation, my name and my deeds are destined to the dusty corners of forgotten history. That thought does not sadden me, for I measure my success in life by the added value my presence brought to those whom I loved, and who loved me. I am not suited for the fame of a king, or the grandiose reputation of a giant among men—like Elminster, who reshapes the world in ways that will affect generations yet to come.

Kings, like my friend Bruenor, add to their society in ways that define the lives of their descendants, and so one such as he will live on in name and deed for as long as Clan Battlehammer survives—for millennia, likely, and hopefully. So, often do I ponder the ways of the king, the thoughts of the ruler, the pride and the magnanimity, the selfishness and the service.

There is a quality that separates a clan leader such as Bruenor from a man who presides over an entire kingdom. For Bruenor, surrounded by the dwarves who claim membership in his clan, kin and kind are one and the same. Bruenor holds a vested interest, truly a friendship, with every dwarf, every human, every drow, every elf, every halfling, every gnome who resides in Mithral Hall. Their wounds are his wounds, their joys his joys. There isn't one he does not know by name, and not one he does not love as family.

The same cannot be true for the king who rules a larger nation. However good his intent, however true his heart, for a king who presides over thousands, tens of thousands, there is an emotional distance of necessity, and the greater the number of his subjects, the greater the distance, and the more the subjects will be reduced to something less than people, to mere numbers. Ten thousand live in this city, a king will know. Five thousand reside in that one, and only fifty in that village. They are not family, nor friends, nor faces he would recognize. He cannot know their hopes and dreams in any particular way, and so, should he care, he must assume and pray that there are indeed common dreams and common needs and common hopes. A good king will understand this shared humanity and will work to uplift all in his wake. This ruler accepts the responsibilities of his position and follows the noble cause of service. Perhaps it is selfishness, the need to be loved and respected, that drives him, but the motivation matters not. A king who wishes to be remembered fondly by serving the best interests of his subjects rules wisely.

Conversely, the leader who rules by fear, whether it be of him or of some enemy he exaggerates to use as a weapon of control, is not a man or woman of good heart. Such was the case in Menzoberranzan, where the matron mothers kept their subjects in a continual state of tension and terror, both of them and their spider goddess, and of a multitude of enemies, some real, some purposefully constructed or nurtured for the sole reason of solidifying the matron mothers' hold on the fearful. Who will ever remember a matron mother fondly, I wonder, except for those who were brought to power by such a vile creature? In the matter of making war, the king will find his greatest legacy—and is this not a sadness that has plagued the reasoning races for all of time? In this, too, perhaps particularly in this, the worth of a king can be clearly measured. No king can feel the pain of a soldier's particular wound, but a good king will fear that wound, for it will sting him as profoundly as it stings the man upon whom it was inflicted. In considering the "numbers" who are his subjects, a good king will never forget the most important number: one. If a general cries victory and exclaims that only ten men died, the good king will temper his celebration with the sorrow for each, one alone repeated, one alone adding weight to his heart.

Only then will he measure his future choices correctly. Only then will he understand the full weight of those choices, not just on the kingdom, but on the one, or ten, or five hundred, who will die or be maimed in his name and for his holdings and their common interest. A king who feels the pain of every man's wounds, or the hunger in every child's belly, or the sorrow in every destitute parent's soul, is one who will place country above crown and community above self. Absent that empathy, any king, even a man of previously stellar temperament, will prove to be no more than a tyrant.

Would that the people chose their kings! Would that they could measure the hearts of those who wish to lead them! For if that choice was honest, if the representation of the would-be king was a clear and true portrayal of his hopes and dreams for the flock and not a pandering appeal to the worst instincts of those who would choose, then all the folk would grow with the kingdom, or share the pains and losses. Like family, or groups of true friends, or dwarf clans, the folk would celebrate their common hopes and dreams in their every action.

But the people do not choose anywhere that I know of in Faerun. By blood or by deed, the lines are set, and so we hope, each in our own nation, that a man or woman of empathy will ascend, that whoever will come to rule us will do so with an understanding of the pain of a single soldier's wound. There is beside Mithral Hall now a burgeoning kingdom of unusual composition. For this land, the Kingdom of Many-Arrows, is ruled by a single orc. Obould is his name, and he has crawled free of every cupboard of expectation that I, or Bruenor, or any of the others have tried to construct about him. Nay, not crawled, but has shattered the walls to kindling and strode forward as something beyond the limitations of his race. Is that my guess or my observation, truly?

My hope, I must admit, for I cannot yet know. And so my interpretation of Obould's actions to this point is limited by my vantage, and skewed by the risk of optimism. But Obould did not press the attack, as we all expected he certainly would, when doing so would have condemned thousands of his subjects to a grisly death. Perhaps it was mere pragmatism: the orc king wisely recognized that his gains could not be compounded, and so he looked down and went into a defensive posture to secure those gains. Perhaps when he has done so, beyond any threat of invasion by the outlying kingdoms, he will regroup and press the attack again. I pray that this is not the case; I pray that the orc king is possessed of more empathy—or even of more selfishness in his need to be revered as well as feared—than would be typical of his warlike race. I can only hope that Obould's ambitions were tempered by a recognition of the price the commoner pays for the folly or false pride of the ruler.

I cannot know. And when I consider that such empathy would place this orc above many leaders of the goodly races, then I realize that I am being foolhardy in even entertaining these fantasies. I fear that Obould stopped simply because he knew that he could not continue, else he might well lose all that he had gained and more. Pragmatism, not empathy, ground Obould's war machine to a stop, it would seem. If that is the case, then so be it. Even in that simple measure of practicality, this orc stands far beyond others of his heritage. If pragmatism alone forces the halt of invasion and the settling of a kingdom, then perhaps such pragmatism is the first step in moving the orcs toward civilization.

Is it all a process, then, a movement toward a better and better way that will lead to the highest form of kingdom? That is my hope. It will not be a straight-line ascent, to be sure. For every stride forward, as with Lady Alustriel's wondrous city of Silverymoon, for example, there will be back-steps.

Perhaps the world will end before the goodly races enjoy the peace and prosperity of the perfect realm. So be it, for it is the journey that matters most. That is my hope, at least, but the flip of that hope is my fear that it is all a game, and one played most prominently by those who value self above community. The ascent to kingship is a road of battle, and not one walked by the gentle man or woman. The person who values community will oft be deceived and destroyed by the knave whose heart lies in selfish ambitions.

For those who walk that road to the end, for those who feel the weight of leadership upon their shoulders, the only hope lies in the realm of conscience.

Feel the pain of your soldiers, you kings. Feel the sorrow of your subjects. Nay, I am not a king. Not by temperament nor by desire. The death of a single subject soldier would slay the heart of King Drizzt Do'Urden. I do not envy the goodly rulers, but I do fear the ones who do not understand that their numbers have names, or that the greatest gain to the self lies in the cheers and the love fostered by the common good.

☙

The point of self-reflection is, foremost, to clarify and to find honesty. Self-reflection is the way to throw self-lies out and face the truth—however painful it might be to admit that you were wrong. We seek consistency in ourselves, and so when we are faced with inconsistency, we struggle to deny.

Denial has no place in self-reflection, and so it is incumbent upon a person to admit his errors, to embrace them, and to move along in a more positive direction. We can fool ourselves for all sorts of reasons. Mostly for the sake of our ego, of course, but sometimes, I now understand, because we are afraid.

For sometimes we are afraid to hope, because hope breeds expectation, and expectation can lead to disappointment. And so I ask myself again, without the protective wall—or at least, conscious of it and determined to climb over it—why do I feel kinship to this man, Artemis Entreri, who has betrayed almost everything that I have come to hold dear? Why do I think about him—ever? Why did I not kill him when I had the chance? What instinct halted the thrust of a scimitar?

I have often wondered, even recently and even as I ponder this new direction, if Artemis Entreri is who I might have been had I not escaped Menzoberranzan. Would my increasing anger have led me down the road he chose, that of passionless killer? It seems a logical thing to me that I might have lost myself in the demands of perfectionism, and would have found refuge in the banality of a life lived without passion.

A lack of passion is perhaps a lack of introspection, and it is that very nature of self-evaluation that would have utterly destroyed my soul had I remained in the city of my birth.

It is only now, in these days when I have at last shed the weight of guilt that for so long burdened my shoulders, that I can say without hesitation that no, had I remained in Menzoberranzan, I would not have become the image of Artemis Entreri. More like Zaknafein, I expect, turning my anger outward instead of inward, wearing rage as armor and not garmenting my frame in the fears of what is in my heart. Zaknafein's was not an existence I desire, nor is it one in which I would have long survived, I am sure, but neither is it the way of Entreri.

So the worries are shed, and we, Entreri and I, are not akin in the ways that I had feared. And yet, I think of him still, and often. It is, I know now, because I suspect that we are indeed akin in some ways, and they are not my fears, but my hopes. Reality is a curious thing. Truth is not as solid and universal as any of us would like it to be; selfishness guides perception, and perception invites justification. The physical image in the mirror, if not pleasing, can be altered by the mere brush of fingers through hair. And so it is true that we can manipulate our own reality. We can persuade, even deceive. We can make others view us in dishonest ways.

We can hide selfishness with charity, make a craving for acceptance into magnanimity, and amplify our smile to coerce a hesitant lover. The world is illusion, and often delusion, as victors write the histories and the children who die quietly under the stamp of a triumphant army never really existed. The robber baron becomes philanthropist in the final analysis, by bequeathing only that for which he had no more use. The king who sends young men and women to die becomes beneficent with the kiss of a baby. Every problem becomes a problem of perception to those who understand that reality, in reality, is what you make reality to be.

This is the way of the world, but it is not the only way. It is not the way of the truly goodly king, of Gareth Dragonsbane who rules in Damara, of Lady Alustriel of Silverymoon, or of Bruenor Battlehammer of Mithral Hall. Theirs is not a manner of masquerading reality to alter perception, but a determination to better reality, to follow a vision, and to trust their course is true, and it therefore follows, that perception of them will be just and kind.

For a more difficult alteration than the physical is the image that appears in the glass of introspection, the pureness or rot of the heart and the soul.

For many, sadly, this is not an issue, for the illusion of their lives becomes self-delusion, a masquerade that revels in the applause and sees in a pittance to charity a stain remover for the soul. How many conquerors, I wonder, who crushed out the lives of tens of thousands, could not hear those cries of inflicted despair beyond the applause of those who believed the wars would make the world a better place? How many thieves, I wonder, hear not the laments of victims and willingly blind themselves to the misery wrought of their violation under a blanket of their own suffered injustices? When does theft become entitlement? There are those who cannot see the stains on their souls. Some lack the capacity to look in the glass of introspection, perhaps, and others alter reality without and within.

It is, then, the outward misery of Artemis Entreri that has long offered me hope. He doesn't lack passion; he hides from it. He becomes an instrument, a weapon, because otherwise he must be human. He knows the glass all too well. I see clearly now, and he cannot talk himself around the obvious stain. His justifications for his actions ring hollow—to him most of all.

Only there, in that place, is the road of redemption, for any of us. Only in facing honestly that image in the glass can we change the reality of who we are. Only in seeing the scars and the stains and the rot can we begin to heal.

I think of Artemis Entreri because that is my hope for the man. It is a fleeting and distant hope to be sure, and perhaps in the end, it is nothing more than my own selfish need to believe that there is redemption and that there can be change. For Entreri? If so, then for anyone. For Menzoberranzan?

Hunter's Blades

The Thousand Orcs

When Thibbledorf Pwent and his small army of battleragers arrived in Icewind Dale with news that Gandalug Battlehammer, the First King and Ninth King of Mithral Hall, had died, I knew that Bruenor would have no choice but to return to his ancestral home and take again the mantle of leadership. His duties to the clan would demand no less, and for Bruenor, as with most dwarves, duties to king and clan usurp everything.

I recognized the sadness on Bruenor's face as he heard the news, though, and knew that little of it was in grieving for the former king. Gandalug had lived a long and amazing life, more so than any dwarf could ever hope. So while he was sad at losing this ancestor he had barely known, that wasn't the source of Bruenor's long look. No, what most troubled Bruenor, I knew, was the duty calling him to return to a settled existence.

I knew at once that I would accompany him, but I knew, too, that I would not remain for long in the safe confines of Mithral Hall.

I am a creature of the road, of adventure. I came to know this after the battle against the drow, when Gandalug was returned to Clan Battlehammer. Finally, it seemed, peace had found our little troupe, but that, I knew so quickly, would prove a double-edged sword.

And so I found myself sailing the Sword Coast with Captain Deudermont and his pirate-chasing crew aboard *Sea Sprite*, with Catti-brie at my side.

It is strange, and somewhat unsettling, to come to the realization that no place will hold me for long, that no "home" will ever truly suffice. I wonder if I am running toward something or away from something. Am I driven, as were the misguided Entreri and Ellifain? These questions reverberate within my heart and soul. Why do I feel the need to keep moving? For what am I searching? Acceptance? Some wider reputation that will somehow grant me a renewed assurance that I had chosen well in leaving Menzoberranzan?

These questions rise up about me, and sometimes bring distress, but it is not a lasting thing. For in looking at them rationally, I understand their ridiculousness.

With Pwent's arrival in Icewind Dale, the prospect of settling in the security and comforts of Mithral Hall loomed before us all once more, and it is not a life I feel I can accept. My fear was for Catti-brie and the relationship we have forged. How would it change? Would Catti-brie desire to make a home and family of her own? Would she see the return to the dwarven stronghold as a signal that she had reached the end of her adventurous road?

And if so, then what would that mean for me?

Thus, we all took the news brought by Pwent with mixed feelings and more than a little trepidation.

Bruenor's conflicted attitude didn't hold for long, though. A young and fiery dwarf named Dagnabbit, one who had been instrumental in freeing Mithral Hall from the duergar those years ago, and son of the famous General Dagna, the esteemed commander of Mithral Hall's military arm, had accompanied Pwent to Icewind Dale. After Bruenor held a private meeting with Dagnabbit, my friend had come out as full of excitement as I had ever seen him, practically hopping with eagerness to be on the road home. And to the surprise of everyone, Bruenor had immediately put forth a special advisement—not a direct order, but a heavy-handed suggestion—that all of Mithral Hall's dwarves who had settled beneath the shadows of Kelvin's Cairn in Icewind Dale return with him.

When I asked Bruenor about this apparent change in attitude, he merely winked and assured me that I'd soon know "the greatest adventure" of my life—no small promise! He still won't talk about the specifics, or even the general goal he has in mind, and Dagnabbit is as tight-lipped as my irascible friend.

But in truth, the specifics are not so important to me. What is important is the assurance that my life will continue to hold adventure, purpose, and goals. That is the secret, I believe. To continually reach higher is to live; to always strive to be a better person or to make the world around you a better place or to enrich your life or the lives of those you love is the secret to that most elusive of goals: a sense of accomplishment. For some, that can be achieved by creating order and security or a sense of home. For some, including many dwarves, it can be achieved by the accumulation of wealth or the crafting of a magnificent item.

For me, I'll use my scimitars.

And so my feet were light when again we departed Icewind Dale, a hearty caravan of hundreds of dwarves, a grumbling (but far from miserable) halfling, an adventurous woman, a mighty barbarian warrior, along with his wife and child, and me, a pleasantly misguided dark elf who keeps a panther as a friend.

Let the snows fall deep, the rain drive down, and the wind buffet my cloak. I care not, for I've a road worth walking!

I am not afraid to die.

There, I said it, I admitted it . . . to myself. I am not afraid to die, nor have I been since the day I walked out of Menzoberranzan.

Only now have I come to fully appreciate that fact, and only because of a very special friend named Bruenor Battlehammer.

It is not bravado that makes such words flow from my lips. Not some needed show of courage and not some elevation of myself above any others. It is the simple truth. I am not afraid to die.

I do not wish to die, and I hold faith that I will fight viciously against any attempts to kill me. I'll not run foolishly into an enemy encampment with no chance of victory (though my friends often accuse me of just that, and even the obvious fact that we are not yet dead does not dissuade them from their barbs). Nay, I hope to live for several centuries. I hope to live forever, with my dear friends all about me every step of that unending journey.

So, why the lack of fear? I understand well enough that the road I willingly walk—indeed, the road I choose to walk—is fraught with peril and presents the very real possibility that one day, perhaps soon, I, or my friends, will be slain. And while it would kill me to be killed, obviously, and kill me even more to see great harm come to any of my dear friends, I will not shy from this road. Nor will they.

And now I know why. And now, because of Bruenor, I understand why I am not afraid to die.

Before, I expected that my lack of fear was due to some faith in a higher being, a deity, an afterlife, and there remains that comforting hope. That is but a part of the equation, though, and a part that is based upon prayers and blind faith, rather than the certain knowledge of that which truly sustains me, which truly guides me, which truly allows me to take every step along the perilous road with a profound sense of inner calm.

I am not afraid to die because I know that I am part of a something, a concept, a belief, that is bigger than all that is me, body and soul.

When I asked Bruenor about this road away from Mithral Hall that he has chosen, I put the question simply: What will the folk of Mithral Hall do if you are killed on the road?

His answer was even more simple and obvious: they'll do better then than if I went home and hid!

That's the way of the dwarves—and it is an expectation they place upon all of their leaders. Even the overprotective ones, such as the consummate bodyguard Pwent, understand deep down that if they truly shelter Bruenor, they have, in effect, already slain the king of Mithral Hall. Bruenor recognizes that the concept of Mithral Hall, a theocracy that is, in fact, a subtle democracy, is bigger than the dwarf, whoever it might be, who is presently occupying the throne. And Bruenor recognizes that kings before him and kings after him will die in battle, tragically, with the dwarves they leave behind caught unprepared for his demise. But countering that seeming inevitability, in the end, is that the concept that is Mithral Hall will rise from the ashes of the funeral pyre.

When the drow came to Mithral Hall, as when any enemy in the past ever threatened the place, Bruenor, as king, stood strong and forthright, leading the charge. Indeed, it was Bruenor Battlehammer, and not some warrior acting on his behalf, who slew Matron Mother Baenre herself, the finest notch he ever put into that nasty axe of his.

That is the place of a dwarf king, because a dwarf king must understand that the kingdom is more important than the king, that the clan is bigger than the king, that the principles of the clan's existence are the correct principles and are bigger than the mortal coil of king and commoner alike.

If Bruenor didn't believe that, if he couldn't honestly look his enemies coldly in the eye without fear for his own safety, then Bruenor should not be king of Mithral Hall. A leader who hides when danger reveals itself is no leader at all. A leader who thinks himself irreplaceable and invaluable is a fool.

But I am no leader, so how does this apply to me and my chosen road? Because I know in my heart that I walk a road of truth, a road of the best intentions (if sometimes those intentions are misguided), a road that to me is an honest one. I believe that my way is the correct way (for me, at least), and in my heart, if I ever do not believe this, then I must work hard to alter my course.

Many trials present themselves along this road. Enemies and other physical obstacles abound, of course, but along with them come the pains of the heart. In despair, I traveled back to Menzoberranzan, to surrender to the drow so that they would leave my friends alone, and in that most basic of errors I nearly cost the woman who is most dear to me her very life. I watched a confused and tired Wulfgar walk away from our group and feared he was walking into danger from which he would never emerge. And yet, despite the agony of that parting, I knew that I had to let him go. At times it is hard to hold confidence that the chosen fork in the road is the right one. The image of Ellifain dying will haunt me forever, I fear, yet I hold in retrospect the understanding that there was nothing I could have truly done differently. Even now knowing the dire consequences of my actions on that fateful day half a century ago, I believe that I would follow the same course, the one that my heart and my conscience forced upon me. For that is all that I can do, all that anyone can do. The inner guidance of conscience is the best marker along this difficult road, even if it is not foolproof.

I will follow it, though I know so well now the deep wounds I might find.

For as long as I believe that I am walking the true road, if I am slain, then I die in the knowledge that for a brief period at least, I was part of something bigger than Drizzt Do'Urden. I was part of the way it should be.

No drow, no man, no dwarf, could ever ask for more than that.

I am not afraid to die.

☙

I have come to view my journey through life as the convergence of three roads. First is the simple physical path, through my training in House Do'Urden to Melee-Magthere, the drow school for warriors, and my continued tutelage under my father, Zaknafein. It was he who prepared me for the challenges, he who taught me the movements to transcend the basics of the drow martial art, indeed to think creatively about any fight. Zaknafein's technique was more about training one's muscles to respond, quickly and in perfect harmony, to the calls of the mind, and even more importantly, the calls of the imagination.

Improvisation, not rote responses, is what separates a warrior from a weapons master.

The road of that physical journey out of Menzoberranzan, through the wilds of the Underdark, along the mountainous trails that led me to Montolio, and from there to Icewind Dale and the loved ones I now share, has intertwined often with the second road. They are inevitably linked.

For the second road was the emotional path, the growth I have come to find in understanding and appreciation, not only of what I desire to be and to have, but of the needs of others, and the acceptance that their way of looking at the world may not coincide with my own. My second road started in confusion as the world of Menzoberranzan came clear to me and made little sense to my views. Again it was Zaknafein who crystallized the beginning steps of this road, as he showed me that there was indeed truth in that which I knew in my heart—but could not quite accept in my thoughts, perhaps—to be true. I credit Catti-brie, above all others, with furthering this journey. From the beginning, she knew to look past the reputation of my heritage and judge me for my actions and my heart, and that was such a freeing experience for me that I could not help but accept the philosophy and embrace it. In doing so I have come to appreciate so many people of various races and various cultures and various viewpoints.

From each I learn, and in learning, with such an open mind, I grow.

Now, after all these adventurous years, I have come to understand that there is indeed a third road. For a long time, I thought it an extension of the second, but now I view this path as independent. It is a subtle distinction, perhaps, but not so in importance.

This third journey began the day I was born, as it does for all reasoning beings. It lay somewhat dormant for me for many years, buried beneath the demands of Menzoberranzan and my own innate understanding that the other two paths had to be sorted before the door to this third could truly open.

I opened that door in the home of Montolio DeBrouchee, in Mooshie's Grove, when I found Mielikki, when I discovered that which was in my heart and soul. That was the first step on the spiritual road, the path more of mystery than of experience, more of questions than of answers, more of faith and hope than of realization.

It is the road that opens only when the needed steps have been taken along the other two. It is the path that requires the shortest steps, perhaps, but is surely the most difficult, at least at first. If the three paths are each divergent and many-forked at their beginning, and indeed, along the way—the physical is usually determined by need, the emotional by want, the spiritual—?

It is not so clear a way, and I fear that for many it never becomes so.

For myself, I know that I am on the right path, but not because I have yet found the answers. I know my way is true because I have found the questions, specifically how, why, and where.

How did I, did anyone, get here? Was it by a course of natural occurrences, or the designs of a creator or creators, or are they indeed one and the same?

In either case, why am I here? Is there indeed even a reason, or is it all pure chance and randomness?

And perhaps the most important question to any reasoning being, where will my journey take me when I have shrugged off this mortal coil?

I view this last and most important road as ultimately private.

These are questions that cannot be answered for me by anyone other than me. I see many people, most people, finding their "answers" in the sermons of others. Words sanctified by age or the perceived wisdom of authors who provide a comfortable ending to their spiritual journey, provide answers to truly troubling questions. No, not an ending, but a pause, awaiting the resumption once this present experience of life as we know it ends.

Perhaps I am being unfair to the various flocks. Perhaps many within have asked themselves the questions and have found their personal answers, then found those of similar ilk with whom to share their revelations and comfort. If that is the case, if it is not a matter of simple indoctrination, then I envy and admire those who have advanced along their spiritual road farther than I.

For myself, I have found Mielikki, though I still have no definitive manifestation of that name in mind. And far from a pause or the ending of my journey, my discovery of Mielikki has only given me the direction I needed to ask those questions of myself in the first place. Mielikki provides me comfort, but the answers, ultimately, come from within, from that part of myself that I feel akin to the tenets of Mielikki as Montolio described them to me.

The greatest epiphany of my life came along this last and most important road: the understanding that all the rest of it, emotional and physical—and material—is naught but a platform. All of our accomplishments in the external are diminished many times over if they do not serve to turn us inward. There and only there lies our meaning, and in truth, part of the answer to the three questions is the understanding to ask them in the first place, and more than that, to recognize their penultimate importance in the course of reason.

The guiding signs of the spiritual journey will rarely be obvious, I believe, for the specific questions found along the road are often changing, and sometimes seemingly unanswerable. Even now, when all seems aright, I am faced with the puzzle of Ellifain and the sadness of that loss. And though I feel as if I am on the greatest adventure of my life with Catti-brie, there are many questions that remain with me concerning our relationship. I try to live in the here and now with her, yet at some point she and I will have to look longer down our shared path. And both of us, I think, fear what we see.

I have to hold faith that things will clarify, that I will find the answers I need.

I have always loved the dawn. I still sit and watch every one, if my situation permits. The sun stings my eyes less now, and less with each rising, and perhaps that is some signal that it, as a representation of the spiritual, has begun to flow more deeply into my heart, my soul, and my understanding of it all.

That, of course, is my hope.

We have to live our lives and view our relationship in the present. That is the truth of my life with Catti-brie, and it is also my fear for that life. To live in the here and now, to walk the wind-swept trails and do battle against whatever foe opposes us. To define our cause and our purpose, even if that purpose is no more than the pursuit of adventure, and to chase that goal with all our hearts and souls. When we do that, Catti-brie and I are free of the damning realities of our respective heritage. As long as we do that, we can live our lives together in true friendship and love, as close as two reasoning beings could ever be.

It is only when we look further down the road of the future that we encounter troubles.

On the mountainous trails north of Mithral Hall, Catti-brie recently had a brush with death and, more poignantly, a brush with mortality. She looked at the end of her life, so suddenly and brutally. She thought she was dead, and believed in that horrible instant that she would never be a mother, that she would bear no children and instill in them the values that guide her life and her road. She saw mortality, true mortality, with no one to carry on her legacy.

She did not like what she saw.

She escaped death, as she has so often done, as I, and all of us, have so often done. Wulfgar was there for her, as he would have been for

any of us, as any of us would have been for him, to scatter the orcs.
And so her mortality was not realized in full.

But still the thought lingers.

And there, in that clearer understanding of the prospects of her
future, in the clearer understanding of the prospect of our future, lies
the rub, the sharp turn in our adventurous road that threatens to spill
all that we have come to achieve into a ravine of deadly rocks.

What future is there between us? When we consider our
relationship day by day, there is only joy and adventure and excitement;
when we look down the road, we see limitations that we, particularly
Catti-brie, cannot ignore. Will she ever bear children? Could she even
bear mine? There are many half-elves in the world, the product of
mixed heritage, human and elf, but half-drow? I have never heard of
such a thing—it was rumored that House Barrison Del'Armgo fostered
such couplings, to add strength and size to their warrior males, but I
know not if that was anything more than rumor. Certainly the results
were not promising, even if that were true!

So I do not know that I could father any of Catti-brie's children,
and in truth, even if it is possible, it is not necessarily a pleasant
prospect, and certainly not one without severe repercussions. Certainly I
would want children of mine to hold so many of Catti-brie's wonderful
qualities: her perceptive nature, her bravery, her compassion, her
constant holding to the course she knows to be right, and, of course,
her beauty. No parent could be anything but proud of a child who
carried the qualities of Catti-brie.

But that child would be half-drow in a world that will not accept
drow elves. I find a measure of tolerance now, in towns where my
reputation precedes me, but what chance might any child beginning in
this place have? By the time such a child was old enough to begin to
make any such reputation, he or she would be undoubtedly scarred by
the uniqueness of heritage. Perhaps we could have a child and keep it
in Mithral Hall all the years.

But that, too, is a limitation, and one that Catti-brie knows all too well.

It is all too confusing and all too troubling. I love Catti-brie—I know that now—and know, too, that she loves me. We are friends above all else, and that is the beauty of our relationship. In the here and in the now, walking the road, feeling the wind, fighting our enemies, I could not ask for a better companion, a better complement to who I am.

But as I look farther down that road, a decade, two decades, I see sharper curves and deeper ravines. I would love Catti-brie until the day of her death, if that day found her infirm and aged while I was still in the flower of my youth. To me, there would be no burden, no longing to go out and adventure more, no need to go out and find a more physically compatible companion, an elf or perhaps even another drow.

Catti-brie once asked me if my greatest limitation was internal or external. Was I more limited by the way people viewed me as a dark elf, or by the way I viewed people viewing me? I think that same thing applies now, only for her. For while I understand the turns our road together will inevitably take, and I fully accept them, she fears them, I believe, and more for my sensibilities than for her own. In three decades, when she nears sixty years of age, she will be old by human standards. I'll be around a hundred, my first century, and would still be considered a very young adult, barely more than a child, by the reckoning of the drow. I think that her brush with mortality is making her look to that point and that she is not much enjoying the prospects—for me more than for her.

And there remains that other issue, of children. If we two were to start a family, our children would face terrific pressures and prejudices and would be young, so very young, when their mother passed away.

It is all too confusing.

I choose, for now, to walk in the present.

Yes, I do so out of fear.

The Lone Drow

I did everything right.

Every step of my journey out of Menzoberranzan was guided by my inner map of right and wrong, of community and selflessness. Even on those occasions when I failed, as everyone must, my missteps were of judgment or simple frailty and were not in disregard of my conscience. For in there, I know, reside the higher principles and tenets that move us all closer to our chosen gods, closer to our definitions, hopes, and understandings of paradise.

I did not abandon my conscience, but it, I fear, has deceived me. I did everything right.

Yet Ellifain is dead, and my long-ago rescue of her is a mockery.

I did everything right.

And I watched Bruenor fall, and I expect that those others I loved, that everything I loved, fell with him.

Is there a divine entity out there somewhere, laughing at my foolishness?

Is there even a divine entity out there, anywhere?

Or was it all a lie, and worse, a self-deception?

Often have I considered community, and the betterment of the individual within the context of the betterment of the whole. This was the guiding principle of my existence, the realization that forced me from Menzoberranzan. And now, in this time of pain, I have come to understand—or perhaps it is just that now I have forced myself to admit—that my belief was also something much more personal. How ironic that in my declaration of community, I was in effect and in fact feeding my own desperate need to belong to something larger than myself.

In privately declaring and reinforcing the righteousness of my beliefs, I was doing no differently from those who flock before the preacher's pulpit. I was seeking comfort and guidance, only I was looking for the needed answers within, whereas so many others seek them without.

By that understanding, I did everything right. And yet, I cannot dismiss the growing realization, the growing trepidation, the growing terror, that I, ultimately, was wrong.

For what is the point if Ellifain is dead, and if she existed in such turmoil through all the short years of her life? For what is the point if I and my friends followed our hearts and trusted in our swords, only for me to watch them die beneath the rubble of a collapsing tower?

If I have been right all along, then where is justice, and where is the reciprocation of a grateful god?

Even in asking that question, I see the hubris that has so infected me. Even in asking that question, I see the machinations of my soul laid bare. I cannot help but ask, am I any different than my kin? In technique, surely, but in effect? For in declaring community and dedication, did I not truly seek exactly the same things as the priestesses I left behind in Menzoberranzan? Did I, like they, not seek eternal life and higher standing among my peers?

As the foundation of Withegroo's tower swayed and toppled, so too have the illusions that have guided my steps.

I was trained to be a warrior. Were it not for my skill with my scimitars, I expect I would be a smaller player in the world around me, less respected and less accepted. That training and talent are all that I have left now; it is the foundation upon which I intend to build this new chapter in the curious and winding road that is the life of Drizzt Do'Urden. It is the extension of my rage that I will turn loose upon the wretched creatures that have so shattered all that I held dear. It is the expression of what I have lost: Ellifain, Bruenor, Wulfgar, Regis, Catti-brie, and, in effect, Drizzt Do'Urden.

These scimitars, Icingdeath and Twinkle by name, become my definition of myself now, and Guenhwyvar again is my only companion. I trust in both, and in nothing else.

I erred, as I knew I would. Rationally, in those moments when I have been able to slip away from my anger, I have known for some time that my actions have bordered on recklessness, and that I would find my end out here on the mountain slopes.

Is that what I have desired all along, since the fall of Shallows? Do I seek the end of pain at the end of a spear?

There is so much more to this orc assault than we believed when first we encountered the two wayward and wounded dwarves from Citadel Felbarr. The orcs have found organization and cooperation, at least to an extent that they save their sharpened swords for a common enemy. All the North is threatened, surely, especially Mithral Hall, and I would not be surprised to learn that the dwarves have already buttoned themselves up inside their dark halls, sealing their great doors against the assault of the overwhelming orc hordes.

Perhaps it is that realization, that these hordes threaten the place that for so long was my home, that so drives me on to strike against the raiders. Perhaps my actions are bringing some measure of discomfort to the invaders, and some level of assistance to the dwarves.

Or is that line of thinking merely justification? Can I admit that possibility to myself at least? Because in my heart I know that even if the orcs had retreated back to their holes after the fall of Shallows, I would not have turned back for Mithral Hall. I would have followed the orcs to the darkest places, scimitars high and ready, Guenhwyvar crouched beside me. I would have struck hard at them, as I do now, taking what little pleasure seems left in my life in the warmth of spilling orc blood.

How I hate them.

Or is it even them?

It is all too confusing to me. I strike hard and in my mind I see Bruenor atop the burning tower, tumbling to his death. I strike hard and in my mind I see Ellifain falling wounded across the room, slumping to her death.

I strike hard, and if I am lucky, I see nothing—nothing but the blur of the moment. As my instincts engulf my rational mind, I am at peace.

And yet, as those immediate needs retreat, as the orcs flee or fall dead, I often find unintended and unwelcome consequences.

What pain I have caused Guenhwyvar these last days! The panther comes to my call unerringly and fights as I instruct and as her instincts guide. I ask her to go against great foes, and there is no complaint. I hear her wounded cry as she writhes in the grip of a giant, but there is no accusation toward me buried within that wail. And when I call upon her again, after her rest in the Astral Plane, she is there, by my side, not judging, uncomplaining.

It is as it was in the Underdark those days after I walked out of Menzoberranzan. She is my only contact to the humanity within me, the only window on my heart and soul. I know that I should be rid of her now, that I should hand her over to one more worthy, for I have no hope that I will survive this ordeal. How great it wounds me to think of the figurine that summons Guenhwyvar, the link to the astral spirit of the panther, in the clutches of an orc.

And yet, I find that I cannot make that trip to Mithral Hall to turn over the panther to the dwarves. I cannot walk this road without her, and it is a road I am unable to turn from.

I am weak, perhaps, or I am a fool. Whichever the case, I am not yet ready to stop this war I wage; I am not yet ready to abandon the warmth of spilled orc blood. These beasts have brought this pain upon me, and I will repay them a thousand thousand times over, until my scimitars slip from my weakened grasp and I fall dying to the stone.

I can only hope that Guenhwyvar has gone beyond the compulsion of the magic figurine, that she has found some free will against its pressure. I believe that she has, and that if an orc pries the figurine from my dead body and somehow discovers how to use it, he will bring to his side the instrument of his death.

That is my hope at least.

Perhaps it is another lie, another justification.

Perhaps I am lost in a web of such soft lies too deep to sift through.

I know only the pain of memory and the pleasure of the hunt. I will take that pleasure, to the end.

How strange it was for me to watch the two elves come to my aid that day at the river. How out of sorts I felt, and how off-balance. I knew the hunting pair were in the area, of course, but to actually confront them on such terms took me to places where I did not dare to venture.

Took me back to the cave in the west, where Ellifain, their friend, lay dead at the end of my bloody blade.

How convenient the situation was to me in that moment of recognition, for there was truth in my advisement that we should flee along separate trails to discourage pursuit. There was justification in my reasoning.

But that cannot hide the truth I know in my own heart. I ran off down a different path because I was afraid, because courage in battle and courage in personal and emotional matters are often two separate attributes, and an abundance of one does not necessarily translate into an ample amount of the other.

I fear little from enemies. I fear more from friends. That is the paradox of my life. I can face a giant, a demon, a dragon, with scimitars drawn and enthusiasm high, and yet it took me years to admit my feelings for Catti-brie, to let go of the fears and just accept our relationship as the most positive aspect of my entire life.

And now I can throw myself into a gang of orcs without regard, blades slashing, a song of battle on my lips, but when Tarathiel and Innovindil presented themselves to me, I felt naked and helpless. I felt like a child again in Menzoberranzan, hiding from my mother and my vicious sisters. I do not think those two meant me any harm; they did not aid me in my battle just so they could find the satisfaction of killing me themselves. They came to me openly, knowing my identity.

But not knowing of my encounter with poor Ellifain, I am fairly certain.

I should have told them. I should have confessed all. I should have explained my pain and my regret, should have bowed before them with sorrow and humility, should have prayed with them for the safekeeping of poor Ellifain's spirit.

I should have trusted them. Tarathiel knows me and once trusted me with one of the precious horses of the Moonwood. Tarathiel saw the truth and believed that I had acted nobly on that long-ago night when the drow raiding party had crept out of the Underdark to slaughter Ellifain's clan. He would have understood my encounter with Ellifain. He would have seen the futility of my position and the honest pain within my heart and soul.

And he should know the fate of his old friend. By all rights, he and Innovindil deserve to know of the death of Ellifain, of how she fell, and perhaps together we could then determine why she fell.

But I couldn't tell them. Not there. Not then. The wave of panic that rolled through me was as great as any I have ever known. All that I could think of was how I might get out of there, of how I might get away from these two allies, these two friends of dead Ellifain.

And so I ran.

With my scimitars, I am Drizzt the Brave, who shies from no battle. I am Drizzt who walked into a verbeeg lair beside Wulfgar and Guenhwyvar, knowing we were outmatched and outnumbered but hardly afraid! I am Drizzt, who survived alone in the Underdark for a decade, who accepted his fate and his inevitable death (or so I thought) rather than compromise those principles that I knew to be the true guiding lights of my existence.

But I am also Drizzt the Coward, fearing no physical challenge but unable to take an emotional leap into the arms of Catti-brie. I am Drizzt the Coward, who flees from Tarathiel because he cannot confess.

I am Drizzt, who has not returned to Mithral Hall after the fall of Shallows because without that confirmation of what I know to be true, that my friends are all dead, I can hold a sliver of hope that somehow some of them managed to escape the carnage. Regis, perhaps, using his ruby pendant to have the orcs carry him to waiting Battlehammer arms. Wulfgar, perhaps, raging beyond sensibility, reverting to his time in the Abyss and a pain and anger beyond control, scattering orcs before him until all those others ran from him and did not pursue.

And Catti-brie with him, perhaps.

It is all folly, I know.

I heard the orcs. I know the truth.

I am amazed at how much I hide behind these blades of mine. I am amazed at how little I fear death at an enemy's hands, and yet, at how greatly I fear having to tell Tarathiel the truth of Ellifain.

Still, I know that to be my responsibility. I know that to be the proper and just course.

I know that.

In matters of the heart, courage cannot overcome cowardice until I am honest with myself, until I admit the truth.

My reasoning in running away from the two elves that day in the river was sound and served to deflect their curiosity. But that reasoning was also a lie, because I cannot yet dare to care again.

I know that.

171

I watched the descent of Obould's sword. With my heart undefended, risking friends once more, I watched, and again my heart was severed. All is a swirl of confusion again, punctuated by pinpricks of pain that find my most vulnerable and sensitive areas, stinging and burning, flashing images of falling friends. I can build the stone wall to block them, I know, in the form of anger. To hide my eyes and hide my heart—yet I am not sure if the relief is worth the price.

That is my dilemma.

The death of Tarathiel was about Tarathiel. That is obvious, I know, but I must often remind myself of that truth. The world is not my playground, not a performance for my pleasure and my pain, not an abstract thought in the mind of Drizzt Do'Urden.

Bruenor's fall was more poignant to Bruenor than it was to me. So was Zaknafein's to Zaknafein, and that of all the others. Aside from that truth, though, there is my own sensibility, my own perception of events, my own pain and confusion. We can only view the world through our own eyes, I think. There are empathy and sympathy; there is often a conscious effort to see as a friend or even an enemy might— this is an important element in the concept of truth and justice, of greater community than our own wants and needs. But in the end, it all, for each of us, comes back to each of us individually, and everything we witness rings more important to each of us than to others, even if what we witness is a critical moment for another.

There is an undeniable selfishness in that realization, but I do not run away from that truth because there is nothing I, or anyone, can do about that truth. When we lose a loved one, the agony is ours as well. A parent watching his or her child suffer is in as much pain, or even more, I am sure, than the suffering child.

And so, embracing that selfishness at this moment, I ask myself if Tarathiel's fall was a warning or a test. I dared to open my heart, and it was torn asunder. Do I fall back into that other being once more, encase my spirit in stone to make it impervious to such pain? Or is this sudden and unexpected loss a test of my spirit, to show that I can accept the cruelty of fate and press on, that I can hold fast to my beliefs and my principles and my hopes against the pain of those images?

I think that we all make this choice all the time, in varying degrees. Every day, every tenday, when we face some adversity, we find options that usually run along two roads. Either we hold our course—the one we determinedly set in better and more hopeful times, based on principle and faith—or we fall to the seemingly easier and more expedient road of defensive posture, both emotional and physical. People and often societies sometimes react to pain and fear by closing up, by sacrificing freedoms and placing practicality above principle. Is that what I have been doing since the fall of Bruenor? Is this hunting creature I have become merely a tactic to forgo the pain?

While in Silverymoon some years ago, I chanced to study the history of the region, to glance at perspectives on the many wars faced by the people of that wondrous community throughout the ages. At those times when the threatened Silverymoon closed up and put aside her enlightened principles—particularly the recognition that the actions of the individual are more important than the reputation of the individual's race—the historians were not kind and the legacy did not shine.

The same will be said of Drizzt Do'Urden, I think, by any who care to take notice.

There is a small pool in the cave where Tarathiel and Innovindil took up residence, where I am now staying with the grieving Innovindil. When I look at my reflection in that pool, I am reminded, strangely, of Artemis Entreri.

When I am the hunting creature, the reactionary, defensive, and closed-hearted warrior, I am more akin to him. When I strike at enemies, not out of community or personal defense, not out of the guiding recognition of right and wrong or good and evil, but out of anger, I am more akin to that closed and unfeeling creature I first met in the tunnels of duergar-controlled Mithral Hall. On those occasions, my blades are not guided by conscience or powered by justice.

Nay, they are guided by pain and powered by anger.

I lose myself.

I see Innovindil across the way, crying still for the loss of her dear Tarathiel. She is not running away from the grief and the loss. She is embracing it and incorporating it into her being, to make it a part of herself, to own it so that it cannot own her.

Have I the strength to do the same?

I pray that I do, for I understand now that only in going through the pain can I be saved.

The Two Swords

I look upon the hillside, quiet now except for the birds.

That's all there is. The birds, cawing and cackling and poking their beaks into unseeing eyeballs. Crows do not circle before they alight on a field strewn with the dead. They fly as the bee to a flower, straight for their goal, with so great a feast before them. They are the cleaners, along with the crawling insects, the rain, and the unending wind. And the passage of time. There is always that. The turn of the day, of the season, of the year.

When it is done, all that is left are the bones and the stones. The screams are gone, the smell is gone. The blood is washed away. The fattened birds take with them in their departing flights all that identified these fallen warriors as individuals.

Leaving the bones and stones, to mingle and mix. As the wind or the rain break apart the skeletons and filter them together, as the passage of time buries some, what is left becomes indistinguishable, perhaps, to all but the most careful of observers. Who will remember those who died here, and what have they gained to compensate for all that they, on both sides, lost?

The look upon a dwarf's face when battle is upon him would argue, surely, that the price is worth the effort, that warfare, when it comes to a dwarven nation, is a noble cause.

Nothing to a dwarf is more revered than fighting to help a friend; theirs is a community bound tightly by loyalty, by blood shared and blood spilled.

And so, in the life of an individual, perhaps this is a good way to die, a worthy end to a life lived honorably, or even to a life made worthy by this last ultimate sacrifice.

I cannot help but wonder, though, in the larger context, what of the overall? What of the price, the worth, and the gain? Will Obould accomplish anything worth the hundreds, perhaps thousands, of his dead? Will he gain anything long-lasting? Will the dwarven stand made out here on this high cliff bring Bruenor's people anything worthwhile? Could they not have slipped into Mithral Hall, to tunnels so much more easily defended?

And a hundred years from now, when there remains only dust, will anyone care?

I wonder what fuels the fires that burn images of glorious battle into the hearts of so many of the sentient races, my own paramount among them. I look at the carnage on the slope and I see the inevitable sight of emptiness. I imagine the cries of pain. I hear in my head the calls for loved ones when the dying warrior knows his last moment is upon him. I see a tower fall with my dearest friend atop it. Surely the tangible remnants, the rubble and the bones, are hardly worth the moment of battle, but is there, I wonder, something less tangible here, something of a greater place? Or is there, perhaps—and this is my fear—something of a delusion to it all that drives us to war, again and again?

Along that latter line of thought, is it within us all, when the memories of war have faded, to so want to be a part of something great that we throw aside the quiet, the calm, the mundane, the peace itself? Do we collectively come to equate peace with boredom and complacency? Perhaps we hold these embers of war within us, dulled only by sharp memories of the pain and the loss, and when that smothering blanket dissipates with the passage of healing time, those fires flare again to life. I saw this within myself, to a smaller extent, when I realized and admitted to myself that I was not a being of comfort and complacency, that only by the wind on my face, the trails beneath my feet, and the adventure along the road could I truly be happy.

I'll walk those trails indeed, but it seems to me that it is another thing altogether to carry an army along beside me, as Obould has done. For there is the consideration of a larger morality here, shown so starkly in the bones among the stones. We rush to the call of arms, to the rally, to the glory, but what of those caught in the path of this thirst for greatness?

Who will remember those who died here, and what have they gained to compensate for all that they, on both sides, lost?

Whenever we lose a loved one, we resolve, inevitably, to never forget, to remember that dear person for all our living days. But we the living contend with the present, and the present often commands all of our attention. And so as the years pass, we do not remember those who have gone before us every day, or even every tenday. Then comes the guilt, for if I am not remembering Zaknafein, my father, my mentor, who sacrificed himself for me, then who is? And if no one is, then perhaps he really is gone. As the years pass, the guilt will lessen, because we forget more consistently and the pendulum turns in our self-serving thoughts to applaud ourselves on those increasingly rare occasions when we do remember! There is always the guilt, perhaps, because we are self-centered creatures to the last. It is the truth of individuality that cannot be denied. In the end, we, all of us, see the world through our own, personal eyes. I have heard parents express their fears of their own mortality soon after the birth of a child. It is a fear that stays with a parent, to a great extent, through the first dozen years of a child's life. It is not for the child that they fear, should they die—though surely there is that worry, as well—but rather for themselves. What father would accept his death before his child was truly old enough to remember him? For who better to put a face to the bones among the stones? Who better to remember the sparkle in an eye before the crow comes a'calling?

I wish the crows would circle and the wind would carry them away, and the faces would remain forever to remind us of the pain. When the clarion call to glory sounds, before the armies anew trample the bones among the stones, let the faces of the dead remind us of the cost. It is a sobering sight before me, the red-splashed stones.

It is a striking warning in my ears, the cawing of the crows.

From a high ridge east of Keeper's Dale, I watched the giants construct their massive battering ram. I watched the orcs practice their tactics—tight lines and sudden charges. I heard the awful cheering, the bloodthirsty calls for dwarf blood and dwarf heads, the feral screams of battle lust.

From that same ridge, I watched the huge ram pulled back by a line of giants, then let loose to swing hard and fast at the base of the mountain on which I stood, at the metal doorway shell of Mithral Hall.

The ground beneath my feet shuddered.

The booming sound vibrated in the air.

They pulled it back and let fly again and again.

Then the shouts filled the air, and the wild charge was on.

I stood there on that ridge, Innovindil beside me, and I knew that my friends, Bruenor's kin, were battling for their homeland and for their very lives right below me. And I could do nothing.

I realized then, in that awful moment, that I should be in there with the dwarves, killing orcs until at last I, too, was cut down. I realized then, in that awful moment, that my decisions of the last few tendays, formed in anger and even more in fear, betrayed the trust of the friendship that Bruenor and I had always held.

Soon after—too soon!—the mountainside quieted. The battle ended.

To my horror, I came to see that the orcs had won the day, that they had gained a foothold inside Mithral Hall.

They had driven the dwarves from the entry hall at least. I took some comfort in the fact that the bulk of the orc force remained outside the broken door, continuing their work in Keeper's Dale. Nor had many giants gone in.

Bruenor's kin were not being swept away; likely, they had surrendered the wider entry halls for the more defensible areas in the tighter tunnels.

That sense of hope did not wash away my guilt, however.

In my heart I understood that I should have gone back to Mithral Hall, to stand with the dwarves who for so long had treated me as one of their own.

Innovindil would hear nothing of it, though. She reminded me that I had not, had never, fled the battle for Mithral Hall.

Obould's son was dead because of my decision, and many orcs had been turned back to their holes in the Spine of the World because of my—of our, Innovindil, Tarathiel, and myself—work in the North.

It is difficult to realize that you cannot win every battle for every friend. It is difficult to understand and accept your own limitations, and with them, the recognition that while you try to do the best you can, it will often prove inadequate.

And so it was then and there, on that mountainside watching the battle, in that moment when all seemed darkest, that I began to accept the loss of Bruenor and the others. Oh, the hole in my heart did not close. It never will. I know and accept that. But what I let go then was my own guilt at witnessing the fall of a friend, my own guilt at not having been there to help him, or there to hold his hand in the end.

Most of us will know loss in our lives. For an elf, drow or moon, wild or avariel, who will see centuries of life, this is unavoidable—a parent, a friend, a brother, a lover, a child even. Profound pain is often the unavoidable reality of conscious existence. How less tolerable that loss will be if we compound it internally with a sense of guilt.

Guilt.

It is the easiest of feelings to conjure, and the most insidious.

It is rooted in the selfishness of individuality, though for goodly folks, it usually finds its source in the suffering of others.

What I understand now, as never before, is that guilt is not the driving force behind responsibility. If we act in a goodly way because we are afraid of how we will feel if we do not, then we have not truly come to separate the concept of right and wrong. For there is a level above that, an understanding of community, friendship, and loyalty. I do not choose to stand beside Bruenor or any other friend to alleviate guilt. I do so because in that, and in their reciprocal friendship, we are both the stronger and the better. Our lives become worth so much more.

I learned that one awful day, standing on a cold mountain stone watching monsters crash through the door of a place that had long been my home.

I miss Bruenor and Wulfgar and Regis and Catti-brie. My heart bleeds for them and yearns for them every minute of every day. But I accept the loss and bear no personal burden for it beyond my own emptiness. I did not turn from my friends in their hour of need, though I could not be as close to them as I would desire. From across that ravine when Withegroo's tower fell, when Bruenor Battlehammer tumbled from on high, I offered to him all that I could: my love and my heart.

And now I will go on, Innovindil at my side, and continue our battle against our common enemy. We fight for Mithral Hall, for Bruenor, for Wulfgar, for Regis, for Catti-brie, for Tarathiel, and for all the goodly folk. We fight the monstrous scourge of Obould and his evil minions.

At the end, I offered to my falling friends my love and my heart. Now I pledge to them my enduring friendship and my determination to live on in a manner that would make the dwarf king stare at me, his head tilted, his expression typically skeptical about some action or another of mine.

"Durned elf," he will say often, as he looks down on me from Moradin's halls.

And I will hear him, and all the others, for they are with me always, no small part of Drizzt Do'Urden.

For as I begin to let go, I find that I hold them all the tighter, but in a way that will make me look up to the imagined halls of Moradin, to the whispered grumbling of a lost friend, and smile.

∞

"Do you know what it is to be an elf, Drizzt Do'Urden?"

I hear this question all the time from my companion, who seems determined to help me begin to understand the implications of a life that could span centuries—implications good and bad when one considers that so many of those with whom I come into contact will not live half that time.

It has always seemed curious to me that, while elves may live near a millennium and humans less than a century, human wizards often achieve levels of understanding and power to rival those of the greatest elf mages. This is not a matter of intelligence, but of focus, it seems clear. Always before, I gave the credit for this to the humans, for their sense of urgency in knowing that their lives will not roll on and on and on.

Now I have come to see that part of the credit for this balance is the elven viewpoint of life, and that viewpoint is not one rooted in falsehood or weakness. Rather, this quieter flow of life is the ingredient that brings sanity to an existence that will see the birth and death of centuries. Or, if preferable, it is a segmented flow of life, a series of bursts.

I see it now, to my surprise, and it was Innovindil's recounting of her most personal relationships with partners both human and elf that presented the notion clearly in my mind. When Innovindil asks me now, "Do you know what it is to be an elf, Drizzt Do'Urden?" I can honestly and calmly smile with self-assurance. For the first time in my life, yes, I think I do know.

To be an elf is to find your distances of time. To be an elf is to live several shorter life spans. It is not to abandon forward-looking sensibility, but it is also to find emotionally comfortable segments of time, smaller life spans in which to exist. In light of that realization, for me the more pertinent question thus becomes, "Where is the range of comfort for such existences?"

There are many realities that dictate such decisions—decisions that, in truth, remain more subconscious than purposeful. To be an elf is to outlive your companions if they are not elves; even if they are, rare is the relationship that will survive centuries. To be an elf is to revel in the precious moments of your children—should they be of only half-elf blood, and even if they are of full blood—and to know that they may not outlive you. In that instance, there is only comfort in the profound and ingrained belief that having these children and these little pockets of joyful time was indeed a blessing, and that such a blessing outweighs the profound loss that any compassionate being would surely feel at the death of an offspring. If the very real possibility that one will outlive a child, even if the child sees the end of its expected life span, will prevent that person from having children, then the loss is doubly sad.

In that context, there is only one answer: to be an elf is to celebrate life.

To be an elf is to revel in the moments, in the sunrise and the sunset, in the sudden and brief episodes of love and adventure, in the hours of companionship. It is, most of all, to never be paralyzed by your fears of a future that no one can foretell, even if predictions lead you to the seemingly obvious, and often disparaging, conclusions.

That is what it is to be an elf.

The elves of the surface, contrary to the ways of the drow, often dance and sing. With this, they force themselves into the present, into the moment, and though they may be singing of heroes and deeds long past or of prophecies yet to come, they are, in their song, in the moment, in the present, grasping an instant of joy or reflection and holding it as tightly as any human might.

A human may set out to make a "great life," to become a mighty leader or sage, but for elves, the passage of time is too slow for such pointed and definitive ambitions. The memories of humans are short, so 'tis said, but that holds true for elves as well. The long-dead human heroes of song no doubt bore little resemblance to the perceptions of the current bards and their audience, but that is true of elves, too, even though those elf bards likely knew the principals of their songs!

The centuries dull and shift the memories, and the lens of time alters images.

A great life for an elf, then, results either from a historical moment seized correctly or, more often, it is a series of connected smaller events that will eventually add up to something beyond the parts. It is a continuing process of growth, perhaps, but only because of piling experiential understanding.

Most of all, I know now, to be an elf is not to be paralyzed by a future one cannot control. I know that I am going to die. I know that those I love will one day die, and in many cases—I suspect, but do not know!—they will die long before I. Certitude is strength and suspicion is worthless, and worry over suspicion is something less than that.

I know, now, and so I am free of the bonds of the future.

I know that every moment is to be treasured, to be enjoyed, to be heightened as much as possible in the best possible way.

I know, now, the failing of the bonds of worthless worry.

I am free.

There is a balance to be found in life between the self and the community, between the present and the future. The world has seen too much of tyrants interested in the former, selfish men and women who revel in the present at the expense of the future. In theoretical terms, we applaud the one who places community first and looks to the betterment of the future.

After my experiences in the Underdark, alone and so involved in simple survival that the future meant nothing more than the next day. I have tried to move myself toward that latter, seemingly desirable goal. As I gained friends and learned what friendship truly was, I came to view and appreciate the strength of community over the needs of the self.

And as I came to learn of cultures that have progressed in strength, character, and community, I came to try to view all of my choices as an historian might centuries from now. The long-term goal was placed above the short-term gain, and that goal was based always on the needs of the community over the needs of the self.

After my experiences with Innovindil, after seeing the truth of friends lost and love never realized, I understand that I have only been half right.

"To be an elf is to find your distances of time. To be an elf is to live several shorter life spans." I have learned this to be true, but there is something more. To be an elf is to be alive, to experience the joy of the moment within the context of long-term desires. There must be more than distant hopes to sustain the joy of life.

Seize the moment and seize the day. Revel in the joy and fight all the harder against despair.

I had something so wonderful for the last years of my life.

I had with me a woman whom I loved, and who was my best of friends. Someone who understood my every mood, and who accepted the bad with the good. Someone who did not judge, except in encouraging me to find my own answers.

I found a safe place for my face in her thick hair. I found a reflection of my own soul in the light in her blue eyes. I found the last piece of this puzzle that is Drizzt Do'Urden in the fit of our bodies.

Then I lost her, lost it all.

And only in losing Catti-brie did I come to see the foolishness of my hesitance. I feared rejection. I feared disrupting that which we had. I feared the reactions of Bruenor and later, when he returned from the Abyss, of Wulfgar.

I feared and I feared and I feared, and that fear held back my actions, time and again.

How often do we all do this? How often do we allow often irrational fears to paralyze us in our movements? Not in battle, for me, for never have I shied away from locking swords with a foe. But in love and in friendship, where, I know, the wounds can cut deeper than any blade.

Innovindil escaped the frost giant lair, and now I, too, am free. I will find her. I will find her and I will hold on to this new friendship we have forged, and if it becomes something more, I will not be paralyzed by fear.

Because when it is gone, when I lay at death's door or when she is taken from me by circumstance or by a monster, I will have no regrets.

That is the lesson of Shallows.

When first I saw Bruenor fall, when first I learned of the loss of my friends, I retreated into the shell of the Hunter, into the instinctual fury that denied pain. Innovindil and Tarathiel moved me past that destructive, self-destructive state, and now I understand that for me, the greatest tragedy of Shallows lies in the lost years that came before the fall.

I will not make that mistake again. The community remains above the self; the good of the future outweighs the immediate desires. But not so much, perhaps. There is a balance to be found, I know now, for utter selflessness can be as great a fault as utter selfishness, and a life of complete sacrifice, without joy, is, at the end, a lonely and empty existence.

Transitions

The Orc King

One of the consequences of living an existence that spans centuries instead of decades is the inescapable curse of continually viewing the world through the focusing prism employed by an historian.

I say "curse"—when in truth I believe it to be a blessing—because any hope of prescience requires a constant questioning of what is, and a deep-seated belief in the possibility of what can be.

Viewing events as might the historian requires an acceptance that my own initial, visceral reactions to seemingly momentous events may be errant, that my "gut instinct" and my own emotional needs may not stand the light of reason in the wider view, or even that these events, so momentous in my personal experience, might not be so in the wider world and the long, slow passage of time.

How often have I seen that my first reaction is based on half-truths and biased perceptions! How often have I found expectations completely inverted or tossed aside as events played out to their fullest!

Because emotion clouds the rational, and many perspectives guide the full reality. To view current events as an historian is to account for all perspectives, even those of your enemy. It is to know the past and to use such relevant history as a template for expectations. It is, most of all, to force reason ahead of instinct, to refuse to demonize that which you hate, and to, most of all, accept your own fallibility.

And so I live on shifting sands, where absolutes melt away with the passage of decades. It is a natural extension, I expect, of an existence in which I have shattered the preconceptions of so many people. With every stranger who comes to accept me for who I am instead of who he or she expected me to be, I roil the sands beneath that person's feet. It is a growth experience for them, no doubt, but we are all creatures of ritual and habit and accepted notions of what is and what is not. When true reality cuts against that internalized expectation—when you meet a goodly drow!—there is created an internal dissonance, as uncomfortable as a springtime rash.

There is freedom in seeing the world as a painting in progress, instead of a place already painted, but there are times, my friend . . .

There are times.

And such is one before me now, with Obould and his thousands camped upon the very door of Mithral Hall. In my heart I want nothing more than another try at the orc king, another opportunity to put my scimitar through his yellow-gray skin. I long to wipe the superior grin from his ugly face, to bury it beneath a spray of his own blood. I want him to hurt—to hurt for Shallows and all the other towns flattened beneath the stamp of orc feet. I want him to feel the pain he brought to Shoudra Stargleam, to Dagna and Dagnabbit, and to all the dwarves and others who lay dead on the battlefield that he created.

Will Catti-brie ever walk well again? That, too, is the fault of Obould.

And so I curse his name, and remember with joy those moments of retribution that Innovindil, Tarathiel, and I exacted upon the minions of the foul orc king. To strike back against an invading foe is indeed cathartic.

That, I cannot deny.

And yet, in moments of reason, in times when I sit back against a stony mountainside and overlook that which Obould has facilitated, I am simply not certain.

Of anything, I fear.

He came at the front of an army, one that brought pain and suffering to many people across this land I name as my home. But his army has stopped its march, for now at least, and the signs are visible that Obould seeks something more than plunder and victory.

Does he seek civilization?

Is it possible that we bear witness now to a monumental change in the nature of orc culture? Is it possible that Obould has established a situation, whether he intended this at first or not, where the interests of the orcs and the interests of all the other races of the region coalesce into a relationship of mutual benefit?

Is that possible? Is that even thinkable?

Do I betray the dead by considering such a thing?

Or does it serve the dead if I, if we all, rise above a cycle of revenge and war and find within us—orc and dwarf, human and elf alike—a common ground upon which to build an era of greater peace?

For time beyond the memory of the oldest elves, the orcs have warred with the "goodly" races. For all the victories—and they are countless!—and for all the sacrifices, are the orcs any less populous now than they were millennia ago?

I think not, and that raises the specter of unwinnable conflict.

Are we doomed to repeat these wars, generation after generation, unendingly? Are we—elf and dwarf, human and orc alike—condemning our descendants to this same misery, to the pain of steel invading flesh?

I do not know.

And yet I want nothing more than to slide my blade between the ribs of King Obould Many-Arrows, to relish in the grimace of agony on his tusk-torn lips, to see the light dim in his yellow, bloodshot eyes.

But what will the historians say of Obould? Will he be the orc who breaks, at long, long last, this cycle of perpetual war? Will he,

inadvertently or not, present the orcs with a path to a better life, a road they will walk—reluctantly at first, no doubt—in pursuit of bounties greater than those they might find at the end of a crude spear?

I do not know.

And therein lies my anguish.

I hope that we are on the threshold of a great era, and that within the orc character, there is the same spark, the same hopes and dreams, that guide the elves, dwarves, humans, halflings, and all the rest. I have heard it said that the universal hope of the world is that our children will find a better life than we. Is that guiding principle of civilization itself within the emotional makeup of goblinkin? Or was Nojheim, that most unusual goblin slave I once knew, simply an anomaly?

Is Obould a visionary or an opportunist?

Is this the beginning of true progress for the orc race, or a fool's errand for any, myself included, who would suffer the beasts to live?

Because I admit that I do not know, it must give me pause. If I am to give in to the wants of my vengeful heart, then how might the historians view Drizzt Do'Urden?

Will I be seen in the company of those heroes before me who helped vanquish the charge of the orcs, whose names are held in noble esteem? If Obould is to lead the orcs forward, not in conquest, but in civilization, and I am the hand who lays him low, then misguided indeed will be those historians, who might never see the possibilities that I view coalescing before me.

Perhaps it is an experiment. Perhaps it is a grand step along a road worth walking.

Or perhaps I am wrong, and Obould seeks dominion and blood, and the orcs have no sense of commonality, have no aspirations for a better way, unless that way tramples the lands of their mortal, eternal enemies.

But I am given pause.

And so I wait, and so I watch, but my hands are near to my blades.

I came from the Underdark, the land of monsters. I lived in Icewind Dale, where the wind can freeze a man solid, or a bog can swallow a traveler so quickly that he'll not likely understand what is happening to him soon enough to let out a cry, unless it is one muffled by loose mud. Through Wulfgar I have glimpsed the horrors of the Abyss, the land of demons, and could there be any place more vile, hate-filled, and tormenting? It is indeed a dangerous existence.

I have surrounded myself with friends who will fearlessly face those monsters, the wind and the bog, and the demons, with a snarl and a growl, a jaw set and a weapon held high. None would face them more fearlessly than Bruenor, of course.

But there is something to shake even that one, to shake us all as surely as if the ground beneath our feet began to tremble and break away.

Change.

In any honest analysis, change is the basis of fear, the idea of something new, of some paradigm that is unfamiliar, that is beyond our experiences so completely that we cannot even truly predict where it will lead us. Change. Uncertainty.

It is the very root of our most primal fear—the fear of death—that one change, that one unknown against which we construct elaborate scenarios and "truisms" that may or may not be true at all. These constructions, I think, are an extension of the routines of our lives. We dig ruts with the sameness of our daily paths, and drone and rail against those routines while we, in fact, take comfort in them. We awake and construct our days of habit, and follow the norms we have built fast, solid, and bending only a bit in our daily existence. Change is the unrolled die, the unused sava piece. It is exciting and frightening only when we hold some power over it, only when there is a potential reversal of course, difficult though it may be, within our control.

Absent that safety line of real choice, absent that sense of some control, change is merely frightening. Terrifying, even.

An army of orcs does not scare Bruenor. Obould Many-Arrows does not scare Bruenor. But what Obould represents, particularly if the orc king halts his march and establishes a kingdom, and more especially if the other kingdoms of the Silver Marches accept this new paradigm, terrifies Bruenor Battlehammer to the heart of his being and to the core tenets of his faith. Obould threatens more than Bruenor's kin, kingdom, and life. The orc's designs shake the very belief system that binds Bruenor's kin, the very purpose of Mithral Hall, the understanding of what it is to be a dwarf, and the dwarven concept of where the orcs fit into that stable continuum. He would not say it openly, but I suspect that Bruenor hopes the orcs will attack, that they will, in the end, behave in accordance with his expectations of orcs and of all goblinkin. The other possibility is too dissonant, too upsetting, too contrary to Bruenor's very identity for him to entertain the plausibility, indeed the probability, that it would result in less suffering for all involved.

I see before me the battle for the heart of Bruenor Battlehammer, and for the hearts of all the dwarves of the Silver Marches.

Easier by far to lift a weapon and strike dead a known enemy, an orc.

In all the cultures I have known, with all the races I have walked beside, I have observed that when beset by such dissonance, by events that are beyond control and that plod along at their own pace, the frustrated onlookers often seek out a beacon, a focal point—a god, a person, a place, a magical item—which they believe will set all the world aright. Many are the whispers in Mithral Hall that King Bruenor will fix it, all of it, and make everything as it had been before the onslaught of Obould. Bruenor has earned their respect many times over, and wears the mantle of hero among his kin as comfortably and deservedly as has any dwarf in the history of the clan. For most of the dwarves here, then, King Bruenor has become the beacon and focal point of hope itself.

Which only adds to Bruenor's responsibility, because when a frightened people put their faith in an individual, the ramifications of incompetence, recklessness, or malfeasance are multiplied many times over. And so becoming the focus of hope only adds to Bruenor's tension. Because he knows that it is not true, and that their expectations may well be beyond him. He cannot convince Lady Alustriel of Silverymoon or any of the other leaders, not even King Emerus Warcrown of Citadel Felbarr, to march in force against Obould. And to go out alone with Mithral Hall's own forces would lead to the wholesale slaughter of Clan Battlehammer. Bruenor understands that he has to wear the mantle not only of hero but of savior, and it is for him a terrible burden.

And so Bruenor, too, has engaged in deflection and wild expectation, has found a focal point on which to pin his hopes. The most common phrase he has spoken throughout this winter has been, "Gauntlgrym, elf."

Gauntlgrym. It is a legend among Clan Battlehammer and all the Delzoun dwarves. It is the name of their common heritage, an immense city of splendor, wealth, and strength that represents to every descendant of the Delzoun tribes the apex of dwarven civilization.

It is, perhaps, history wound with myth, a likely unintentional lionizing of that which once was. As heroes of old take on more gigantic proportions with each passing generation, so too does this other focal point of hope and pride expand.

"Gauntlgrym, elf," Bruenor says with steady determination. All of his answers lie there, he is certain. In Gauntlgrym, Bruenor will find a path to unravel the doings of King Obould. In Gauntlgrym, he will discover how to put the orcs back in their holes, and more importantly, how to realign the races of the Silver Marches into proper position, into places that make sense to an old, immovable dwarf.

He believes that we found this magical kingdom on our journey here from the Sword Coast. He has to believe that this unremarkable sinkhole in a long-dead pass was really the entrance to a place where he can find his answers.

Otherwise he has to become the answer for his anxious people.

And Bruenor knows that their faith is misplaced, for at present, he has no answer to the puzzle that is Obould.

Thus, he says, "Gauntlgrym, elf," with the same conviction that a devout believer will utter the name of his savior god.

We will go to this place, this hole in the ground in a barren pass in the west. We will go and find Gauntlgrym, whatever that may truly mean. Perhaps Bruenor's instincts are correct—could it be that Moradin told him of this in his days of near death? Perhaps we will find something entirely different, but that will still bring to us, to Bruenor, the clarity he needs to find the answers for Mithral Hall.

Fixated and desperate as he is, and as his people are, Bruenor doesn't yet understand that the name he has affixed to our savior is not the point. The point is the search itself, for solutions and for the truth, and not the place he has determined as our goal.

"Gauntlgrym, elf."

Indeed.

We construct our days, bit by bit, tenday by tenday, year by year.

Our lives take on a routine, and then we bemoan that routine.

Predictability, it seems, is a double-edged blade of comfort and boredom.

We long for it, we build it, and when we find it, we reject it.

Because while change is not always growth, growth is always rooted in change. A finished person, like a finished house, is a static thing. Pleasant, perhaps, or beautiful or admirable, but not for long exciting.

King Bruenor has reached the epitome, the pinnacle, the realization of every dream a dwarf could fathom. And still King Bruenor desires change, though he would refuse to phrase it that way, admitting only his love of adventure. He has found his post, and now seeks reasons to abandon that post at every turn. He seeks, because inside of him he knows that he must seek to grow. Being a king will make Bruenor old before his time, as the old saying goes.

Not all people are possessed of such spirits. Some desire and cling to the comfort of the routine, to the surety that comes with the completion of the construction of life's details. On the smaller scale, they become wedded to their daily routines. They become enamored of the predictability. They calm their restless souls in the confidence that they have found their place in the multiverse, that things are the way they are supposed to be, that there are no roads left to explore and no reason to wander.

On the larger scale, such people become fearful and resentful—sometimes to extremes that defy logic—of anyone or anything that intrudes on that construct. A societal change, a king's edict, an attitude shift in the neighboring lands, even events that have nothing to do with them personally, can set off a reaction of dissonance and fear. When Lady Alustriel initially allowed me to walk the streets of Silverymoon openly, she found great resistance.

Her people, well protected by one of the finest armies in all the land and by a leader whose magical abilities are renowned throughout the world, did not fear Drizzt Do'Urden. Nay, they feared the change that I represented. My very presence in Silverymoon infringed upon the construct of their lives, threatened their understanding of the way things were, threatened the way things were supposed to be. Even though, of course, I posed no threat to them whatsoever.

That is the line we all straddle, between comfort and adventure.

There are those who find satisfaction, even fulfillment, in the former, and there are those who are forever seeking.

It is my guess, and can only be my guess, that the fears of the former are rooted in fear of the greatest mystery of all, death. It is no accident that those who construct the thickest walls are most often rooted firmly, immovably, in their faith. The here and now is as it is, and the better way will be found in the afterlife. That proposition is central to the core beliefs that guide the faithful, with, for many, the added caveat that the afterlife will only fulfill its promise if the here and now remains in strict accord with the guiding principles of the chosen deity.

I count myself among the other group, the seekers. Bruenor, too, obviously so, for he will ever be the discontented king. Catti-brie cannot be rooted. There is no sparkle in her eyes greater than the one when she looks upon a new road. And even Regis, for all his complaints regarding the trials of the road, wanders and seeks and fights. Wulfgar, too, will not be confined. He has seen his life in Mithral Hall and has concluded, rightfully and painfully, that there is for him a better place and a better way. It saddens me to see him go. For more than a score of years he has been my friend and companion, a trusted arm in battle and in life. I miss him dearly, every day, and yet when I think of him, I smile for him. Wulfgar has left Mithral Hall because he has outgrown all that this place can offer, because he knows that in Icewind Dale he will find a home where he will do more good—for himself and for those around him.

I, too, hold little faith that I will live out my days in Bruenor's kingdom. It is not just boredom that propels my steps along paths unknown, but a firm belief that the guiding principle of life must be a search not for what is, but for what could be. To look at injustice or oppression, at poverty or slavery, and shrug helplessly, or worse to twist a god's "word" to justify such states, is anathema to the ideal, and to me, the ideal is achieved only when the ideal is sought. The ideal is not a gift from the gods, but a promise from them.

We are possessed of reason. We are possessed of generosity. We are possessed of sympathy and empathy. We have within us a better nature, and it is one that cannot be confined by the constructed walls of anything short of the concept of heaven itself. Within the very logic of that better nature, a perfect life cannot be found in a world that is imperfect.

So we dare to seek. So we dare to change. Even knowing that we will not get to "heaven" in this life is no excuse to hide within the comfort of routine. For it is in that seeking, in that continual desire to improve ourselves and to improve the world around us, that we walk the road of enlightenment, that we eventually can approach the gods with heads bowed in humility, but with confidence that we did their work, that we tried to lift ourselves and our world to their lofty standards, the image of the ideal.

Œ

The questions continue to haunt me. Are we watching the birth of a civilization? Are the orcs, instead of wanting us dead, wishing to become more like us, with our ways, our hopes, our aspirations?

Or was that wish always present in the hearts of the primitive and fierce race, only they saw not how to get to it? And if this is the case, if the orcs are redeemable, tamable, how then are we best to facilitate the rise of their more civilized culture? For that would be an act of great self-defense for Mithral Hall and all of the Silver Marches.

Accepting the premise of a universal desire among rational beings, a commonality of wishes, I wonder, then, what might occur should one kingdom stand paramount, should one city-state somehow attain unquestioned superiority over all the rest. What responsibilities might such predominance entail? If Bruenor has his way, and the Silver Marches rise up and drive Obould's orcs from the land and back to their individual tribes, what will be our role, then, in our resulting, unquestioned dominance?

Would the moral road be the extermination of the orcs, one tribe at a time? If my suspicions regarding Obould are correct, then that I cannot reconcile. Are the dwarves to become neighbors or oppressors?

It is all premised on a caveat, of course, on a hunch—or is it a deep-rooted prayer in the renegade soul of Drizzt Do'Urden? I desperately want to be right about Obould—as much as my personal desires might urge me to kill him!—because if I am, if there is in him a glint of rational and acceptable aspirations, then surely the world will benefit.

These are the questions for kings and queens, the principal building blocks of the guiding philosophies for those who gain power over others. In the best of these kingdoms—and I name Bruenor's among that lot—the community moves constantly to better itself, the parts of the whole turn in harmony to the betterment of the whole. Freedom and community live side by side, a tandem of the self and the bigger tapestry. As those communities evolve and ally with other like-minded kingdoms, as roads and trade routes are secured and cultures exchanged, what of the diminishing few left behind? It is incumbent, I believe, for the powerful to bend and grasp the hand of the weak, to pull them up, to share in the prosperity, to contribute to the whole. For that is the essence of community. It is to be based on hope and inspiration and not on fear and oppression.

But there remains the truth that if you help an orc to stand, he will likely stab your heart on the way to his feet.

Ah, but it is too much, for in my heart I see the fall of Tarathiel and want to cut the vicious orc king apart! It is too much because I know of Innovindil's fall! Oh, Innovindil, I pray you do not think less of me for my musing!

I feel the sting of paradox, the pain of the irresolvable, the stark and painful imperfections of a world of which I secretly demand perfection. Yet for all the blemishes, I remain an optimist, that in the end the ideal will prevail. And this, too, I also know, and it is why my weapons sit comfortably in my hands. Only from a position of unquestioned strength can true change be facilitated. For it is not in the hands of a rival to effect change. It is not in the hands of the weaker to grant peace and hope to the stronger.

I hold faith in the kingdom of common voices that Bruenor has created, that Alustriel has similarly created in Silverymoon. I believe that this is the proper order of things—though perhaps with some refining yet to be found—for theirs are kingdoms of freedom and hope, where individual aspirations are encouraged and the common good is shared by all, in both benefit and responsibility. How different are these two places from the darkness of Menzoberranzan, where the power of House presided over the common good of the community, and the aspirations of the individual overwhelmed the liberty, even the life, of others.

My belief in Mithral Hall as nearer the ideal brings with it a sense of Mithral Hall's responsibilities, however. It is not enough to field armies to thwart foes, to crush our enemies under the stamp of well-traveled dwarven boots. It is not enough to bring riches to Mithral Hall, to expand power and influence, if said power and influence is to the benefit only of the powerful and influential.

To truly fulfill the responsibilities of predominance, Mithral Hall must not only shine brightly for Clan Battlehammer, but must serve as a beacon of hope for all of those who glimpse upon it. If we truly believe our way to be the best way, then we must hold faith that all others—perhaps even the orcs!—will gravitate toward our perspectives and practices, that we will serve as the shining city on the hill, that we will influence and pacify through generosity and example instead of through the power of armies.

For if it is the latter, if dominance is attained and then maintained through strength of arm alone, then it is no victory, and it cannot be a permanent ordering. Empires cannot survive, for they lack the humility and generosity necessary to facilitate true loyalty.

The wont of the slave is to throw off his shackles. The greatest aspiration of the conquered is to beat back their oppressors. There are no exceptions to this. To the victors I warn without doubt that those you conquer will never accept your dominion. All desire to emulate your better way, even if the conquered agree with the premise, will be overwhelmed by grudge and humiliation and a sense of their own community. It is a universal truth, rooted in tribalism, perhaps, and in pride and the comfort of tradition and the sameness of one's peers.

And in a perfect world, no society would aspire to dominance unless it was a dominance of ideals. We believe our way is the right way, and thus we must hold faith that others will gravitate similarly, that our way will become their way and that assimilation will sheathe the swords of sorrow. It is not a short process, and it is one that will be played out in starts and stops, with treaties forged and treaties shattered by the ring of steel on steel.

Deep inside, it is my hope that I will find the chance to slay King Obould Many-Arrows.

Deeper inside, it is my prayer that King Obould Many-Arrows sees the dwarves standing higher on the ladder in pursuit of true civilization, that he sees Mithral Hall as a shining city on the hill, and that he will have the strength to tame the orcs long enough for them to scale the rungs of that same ladder.

The Pirate King

A million, million changes—uncountable changes!—every day, every heartbeat of every day. That is the nature of things, of the world, with every decision a crossroad, every drop of rain an instrument both of destruction and creation, every animal hunting and every animal eaten changing the present just a bit.

On a larger level, it's hardly and rarely noticeable, but those multitude of pieces that comprise every image are not constants, nor, necessarily, are constant in the way we view them.

My friends and I are not the norm for the folk of Faerun. We have traveled half the world, for me both under and above. Most people will never see the wider world outside of their town, or even the more distant parts of the cities of their births. Theirs is a small and familiar existence, a place of comfort and routine, parochial in their church, selective in their lifelong friends.

I could not suffer such an existence. Boredom builds like smothering walls, and the tiny changes of everyday existence would never cut large enough windows in those opaque barriers.

Of my companions, I think Regis could most accept such a life, so long as the food was plentiful and not bland and he was given some manner of contact with the goings-on of the wider world outside. I have often wondered how many hours a halfling might lie on the same spot on the shore of the same lake with the same unbaited line tied to his toe.

Has Wulfgar moved back to a similar existence? Has he shrunk his world, recoiling from the harder truths of reality?

It's possible for him, with his deep emotional scars, but never would it be possible for Catti-brie to go with him to such a life of steadfast routine. Of that I'm most certain. The wanderlust grips her as it grips me, forcing us along the road—even apart along our separate roads, and confident in the love we share and the eventual reunions.

And Bruenor, as I witness daily, battles the smallness of his existence with growls and grumbles. He is the king of Mithral Hall, with riches untold at his fingertips. His every wish can be granted by a host of subjects loyal to him unto death. He accepts the responsibilities of his lineage, and fits that throne well, but it galls him every day as surely as if he was tied to his kingly seat. He has often found and will often find again excuses to get himself out of the hall on some mission or other, whatever the danger.

He knows, as Catti-brie and I know, that stasis is boredom and boredom is a wee piece of death itself.

For we measure our lives by the changes, by the moments of the unusual. Perhaps that manifests itself in the first glimpse of a new city, or the first breath of air on a tall mountain, a swim in a river cold from the melt or a frenzied battle in the shadows of Kelvin's Cairn. The unusual experiences are those that create the memories, and a tenday of memories is more life than a year of routine. I remember my first sail aboard *Sea Sprite*, for example, as keenly as my first kiss from Catti-brie, and though that journey lasted mere tendays in a life more than three-quarters of the way through a century, the memories of that voyage play out more vividly than some of the years I spent in House Do'Urden, trapped in the routine of a drow boy's repetitive duties.

It's true that many of the wealthier folk I have known, lords of

Waterdeep even, will open their purses wide for a journey to a far-off place of respite. Even if a particular journey does not go as anticipated for them, with unpleasant weather or unpleasant company, or foul food or even minor illnesses, to a one, the lords would claim the trip worth the effort and the gold. What they valued most for their trouble and treasure was not the actual journey, but the memory of it that remained behind, the memory of it that they will carry to their graves. Life is in the experiencing, to be sure, but it's just as much in the recollection and in the telling!

Contrastingly, I see in Mithral Hall many dwarves, particularly older folk, who revel in the routine, whose every step mirrors those of the day before. Every meal, every hour of work, every chop with the pick or bang with the hammer follows the pattern ingrained throughout the years. There is a game of delusion at work here, I know, though I wouldn't say it aloud. It's an unspoken and internal logic that drives them ever on in the same place. It's even chanted in an old dwarven song:

> For this I did on yesterday
> And not to Moradin's Hall did I fly
> So's to do it again'll keep me well
> And today I sha'not die.

The logic is simple and straightforward, and the trap is easily set, for if I did these things the day before and do these same things today, I can reasonably assume that the result will not change.

And the result is that I will be alive tomorrow to do these things yet again.

Thus do the mundane and the routine become the—false—assurance of continued life, but I have to wonder, even if the premise were true, even if doing the same thing daily would ensure immortality, would a year of such existence not already be the same as the most troubling possibility of death?

From my perspective, this ill-fated logic ensures the opposite of that delusional promise! To live a decade in such a state is to ensure the swiftest path to death, for it is to ensure the swiftest passage of the decade, an unremarkable recollection that will flitter by without a pause, the years of mere existence. For in those hours and heartbeats and passing days, there is no variance, no outstanding memory, no first kiss.

To seek the road and embrace change could well lead to a shorter life in these dangerous times in Faerun. But in those hours, days, years, whatever the measure, I will have lived a longer life by far than the smith who ever taps the same hammer to the same familiar spot on the same familiar metal.

For life is experience, and longevity is, in the end, measured by memory, and those with a thousand tales to tell have indeed lived longer than any who embrace the mundane.

I put Regis at ease as we walked out of Longsaddle. I kept my demeanor calm and assuring, my stride solid and my posture forward-leaning. Yet inside, my stomach churned and my heart surely ached. What I saw in the once-peaceful village shook me profoundly. I had known the Harpells for years, or thought so, and I was pained to see that they were walking a path that could well lead them to a level of authoritarian brutishness that would have made the magistrates at Luskan's wretched Prisoner's Carnival proud.

I cannot pretend to judge the immediacy and criticality of their situation, but I can certainly lament the potential outcome I so clearly recognized.

I wonder, then, where is the line between utilitarian necessity and morality? Where does one cross that line, and more importantly, when, if ever, is the greater good not served by the smaller victories of, or concessions to, basic standards of morality?

This world in which I walk often makes such distinctions based on racial lines. Given my dark elf heritage, I certainly know and understand that. Moral boundaries are comfortably relaxed in the concept of "the other." Cut down an orc or a drow with impunity, indeed, but not so a dwarf, a human, an elf?

What will such moral surety do in light of King Obould should he consider his unexpected course? What did such moral surety do in light of myself? Is Obould, am I, an anomaly, the exception to a hard and fast rule, or a glimpse of wider potential?

I know not.

Words and blades, I kept in check in Longsaddle. This was not my fight, since I had not the time, the standing, or the power to see it through to any logical conclusion. Nor could I and Regis have done much to alter the events at hand. For all their foolishness, the Harpells are a family of powerful magic-users. They didn't ask for permission from or the opinion of a dark elf and halfling walking a road far from home.

Is it pragmatism, therefore, to justify my lack of action, and my subsequent assurances to Regis, who was so openly troubled by what we had witnessed?

I can lie to him—or at least, conceal my true unease—but I cannot do so to myself. What I saw in Longsaddle wounded me profoundly; it broke my heart as much as it shocked my sensibilities.

It also reminded me that I am one small person in a very large world. I hold in reserve my hope and faith in the general weal of the family Harpell. This is a good and generous family, grounded in morality if not in common sense. I cannot consider myself so wrong in trusting in them. But still . . .

Almost in answer to that emotional turmoil, I now find a situation not so different waiting for me in Luskan, but one from a distinctly opposing perspective. If Captain Deudermont and this young Waterdhavian lord are to be believed, then the authorities in Luskan have gone over to a dangerous place. Deudermont intends to lead something not quite a revolution, since the Hosttower of the Arcane is not the recognized leadership of the city.

Is Luskan now what Longsaddle will become as the Harpells

consolidate their power with clever polymorphs and caged bunnies? Are the Harpells susceptible to the same temptations and hunger for greater power that has apparently infected the hierarchy of the Hosttower? Is this a case of better natures prevailing? My fear is that any ruling council where the only check against persecuting power is the better nature of the ruling principles is doomed to eventual, disastrous failure. And so I ride with Deudermont as he begins his correction of that abuse.

Here, too, I find myself conflicted. It is not a lament for Longsaddle that drives me on in Luskan; I accept the call because of the man who calls. But my words to Regis were more than empty comforts. The Harpells were behaving with brutality, it seemed, but I hold no doubt that the absence of suffocating justice would precipitate a level of wild and uncontrollable violence between the feuding clerics.

If that is true, then what will happen in Luskan without the power behind the throne? It is well understood that the Arcane Brotherhood keeps under its control the five high captains, whose individual desires and goals are often conflicting. These high captains were all men of violence and personal power before their ascent. They are a confederation whose individual domains have never been subservient to the betterment of the whole of Luskan's populace.

Captain Deudermont will wage his battle against the Hosttower.

I fear that defeating Arklem Greeth will be the easier task than replacing the control exerted by the archmage arcane.

I will be there beside Deudermont, one small person in a very large world. And as we take actions that will no doubt hold important implications for so many people, I can only hope that Deudermont and I, and those who walk with us, will create good results from good desires.

If so, should I reverse my steps and return to Longsaddle?

I am often struck by the parallel courses I find in the wide world.

My life's road has led me to many places, back and forth from

Mithral Hall to the Sword Coast, to Icewind Dale and the Snowflake Mountains, to Calimport and to the Underdark. I have come to know the truth of the old saying that the only constant is change, but what strikes me most profoundly is the similarity of direction in that change, a concordance of mood, from place to place, in towns and among people who have no, or at least only cursory, knowledge of each other.

I find unrest and I find hope. I find contentment and I find anger. And always, it seems, I'm met with the same general set of emotions among the people from place to place. I understand there is a rationality to it all, for even peoples remote from each other will share common influences: a difficult winter, a war in one land that affects commerce in another, whispers of a spreading plague, the rise of a new king whose message resonates among the populace and brings hope and joy even to those far removed from his growing legend. But still, I often feel as though there is another realm of the senses. As a cold winter might spread through Icewind Dale and Luskan, and all the way to the Silver Marches, so too, it seems, does mood spiderweb the paths and roads of the Realms. It's almost as if there is a second layer of weather, an emotional wave that rolls and roils its way across Faerun.

There is trepidation and hopeful change in Mithral Hall and the rest of the Silver Marches, a collective holding of breath where the coin of true peace and all-out war spins on its edge, and not dwarf nor elf nor human nor orc knows on which side it will land. There is a powerful emotional battle waging between the status quo and the desire to embrace great and promising change.

And so I found this same unsettling dynamic in Longsaddle, where the Harpells are engaged in a similar state of near disaster with the rival factions of their community. They hold the coin fast, locked in spells to conserve what is, but the stress and strain are obvious to all who view.

And so I found this same dynamic in Luskan, where the potential change is no less profound than the possible—and none too popular— acceptance of an orc kingdom as a viable partner in the league of nations that comprise the Silver Marches.

A wave of unrest and edginess has gripped the land, from Mithral Hall to the Sword Coast—palpably so. It's as if the people and races of the world have all at once declared the unacceptability of their current lot in life, as if the sentient beings have finished their collective exhale and are now taking in a new breath.

I head to Icewind Dale, a land of tradition that extends beyond the people who live there, a land of constants and of constant pressure. A land not unaccustomed to war, a land that knows death intimately. If the same breath that brought Obould from his hole, that brought out ancient hatreds among the priests of Longsaddle, that led to the rise of Deudermont and the fall of Arklem Greeth, has filled the unending winds of Icewind Dale, then I truly fear what I may find there, in a place where the smoke of a gutted homestead is almost as common as the smoke of a campfire, and where the howl of the wolf is no less threatening than the war cry of a barbarian, or the battle call of an orc, or the roar of a white dragon. Under the constant struggle to simply survive, Icewind Dale is on edge even in those times when the world is in a place of peace and contentment. What might I find there now, when my road has passed through lands of strife and battle?

I wonder sometimes if there is a god, or gods, who play with the emotions of the collective of sentient beings as an artist colors a canvas. Might there be supernatural beings watching and taking amusement at our toils and tribulations? Do these gods wave giant wands of envy or greed or contentment or love over us all, that they can then watch at their pleasure, perhaps even gamble on the outcome?

Or do they, too, battle among themselves, reflections of our own failures, and their victories and failures similarly extend to us, their insignificant minions?

Or am I simply taking the easier route of reasoning, and ascribing what I cannot know to some irrationally defined being or beings for the sake of my own comfort? This trail, I fear, may be no more than warm porridge on a wintry morning.

Whatever it is, the weather or the rise of a great foe, folk demanding to partake of advancements in comfort or the sweep of a plague, or some unseen and nefarious god or gods at play, or whether, perhaps, the collective I view is no more than an extension of my own inner turmoil or contentment, a projection of Drizzt upon the people he views . . . whatever it may be, this collective emotion seems to me a palpable thing, a real and true motion of shared breath.

They are two men I love dearly, two men I truly respect, and as such, I'm amazed when I step back and consider the opposite directions of the roads of Wulfgar and Deudermont. Indeed, they are both true warriors, yet they have chosen different foes to battle.

Deudermont's road, I think, was wrought of frustration.

He has spent more than two decades sailing the Sword Coast in pursuit of pirates, and no person in the memories of old elves has ever been so successful at such a dangerous trade. All honors were bestowed upon *Sea Sprite* when she put in to any of the major cities, particularly the all-important Waterdeep. Captain Deudermont dined with lords, and could have taken that title at his whim, bestowed by the grateful noblemen of Waterdeep for his tireless and effective service.

But for all that, it was upon learning the truth of the newest pirate advances, that the Hosttower of the Arcane supported them with magic and coin, that Captain Deudermont had to face the futility of his lifelong quest. The pirates would outlive him, or at least, they would not soon run out of successors.

Thus was Deudermont faced with an untenable situation and a lofty challenge indeed. He didn't shy, he didn't sway, but rather took his ship straight to the source to face this greater foe. His reaction to a more terrible and wider world was to fight for control of that which seemed uncontrollable. And with such courage and allies, he may actually

succeed, for the specter of the Hosttower of the Arcane is no more, Arklem Greeth is no more, and the people of Luskan have rallied to Deudermont's noble cause.

How different has been Wulfgar's path. Where Deudermont turned outward to seek greater allies and greater victories, Wulfgar turned inward, and returned his thoughts to a time and place more simple and straightforward. A time and place no less harsh or dangerous, to be sure, but one of clear definition, and one where a victory does not mean a stalemate with a horde of orcs, or a political concession for the sake of expediency. In Wulfgar's world, in Icewind Dale, there is no compromise. There is perfection of effort, of body, of soul, or there is death. Indeed, even absent mistakes, even if perfection is achieved, Icewind Dale can take a man, any man, at a whim. Living there, I know, is the most humbling of experiences.

Still, I have no doubt that Wulfgar will defeat Icewind Dale's winter season. I have no doubt that upon his return to the Tribe of the Elk at the spring equinox, he will be greeted as family and friend, to be trusted. I have no doubt that Wulfgar will one day again be crowned as chief of his tribe, and that, should a terrible enemy rise up in the dale, he will stand forward, with all the inspired tribes gratefully at his back, cheering for the son of Beornegar.

His legend is secured, but hardly fully written.

So one of my friends battles a lich and an army of pirates and sorcerers, while the other battles inner demons and seeks definition of a scattered and unique existence. And there, I think, rests the most profound difference in their respective roads. For Deudermont is secure in his time and place, and reaches from solid foundation to greater endeavors. He is confident and comfortable with, above all others, Deudermont. He knows his pleasures and comforts, and knows, too, his enemies within and without. Because he understands his limitations, so he can find the allies to help him step beyond them. He is, in spirit, that which Wulfgar will become, for only after one has understanding and acceptance of the self can one truly affect the external.

I have looked into the eyes of Wulfgar, into the eyes of the son of Beornegar, into the eyes of the son of Icewind Dale.

I fear for him no longer—not in body, not in soul.

And yet, even though Wulfgar seeks as a goal to be where Deudermont already resides, it's Deudermont for whom I now fear. He steps with confidence and so he steps boldly, but in Menzoberranzan we had a saying, "Noet z'hin lil'avinsin."

"Boldly stride the doomed."

The Ghost King

Where does reason end and magic begin? Where does reason end and
faith begin? These are two of the central questions of sentience, so I
have been told by a philosopher friend who has gone to the end of his
days and back again. It is the ultimate musing, the ultimate search, the
ultimate reality of who we are. To live is to die, and to know that you
shall, and to wonder, always wonder.

This truth is the foundation of the Spirit Soaring, a cathedral,
a library, a place of worship and reason, of debate and philosophy.
Her stones were placed by faith and magic, her walls constructed of
wonderment and hope, her ceiling held up by reason. There, Cadderly
Bonaduce strides in profundity and demands of his many visitors,
devout and scholarly, that they do not shy from the larger questions
of existence, and do not shield themselves and buffet others with
unreasoned dogma.

There is now raging in the wider world a fierce debate—just such a
collision between reason and dogma. Are we no more than the whim
of the gods or the result of harmonic process? Eternal or mortal, and if
the former, then what is the relationship of that which is forever more,
the soul, to that which we know will feed the worms? What is the next

progression for consciousness and spirit, of self-awareness and—or—the loss of individuality in the state of oneness with all else? What is the relationship between the answerable and the unanswerable, and what does it bode if the former grows at the expense of the latter?

Of course, the act of simply asking these questions raises troubling possibilities for many people, acts of punishable heresy for others, and indeed even Cadderly once confided in me that life would be simpler if he could just accept what is, and exist in the present. The irony of his tale is not lost on me. One of the most prominent priests of Deneir, young Cadderly remained skeptical even of the existence of the god he served. Indeed he was an agnostic priest, but one mighty with powers divine. Had he worshipped any god other than Deneir, whose very tenets encourage inquisition, young Cadderly likely would never have found any of those powers, to heal or to invoke the wrath of his deity.

He is confident now in the evermore, and in the possibility of some Deneirrath heaven, but still he questions, still he seeks.

At Spirit Soaring, many truths—laws of the wider world, even of the heavens above—are being unraveled and unrolled for study and inquisition. With humility and courage, the scholars who flock there illuminate details of the scheme of our reality, argue the patterns of the multiverse and the rules that guide it, indeed, realign our very understanding of Toril and its relationship to the moon and the stars above.

For some, that very act bespeaks heresy, a dangerous exploration into the realms of knowledge that should remain solely the domain of the gods, of beings higher than us. Worse, these frantic prophets of doom warn, such ponderings and impolitic explanations diminish the gods themselves and turn away from faith those who need to hear the word. To philosophers like Cadderly, however, the greater intricacy, the greater complexity of the multiverse only elevates his feelings for his god. The harmony of nature, he argues, and the beauty of universal law and process bespeak a brilliance and a notion of infinity beyond that realized in blindness or willful, fearful ignorance.

To Cadderly's inquisitive mind, the observed system supporting divine law far surpasses the superstitions of the Material Plane.

For many others, though, even some of those who agree with Cadderly's search, there is an undeniable level of discomfort.

I see the opposite in Catti-brie and her continued learning and understanding of magic. She takes comfort in magic, she has said, because it cannot be explained. Her strength in faith and spirituality climbs beside her magical prowess. To have before you that which simply is, without explanation, without fabrication and replication, is the essence of faith.

I do not know if Mielikki exists. I do not know if any of the gods are real, or if they are actual beings, whether or not they care about the day-to-day existence of one rogue dark elf. The precepts of Mielikki— the morality, the sense of community and service, and the appreciation for life—are real to me, are in my heart. They were there before I found Mielikki, a name to place upon them, and they would remain there even if indisputable proof were given to me that there was no actual being, no physical manifestation of those precepts.

Do we behave out of fear of punishment, or out of the demands of our heart? For me, it is the latter, as I would hope is true for all adults, though I know from bitter experience that such is not often the case. To act in a manner designed to catapult you into one heaven or another would seem transparent to a god, any god, for if one's heart is not in alignment with the creator of that heaven, then . . . what is the point?

And so I salute Cadderly and the seekers, who put aside the ethereal, the easy answers, and climb courageously toward the honesty and the beauty of a greater harmony.

As the many peoples of Faerun scramble through their daily endeavors, march through to the ends of their respective lives, there will be much hesitance at the words that flow from Spirit Soaring, even resentment and attempts at sabotage. Cadderly's personal journey to explore the cosmos within the bounds of his own considerable intellect will no doubt foster fear, in particular of the most basic and terrifying concept of all, death.

From me, I show only support for my priestly friend. I remember my nights in Icewind Dale, tall upon Bruenor's Climb, more removed from the tundra below, it seemed, than from the stars above. Were my ponderings there any less heretical than the work of Spirit Soaring? And if the result for Cadderly and those others is anything akin to what I knew on that lonely mountaintop, then I recognize the strength of Cadderly's armor against the curses of the incurious and the cries of heresy from less enlightened and more dogmatic fools.

My journey to the stars, among the stars, at one with the stars, was a place of absolute contentment and unbridled joy, a moment of the most peaceful existence I have ever known.

And the most powerful, for in that state of oneness with the universe around me, I, Drizzt Do'Urden, stood as a god.

I know she is in constant torment, and I cannot go to her. I have seen into the darkness in which she resides, a place of shadows more profound and more grim than the lower planes. She took me there, inadvertently, when I tried to offer some comfort, and there, in so short a time, I nearly broke.

She took Regis there, inadvertently, when he tried to reach her with the ruby, and there he broke fully. He threw the drowning Catti-brie a rope and she pulled him from the shore of sanity.

She is lost to me. Forever, I fear. Lost in an oblivious state, a complete emptiness, a listless and lifeless existence. And those rare occasions when she is active are perhaps the most painful of all to me, for the depth of her delusions shines all too clearly. It's as if she's reliving her life, piecemeal, seeing again those pivotal moments that shaped this beautiful woman, this woman I love with all my heart. She

stood again on the side of Kelvin's Cairn back in Icewind Dale, living again the moment when first we met, and while that to me is among my most precious of memories, that fact made seeing it play out again through the distant eyes of my love even more painful.

How lost must my beloved Catti-brie be to have so broken with the world around her?

And Regis, poor Regis. I cannot know how deeply into that darkness Catti-brie now resides, but it's obvious to me that Regis went fully into that place of shadows. I can attest to the convincing nature of his delusions, as can Bruenor, whose shoulder now carries the scar of my blade as I fought off imaginary monsters. Or were they imaginary? I cannot begin to know. But that is a moot point to Regis, for to him they are surely real, and they're all around him, ever clawing at him, wounding him and terrifying him relentlessly.

We four—Bruenor, Catti-brie, Regis, and I—are representative of the world around us, I fear. The fall of Luskan, Captain Deudermont's folly, the advent of Obould—all of it were but the precursors. For now we have the collapse of that which we once believed eternal, the unraveling of Mystra's Weave. The enormity of that catastrophe is easy to see on the face of the always calm Lady Alustriel. The potential results of it are reflected in the insanity of Regis, the emptiness of Catti-brie, the near-loss of my own sanity, and the scar carried by King Bruenor.

More than the wizards of Faerun will feel the weight of this dramatic change. How will diseases be quelled if the gods do not hear the desperate pleas of their priests? How will the kings of the world fare when any contact to potential rivals and allies, instead of commonplace through divination and teleportation, becomes an arduous and lengthy process? How weakened will be the armies, the caravans, the small towns, without the potent power of magic-users among their ranks? And what gains will the more base races, like goblins and orcs, make in the face of such sudden magical weakness? What druids will tend the fields?

What magic will bolster and secure the exotic structures of the

world? Or will they fall catastrophically as did the Hosttower of the
Arcane, or long-dead Netheril?

Not so long ago, I had a conversation with Nanfoodle, the gnome
in Mithral Hall. We discussed his cleverness in funneling explosive
gasses under the mountain ridge where Obould's giant allies had set
up devastating artillery. Quite an engineering feat by the gnome and
his crew of dwarves, and one that blew the mountain ridge apart more
fully than even a fireball from Elminster could have done. Nanfoodle
is much more a follower of Gond, the god of inventions, than he is a
practitioner of the Art. I asked him about that, inquiring as to why he
tinkered so when so much of what he might do could be accomplished
more quickly by simply touching the Weave.

I never got an answer, of course, as that is not Nanfoodle's wont.
Instead, he launched into a philosophical discussion of the false comfort
we take in our dependence on, and expectation of, "that which is."

Never has his point been more clear to me than it is now, as I see
"that which is" collapsing around us all. Do the farmers around the
larger cities of Faerun, around Waterdeep and Silverymoon, know
how to manage their produce without the magical aid of the druids?
Without such magical help, will they be able to meet the demands of
the large populations in those cities? And that is only the top level
of the problems that will arise should magic fail! Even the sewers of
Waterdeep are complicated affairs, built over many generations, and
aided at certain critical points, since the city has so expanded, by the
power of wizards, summoning elementals to help usher away the waste.
Without them—what?

And what of Calimport? Regis has told me often that there are
far too many people there, beyond any sensible number for which the
ocean and desert could possibly provide. But the fabulously rich Pashas
have supplemented their natural resources by employing mighty clerics
to summon food and drink for the markets, and mighty wizards to
teleport in fresh sustenance from faraway lands.

Without that aid, what chaos might ensue?

And, of course, in my own homeland of Menzoberranzan, it is magic that keeps the kobolds enslaved, magic that protects the greater Houses from their envious rivals, and magic that holds together the threads of the entire society. Lady Lolth loves chaos, they say, and so she may see it in the extreme if that magic fades!

The societies of the world have grown over the centuries. The systems we have in place have evolved through the many generations, and in that evolution, I fear, we have long forgotten the basic foundations of society's structures. Worse, perhaps, even relearning those lost arts and crafts will not likely suffice to meet the needs of lands grown fatter and more populous because of the magical supplements to the old ways. Calimport could never have supported her enormous population centuries ago.

Nor could the world, a much wider place by far, have attained such a level of singularity, of oneness, of community, as it has now. For people travel and communicate to and with distant lands much more now than in times long past. Many of the powerful merchants in Baldur's Gate are often seen in Waterdeep, and vice versa. Their networks extend over the leagues because their wizards can maintain them. And those networks are vital in ensuring that there will be no war between such mighty rival cities. If the people of Baldur's Gate are dependent upon the craftsmen and farmers of Waterdeep, then they will want no war with that city!

But what happens if it all collapses? What happens if "that which is" suddenly is not? How will we cope when the food runs out, and the diseases cannot be defeated through godly intervention?

Will the people of the world band together to create new realities and structures to fulfill the needs of the masses?

Or will all the world know calamity, on a scale never before seen?

The latter, I fear. The removal of "that which is" will bring war and distance and a world of pockets of civilization huddled defensively in corners against the intrusion of murderous insanity.

I look helplessly at Catti-brie's lifelessness, at Regis's terror, and at Bruenor's torn shoulder and I fear that I am seeing the future.

∾

We live in a dangerous world, and one that seems more dangerous now that the way of magic is in transition, or perhaps even collapse. If Jarlaxle's guess is correct, we have witnessed the collision of worlds, or of planes, to the point where rifts will bring newer and perhaps greater challenges to us all.

It is, I suspect, a time for heroes.

I have come to terms with my own personal need for action.

I am happiest when there are challenges to be met and overcome.

I feel in those times of great crisis that I am part of something larger than myself—a communal responsibility, a generational duty—and to me, that is great comfort.

We will all be needed now, every blade and every brain, every scholar and every warrior, every wizard and every priest. The events in the Silver Marches, the worry I saw on Lady Alustriel's face, are not localized, but, I fear, resonate across the breadth of Toril. I can only imagine the chaos in Menzoberranzan with the decline of the wizards and priests; the entire matriarchal society might well be in jeopardy, and those greatest of Houses might find themselves besieged by legions of angry kobolds.

Our situation on the World Above is likely to be no less dire, and so it is the time for heroes. What does that mean, to be a hero? What is it that elevates some above the hordes of fighters and battle-mages? Certainly circumstance plays a role—extraordinary valor, or action, is more likely in moments of highest crisis.

And yet, in those moments of greatest crisis, the result is, more often than not, disaster. No hero emerges. No savior leads the charge across the battlefield, or slays the dragon, and the town is immersed in flames.

In our world, for good or for ill, the circumstances favorable to creating a hero have become all too common.

It is not, therefore, just circumstance, or just good fortune.

Luck may play a part, and indeed some people—I count myself among them—are more lucky than others, but since I do not believe that there are blessed souls and cursed souls, or that this or that god is leaning over our shoulders and involving himself in our daily affairs, then I do know that there is one other necessary quality for those who find a way to step above the average.

If you set up a target thirty strides away and assemble the hundred best archers in any given area to shoot at it, they'd all hit the mark. Add in a bet of gold and a few would fall away, to the hoots of derision from their fellows.

But now replace the target with an assassin, and have that assassin holding at dagger-point the person each successive archer most loves in the world. The archer now has one shot. Just one. If he hits the mark—the assassin—his loved one will be saved. If he misses the assassin, it is certain doom for his beloved.

A hero will hit that mark. Few mere archers would.

That is the extra quality involved, the ability to hold poise and calm and rational thought no matter how devastating the consequences of failure, the ability to go to that place of pure concentration in times most emotionally and physically tumultuous.

Not just once and not by luck. The hero makes that shot.

The hero lives for that shot. The hero trains for that shot, every day, for endless hours, with purest concentration.

Many fine warriors live in the world, wielding blade or lightning bolt, who serve well in their respective armies, who weather the elements and the enemies with quiet and laudable stoicism.

Many are strong in their craft, and serve with distinction.

But when all teeters precariously on the precipice of disaster, when victory or defeat rests upon matters beyond simple strength and courage and valor, when all balances on that sword-edged line between victory or defeat, the hero finds a way—a way that seems impossible to those who do not truly understand the give and take of battle, the ebb and flow of sword play, the logical follow-up to counter an enemy's advantage.

For a warrior is one trained in the techniques of various weaponry, one who knows how to lift a shield or parry a thrust and properly counter, but a true warrior, a hero, extends beyond those skills. Every movement is instinctual, is engrained into every muscle to flow with perfect and easy coordination. Every block is based on clear thinking—so clear that it is as much anticipatory as reflexive. And every weakness in an opponent becomes apparent at first glance.

The true warrior fights from a place of calm, of controlled rage and quelled fear. Every situation comes to sharpened focus, every avenue of solution shines its path clearly. And the hero goes one step beyond that, finding a way, any way, to pave a path of victory when there is no apparent route.

The hero finds a way, and when that way is shown, however difficult the path, the hero makes the thrust or the block or the last frantic riposte, stealing his opponent's victory. As when Regis used his ruby pendant to paralyze a battle-mage in Luskan. As when Wulfgar threw himself at the yochlol to save Catti-brie. As when Catti-brie made that desperate shot in the sewers of Calimport to drive off Entreri, who had gained the advantage over me. As when Bruenor used his cunning, his strength, and his unshakable will to defeat Shimmergloom in the darkness of Mithral Hall.

Certain doom is a term not known in the vocabulary of the hero, for it is precisely at those times when doom seems most certain—when Bruenor rode the flaming shadow dragon down to the depths of Garumn's Gorge—that the warrior who would be hero elevates himself above the others. It is, instinctually, not about him or his life.

The hero makes the shot.

We are all to be tested now, I fear. In this time of confusion and danger, many will be pulled to the precipice of disaster, and most will fall over that dark ledge. But a few will step beyond that line, will find a way, and will make that shot.

In those moments, however, it is important to recognize that reputation means nothing, and while past deeds might inspire confidence, they are no guarantee of present or future victory. I hope that Taulmaril is steady in my hands when I stand upon that precipice, for I know that I walk into the shadows of doom, where black pits await, and I need only to think of broken Regis or look at my beloved Catti-brie to understand the stakes of this contest.

I hope that I am given that shot at this assassin, whomever or whatever it may be, who holds us all at dagger-point, for if so, I intend to hit the mark.

For that is the last point to make about the hero. In the aforementioned archery contest, the hero wants to be the one chosen to take that most critical shot. When the stakes are highest, the hero wants the outcome to be in his hands. It's not about hubris, but about necessity, and the confidence that the would-be hero has trained and prepared for exactly that one shot.

The recognition of utter helplessness is more than humbling; it is devastating. On those occasions when it is made clear to someone, internally, that willpower or muscle or technique will not be enough to overcome the obstacles placed before him, that he is helpless before those obstacles, there follows a brutal mental anguish.

When Wulfgar was taken by Errtu in the Abyss, he was beaten and physically tortured, but on those few occasions I was able to coax my friend to speak of that time, those notes he sang most loudly in despair were those of his helplessness. The demon, for example, would make him believe that he was free and was living with the woman he loved, then would slaughter her and their illusionary children before Wulfgar's impotent gaze.

That torture created Wulfgar's most profound and lasting scars.

When I was a child in Menzoberranzan, I was taught a lesson universal to male drow. My sister Briza took me out to the edge of our cavern homeland where a gigantic earth elemental waited. The beast was harnessed and Briza handed me the end of the rein.

"Hold it back," she instructed.

I didn't quite understand, and when the elemental took a step away, the rope was pulled from my hand. Briza struck me with her whip, of course, and no doubt, she enjoyed it.

"Hold it back," she said again.

I took the rope and braced myself. The elemental took a step and I went flying after it. It didn't even know that I existed, or that I was tugging with all my insignificant strength to try to hinder its movement.

Briza scowled as she informed me that I would try again.

This test must be a matter of cleverness, I decided, and instead of just bracing myself, I looped the rope around a nearby stalagmite, to Briza's approving nods, and dug in my heels.

The elemental, on command, took a step and whipped me around the stone as if I were no more than a bit of parchment in a furious gale. The monster didn't slow, didn't even notice.

In that moment, I was shown my limitations, without equivocation. I was shown my impotence.

Briza then held the elemental in place with an enchantment and dismissed it with a second one. The point she was trying to make was that the divine magic of Lolth overwhelmed both muscle and technique. This was no more than another subjugation tactic by the ruling matron mothers, to make the males of Menzoberranzan understand their lowly place, their inferiority, particularly to those more in Lolth's favor.

For me, and I suspect for many of my kin, the lesson was more personal and less societal, for that was my first real experience encountering a force supremely beyond my willpower, utterly beyond my control. It wasn't as if had I tried harder or been more clever I might have changed the outcome. The elemental would have stepped away unhindered and unbothered no matter my determination.

To say I was humbled would be an understatement. There, in that dark cavern, I learned the first truth of both mortality and mortal flesh.

And now I feel that terrible measure of impotence again.

When I look at Catti-brie, I know that she is beyond my ability to help. We all dream about being the hero, about finding the solution, about winning the moment and saving the day. And we all harbor, to some degree, the notion that our will can overcome, that determination and strength of mind can push us to great ends—and indeed they can.

To a point.

Death is the ultimate barrier, and when faced with impending death, personally or for someone you love, a mortal being will encounter, most of all, ultimate humility.

We all believe that we can defeat that plague or that disease, should it befall us, through sheer willpower. It is a common mental defense against the inevitability we all know we share. I wonder, then, if the worst reality of a lingering death is the sense that your own body is beyond your ability to control.

In my case, the pain I feel in looking at Catti-brie is manifold, and not least among the variations is my own sense of helplessness. I deny the looks that Cadderly and Jarlaxle exchanged, expressions that revealed their hearts and minds. They cannot be right in their obvious belief that Catti-brie is beyond our help and surely doomed!

I demand that they are not right.

And yet I know that they are. Perhaps I only "know" because I fear beyond anything I have ever known that they are correct, and if they are, then I will know no closure. I cannot say good-bye to Catti-brie because I fear that I already have.

And thus, in moments of weakness, I lose faith and know that they are right. My love, my dearest friend, is lost to me forever—and there again lurches my stubbornness, for my first instinct was to write "likely forever." I cannot admit the truth even as I admit the truth!

So many times have I seen my friends return from the brink of death: Bruenor on the back of a dragon. Wulfgar from the Abyss. Catti-brie from the dark plane of Tarterus. So many times have the odds been beaten. In the end, we always prevail!

But that is not true. And perhaps the cruelest joke of all is the confidence, the surety, that our good fortune and grand exploits have instilled in my friends, the Companions of the Hall.

How much worse becomes the cruel reality when at last we are touched by inescapable tragedy.

I look at Catti-brie and I am reminded of my limitations. My fantasies of saving the moment and the day are dashed against jagged and immovable rocks. I want to save her and I cannot. I look at Catti-brie, wandering lost, and in those moments when I can accept that this state is forever, my hopes become less about victory and more about . . .

I can hardly think it. Have I truly been reduced to hoping that this woman I love will pass on quickly and peacefully?

And still the fight goes on around us. I am sure, in this world gone mad. And still will my scimitars be put to use in a struggle that has, I fear, only just begun. And still will I be needed to mediate between Bruenor and Jarlaxle, Cadderly and Jarlaxle. I cannot skulk away and be alone with my mounting grief and pain. I cannot abrogate my responsibilities to those around me.

But it all, so suddenly, seems less important to me. Without Catti-brie, what is the point of our fight? Why defeat the dracolich when the outcome will not change, since we are all doomed in the end? Is it not true that that which we deem important is, in the grand scheme of the millennia and the multiverse, utterly and completely irrelevant?

This is the demon of despair wrought of impotence. More profound than the helplessness created by Shimmergloom the shadow dragon's dark cloud of breath. More profound than the lesson of the drow matron mothers. For that question. "What is the point?" is the most insidious and destructive of all.

I must deny it. I cannot give in to it. for the sake of those around me and for the sake of myself, and yes, for the sake of Catti-brie, who would not allow me to surrender to such a concept.

Truly this inner turmoil tests me more than any demon, any dragon, any horde of ravaging orcs ever could.

For as this dark moment shows me the futility, so too it demands of me the faith—the faith that there is something beyond this mortal coil, that there is a place of greater understanding and universal community than this temporary existence.

Else it is all a sad joke.

Neverwinter

Gauntlgrym

It is time to let the waters of the past flow away to distant shores. Though never to be forgotten, those friends long gone must not haunt my thoughts all the day and night. They will be there, I take comfort in knowing, ready to smile whenever my mind's eye seeks that comforting sight, ready to shout a chant to a war god when battle draws near, ready to remind me of my folly when I cannot see that which is right before me, and ready, ever ready, to make me smile, to warm my heart.

But they will ever be there, too, I fear, to remind me of the pain, of the injustice, of the callous gods who took from me my love in just that time when I had at last found peace. I'll not forgive them.

"Live your life in segments," a wise elf once told me, for to be a long-lived creature who might see the dawn and dusk of centuries would be a curse indeed if the immediacy and intensity of anticipated age and inevitable death is allowed to be forgotten.

And so now, after twenty-five years, I lift my glass in toast to those who have gone before: to Deudermont, to Cadderly, to Regis, perhaps to Wulfgar (for I know not of his fate), and most of all, to Catti-brie, my love, my life—nay, the love of that one segment of my life.

By circumstance, by fate, by the gods . . .

I'll never forgive them.

So certain and confident these words of declared freedom read, yet my hand shakes as I pen them. It has been a quarter of a century since the catastrophe of the Ghost King, the fall of Spirit Soaring, and the deat . . . the loss of Catti-brie, but that awful morning seems as if it was only this very morning, and while so many memories of my life with Catti seem so far away now, almost as if I am looking back at the life of another drow, one whose boots I inherited, that morning when the spirits of my love and Regis rode from Mithral Hall on a ghostly unicorn, rode through the stone walls and were lost to me, that morning of the deepest pain I have ever known, remains to me an open, bleeding, and burning wound.

But no more, I declare.

That memory I now place on the flowing waters, and look not behind me as it recedes.

I go forward, on the open road with friends old and new. Too long have my blades been still, too clean are my boots and cape. Too restless is Guenhwyvar. Too restless is the heart of Drizzt Do'Urden.

We are off to Gauntlgrym, Bruenor insists, though I think that unlikely. But it matters not, for in truth, he is off to close his life and I am away to seek new shores. Clean shores, free of the bonds of the past, a new segment of my life.

It is what it is to be an elf.

It is what it is to be alive, for though this exercise is most poignant and necessary in those races living long, even the short-lived humans divide their lives into segments, although they rarely recognize the transient truth as they move through one or another stage of their existence. Every person I have known tricks himself into thinking that this current way of things will continue on, year after year. It is so easy to speak of expectations, of what will be in a decade, perhaps, and to be convinced that the important aspects of one's life will remain as they are, or will improve as desired.

"This will be my life in a year!"

"This will be my life in five years!"

"This will be my life in ten years!"

We all tell ourselves these hopes and dreams and expectations, and with conviction, for the goal is needed to facilitate the journey. But in the end of that span, be it one or five or ten or fifty years hence, it is the journey and not the goal, achieved or lost, that defines who we are. The journey is the story of our life, not the achievement or failure at its end, and so the more important declaration by far, I have come to know, is, "This is my life now."

I am Drizzt Do'Urden, once of Mithral Hall, once the battered son of a drow matron, once the protégé of a wondrous weapons-master, once loved in marriage, once friend to a king and to other companions no less wonderful and important. Those are the rivers of my memory, flowing now to distant shores, for now I reclaim my course and my heart.

But not my purpose, I am surprised to learn, for the world has moved beyond that which I once knew to be true, for the Realms have found a new sense of darkness and dread that mocks he who would deign to set things aright.

Once I would have brought with me light to pierce that darkness. Now I bring my blades, too long unused, and I welcome that darkness.

No more, I declare! I am rid of the open wound of profound loss, so say I!

I lie.

The fights are increasing and it pleases me.

The world around me has grown darker, more dangerous . . . and it pleases me.

I have just passed a period of my life most adventurous and yet, strangely, most peaceful, where Bruenor and I have climbed through a hundred hundred tunnels and traveled as deep into the Underdark as I have been since my last return to Menzoberranzan. We found our battles of course, mostly with the oversized vermin that inhabit such places, a few skirmishes with goblins and orcs, a trio of trolls here, a clan of ogres there. Never was there any sustained battle, though, never anything to truly test my blades, and indeed, the most perilous day I have known since our departure from Mithral Hall those many years ago was when an earthquake threatened to bury us in some tunnels.

No more is that the case, I find, and it pleases me. Since the day of cataclysm, a decade ago, when the volcano roared forth and painted a line of devastation from the mountain all the way to the sea, burying Neverwinter in its devastating run, the tone of the region has changed. It is almost as if that one event had sent forth a call for conflict, a clarion call for sinister beings.

In a sense, it did just that. The loss of Neverwinter in essence severed the northland from the more civilized regions to the south, where Waterdeep has now become the vanguard against the wild regions. Traders do not regularly travel through the region, except by sea, and the lure of Neverwinter's former treasures has pulled adventurers, often unsavory, often unprincipled, to the devastated city in great numbers.

Some are trying to rebuild now, desperate to restore the important port and the order it once imposed upon these inhospitable lands. They battle as much as they build. They carry a carpenter's hammer in one hand, a warhammer in the other.

For enemies abound: Shadovar; strange zealots to a devil god; opportunistic highwaymen; goblinkin and giantkind and monsters alive and undead. And other things, darker things from deeper holes.

In the years since the cataclysm, the region has grown darker by far. And it pleases me.

When I am in battle, I am free. When my blades cut low a scion of evil, only then do I feel as if there is purpose and accomplishment. Many times have I wondered if this rage within is just a reflection of a heritage I have never truly shaken. The focus of battle, the intensity of the fight, the satisfaction of victory ... are they all merely an admission by Drizzt Do'Urden that he is, after all, drow?

And if that is the truth, then what did I actually know about my homeland and my people, and what did I merely paste onto a caricature I had created of a society whose roots lay in passions and lust I had not yet begun to understand or experience?

Was there, I wonder and I fear, some deeper wisdom to the matron mothers of Menzoberranzan, some understanding of drow joy and need that perpetuated the state of conflict and battle in the drow city?

It seems a ridiculous thought, and yet, only through battle have I endured the pain. Only through battle have I found again a sense of accomplishment, of forward movement, of bettering community.

This truth surprises me, angers me, and paradoxically, even as it offers me hope to continue, it hints at some notion that perhaps I should not, that this existence is only a futile thing, after all, a mirage, a self-delusion.

Like Bruenor's quest. I doubt he'll find Gauntlgrym. I doubt it exists and I doubt that he believes he'll find it, or that he ever believed he would find it!

And yet he pores over his collection of maps and clues daily, and leaves no hole unexplored. It is his purpose; the search gives meaning to the life of Bruenor Battlehammer. Indeed, it seems the nature of the dwarf, and of the dwarves, who are always talking of things gone by and reclaiming the glory that once was.

What is the nature of the drow, then?

Even before I lost her, my love Catti-brie, and my dear halfling friend, I knew that I was no creature of calm and respite; I knew that my nature was that of the warrior. I knew that I was happiest when adventure, and battle, summoned me forth, demanding of those skills I had spent my entire life perfecting.

I relish it more now—is that because of my pain and loss, or is it merely a truer reflection of my heritage?

And if that is the case, will the cause of battle widen, will the code that guides my scimitars weaken to accommodate more moments of joy? At what point, I wonder and I fear, does my desire for battle, that which is in my heart, interfere with that which is in my conscience? Is it easier to justify drawing my blades?

That is my true fear, that this rage within me will come forth in all its madness, explosively, randomly, murderously.

My fear?

Or my hope?

Neverwinter

And now I am alone, more so than I have been since the days following the death of Montolio those many years ago. Even on that later occasion when I traveled back into the Underdark to Menzoberranzan, forsaking my friends in the foolish belief that I was unfairly endangering them, it was not like this. For though I physically walked alone into the Underdark, I did not go without the emotional support that they were there beside me, in spirit. I went with full confidence that Bruenor and Catti-brie and Regis remained alive and well—indeed, more well, I believed, because I had left them.

But now I am alone. They are gone, one and all. My friends, my family.

There remains Guenhwyvar, of course, and she is no small thing to me—a true and loyal companion, someone to listen to my laments and my joys and my pondering. But it is not the same. Guen can hear me, but is there anything I would hear from her? She can share my victories, my joys, my trials, but there is no reciprocation. After knowing the love of friends and family, I cannot so fool myself again, as I did in those first days after I left Menzoberranzan, as to believe that the wonderful Guenhwyvar is enough.

My road takes me from Gauntlgrym as it once took me from Mithral Hall, and I doubt I shall return—certainly I will not return to stand and stare at the cairn of Bruenor Battlehammer, as I rarely visited the graves of Catti-brie and Regis during my years in Mithral Hall. A wise elf lady once explained to me the futility of such things, as she taught me that I must learn to live my life as a series of shorter spans. It is the blessing of the elven peoples to live through the dawn and sunset of centuries, but that blessing can serve too as a curse. Few elves partner for life, as is common among the humans, for example, because the joy of such a partnership can weigh as an anchor after a hundred years or two hundred.

"Treat each parting as a rebirth," Innovindil said to me. "Let go of that which is past and seek new roads. Perhaps never to forget your lost friends and family and lovers, but place them in your memory warmly and build again those things that so pleased you."

I have gone back to Innovindil's lessons many times over the last few decades, since Wulfgar left Mithral Hall and since Catti-brie and Regis were lost to me. I have recited them as a litany against the rage, the pain, the sadness . . . a reminder that there are roads yet to walk.

I was deluding myself, I now know.

For I hadn't let go of my dear friends. I hadn't lost hope that someday, one day, some way, I would raze a giant's lair beside Wulfgar once more, or would fish beside Regis on a lazy summer's day on the banks of Maer Dualdon, or I would would spend the night in Catti-brie's warm embrace. I tasked Jarlaxle with finding them, not out of any real hope that he would, but because I couldn't bear to relinquish the last flicker of hope for these moments, these soft joys I once knew.

And now Bruenor is gone and the Companions of the Hall are no more.

I watched him take his last breath. There is closure. There is finality. And only through Bruenor had I kept the dream of Catti-brie and Regis, and even Wulfgar, alive. Only through his determination and steadfastness did I allow myself to believe that somehow, some magical way, they might still be out there. The journey to Icewind Dale should have disavowed me of that notion, and did so to some extent (and also pushed Bruenor, at long last, into a state of resignation), and whatever little flickers remained within my heart were snuffed out when I watched my dearest friend breathe his last.

So I am alone. The life I had known is ended.

I surely feel the sadness, the regret at things that could not be, the loneliness. At every turn, I want to call out to Bruenor to tell him my news, only to remember that, alas, he is not there. All of it is there; all of the pain that one would expect.

But there is something else, something unexpected, something surprising, something bringing with it more than a bit of confusion and even guilt.

As I turned my back on Gauntlgrym and the grave of King Bruenor Battlehammer, pushing up in my emotions beside the pain and the rage and the helplessness was . . . a deep sense of relief.

I am ashamed to admit this, but to deny it would be to lie, and worse, to lie to myself. For at long last, I have a sense of finality. It is time for the past to rest and for me to move forward. It is time, as Innovindil explained to me in a forest far from here, for me to begin anew.

Certainly I'm not relieved that Bruenor has passed. Nor Thibbledorf Pwent, for that matter. A better friend than Bruenor I have never known and I would wish him back to my side in an instant, were that possible.

But in the larger sense, the greater perspective of my life, I have been ready to let go of Catti-brie and Regis and Wulfgar for a long time now—not to forget them. I'll never forget them, never want to forget them! They are embedded in my heart and soul and walk with Drizzt Do'Urden every step of his way. But I accepted their loss—my loss—years, even decades, ago, and it was only the stubbornness of an old dwarf, refusing to let go, insisting that they were still to be found and that our wondrous years together would be restored, that forced me, too, to hang on.

I am alone now. I am free.

What an awful thought! How disloyal am I, then, to feel any eagerness in looking forward, to a new road, a third life, taking the painful lessons of my first existence in Menzoberranzan along with the wondrous joys of my second life beside the Companions of the Hall. Now I am hardened by the whips of the drow matrons and softened by the honest love of friends, and settled in what I know is, what should be, and what should never be. As my second life so exceeded my first in joy and purpose, could my third not climb higher still?

I don't know, and truly I understand how fortunate I was in finding these four amazing companions to share a road. Will I find such friends, ready to sacrifice all for me, again? Will I love again? Even if I do, will it be the same intensity of that which I knew with Catti-brie?

I know not, but I'm not afraid to find out. That is my freedom now, to walk my road with eyes wide and heart open, without regret and with a true understanding of how blessed my existence has been.

And there is one other freedom now: for the first time in decades, I awaken to discover that I am not angry. Strangely so. I feel as if the rage that has for so long kept my muscles tightened has at last relaxed.

This, too, stings me with pangs of guilt, and I am sure that those around me will often hear me muttering to myself in confusion. Perhaps I am simply deluding myself. Perhaps the loss of Bruenor has pushed me past the bounds of sensibility, where the level of pain has become intolerable and so I trick myself into something wholly converse.

Perhaps.

Perhaps not.

I can only shrug and wonder.

I can only feel and accept.

I am alone now.

I am free.

Long has it occurred to me that I am a creature of action, of battle, and of adventure. In times of peace and calm, like my friend Bruenor, I find myself longing for the open road, where bandits rule and wild orcs roam. For so many years, I stubbornly clung to the battle and the adventure. I admit my thrill when King Bruenor decided to quietly abdicate and go on his search for the legendary Gauntlgrym.

In that quest, we found the open road, the wilderness, the adventure, and indeed, the battles.

But something was missing. I couldn't quite place it, but for a long while now, indeed back to the early days of King Bruenor's reign of reclaimed Mithral Hall, there remained a sharp edge missing, that edge that scraped my skin and kept me wholly alive.

Anyone who has ever stood on the edge of a cliff understands this. One can bask in the views, and feel the thrill of being a part of something bigger and grander.

But for all the beauty and awe-inspiring grandeur, it is the feel of the wind that completes the sensation, particularly if it is a swirling and gusting breeze. For then comes the greatest affirmation of life: the sensation of fear, the recognition of how fleeting it all can be.

When I stand on the edge of that cliff, on the precipice of disaster, and I lean against that wind, I am truly alive. I have to be quick to realign my balance and my footing as the wind swirls. If I wish to stay on my perch, indeed to stay alive, I have to remain quicker than the whims of the wind.

In the past I'd stubbornly kept tight the battles and the adventures, and ever turned my eye to the open and dangerous road, but it was

not until very recently that I came to understand that which was truly missing: the thrill of the risk.

The thrill of the risk. The edge of that high precipice. Not the risk itself, for that was ever there, but the thrill of that risk . . .

In truth, it was not until my midnight ride back from Luskan that I realized how long I'd missed that thrill.

When first I left Dahlia, I was afraid for her, but that dissipated almost immediately, replaced by a sense of invincibility that I have not known in decades, in a century perhaps. I knew that I would get over Luskan's guarded wall, that I would find Beniago and that I would bend him to my need. I knew that I would win out. I knew that I would be quicker than the wind.

Why?

The risk was ever there, but for so many years, the thrill of that risk was not, because of the untenable price of defeat. For the cost of having friends so dear and a wife so beloved is . . . vulnerability.

I can accept the wind blowing Drizzt Do'Urden from the cliff. Such a price is not too high. But to watch Catti-brie fall before me?

Then I am not invincible. Then there is simply the risk, and not the thrill of living on the edge of that dangerous cliff.

No more.

For when I rode to Luskan, I was invincible. The walls could not stop me. Beniago could not stop me.

And now I understand that when I lost my friends, my family, my home, I lost, too, my vulnerability, and gained back in return the thrill of danger, the freedom not only to walk on the edge of that high cliff, but to dance there, to taunt the wind.

What a strange irony.

But what, then, of Dahlia?

She fascinates me. She teases me with her every movement and every word. She lures me—to where I do not know!

On my ride, in my unbridled joy, in the thrill of adventure and battle and yes, risk. I knew that she would survive. I knew it! Even when all reason warned me that the poison would take her long before I could return, somewhere deep inside of me, I just knew that she would not be lost to me. Not then, not like that. Her fate could not be written such; her death would not be so crude or mundane.

But what if I was proven wrong? What if she had been taken from me, like those before? Surely Dahlia dances more wildly on the edge of that cliff than I do. She is fearless to the point of utter recklessness—in the short time I have known her, I have seen that all too clearly.

And yet, that risk does not frighten me.

Surely I don't want her to die. The fascination, the attraction, is all too real and all too powerful. I want to know her, to understand her. I want to yell at her and kiss her all at once. I want to test her in battle and in passion!

She is as erratic as she is erotic, changing her tone as easily as she alters her appearance. I think it a game she plays, a way to keep friends and enemies alike off-balance. But I cannot be sure, and that, too, is part of her never-ending seduction. Is she teasing me with seemingly erratic behavior, or is Dahlia truly erratic? Is she the actor or the role?

Or perhaps there is a third answer: am I so desperate to know this unpredictable doppelganger that I am reading too much into her every word? Am I seeking, and thus seeing, deeper meaning than she intends as I scour for clues to what lies in her heart?

A carefully guarded heart. But why?

Another mystery to unravel . . .

I knew she would not be lost to me, but how? How did my instincts counter my reason so fully? Given all that has passed in my life, shouldn't I have expected the worst outcome regarding Dahlia? Given the losses I have endured, shouldn't I have feared exactly that in a desperate situation?

And yet I did not. I reveled in the midnight ride, in the adventure and the thrill of the risk.

Is it Dahlia's competency, her swagger, her own fearlessness, affecting my heart? Or is it, perhaps, that I do not love her—not as I loved Catti-brie, or Bruenor, Wulfgar, and Regis?

Or is it something more, I wonder? Perhaps Innovindil's lesson reached me more deeply than I had known. Logically, rationally, I can see Innovindil's viewpoint, that we elves have to live our lives in shorter segments because of the short-lived races with whom we naturally interact. But could it be that Innovindil's lessons have sparked within me a confidence that I will go on, that there is more road before me? Although those I deeply loved are removed from my side, I will find others to share the leagues and the fights?

It is all of that, I expect, and perhaps something more. Perhaps each loss has hardened my heart and numbed me to the pain. The loss of Bruenor stung less than those of Catti-brie and Regis, and less than my knowledge that Wulfgar, too, has surely passed on. There are other reasons, I am confident. Bruenor's last words to me, "I found it, elf," reflected a full life's journey, to be sure. What dwarf could ask for more than that which King Bruenor Battlehammer knew? His final battle alone, his victory over the pit fiend while immersed in the power of dwarven kings of old, would surely fill to bursting the heart of any dwarf.

So I did not cry for Bruenor, though I surely miss him no less than any of the others.

There is no one answer, then. Life is a complicated journey, and few are the direct lines from feeling to consequence and consequence to anticipation. I will try to unravel it all, of course, as that is my nature. But in the end, I am left with only one inescapable truth: the joy of that midnight ride, of bargaining with Beniago at the end of a scimitar, of reckless adventure.

The edge of the cliff.

This is the promise made to Drizzt Do'Urden by my lady Dahlia the erotic, the erratic.

And this is the legacy given to Drizzt Do'Urden by my old Companions of the Hall.

Do you see me now, Catti-brie?

Do you see me now, Bruenor?

Do you see me now, Regis?

Do you see me now, Wulfgar?

Because I see you. You walk with me. You are in my thoughts every day, all four, and I see you smile when I smile and frown when I hurt. I believe this. I sense this.

I pray for this.

Charon's Claw

I am past the sunset of my second century of life and yet I feel as if
the ground below me is as the shifting sands. In so many ways, I find
that I am no more sure of myself than I was those many decades ago
when I first walked free of Menzoberranzan—less sure, in truth, for
in that time, my emotions were grounded in a clear sense of right and
wrong, in a definitive understanding of truth against deception.

Perhaps my surety then was based almost solely on a negative: when
I came to recognize the truth of the city of Menzoberranzan about me,
I knew what I could not accept, knew what did not ring true in my
heart and soul, and demanded the notion of a better life, a better way.
It was not so much that I knew what I wanted, for any such concepts
of the possibilities beyond Menzoberranzan were surely far beyond my
experience.

But I knew what I did not want and what I could not accept.

Guided by that inner moral compass, I made my way, and my beliefs
seemed only reinforced by those friends I came to know, not kin, but
surely kind.

And so I have lived my life, a goodly life, I think, with the power
of righteousness guiding my blades. There have been times of doubt,

of course, and so many errors along the way. Again, there stood my friends, to guide me back to the correct path, to walk beside me and support me and reinforce my belief that there is a community greater than myself, a purpose higher and more noble than the simple hedonism so common in the land of my birth.

Now I am older.

Now, again, I do not know.

For I find myself enmeshed in conflicts I do not understand, where both sides seem equally . . . wrong.

This is not Mithral Hall defending her gates against marauding orcs. This is not the garrison of Ten Towns holding back a barbarian horde, or battling the monstrous minions of Akar Kessell. In all the Realms now, there is conflict and shadow and confusion, and a sense that there is no clear path to victory. The world has grown dark, and in a dark place, so dark rulers can arise.

I long for the simplicity of Icewind Dale.

For down here in the more populous lands, there is Luskan, full of treachery and deceit and unbridled greed. There are a hundred "Luskans" across the Realms, I fear, for in the tumult of the Spellplague and the deeper and more enduring darkness of the Shadowfell, the return of the shades and the Empire of Netheril, those structures of community and society could not hold unscathed. Some see chaos as an enemy to be defeated and tamed; others, I know from my earliest days, see chaos as opportunity for personal gain.

For down here, there are the hundreds of communities and clusters of farms depending on the protection of the city garrisons, who will not come. Indeed, under the rule of despot kings or lords or high captains alike, those communities so oft become the prey of the powerful cities.

For down here, there is Many Arrows, the orc kingdom forced upon the Silver Marches by the hordes of King Obould in that long-ago war—though even now, a century hence, it remains a trial, a test, whose outcome cannot be predicted. Did King Bruenor, with his courage in signing the Treaty of Garumn's Gorge, end the war, or merely delay a larger one?

It is always confusion, I fear, always those shifting sands.

Until I draw my blades, and that is the dark truth of who I have become. For when my scimitars are in hand, the battle becomes immediacy, the goal survival and the greater politic that once guided my hand is a fleeting vision, a thin and drifting campfire's smoke out on the horizon. I live in a land of many Akar Kessells, but so few, it seems, places worth defending!

Perhaps among the settlers of Neverwinter City there exists such a noble defense as that I helped wage in Ten Towns, but there live, too, in the triad of interests, the Thayans and their undead hordes and the Netherese, many persons no less ruthless and no less self-interested. Indeed, no less wrong.

How might I engage my heart in such a conflict as the morass that is Neverwinter? How might I strike with conviction, secure in the knowledge that I fight for the good of the land?

I cannot. Not now. Not with competing interests equally dark.

But no more am I surrounded by friends of similar weal, it seems. Were it my choice alone, I would flee this land, perhaps to the Silver Marches and (hopefully) some sense of goodliness and hope. To Mithral Hall and Silverymoon, who cling still to the heartsong of King Bruenor Battlehammer and Lady Alustriel, or perhaps to Waterdeep, shining still, where the lords hold court for the benefit of their city and citizens.

But Dahlia will not be so persuaded to leave. There is something here, some old grudge that is far beyond my comprehension. I followed her to Sylora Salm willingly, settling my own score as she settled hers. And now I follow her again, or I abandon her, for she will not turn aside. When Artemis Entreri mentioned that name, Herzgo Alegni, such an anger came over Dahlia, and such a sadness, I think, that she will hear of no other goal.

Nor will she hear of any delay, for winter is soon to be thick about us. No storm will slow her, I fear; no snow will gather deep enough that stubborn Dahlia will not drive through it, to Neverwinter City, to wherever she must go to find this Netherese lord, this Herzgo Alegni.

I had thought her hatred of Sylora Salm profound, but nay. I know now, it cannot measure against the depths of Dahlia's loathing of this tiefling Netherese warlord. She will kill him, so she says, and when I threatened to leave her to her own course, she did not blink and did not hesitate, and did not care enough to offer me a fond farewell.

So again I am drawn into a conflict I do not understand. Is there a righteous course to be found here? Is there a measure of right and wrong between Dahlia and the Shadovar? By the words of Entreri, it would seem that this tiefling is a foul beast deserving of a violent end, and surely the reputation of Netheril supports that notion.

But am I now so lost in my choice of path that I take the word of Artemis Entreri as guidance? Am I now so removed from any sense of correctness, from any communities so designed, that it falls to this?

The sands shift beneath my feet. I draw my blades, and in the desperation of battle, I will wield them as I always have. My enemies will not know the tumult in my heart, the confusion that I have no clear moral path before me. They will know only the bite of Icingdeath, the flash of Twinkle.

But I will know the truth of it.

Does this reluctance to pursue Alegni reflect in me a distrust of Dahlia, I wonder? She is certain in her course—more certain than I have ever seen her, or seen anybody, for that matter. Even Bruenor, in his long-ago quest to regain Mithral Hall, did not stride so determinedly. She will kill this tiefling or she will die trying. A sorry friend, a sorrier lover, am I indeed if I do not accompany her.

But I do not understand. I do not see the path clearly. I do not know what greater good I serve. I do not fight in the hopes of betterment of my corner of the world.

I just fight.

On the side of Dahlia, who intrigues me.

On the side of Artemis Entreri, so it would seem.

Perhaps in another century, I will return to Menzoberranzan, not as an enemy, not as a conqueror, not to tear down the structures of that society I once held as most vile.

Perhaps I will return because I will belong.

This is my fear, of a life wasted, of a cause misbegotten, of a belief that is, in the end, an empty and unattainable ideal, the foolish designs of an innocent child who believed there could be more.

Bruenor has not been gone from my side for long, but oh, how dearly do I miss him!

ᘒ

My thoughts slip past me: slithering snakes they seem, rushing all about, winding over each other and unwinding, coiling and darting. Always just ahead, a turning thread, just out of reach.

Diving down dark holes where I cannot follow.

One of the most common truths of life is that we all take for granted things that simply are. Whether it's a spouse, a friend, family, or home, after enough time has passed, that person, place, or situation becomes the accepted norm of our lives, and so, the expected norm of our lives.

It is not until we confront the unexpected, not until the normal is no more, that we truly come to appreciate what once we had.

I have said this, I have known this, I have felt this so many times . . .

But I find myself off-balance again, and the snakes slide past, teasing me, and I cannot catch them, cannot sort through their intertwined bodies.

So it is with the ill person who suddenly must face mortality, when the paralyzing shackles of the concept of forever are sundered, and every drip of sand in the hourglass crystallizes into a moment of importance. I have met several people in my travels who, when told by a cleric that they had not long to live, insisted to me that their disease was the greatest event of their existence, insisted that colors became more vivid, sounds more acute and meaningful and pleasurable, and friendships more endearing.

The shattering of the normal routine brings life to this person, so paradoxically, considering that the catalyst is, after all, the anticipated imminence of death.

But though we know, though we are seasoned, we cannot prepare. The snakes move too quickly!

I felt this tearing of the fabric of the static canvas that had become my life when Catti-brie became afflicted by the Spellplague, and then, even more profoundly, when she and Regis were taken from me. All my sensibilities screamed at me; it wasn't supposed to be like that. So many things had been sorted through hard work and trial, and we four remaining Companions of the Hall were ready for our due and just reward: adventures and leisure of our choosing.

I don't know that I took those two dear friends for granted, though losing them so unexpectedly and abruptly surely tore apart the romantic tapestry I had painted about me.

A tapestry full of holes, and with snakes, flowing rivers of discordant thought, sliding all about. I remember my confusion, my rage, helpless rage . . . I grabbed Jarlaxle because I needed something to hold, some solid object and solid hope to stop the stones from shifting under my feet.

So too with the departure of Wulfgar, whose choice to leave us was not really unexpected.

So too with Bruenor. We walked a road together that we knew would end as it ended. The only question was whether he or I would die first at the end of an enemy's spear.

I feel that I long ago properly insulated myself against this trap of simply accepting what was with the false belief that what was would always be.

In almost every case.

Almost, I see now.

I speak of the Companions of the Hall as if we were five, then four when Wulfgar departed. Even now as I recognize my error, I found at my fingertips the same description when I penned, "we four."

We were not five in the early days, but six.

We were not four when Wulfgar departed, but five.

We were not two when Catti-brie and Regis were taken from us, but three.

And the one whom I seldom consider, the one whom I fear I have too often taken for granted, is the one most joined to the heart of Drizzt Do'Urden.

And now the snakes return, tenfold, just out of grasp, and I stagger because the ground beneath my feet is not firm, because the stones buckle and roll, because the balance I have known has been torn from me.

I cannot summon Guenhwyvar.

I do not understand—I have not lost hope!—but for the first time, with the onyx figurine in hand, the panther, my dear friend, will not come to my call, nor do I sense her presence, roaring back at me across the planescape. She went through to the Shadowfell with Herzgo Alegni, or went somewhere, disappearing into the black mist on the winged bridge of Neverwinter.

I sensed the distance soon after, a vast expanse between us, too far to reach with the magic of the idol.

I do not understand.

Was not Guenhwyvar eternal? Was she not the essence of the panther? Such essence cannot be destroyed, surely!

But I cannot summon her, cannot hear her, cannot feel her about me and in my thoughts.

What road is this, then, that I find myself upon? I have followed a trail of vengeance beside Dahlia—nay, behind Dahlia, for little can I doubt that it is she who guides my strides. So do I cross the leagues to kill Sylora Salm, and I cannot consider that an illegitimate act, for it was she who freed the primordial and wreaked devastation on Neverwinter City. Surely defeating Sylora was a just and worthy cause.

And so back again have I traveled to Neverwinter City to exact revenge upon this tiefling, Herzgo Alegni—and I know not the crime, even! Do I justify my battle with my knowledge of his enslavement of Artemis Entreri?

In the same breath, can I justify freeing Artemis Entreri? Perhaps it is that his enslavement was really imprisonment, atonement for a life ill lived. Was this Alegni then a gaoler tasked with controlling the assassin?

How can I know?

I shake my head as I consider the reality of my road, that I have as my lover an elf I do not understand, and one who has no doubt committed acts beside which I would never willingly associate myself. To delve into Dahlia's past would reveal much, I fear—too much, and so I choose not to probe.

So be it.

And so it is true with Artemis Entreri, except that I have chosen simply to allow for his redemption, to accept what he was and who he was and hope that perhaps, by my side, he will make amends. There was always within him a code of honor, a sense of right and wrong, though horribly stilted through the prism of his pained eyes.

Am I a fool, then? With Dahlia? With Entreri? A fool of convenience? A lonely heart alone in a world too wide and too wild? An angry heart too scarred to linger on hopes I now know to be false?

There's the rub, and the most painful thought of all.

These are the questions I would ask of Guenhwyvar. Of course she could not answer, and yet, of course she could. With her eyes, her simple glance, her honest scrutiny reminding me to look within my own heart with similar honesty.

The cobblestones twist and turn beneath my feet. I should fear that unexpected winding, these turns left and right to places not of my own choosing.

I should, and yet I cannot deny the thrill of it all, of Dahlia, more wild than the road, and of Entreri, that tie to another life, it seems, in another world and time. The presence of Artemis Entreri surely complicates my life, and yet it brings me to a simpler time.

I have heard their banter and seen their glances to each other. They are more alike, Entreri and Dahlia, than either to me; they share something I do not understand.

My heart tells me that I should leave them.

But it is a distant voice, as distant, perhaps, as Guenhwyvar.

The Last Threshold

I did not think it possible, but the world grows grayer still around me, and more confusing.

How wide was the line twixt darkness and light when first I walked out of Menzoberranzan. So full of righteous certitude was I, even when my own fate appeared tenuous. But I could thump my fist against the stone and proclaim, "This is the way the world works best. This is right and this is wrong!" with great confidence and a sense of internal contentment.

And now I travel with Artemis Entreri.

And now my lover is a woman of . . .

Thin grows that line twixt darkness and light: what once seemed a clear definition fast devolves into an obfuscating gray fog.

In which I wander, and with a strange sense of detachment.

It has always been there, of course. It is not the world that has changed, merely my understanding of it. There have always been, there will always be, thieves like Farmer Stuyles and his band of highwaymen. By the letter of the law, they are outlaws indeed, but does not the scale of immorality sink more strongly at the feet of the feudal lords of

Luskan and even of Waterdeep, whose societal structures put men like Stuyles into an untenable position?

So on the surface, even that dilemma seems straightforward, and yet, when Stuyles and his band act, are they not assailing, assaulting, perhaps even killing, mere delivery boys of the puppet masters, similarly desperate men and women working within the shaken structures of society to feed their own?

Where then might the moral scale tip?

And perhaps more importantly, from my own perspective and my own choices in life, where then might I best follow the tenets and truths I hold dear? What scale best serves me, what scale must I seek, if options of scale abound?

Shall I be a singular player in a society of one, taking care of my personal needs in a manner attuned with that which I believe to be right and just? A hermit, then, living among the trees and the animals, akin to Montolio DeBrouchee, my long-lost mentor. This would be the easiest course, but would it suffice to assuage a conscience that has long declared community above self?

Shall I be a large player in a small pond, where my every conscience-guided move sends waves to the surrounding shores? Both of these choices seem best to describe my life to date, I think, through the last decades beside Bruenor, and with Thibbledorf and Jessa and Nanfoodle, where our concerns were our own. Our needs remained aside from the surrounding communities, for the most part, as we sought Gauntlgrym and carved our measures of personal need and occasional comforts.

Shall I venture forth to a lake, where my waves become ripples, or an ocean of society, where my ripples might well become indistinguishable among the tides of the dominant civilizations?

Where, I wonder and I fear, does hubris end and reality overwhelm? Is this the danger of reaching too high, or am I bounded by fear, which will hold me too low?

Once again I have surrounded myself with powerful companions, though less morally aligned than my previous troupe and so less easily controlled. With Dahlia and Entreri, this intriguing dwarf who calls herself Ambergris and this monk of considerable skill, Afafrenfere, I have little doubt that we might insert ourselves forcefully into some of the more pressing issues of the wider region of the northern Sword Coast.

But I do not deceive myself regarding the risk in this. I know who Artemis Entreri was, whatever I might hope he now will be. Dahlia, for all of those qualities that intrigue me, is a dangerous sort and haunted by demons of which scale I have only begun to comprehend. And now I find myself even more off-balance before her, for the revelation of this strange young tiefling as her son has put her into a place of dangerous turmoil.

Ambergris—Amber Gristle O'Maul of the Adbar O'Mauls—might be the most easily trusted of the bunch, and yet when first I met her, she was part of a band that had come to slay me and imprison Dahlia in support of forces dark indeed! And Afafrenfere . . . well, I simply do not know.

Which leads me to my road, my own road, a road of my conscious choosing and directed by my conscience and by my determination of the level of my responsibility to this world, to this community, about me. My own road—perhaps some of these new companions will choose to follow that lead, perhaps not.

What I do know with certainty, given what I have come to know of these companions, is that in terms of my moral obligations to those truths I hold dear, I cannot follow them. Whether I can or should convince them to follow me is a different question altogether.

Freedom. I talk about this concept often, and so often, in retrospect, do I come to know that I was confused about the meaning of the word. Confused or self-deluded, I fear.

257

"I am alone now. I am free!" I proclaimed when Bruenor lay cold under the stones of his cairn in Gauntlgrym.

And so I believed those words, because I did not understand that buried within my confusion over the battling shadows and sunlight of the new world about me, I was in fact heavily shackled by my own unanswered emotions. I was free to be miserable, perhaps, but in looking back upon those first steps out of Gauntlgrym, that would seem the extent of it.

I came to suspect this hidden truth, and so I pressed northward to Port Llast.

I came to hope that I was correct in my assessment and my plans when that mission neared completion and we set out from Port Llast.

But for all my hopes and suspicions, it wasn't until the caravan led by myself and Farmer Stuyles approached the gate of Port Llast that I came to fully realize the truth of that quiet irritation which had driven me along. I asked myself of the road I would choose, but that question was wholly irrelevant.

For the road that I find before me determines my actions and not the other way around.

Had I not gone to Port Llast to try to help, had I not remembered the plight of Farmer Stuyles and so many others, then I would be abandoning that which is so clear in my heart, and there is no greater shackle than self-deception. A man who denies his heart through fear of personal consequence (whether regarding physical jeopardy, or self-doubt, or simply of being ostracized) is not free. To go against your mores, against that which you know is right and true, creates a prison stronger than adamantine bars and thick stone walls. Every instance of putting expediency above the cries of conscience throws another heavy chain out behind, to drag forevermore.

Perhaps I wasn't wrong when I proclaimed my freedom after the last of my companions had departed this world, but I was surely only part of the way there. Now I am without obligation to anyone but myself, but that obligation to follow that which is in my heart is the most important one of all.

So now I say again, I am free, and say it with conviction. Because now I accept and embrace again that which is in my heart, and understand those tenets to be the truest guidepost along this road. The world may be shadowed in various shades of gray, but the concept of right and wrong is not so subtle for me, and has never been. And when that concept collides against the stated law, then the stated law be damned.

Never have I walked more purposefully than in my journey to find and retrieve Farmer Stuyles and his band. Never have fewer doubts slowed my steps.

It was the right thing to do.

My road presented this opportunity before me, and what a fraud I would have been to turn my back on these demands of my heart.

I knew all of that as I descended beside Stuyles along the road to Port Llast's welcoming gate. The expressions from the wall, and those among the caravan, all confirmed to me that this seemingly simple solution for the problems of both these peoples was the correct, the just, and the best answer.

The road had brought me here. My heart had shown me the footsteps of Drizzt Do'Urden along that road. In following that conscience-dictated trail, I can claim now, with confidence, that I am free.

How amazing to me that an early confirmation of my trail came not in the cheers of the citizens of Port Llast, nor from the relief I noted so commonly among Stuyles's refugee band that they would at last be finding a place to call a home, but in the slight nod and approving look of Artemis Entreri!

He understood my scheme, and when Dahlia publicly denounced it, he offered his quiet support—I know not why!—with but a look and a nod.

I would be a liar if I insisted that I wasn't thrilled to have Artemis Entreri beside me for this journey. Is he a redeemed man? Unlikely, and

I remain wary of him, to be sure. But in this one instance, he showed me that there is indeed something more there within his broken and scarred heart. He'll never admit his own thrill at finding this solution, of course, no more than he returned from our first foray against the sahuagin with a satisfied grin upon his ever-dour face.

But that nod told me something.

And that something makes this choice of mine—nay, makes these choices of mine, for I coerced Entreri into coming north with me in the first place, as I accepted his offer of help against Herzgo Alegni previously, and even trusted his guidance through the sewers of Neverwinter—all the more important and supportive of that which I now know to be true.

I am choosing correctly because I am following my conscience above all else, because my fears cannot sway me any longer.

Thus, I am free.

Equally important, I am content, because my faith has returned that the great cycle of civilization inexorably moves the races of Faerun toward a better destination. Ever will there be obstacles—the Spellplague, the fall of Luskan to pirates, the advent of the Empire of Netheril, the cataclysm that leveled Neverwinter—but the bigger tale is one of trudging forward, of grudging resolve and determination, of heroes small and large. Press on, soldier on, and the world grows tamer and freer and more comfortable for more people.

This is the faith that guides my steps.

Where before I saw uncertainty and walked with hesitancy, now I see opportunity and adventure. The world is broken—can I fix it all?

I know not, but with a wide smile, I expect that trying to do so will be the grandest adventure of all.

My journey from Luskan to Calimport and back again proved, at the same time, to be the least eventful and most memorable of any voyage I have known. We encountered no storms, no pirates, and no trouble with the ship whatsoever. The activities on *Minnow Skipper's* deck were nothing beyond routine throughout the entire journey.

But on an emotional level, I watched a fascinating exchange play out over the tendays and months, from the purest hatred to the deepest guilt to a primal need for a resolution that seemed untenable in a relationship irreparable.

Or was it?

When we battled Herzgo Alegni, Dahlia believed that she was facing her demon, but that was not the case. In this journey, standing before Effron, she found her demon, and it was not the broken young tiefling, but the tear in her own heart. Effron served as merely a symbol of that, a mirror looking back at her, and at what she had done.

No less was true from Effron's perspective. He was not saddled with the guilt, perhaps, but surely he was no less brokenhearted. He had suffered the ultimate betrayal, that of a mother for her child, and had spent his lifetime never meeting the expectations and demands of his brutal father. He had grown under the shadow of Herzgo Alegni, without a buffer, without a friend. Who could survive such an ordeal unscarred?

Yet for all the turmoil, there is hope for both, I see. Capturing Effron in Baldur's Gate (and we will all be forever indebted to Brother Afafrenfere!) forced Dahlia and her son together in tight quarters and for an extended period. Neither found anywhere to hide from their respective demons; the focal point, the symbol, the mirror, stood right there, each looking back at the other.

So Dahlia was forced to battle the guilt within herself. She had to honestly face what she had done, which included reliving days she would better leave unremembered. She remains in turmoil, but her burden has greatly lifted, for to her credit, she faced it honestly and forthrightly.

Isn't that the only way?

And greater is her release because of the generosity—or perhaps it is a need he doesn't even yet understand—of Effron. He has warmed to her and to us—he revealed to me the location of Guenhwyvar, which stands as a stark repudiation of the life he had known before his capture in Baldur's Gate. I know not whether he has forgiven Dahlia, or whether he ever will, but his animosity has cooled, to be sure, and in the face of that, Dahlia's step has lightened.

I observe as one who has spent the bulk of my days forcing honesty upon myself. When I speak quietly, alone under the stars or, in days former (and hopefully future), when I write in these very journals, there is no place for me to hide, and I want none! That is the point. I must face my failings most of all, without justification, without caveat, if ever I hope to overcome them.

I must be honest.

Strangely, I find that easier to do when I preach to an audience of one: myself. I never understood this before, and don't know if I can say that this was true in the time of my former life, the life spent beside the brutally blunt Bruenor and three other friends I dearly trusted. Indeed, as I reflect on it now, the opposite was true. I was in love with Catti-brie for years before I ever admitted it, not just openly, but privately! Catti-brie knew it on our first journey to Calimport, when we sailed to rescue Regis, and her hints to me woke me to my own lie.

She woke me because I was willfully asleep, and I slumbered because I was afraid of the consequences of admitting that which was in my heart.

Did I owe her more trust than that? I think I did, and owed it to Wulfgar, too, and it is that price, the price the others had to pay, which compounds my responsibility.

Certainly there are times when the truth of one's heart need not be shared, when the wound inflicted might prove worse than the cost of the deception. And so, as we see Luskan's skyline once more, I look upon Dahlia and I am torn.

Because I know now the truth of that which is in my heart. I hid it, and fought it, and buried it with every ounce of rationale I could find, because to admit it is to recognize, once more, that which I have lost, that which is not coming back.

I found Dahlia because I was alone. She is exciting. I cannot deny, and intriguing, I cannot deny, and I am the better for having traveled beside her. In our wake, given the events in Neverwinter, in Gauntlgrym, in Port Llast, and with Stuyles's band, we are leaving the world a better place than we found it. I wish to continue this journey, truly, with Dahlia and Ambergris, Afafrenfere, and even with Effron (perhaps most of all, with Effron!) and even with Artemis Entreri. I feel that I am walking a goodly road here.

But I do not love her.

I determined that I did love her because of that which burned too hotly within my loins, and even more so because of that which remained too cold within my heart. I heard again Innovindil's advice, to live my life in shorter and more intense bursts, to be reborn with each loss into a new existence with new and exciting relationships.

There may be some truth to that advice—for some of the elven people, all of it might be true.

But not for me (I hope and I fear). I can replace my companions, but I cannot replace those friends, and most of all, I cannot fill the hole left by the passing of Catti-brie.

Not with Dahlia.

Not with anyone?

I have avoided sharing this truth because of Dahlia's current emotional state. I believe Effron when he said that she sought Artemis Entreri's bed. It did not surprise me, but what did surprise me was how little that information bothered me.

Catti-brie is with me still, in my thoughts and in my heart. I'll not try to shield myself from her with the company of another.

Perhaps the passing of time and the turns in my road will show me the ultimate wisdom of Innovindil's words. But there is a profound difference between following your heart and trying to guide it.

And now my road is clear, in any case, and that road is to retrieve another friend most dear. I am coming for you, Guenhwyvar. I will have you by my side once more. I will walk the starry nights beside you.

Or I will die trying.

That is my pledge.

I found, to my surprise, that I had lost the focal point of my anger.

The anger, the frustration, the profound sense of loss yet again, remained, simmering within me, but the target of that anger dispersed into a more general distaste for the unfairness and harshness of life itself.

I had to keep reminding myself to be mad at Draygo Quick!

What a strange realization that became, an epiphany that rolled over me like a breaking wave against Luskan's beach. I remember the moment vividly, as it happened all at once (whereas the loss of the focal point took many months). I rested in my chamber at Draygo Quick's grand residence, relaxing in luxury, eating fine food, and with my own small wine rack that Draygo's staff had recently provided, when I was struck dumb by my affinity toward Draygo Quick—or if not affinity, perhaps, then my complete absence of anger toward him.

How had that happened?

Why had that happened?

This Netherese lord had imprisoned me in the most terrible of circumstances, chained in filth in a dark and rank dungeon cell. He hadn't tortured me overtly, although the handling by his servants had often been harsh, including slaps and punches and more than a few kicks to my ribs. And weren't the mere realities of my incarceration in and of themselves a manner of grotesque torture?

This Netherese lord had set a medusa upon my companions, upon my lover, and upon my only remaining tie to those coveted bygone days. They were gone. Dahlia, Entreri, Ambergris, and Afafrenfere, turned to stone and dead by the machinations of Draygo Quick.

Yet, we had invaded his home . . . that mitigating notion seemed ever present in my mind, and only grew in strength, day by day, as my own conditions gradually improved.

And that was the key of it all, I came to recognize. Draygo Quick had played a subtle and tantalizing game with my mind, and with Effron's mind, slowly improving our lives. Bit by bit, and literally at first, bite by bite, with improving food in terms of both quality and quantity.

It is difficult for a starving man to slap the hand that is feeding him.

And when basic needs like sustenance dominate your thoughts, it is no less difficult to remember to maintain anger, or remember why.

Tasty bites delivered with soothing words steal those memories, so subtly, so gradually (although every improvement felt momentous indeed), that I remained oblivious to my own diminishing animosity toward the old warlock shade.

Then came the epiphany, that day in my comfortably appointed room in the castle of Draygo Quick. Yet even with the stark recollection of the unfolding events, I found it impossible to summon the level of rage I had initially known, and hard to find anything more than a simmer.

I am left to sit here, wondering.

Draygo Quick comes to me often, daily even, and there are weapons I might fashion—of a broken wine bottle, for example.

Should I make the attempt?

The possibility of gaining my freedom through violence seems remote at best. I haven't seen Effron in tendays and have no idea of where or how to find him. I know not if he is even still within the castle, or if he is even still alive. I have no idea of how to find Guenhwyvar, nor do I even possess the onyx figurine any longer.

And even if I struck dead the old warlock and gained an escape from the castle, then what? How would I begin to facilitate my return to Faerun, and what would be there for me, in any case?

None of my old friends, lost to the winds. Not Dahlia, or even Artemis Entreri. Not Guenhwyvar or Andahar.

To strike at Draygo Quick would be the ultimate act of defiance, and one made by a doomed drow.

I look at the bottles nestled in their diagonal cubbies in the wine rack now and in them I see that the promise of deadly daggers is well within my reach. Draygo Quick comes to me alone now, without guard, and even if he had his finest soldiers beside him, I have been trained to strike faster than they could possibly block. Perhaps the old warlock has magical wards enacted about him to defeat such an attack, perhaps not, but in striking so, I would be making a cry of freedom and a denial against this warlock who took so much from me, who imprisoned Guenhwyvar and cost me my companions when we came for her.

But I can only shake my head as I stare at those potential daggers, for I will not so fashion the bottles. It is not fear of Draygo Quick that stays my hand. It is not the desperation of such an act, the near surety that even if successful, I would be surely bringing about my own demise, and likely in short order.

I won't kill him, I know.

Because I don't want to.

And that, I fear, might be the biggest epiphany of all.

Companions and
Companions Codex

The Companions

So many times have I pondered the long road I have walked, and likely will still walk. I hear Innovindil's words often, her warning that a long-lived elf must learn to live her life to accommodate the mortality of those she may come to know and love. And so, when a human passes on, but the elven lover remains, it is time to move on, time to break emotionally and completely and begin anew.

I have found this a difficult proposition, indeed, and something I cannot easily resolve. In my head, Innovindil's words ring with truth. In my heart . . .

I do not know.

As unconvinced as I am about this unending cycle, it occurs to me that measuring the life span of a human as a guideline is also a fool's errand, for indeed, do not these shorter-lived races live their lives in bursts, in fits and starts, abrupt endings and moments of renewal? Childhood friends, parted for mere months, may reunite only to discover that their bonds have frayed. Perhaps one has entered young adulthood, while the other remains in the thrall of childhood joys. Many times did I witness this in Ten Towns (though surely it was less frequent among the more regimented lives of Bruenor's kin in Mithral

Hall), where a pair of boys, the best of friends, would turn corners away from each other, one pursuing a young lady who intrigued him in ways he could not have previously imagined, the other holding fast to childish games and less complicated joys.

On many occasions, this parting proved more than a temporary split, for never again would the two see each other in the previous light of friendship. Never again.

Nor is this limited to the transition of childhood to young adulthood. Far from it! It is a reality we all rarely seem to anticipate. Friends find different roads, vowing to meet again, and many times—nay, most times!—is that vow unrealized. When Wulfgar left us in Mithral Hall, Bruenor swore to visit him in Icewind Dale, and yet, alas, such a reunion never came to pass.

And when Regis and I did venture north of the Spine of the World to visit Wulfgar, we found for our efforts a night, a single night, of reminiscing. One night where we three sat about a fire in a cave Wulfgar had taken as his home, speaking of our respective roads and recalling adventures we had long ago shared.

I have heard that such reunions can prove quite unpleasant and full of awkward silence, and fortunately, that was not the case that night in Icewind Dale. We laughed and resolved that our friendship would never end. We prodded Wulfgar to open up his heart to us, and he did, recounting the tale of his journey back to the north from Mithral Hall, when he had returned his adoptive daughter to her true mother. Indeed, in that case, the years we had spent apart seemed to melt away, and we were three friends uninterrupted, breaking bread and sharing tales of great adventure.

And still, it was but one single night, and when I awoke in the morn, to find that Wulfgar had prepared a breakfast, we two knew that our time together had come to an end. There was no more to say, no stories left which hadn't been told. He had his life now, in Icewind Dale, while the road for me and Regis was back to Luskan, and to Mithral Hall beyond that. For all the love between us, for all the shared experiences, for all the vows that we would meet again, we had reached the end of our lives together. And so we parted, and in that last hug, Wulfgar had promised Regis that he would find him on the banks of Maer Dualdon one day, and would even sneak up and bait the hook of his fishing pole!

But of course, that never happened, because while Innovindil advised me, as a long-lived elf, to break my life into the shorter life spans of those humans I would know, so too do humans live their lives in segments. Best friends today vow to be best friends when they meet again in five years, but alas, in five years, they are often strangers. In a few years, which seems not a long stretch of time, they have often made for themselves new lives with new friends, and perhaps even new families. This is the way of things, though few can accurately anticipate it and fewer still will admit it.

The Companions of the Hall, the four dear friends I came to know in Icewind Dale, sometimes told me of their lives before. Wulfgar and Catti-brie were barely adults when I came into their lives, but Bruenor was an old dwarf even then, with adventures that had spanned centuries and half the world, and Regis had lived for decades in exotic southern cities, with as many wild adventures behind him as those yet to come.

Bruenor spoke to me often about his clan and Mithral Hall, as dwarfs are wont to do, while Regis, with more to hide, likely, remained cryptic of his earlier days (days that had set Artemis Entreri on his trail, after all!). But even with the exhaustive stories Bruenor told to me, of his father and grandfather, of the adventures he had known in the tunnels about Mithral Hall, of the founding of Clan Battlehammer in Icewind Dale, it rarely occurred to me that he had once known friends as important to him as I had become.

Or had he? Isn't that the mystery and the crux of Innovindil's claims, when all is stripped bare? Can I know another friend to match the bond I shared with Bruenor? Can I know another love to match that which I found in Catti-brie's arms?

What of Catti-brie's life before I met her on the windswept slope on Kelvin's Cairn, or before she had come to be adopted by Bruenor? How well had she known her parents, truly? How deeply had she loved them? She spoke of them only rarely, but that was because she simply could not remember. She had been but a child, after all . . .

And so I find myself in another of the side valleys running alongside Innovindil's proposed road: that of memory. A child's feelings for her mother or father cannot be questioned. To look at the child's eyes as she stares at one of her parents is to see true and deep love. Catti-brie's eyes shone like that for her parents, no doubt.

Yet she could not tell me of her birth parents, for she could not remember!

She and I spoke of having children of our own, and oh, but I wish that had come to pass! For Catti-brie, though, there hovered about her the black wings of a great fear, that she would die before her child, our child, was old enough to remember her, that her child's life would parallel her own in that one, terrible way. For though she rarely spoke of it, and though she had known a good life under the watchful gaze of benevolent Bruenor, the loss of her parents—even parents she could not remember—forever weighed heavily upon Catti-brie. She felt as if a part of her life had been stolen from her, and cursed her inability to remember in greater detail more profoundly than the joy she found in recalling the smallest bits of that life lost.

Deep are those valleys beside Innovindil's road.

Given these truths, given that Catti-brie could not even remember two she had loved so instinctively and wholly, given the satisfied face of Wulfgar when Regis and I found him upon the tundra of Icewind Dale, given the broken promises of finding old friends once more or the awkward conversations which typically rule such reunions, why, then, am I so resistant to the advice of my lost elven friend?

I do not know.

Perhaps it is because I found something so far beyond the normal joining one might know, a true love, a partner in heart and soul, in thought and desire.

Perhaps I have not yet found another to meet that standard, and so I fear it cannot ever be so again.

Perhaps I am simply fooling myself—whether wrought of guilt or sadness or frustrated rage, I amplify and elevate in my memory that which I had to a pedestal that no other can begin to scale.

It is the last of these possibilities which terrifies me, for such a deception would unravel the very truths upon which I stand, the very hopes that lift me from my bed each morning, the very memories which carry me through each day. I have felt this sensation of love so keenly—to learn that there were no gods or goddesses, no greater design to all that is beyond that which I already know, no life after death, even, would pain me less, I believe, than to learn that there is no lasting love.

And thus do I deny the clear truth of Innovindil's advice, because in this one instance, I choose to let that which is in my heart overrule that which is in my head.

For I have come to know that to do otherwise, for Drizzt Do'Urden, would be to walk a barren road.

The world moves along outside the purview or influence of my personal experience. To return to Icewind Dale is to learn that the place has continued, with new people replacing those who are gone, through immigration and emigration, birth and death. Some are descendants of those who lived here before, but in this transient place of those who flee the boundaries of society, many, many more are those who have come here anew from other lands.

Similarly, new buildings have arisen, while others have fallen. New boats replace those which have been surrendered to the three great lakes of the area.

There is a reason and logic to the place and a wondrous symmetry. In Icewind Dale, it all makes sense. The population of Ten Towns grows and shrinks, but mostly remains stable to that which the region can support.

This is an important concept in the valuation of the self, for far too many people seem oblivious to the implications of this most basic truth: the world continues outside of their personal experience. Oh, perhaps they do not consciously express such a doubt of this obvious truth, but I have met more than one who has postulated that this existence is a dream—his dream and the rest of us, therefore, are mere components within the reality of his creation. Indeed, I have met many who act that way, whether they have thought it out to that level of detail or not.

I speak, of course, of empathy, or in the cases stated, of the lack thereof. We are in constant struggle, the self and the community, where in our hearts we need to decide where one line ends and another begins. For some, this is a matter of religion, the unquestioned edicts of a professed god, but for most, I would hope, it is a realization of the basic truth that the community, the society, is a needed component in the preservation of the self, both materially and spiritually.

I have considered this many times before, and professed my belief in community, and indeed, it was just that belief that stood me up again when I was beaten down with grief, when I led my newfound companions out of Neverwinter to serve the greater good of a worthy place called Port Llast. This, to me, is not a difficult choice: to serve the community is to serve the self. Even Artemis Entreri, that most cynical of creatures, could hardly disguise the sense of satisfaction he felt when we pushed the Sahuagin sea devils back under the surf for the good of the goodly folk of Port Llast.

As I consider my own roots and the various cultures through which I have passed, however, there is a more complicated question regarding this equation: What is the role of the community to the self? And what of the smaller communities within the larger? What are their roles, or their responsibilities?

Surely common defense is paramount to the whole, but the very idea of community needs to go deeper than that. What farming community would survive if the children were not taught the ways of the fields and cattle? What dwarven homeland would thrive through the centuries

if the dwarflings were not tutored in the ways of stone and metal?
What elven clan could dance in the forest for centuries untold if not
for the training given the children, the ways of the stars and the winds?

And there remain many tasks too large for any one man, or woman,
or family, critical to the prosperity and security of any town or city. No
one man could build the wall about Luskan, or the docks of Baldur's
Gate, or the great archways and wide boulevards of Waterdeep, or the
soaring cathedrals of Silverymoon. No one church, either, and so these
smaller groupings within the larger societies need contribute, for the
good of all, whether citizens of their particular flock or group, or not.

But what then of the concentration of power which might
accompany the improvements and the hierarchical regimentation that
may result within any given community? In singular societies, such as
a dwarven clan, this is settled through the bloodlines and proper heirs,
but in a great city of mixed heritage and various cultures, the allocation
of power is certainly less definitive. I have witnessed lords willing to
allow their peasants to starve, while food rots in their own larders,
for it is far too plentiful for their singular house to possibly consume.
I have seen, as with Prisoner's Carnival in Luskan, magistrates who
use the law as a weapon for their own ends. And even in Waterdeep,
whose lords are considered among the most beneficent in all the
world, lavish palaces look down upon hovels and shanties, or orphaned
children shivering in the street.

Once again, and to my surprise, I look to Ten Towns as my
preferred example, for in this place, where the population remains
fairly steady, if the individuals constantly change, there is logical and
reasoned continuity. Here the ten communities remain distinct and
choose among them their respective leaders through various means, and
those leaders have voice at the common council.

The irony of Icewind Dale is that these communities, full of solitary
folk (often numbering among their citizens many who fled the law or
some gang, using Ten Towns as a last refuge), full of those who could
not, supposedly, live among the civilized societies, are in truth among

the most cooperative places I have ever known. The individual fishing boats on Maer Dualdon might vie fiercely for favored spots, but when the winter sets in, none in Ten Towns starve while others feast heartily. None in Ten Towns freeze in the empty street when there is room near a hearth—and there is always such room to be found. Likely it is the ferocity of the land, where all understand that numbers alone keep them safe from the yetis and the goblinkin and giantkind.

And that is the point of community: common need and common good, the strength of numbers, the tenderness of a helping hand, the ability to work as one to attain greater heights for all, the widening of horizons beyond one's own perspective and one's own family, the enrichment of life itself.

O, but there are many who would not agree with me, who view the responsibilities to the community, be it in tithe of food, wealth, or time, as too cumbersome or infringing upon their personal liberties . . . which I find too oft defined as personal desires and greed in the disguise of prettier words.

To them I can only insist that the ultimate loss exceeds the perceived gain. What good your gold if your neighbor will not lift you when you have fallen?

What length your memory, spoken in fondness, when you are gone?

Because in the end, that is the only measure, methinks. In the end, when life's last flickers do fade, all that remains is memory, and richness then, in the final measure, is not weighed in gold coins, but in the number of people you have touched, the tears of those who will mourn your passing and who will continue to celebrate your life.

I could not have planned my journey. Not any particular journey to a town or a region, but the journey of my life, the road I've walked from my earliest days. I often hear people remark that they have no regrets about choices they've made because the results of those choices have made them who they are.

I can't say that I agree fully with such sentiments, but I certainly understand them. And in that same reflection, I admit that hindsight is easy, but decisions made in the moment are often much more difficult, the "right" choice often much harder to discern.

Which circles me back to my original thought: I could not have planned out this journey I have taken, these decades of winding roads. Even on those occasions when I purposely strove in a determined direction, as when I walked out of Menzoberranzan, I could not begin to understand the long-term ramifications of my choice. Indeed on that occasion, I thought that I would likely meet my death, soon enough. It wasn't a suicide choice, of course—never that!—but merely a decision that the long odds were worth the gamble when weighed against the certainty of life in Menzoberranzan (which seemed to me a form of emotional suicide).

Never did I think those first steps would lead me out of the Underdark to the surface world. And even when that course became evident, I could not have foreseen the journeys that lay ahead—the love of Montolio, and then the home and family I found in Icewind Dale. On that day I walked away from Menzoberranzan, the suggestion that my best friend would be a dwarf and I would marry a human would have elicited a perplexed and incredulous look indeed!

Imagine Drizzt Do'Urden of Daermon N'a'shezbaernon sitting at the right hand of King Bruenor Battlehammer of Mithral Hall, fighting beside King Bruenor against the raiding drow of Menzoberranzan! Preposterous!

But true.

This is life, an adventure too intricate, too interconnected to too many variables to be predictable. So many people try to outline and determine their path, rigidly unbending, and for them I have naught but a sigh of pity. They set the goal and chase it to the exclusion of all else. They see the mark of some imagined finish line and never glance left or right in their singular pursuit.

There is only one certain goal in life: death.

It is right and necessary and important to set goals and chase them. But to do so singularly, particularly regarding those roads which will take many months, even years, to accomplish is to miss the bigger point. It is the journey that is important, for it is the sum of all those journeys, planned or unexpected, which makes us who we are. If you see life as a journey to death, if you truly understand that ultimate goal, then it is the present which becomes most important, and when the present takes precedence above the future, you have truly learned to live.

One eye toward the future, one eye firmly rooted in the present journey, I say.

I have noted before and do so again—because it is a valuable lesson that should often be reinforced—that many who are faced with impending death, a disease that will likely take them in a year's time, for example, quite often insist that their affliction is the best thing that ever happened to them. It took the immediacy of mortality to remind them to watch the sunrise and the sunset, to note the solitary flower among the rocks, to appreciate those loved ones around them, to taste their food and revel in the feel of a cool breeze.

To appreciate the journey is to live in the present, even as you aim for the future.

There are unintended consequences to be found, in any case. We do not usually choose to love those who become important to us. Oh, perhaps we choose our mate, but that is but one of a myriad of beloved we will know. We do not choose our parents or our siblings, but typically these people will become beloved to us. We do not choose our neighbors in our youth, and our city or kingdom is determined for us, initially at least. Few are those who break from that societal bond. I did, but only because of the extreme nature of Menzoberranzan. Had I been born and raised in Baldur's Gate, and that city became involved in a war with Waterdeep, under whose flag would I fight? Almost assuredly the place of my birth, the place of my kin and kind. This would not be a neutral choice, and would be one, almost assuredly, influenced by past events large and small, by past emotional attachments of which I might not even be consciously aware. I would fight for my home, most of all, because it was my home!

And not one I had purposely chosen.

This is even truer regarding religion, I have found. For most people, at least. Children are typically raised within the guidelines of their family's religion; this moral code becomes a part of their very identity, true to the core of who they are. And though the ultimate morality of most of the religions is identical, the particulars, whether in ritual or minor tenet, often are not. Even these seemingly minor discrepancies go to the heart of the tribal bonds of every sentient being, and few can step above their partisan outlook to evaluate a conflict at hand, should there be one, through the eyes of the opposing people.

These are journeys that we do not individually determine, full of beloved people we did not consciously choose to love. Familiarity may breed contempt, as the old saying goes, but in truth, familiarity breeds family and familial love, and that bond is powerful indeed. It would take extraordinary circumstances, I expect, for a brother to fight against a brother. And sadly, most wars are not waged over extraordinary moral quandaries or conflicting philosophies.

And so the bond will usually hold in the face of such conflict. To pass through childhood beside our siblings is to forge a special bond which those outside that family group cannot enter. A wise drow once told me that the surest way to rally citizens about their king is to threaten him, for even if those same citizens loathed the man, they would not loathe their homeland, and when such a threat is made, it is made upon that homeland most of all.

I find that such parochialism is true more often for humans and the shorter-living races than it is for elves, drow or surface, and for a very simple reason: rarely are elven children raised together. A child of the elven folk is more likely to have a sibling a century older than he is to have one passing through childhood beside him.

Our journeys are unique, but they are not in isolation. The roads of a thousand thousand individuals crisscross, and each intersection is a potential side street, a wayward path, a new adventure, an unexpected emotional bond.

Nay, I could not have planned this journey I have taken. For that, I am truly glad.

Is there any greater need within the social construct than that of trust? Is there any more important ingredient to friendship or to the integrity of a team?

And yet, throughout a person's life, how many others might he meet in whom he can truly trust? The number is small, I fear. Yes, we will trust many others with superficial tasks and confidences at a certain level, but when we each dig down to emotions that entail true vulnerability, that number of honest confidants shrinks dramatically.

That has ever been the missing ingredient in my relationship with Dahlia, and in my companionship with Artemis Entreri. As I consider it now, I can only laugh at the reality that I trust Entreri more than Dahlia, but only in that I am trusting him with matters of mutual benefit. Were I in dire peril, would either rush to my aid?

I think they would if there was any hope of victory, but if their help meant true sacrifice, wherein either of them had to surrender his or her own life to save mine . . . well, I would surely perish.

Is it possible that I have grown so cynical and dark in my heart that I could accept that?

Who am I, then, and who might I become? I have forgotten that I have known friends who would push me out of the way of a speeding arrow, even if that meant catching the missile in their own body. So it was with the Companions of the Hall, all of us for each of us.

Even Regis. So often did we tease Regis, who was ever hiding in the shadows when battle was joined, but we knew with full confidence that our halfling friend would be there when the tide turned against us, and indeed, I have no doubt that my little friend would leap high to intercept the arrow before it reached my bosom at the willing price of his own life.

I cannot say the same of this second group with whom I adventured. Entreri would not give his life for me, nor would Dahlia, I expect (though in truth, with Dahlia I never know what to expect!). Afafrenfere the monk was capable of such loyalty, as was Ambergris the dwarf of Adbar, though whether I had earned that level of companionship with them or not I do not know. And Effron the twisted warlock? I cannot be certain, though I surely doubt that one who dabbles in arts so dark is a man of generous heart.

Perhaps with time, this second adventuring group would grow as close as the Companions of the Hall, and perhaps in that tightening bond there would come selfless acts of the highest courage.

But should I spend a hundred years beside them, might I ever expect the same level of sacrifice and valor that I had known with Bruenor, Catti-brie, Regis, and Wulfgar? In a desperate battle against seemingly unwinnable odds, could I move ahead to flank our common enemy with full confidence that when it came to blows, these others would be there beside me, all in to victory or death? That was what I knew would happen with the Companions of the Hall, but with my newfound "friends"?

No. Never.

This is the bond that would never materialize, the level of love and friendship that rises above all else—all else, even the most basic instinct of personal survival.

When I had learned of Dahlia's indiscretion, her illicit affair with Entreri, I was not surprised, and not merely because of my own role in driving her away, my inattentiveness to her. She made of me a cuckold, something Catti-brie would never have done, under any circumstance. And I was not surprised at the revelation, for this basic difference between the two women was clear for me to see all along. Perhaps I deluded myself in the beginning with Dahlia, blinded by intrigue and lust, or by the quaint notion that I could somehow repair the wounds within her, or most likely of all, by my need to replace that which I had lost, but I always knew the truth.

When Effron told me of her dalliance with Entreri, I believed him immediately because it resonated with my honest understanding of my relationship and of this woman. I was neither surprised nor terribly wounded because this was who I knew Dahlia to be. However I lied to myself, however I tried to believe the best of the woman, this was who I knew Dahlia to be.

I wanted to remake the Companions of the Hall. More than anything in all the world, I wanted to know again the level of friendship and trust—honest and deep, to the heart and to the soul—that I had known for those years with my dearest friends. The world can never brighten for me until I have found that, and yet I fear that what I once knew was unique, derived of circumstances I cannot replicate.

In joining with Entreri and the others, I tried to salve that wound and re-create the joy of my life.

But in considering the new band of adventurers, there entails the inevitable comparison, and in that, all that I have accomplished is to rip the scab from the unhealed wound.

I find that I am lonelier than ever before.

Night of the Hunter

Do people really change?

I've thought about this question so many times over the last decades—and how poignant it seemed to me when I happened once more upon Artemis Entreri, shockingly alive, given the passage of a century.

I came to travel with him, to trust him even; does that mean that I came to believe that he had "changed"?

Not really. And now that we have once more parted ways, I don't believe there to be a fundamental difference in the man as compared to the Entreri I fought beside in the undercity of Mithral Hall when it was still in the hands of the duergar, or the Entreri I pursued to Calimport when he had abducted Regis. Fundamentally, he is the same man, as, fundamentally, I am the same drow.

A person may learn and grow, and thus react differently to a recurring situation—that is the hope I hold for all people, for myself, for societies, even. Is that not the whole point of gaining experience, to use it to make wiser choices, to temper destructive instincts, to find better resolutions? In that regard, I do believe Artemis Entreri to be a changed man, slower in turning to the dagger for resolution, though no less deadly when he needs it. But fundamentally, regarding that which is in the man's heart, he is the same.

I know that to be true of myself, although, in retrospect, I walked a very different path over the last few years than that I purposefully strode for the majority of my life. Darkness found my heart, I admit. With the loss of so many dear friends came the loss of hope itself and so I gave in to the easier path—although I had vowed almost every day that such a cynical journey would not be the road of Drizzt Do'Urden.

Fundamentally, though, in my heart, I did not change, and so when faced with the reality of the darkened road, when it came time for me to admit the path to myself, I could not go on.

I cannot say that I miss Dahlia, Entreri, and the others of that group. My heart does not call out for me to go and find them, surely—but I am not so certain that I could confidently claim such a casual attitude about my decision to part ways had it not been for the return of those friends I hold most dear! How can I regret parting with Dahlia when the fork in our road led me directly back to the arms of Catti-brie?

And thus, here I stand, together once more beside the Companions of the Hall, rejoined with the truest and dearest friends I have ever known, and could ever hope to know. Have they changed? Have their respective journeys through the realm of death itself brought to these four friends a new and guiding set of principles that will leave me sorely disappointed as I come to know them once more?

That is a fear I hold, but hold afar.

For, again, people do not fundamentally change, so I believe. The warmth of Catti-brie's embrace is one inspiring confidence that I am right. The mischievous grin of Regis (even with the mustache and goatee) is one I have seen before, and though it now promises to me something new and something more, all of that comes in the form of a big-hearted halfling who remains quite familiar to me. And Bruenor's call that night under the stars atop Kelvin's Cairn, and his reaction to Wulfgar . . . aye, that was Bruenor, true to the thick bone and thick head!

All that said, in these first days together, I have noted a change in Wulfgar's step, I admit. There is a lightness there I have not seen before, and—curiously, I say, given the description I have been told of his reluctance to leave Iruladoon for the mortal world once more—a smile that never seems to leave his face.

But he is Wulfgar, surely, the proud son of Beornegar. He has found some enlightenment, it would seem, though in what way I cannot say, though the direction of that new reality seems clear upon his face. Enlightened and lightened. I see no burden there. I see amusement and joy, as if he views this all as a grand adventure on borrowed time, and I cannot deny the health of that perspective!

They are back. We are back. The Companions of the Hall. We are not as we once were, but our hearts remain true, our purpose joined, and our trust for each other undiminished and thus, unbridled.

I am very glad of that!

And, in a curious way (and a surprising way to me), I hold no regrets for the last few years of my journey through a life confusing, frightening, and grand all at once. My time with Dahlia, and particularly with Entreri, was one of learning, I must believe. To see the world through a cynical perspective did not hurl me back to the days of my youth in Menzoberranzan, and thus encapsulate me in darkness, but rather, has offered to me a more complete understanding of the consequence of choice, for I broke free of the cynicism before knowing what fate awaited me atop Bruenor's Climb.

I am not so self-centered as to believe that the world about me is created for the purpose of . . . me! We all play such self-centered games at times, I suppose, but in this case, I will allow myself one moment of self-importance, to accept the reunion of the Companions of the Hall as a reward to me. Put whatever name you wish upon the gods and goddesses, or the fates or the coincidences and twists that move the world along its path—it matters not. In this one instance, I choose to believe in a special kind of justice.

Indeed, it is a foolish and self-serving claim, I know.

But it feels good.

I am haunted by the expression on Bruenor's face and by the words of Catti-brie. "The burden you carry blurs your judgment," she told me, and without reservation. "As you see yourself, you hope to find in others—in orcs and goblins, even."

She alone said this, but Bruenor's expression and wholehearted nod certainly agreed with Catti-brie's assessment. I wanted to argue, but found I could not. I wanted to scream against them both, to tell them that no, fate is not predetermined by nature, that a reasoning being could escape the determinations of heredity, that rationale could overwhelm instinct.

I wanted to tell them that I had escaped.

And so, in that roundabout reasoning-turned-admission, Catti-brie's words of my burden ultimately rang true to me, and so, were I not bound by my own experiences, and the uncertainty that has followed me every step out of Menzoberranzan, even these many decades later, my determined expression would likely have matched Bruenor's own.

Was the Treaty of Garumn's Gorge a mistake? To this day, I still do not know, but I find now, in light of this discussion, that my ambiguous stance relies more on the suffering that was averted for the dwarves and elves and humans of the Silver Marches, and less by the benefit to the orcs. For in my heart, I suspect that Bruenor is right, and that Catti-brie's newfound understanding of the nature of orcs is being confirmed by that which Bruenor relates of the goings-on in the Silver Marches. The Kingdom of Many Arrows holds as an entity, so he claims, but the peace it promotes is a sham. And perhaps, I must admit, that peace only facilitates the orc raiders and allows them more freedom than they would find if Many Arrows did not exist.

But still, with all the revelations and epiphanies, it hurts, all of this, and the apparent solution seems a chasm too far for me to jump. Bruenor is ready to march to Mithral Hall, rouse the dwarves and raise an army, and with that force wage open war on the Kingdom of Many Arrows.

Bruenor is determined to begin a war. So determined is he that he will put aside the suffering, the death, the disease, the utter misery that such a conflict will wreak on the land, so that, as he puts it, he might right the wrong he caused that century ago.

I cannot start a war. Even were I to fully embrace what Catti-brie has claimed, even were I to believe that her every word came from the mouth of Mielikki herself, I cannot start a war!

I will not, I say (and I fear), nor will I allow Bruenor to do so. Even if his words about the nature of orcs are true—and likely they are—then the current situation still, in my view, remains better than the open conflict he so desires. Perhaps as I am bound to caution because of my burden of personal experience, so Bruenor is bound by guilt to try to correct that which he sees as his chance at redemption.

Is that any less a burden?

Nay, I think, and likely it is more so.

He will run headlong into misery, for himself, for his legacy, and for all the goodly folk of the Silver Marches. That is my fear, and as such, as a friend, I must stop him if I can.

I can only wince at the possibilities illuminated by this course, for never have I seen Bruenor more determined, more sure of his steps. So much so, that should I try to dissuade him, I fear we might come to blows!

As indeed, I fear my road back to Mithral Hall. My last visit was not pleasant, and not one I often consider, for it pains me to realize that I, a ranger, have worked openly against dwarves and elves for the sake of orcs. For the sake of the "peace," I tell myself, but in the end, that dodge can hold true only if Catti-brie's admonition, if Mielikki's claim, is not true. If orcs are not to be counted among the reasoning beings born of a choice in their road, then . . .

I will follow Bruenor to Mithral Hall. If the orc raiders are as prevalent as Bruenor insists, then I am sure I will find good use for my blades, and likely at Bruenor's side, vigilant hunters striking without hesitation or guilt.

But I will not start a war.

That chasm is too wide.

Am I wrong, then, in hoping that the decision is taken from us before we ever arrive? In hoping that the Kingdom of Many Arrows proves Catti-brie's point in no uncertain terms?

"Where's the babies' room!" I hear her again, often in my thoughts, in that Dwarvish brogue of old, and with the ferocity befitting a daughter of King Bruenor Battlehammer. And though Catti-brie carried this accent for many years, and can fight as well as any, this time her cheer rang discordantly, painfully, in my ears.

What of Nojheim, then, the goblin I once knew who seemed a decent sort undeserving of his harsh fate?

Or am I really saying, what, then, of Drizzt?

I want to deny the message of Mielikki: once I claimed the goddess as that which was in my heart, a name for what I knew to be true and right. And now I want to deny it, desperately so, and yet I cannot. Perhaps it is the harsh truth of Faerun that goblinkin and evil giantkind are just that, evil, by nature and not nurture.

And likely, my perception of this truth has been distorted by my own determined escape from the seemingly inevitable path I was born to follow, and perhaps distorted in dangerous ways.

On a very basic level, this message wounds me, and that wound is the burden. Is there, in this instance, no place for optimism and an insistence that there is good to be found? Does that outlook, the guiding philosophy of my existence, simply have no place in the darkness of an orc's heart?

Can I start a war?

I walk this road tentatively, but also eagerly, for I am filled with conflict. I wish to know. I must know!

I am afraid to know.

Alas, so much has changed, but so much remains the same. The Spellplague is gone, yet trouble seems ever to be brewing behind us in our wake, and yet we walk a road into deeper darkness, into

Gauntlgrym for the sake of a lost friend, and then, if we survive, into the midst of a brewing storm.

For all of that, have I ever been happier?

Even in this crazy world, where magic runs in wild cycles and wilder circles, where orcs appear suddenly by the tens of thousands and pirates become kings, there are moments of clarity and predictability, where the patterns align into expected outcomes. These I call the rhymes of history.

Regis came to us just ahead of pursuit, a dangerous foe indeed.

The rhyme of history, the comfort of predictability!

He is very different in this second life, this halfling friend of ours. Determined, skilled, practiced with the blade, Regis has lived his second life with purpose and focused on a clear goal. And when the lich arrived at our encampment that dark night in the wilderlands of the Crags, this most fearsome monster—indeed, a monster I do not think we could have defeated had not Catti-brie used the dweomer the Harpells had fortunately provided!—Regis did not flee. Nay, he called out for us to flee while he continued to try to battle the vile lich.

But for all of those alterations, the whole of the experience rang with the comfort of familiarity.

The rhyme of history.

I have heard this truth of reasoning beings mentioned often, particularly among the elves, and most particularly among the eldest of the elves, who have seen the sunrise and sunset of several centuries. Little surprises them, even the tumultuous events like the Time of Troubles and the Spellplague, for they have heard the rhyme many times. And this expected reality is so particularly concerning the rise and fall of kingdoms and empires. They follow a course, an optimistic climb, an ascent through the glories of possibility. Sometimes they get there, sparkling jewels in periods of near perfection—the height of

Myth Drannor, the glory of Waterdeep, and yes, I would include the rebirth of Clan Battlehammer in Mithral Hall. This is the promise and the hope.

But the cycle wheels along and far too often, the fall is as predictable as the rise.

Is it the ambition or the weakness of sentient races, I wonder, that leads to this cycle, this rise and fall, of cultures and kingdoms? So many begin beneficent and with grand hopes. A new way, a new day, a bright sunrise, and a thousand other hopeful clichés . . .

And each and every way, it seems, falls to stagnation, and in that stagnation do evil men rise, through greed or lust for power. Like canker buds do they find their way in any government, slipping through seams in the well-intended laws, coaxing the codes to their advantage, finding their treasures and securing their generational well-being at the expense of all others, and ever blaming the helpless, who have no voice and no recourse. To the laborers do they cry, "Beware the leech!" and the leech is the infirm, the elderly, the downtrodden.

So do they deflect and distort reality itself to secure their wares, and yet, they are never secure, for this is the truest rhyme of history, that when the theft is complete, so will the whole collapse, and in that collapse will fall the downtrodden and the nobility alike.

And the misery and pain will feast in the fields and in the sea and in the forest about, in the laborers and the farmers and the fishermen and the hunters, and in those who sow and those who eat.

For the rhyme of history is a sullen one, I fear, ringing as a klaxon of warning, and fading fast into distant memory, and even to fable, while the new cankers burst from their pods and feast.

It need not be like this, but too often it is. It was my hope and dream of something new and better, and something lasting, which led to the Treaty of Garumn's Gorge, a path I am coming to lament.

And so I should be despondent.

But, nay, far from it, for I have witnessed divine justice now, and am blessed in the glories of those things most valuable: the truest friends and family anyone could know. With open eyes and open hearts we go, the Companions of the Hall, and well aware of the rhyme of history, and determined that those sad notes will give way to triumphant bars and soothing melodies of hope and justice.

The world is chaos, but we are order.

The world is shadow, but we are determined to shine as light.

Once, not long ago, I had to coax my former companions to good deeds and selfless acts; now I am surrounded by those who drive me to the same.

For even the too-often dark truth of the rhyme of history cannot overwhelm the unceasing optimism that there is something more and better, a community for all, where the meek need not fear the strong.

We'll find our way, and those lesser rhymes will find discordant notes, as with this lich Regis dragged upon us, this Ebonsoul creature who thought himself beyond us.

For this was part of the play, and a part expected had we looked more carefully at our halfling friend, had we remembered the truth of Rumblebelly—that same Regis who brought upon us one day long past the darkness that once was Artemis Entreri (once was, I say!).

And so we now look more carefully as we tread, for with Regis, there is something about him—an aura, a mannerism, perhaps, or a willingness to take a chance, often foolishly?—that throws a towrope to trouble.

So be it; perhaps, as the old saying goes, that is part of his charm.

He drags the shark to its doom, I say.

Words blurted in fast reaction so oft ring true.

From the heart, they flow, and give voice to raw emotions before the speaker can thoughtfully intervene, out of tact or fear. Before the natural guards arise to self-censor, to protect the speaker from embarrassment or retribution. Before the polite filters catch the words to protect the sensibilities of others, to veil the sharp truth before it can stab.

Bruenor calls this fast reaction "chewing from yer gut."

We all do it. Most try not to do it, audibly at least, and in matters of tact and etiquette that is a good thing.

But sometimes chewing from your gut can serve as an epiphany, an admission of sorts to that which is actually in your heart, despite the reservations one might have gained among polite company.

So it was that day in the chambers of upper Gauntlgrym when I said that I would not leave Entreri to his drow captors. I did not doubt my course from the moment Thibbledorf Pwent revealed the situation to me. I would go to find Artemis Entreri, and I would free him—and the others, if they, too, had been taken.

It was that simple.

And yet, when I look back on that moment, there was nothing simple about it at all. Indeed, I find my resolution and determination truly surprising, and for two very different reasons.

First, as my own words rang in my ears, they revealed to me something I had not admitted: that I cared for Artemis Entreri. It wasn't just convenience that had kept me beside him, nor my own loneliness, nor my (flawed) desire to bring him and the others to the path of righteousness. It was because I cared, and not just for Dahlia, but for Entreri as well.

I have many times flirted with this point through the years. When I learned that Artemis Entreri had become friends to Jarlaxle, I hoped that Jarlaxle would lead the man from his personal demons. I wished Entreri well, meaning that I hoped he would find a better life and a better way. That thought has often flitted about my consciousness, a quiet hope.

But still this particular instance of chewing from my gut surprised me on this matter because of the depth it revealed of my feelings toward the man.

I had my friends with me, after all, the Companions of the Hall, the group of my dearest friends, yea, my family, the only family I had ever known. My chewed-from-the-gut proclamation that I was going after Entreri was much more than a personal declaration, because of course these beloved companions would go along with me. Presumably, it follows that I was willing to put my dearest friends, even Catti-brie, into such obvious and dire jeopardy for the sake of Artemis Entreri!

That, I think, is no small thing, and looking at it in retrospect reveals to me much more than my desire to free Artemis Entreri.

When I first ventured to Icewind Dale, those around me thought me a bit reckless. Even Bruenor, who leaped onto a shadow dragon's back with a keg of flaming oil strapped to his own back, often shook his head and muttered "durned elf" at my battle antics!

I fought as if I had nothing to lose, because in my heart and mind, I had nothing to lose. But then, so suddenly, I learned that I had so much to lose, in these friends I had come to know and love, in this woman who would be my wife.

This is not a new revelation to me—indeed, I have spent the better part of a century seeking freedom from these self-imposed restraints, and indeed, I thought I had found such freedom when Bruenor, the last of my companions, passed on to Dwarfhome. Even in my great lament at his passing, I felt as if I was finally free.

And then my friends, my family—my constraints?—returned to me. What did it mean? Surely I was glad, thrilled, overjoyed, but was I doomed to return to that place of caution I had known before?

But in that simple chewed-from-the-gut moment, my insistence that I, that we, would go and free Entreri and the others, no matter the odds, I knew without doubt that my beloved friends had not brought my emotional shackles back with them. Perhaps it was their transformation, their literal passage through death, which had bolstered my own faith and resolve and willingness to engage the adventure. Perhaps this courage stemmed from my growing acceptance that these friends had been lost to me, and so I had not reclaimed the fear that they could be lost to me.

More likely, it was something more, something rooted in the twining of my core beliefs. In the course of events, you do what you think is right and proper, and hold faith that such a course will lead to good ends. To believe less . . . if this is what I truly hold in my heart and proclaim, then what a coward I would be to deny such a course out of fear, any fear, even fear for the safety of my beloved companions.

I spoke purely on reflex to the news of Entreri's capture, spouting from the gut the course I knew to be correct, but when I went back and examined that moment, I discovered much more about myself indeed.

And much more about my friends, for the second revelation in that moment came with their response. They did not hesitate in the least, and indeed were eager for the fight—as eager as I. Even within Regis, there was no fear. This was the course, the correct path, and so we would walk it.

And so we did. I have not walked this lightly in decades, since long before Catti-brie was first lost to me in the advent of the Spellplague. So many times have I strived for this freedom, wandering from Mithral Hall with Catti-brie after its reclamation, time and again resolving to find joy.

But this was different. This wasn't a considered thought, a spoken determination or pledge. This was what I have been seeking, come full circle from the time when Wulfgar and I entered the lair of the verbeeg named Biggrin. This choice was without a second thought— there was a problem and so we would go and fix it, and we would go brimming with confidence in ourselves, with faith in each other.

"Think we might be warnin' them drow that they'll get some more o' their kin and make it more of a fight?" Bruenor had joked, but it almost didn't seem like a joke at that time.

Because we knew in our hearts that we'd prove victorious.

Because no other outcome was acceptable.

It was just that simple.

Yet these were dark elves in the road ahead, a sizable number, and a band that had already managed to somehow defeat and capture Artemis Entreri and the others, and so as we began our steps, doubts crept in.

Not doubts regarding our chosen course, but doubts about whether or not we could succeed.

And doubts regarding how high the price might prove.

But this is our way.

This is our creed.

This is the mantra of the Companions of the Hall.

It can be no other way.

And since we knew our course to be true, doubts could not equal regret.

No matter the price.

Rise of the King

How much easier sound my footfalls when I know I am walking a road of righteousness, when I know that my course is true. Without doubt, without hesitation, I stride, longing to get to the intended goal, knowing that when I have arrived there I will have left in my wake a better path than that which I walked.

Such was the case in my road back to Gauntlgrym, to rescue a lost friend. And such was the case leaving that dark place, to Port Llast to return the rescued captives to their homes and proper place.

And so now the road to Longsaddle, where Thibbledorf Pwent will be freed of his curse. Without hesitation, I stride.

What of our intended journey after that, to Mithral Hall, to Many Arrows . . . to start a war?

Will my steps slow as the excitement of adventuring with my old friends ebbs under the weight of the darkness before us? And if I cannot come to terms with Catti-brie's assertions of goblinkin as irredeemable, or cannot agree with Bruenor's insistence that the war has already begun in the form of orc raids, then what does this discordance portend for the friendship and unity of the Companions of the Hall?

I will not kill on the command of another, not even a friend. Nay, to free my blades, I must be convinced heart and soul that I strike for justice or defense, for a cause worth fighting for, worth dying for, and most importantly, worth killing for.

That is paramount to who I am and to how I have determined to live my life. It is not enough for Bruenor to declare war on the orcs of Many Arrows and begin its prosecution. I am not a mercenary, for gold coins or for friendship. There must be more.

There must be my agreement with the choice.

I will enjoy the journey to Mithral Hall, I expect. Surrounding me will be those friends I hold most dear, as we walk the new ways together again. But likely my stride will be a bit tighter, perhaps a bit heavier, the hesitance of conscience pressing down.

Or not conscience, perhaps, but confusion, for surely I am not convinced, yet neither am I unconvinced!

Simply put, I am not sure. Because even though Catti-brie's words, so she says and so I believe, come from Mielikki, they are not yet that which I feel in my own heart—and that must be paramount. Yes, even above the whispers of a goddess!

Some would call that insistence the height of hubris, and pure arrogance, and perhaps they would be right in some regard to place that claim upon me. To me, though, it is not arrogance, but a sense of deep personal responsibility. When first I found the goddess, I did so because the description of Mielikki seemed an apt name for that which I carried in my thoughts and heart. Her tenets aligned with my own, so it seemed. Else, she would mean no more to me than any other in the named pantheon of Toril's races.

For I do not want a god to tell me how to behave. I do not want a god to guide my movements and actions—nay! Nor do I want a god's rules to determine that which I know to be right or to outlaw that which I know to be wrong!

For I surely do not need to fear the retribution of a god to keep my path aligned with what is in my heart. Indeed, I see such justifications for behavior as superficial and ultimately dangerous. I am a reasoning being, born with conscience and an understanding of what is right and what is wrong. When I stray from that path, the one most offended is not some unseen and extra-worldly deity whose rules and mores are relayed, and often subjectively interpreted—inevitably by mortal priests and priestesses with humanoid failings. Nay, the one most wounded by the digressions of Drizzt Do'Urden, is Drizzt Do'Urden!

It can be no other way. I did not hear the call of Mielikki when I fell into the gray-toned company of Artemis Entreri, Dahlia, and the others. It was not the instructions of Mielikki that made me, at long last, turn away from Dahlia on the slopes of Kelvin's Cairn, not unless those instructions are the same ones etched upon my heart and my conscience.

Which, if true, brings me back full circle to the time when I found Mielikki.

At that moment, I did not find a supernatural mother to hold the crossbar to the strings supporting a puppet named Drizzt.

At that moment, I found a name for that which I hold as true. And so, I insist, the goddess is in my heart, and I need look no further than there to determine my course.

Or perhaps I am just arrogant.

So be it.

I have lived through two centuries, and much of those years have known conflict—battle and war, monstrous ambushes and unexpected dangers.

Yet if I add together all of the actual fighting I have done in my life, that total measure of time would pale against the number of practice hours I might devote to my fighting in a single tenday! Indeed, how many hundreds of hours, thousands of days of time, have I spent in turning my weapons against imaginary opponents, training my muscles to bring the blade to bear as fast as I can manage, in perfect balance, at the right angle, at the right moment?

In a single session of training, I might execute a middle thrust more times than in all the fights I have ever known, combined. This is the way of the warrior, the only way, and the way, I have come to know as truth, of anyone and everyone who deigns to rise to excellence, the way of anyone and everyone who seeks perfection even while knowing that there is no such thing.

For there is no perfect strike, no perfect defense, no perfection of the muscles. The word itself defines a state that cannot be improved, but such is not the case, is never the case with muscle and mind and technique.

So there is no state of perfection, but to seek it is not folly, nay, for it is that very seeking, the relentless journey, which defines the quality of the warrior.

When you see the journey and focus not merely on the goal, you learn humility.

A warrior must be humble.

Too often do people too greatly measure their lives by their goals, and, subsequently, by that which they consider accomplishments. I have reflected on this many times in my life and so the wisdom of years has taught me to constantly move the goal just beyond my stretching reach. For is the downside to achievement complacency? I have come to believe that too often do we name a goal and achieve it, then think the journey at its end.

I seek perfection, with my blades, with my body. I know there is no such thing, and that knowledge drives me forward, every day, and never inspires frustration or regret. My goal is unattainable, but the truth is that it is my journey toward that goal which is more important.

This is true of every goal of every person, but rarely do we see it. We seek goals as if their achievement will grant magical happiness and unending fulfillment, but is that ever the case? Bruenor would find Mithral Hall, and so he did—and how many years subsequent to that achievement did my dwarf friend seek ways to un-discover the hall?

At least, to remove himself from the goal he had set, as he sought new adventures, new roads, and new goals, and ultimately abdicated his throne in Mithral Hall altogether!

As this is true for the king, so it is true for the commoner, so it is true for almost everyone, living their lives in a mad rush for the next "if only," and in doing so, missing the most important truth of all.

The journey is more important than the goal, for while the goal might be worthwhile, the journey is, in fact, the thread of your life.

And so I set an unreachable goal: perfection of the body, perfection in battle.

That lifelong quest keeps me alive.

How many times have I narrowly escaped the bite of a monstrous maw, or the murderous edge of an enemy's blade? How many times have I won out because of the memory within my muscles, their ability to move as I need of them before I register the thought to move them? The relentless practice, the slow dance, the swift dance, the repetition of repetition, ingrains carefully considered movements to the point of mere reflex. When I dance, I see in my mind's eye the angle of my opponent's attack, the balance of his feet, the posture of his form. I close my eyes and put the image there in my mind, and react to that image with my body, carefully calculating the proper response, the correct parry or riposte, the advantage and opening.

Many heartbeats will pass in that single imagined movement, and many times will many heartbeats pass as the movement is executed again and again, and altered, perhaps, as better angles present themselves to my practiced imagination. Over and over, I will do this same dance. The pace increases—what took fifty heartbeats will take forty-nine, then forty-eight, and down the line.

And when in real combat my eyes register the situation pictured in my mind's eye during practice, the response will happen without conscious thought, a flicker of recognition demanding reflexive counters that might be fully played before the time span of a single beat of my heart.

This is the way of the warrior, honing the muscles to act correctly upon the slightest call, and training the mind to trust.

Aye, there's the rub of it all! Training the body is easy, and it is useless if the mind, too, cannot be properly conditioned.

This is the calm of the hero.

From my experiences and encounters, from speaking to warriors, wizards, priests, from watching incredible courage under incredible duress, I have come to believe that in this regard, there are three kinds of people: those who run from danger, those who freeze when in danger, and those who run into danger. This is no great revelation to anyone, I expect, nor would I expect anyone to believe of himself or herself anything but the latter of those three choices!

But that reaction, to run toward danger, to face it forthright and calmly, is the least likely among all the races, even the drow and even the dwarves.

The moment of surprise stuns the sensibilities. Often will a person caught in a sudden emergency spend too long in simply processing the truth of the moment, denying its reality as that very reality overwhelms the onlooker.

"It cannot be!" are among the most common of final words.

Even when the situation is consciously accepted, too many thoughts often blur the reaction. When faced with a grievously wounded companion, for example, a person's fears of unintentionally doing something harmful can hold back the bandage while the friend bleeds out.

When battle is joined, the situation becomes even more complicated, for there is also the matter of conscience and fear. Archers who can hit a target from a hundred paces often miss an enemy at much closer range, a much easier shot. Perhaps it is conscience, a nerve in a person's soul telling him that he is not a killer, that he should not kill. Perhaps it is fear, since the consequences of missing the mark could soon thereafter prove fatal to the shooter!

In the drow martial academy of Melee-Magthere, when I began

my training, one of our first classes involved an unexpected attack by duergar marauders. The raiders burst through the doors of the training hall and took down the instructors in a matter of eye-blinks, leaving the students, young drow all, to fend or to die.

I witnessed dark elves of noble houses fleeing out the back of the chamber—some threw down their weapons as they went, screaming in terror. Others stood dumbfounded, easy kills for the enemy gray dwarves (had it been an actual ambush).

A few leaped in for the battle. I was among that group. It wasn't courage that drove my feet forward, but instant calculation—for I understood that my duty, my best chance for doing the greatest good for Menzoberranzan and my fellows at the Academy, and indeed, my best chance for surviving, lay forward, in the fight, ready to do battle. I don't know how, but in that moment of sudden and overpowering stress, my mind overcame my heart, my fears fell away beneath the call of my duty.

This expression and reaction, the masters of the academy called "the calm of the hero," and we who faced the duergar properly were acknowledged, if not applauded.

For those who ran or froze, there came angry recriminations, but none were summarily dismissed from the Academy, a clear signal that the masters had expected as much. Nay, those who failed were trained— we were all trained—hour after hour, long day after day, endlessly, relentlessly, brutally.

This test was repeated many months later, in the form of another unexpected battle with a different enemy in a different location.

Now many more of us had been taught what some of us had instinctively known, and relying on that training, few fled and fewer froze in place. Our enemy in that battle in a wide tunnel just outside the city was a band of goblins, and this time, unlike with the duergar, they had been instructed to actually attack us.

But this time, unlike with the duergar, the ambushers met a force that had trained under skilled masters, not just physically, but mentally. Hardly a scratch showed on black drow skin when the last goblin fell dead.

Those dark elves who fled or froze, however, would get no more chances in Melee-Magthere. They were not possessed of the mind of a warrior and so they were dismissed, summarily.

Many, I later learned, were also dismissed from their houses and families in shame.

In the cold and heartless calculations of the Spider Queen and her wicked matrons, there is no place in Menzoberranzan for those who cannot learn the way of the warrior.

Watching Regis these last tendays reminded me of those days in Melee-Magthere. My halfling friend returned to mortal life determined that he would rewrite the impulses in his heart and brain, that he would teach himself the way of the warrior. When I consider my own experiences, and the progress of those many dark elves who failed the first encounter with the gray dwarves, but fought well against the goblins, I nod and understand better the truth of this new and formidable companion.

Regis sometimes calls himself Spider Parrafin, the name he found in this new life, but in the end, he is Regis, the same Regis we knew before, but one who through determination and the pursuit of an unattainable goal has found confidence enough in himself to walk the road of the warrior.

He has confided to me that he still has doubts and fears, at which I laughed.

For that, my halfling friend, is a truth universal to all the folk of all the reasoning races.

⁓

It itches on the collective consciousness of a society, nagging and nattering, whispering unease.

The tiny bubbles of criticism appear, about the bottom of the pot at first, hanging on, secret.

Quiet.

They dart upward, roiling the surface, just a few, then a few more, then a cascade.

This is the critical moment, when the leaders must step forth as one to calm the brew, to lift the pot from the fire, but too often, I fear, it is the ambitious opposition to these leaders stoking the flames among the citizenry, poking the folk with one malicious whisper after another.

Veracity matters not; the emotional response takes hold and will not let go.

The bubbles become a boil, the heat flowing through the water and wafting up into the air on the souls of the many who will surely die in this symphony of hatred, this expression of rage seeking focus.

This war.

I have seen it over and over through the decades, in campaigns sometimes worthy, but most often involving nefarious designs beneath the lies and feigned purposes. And in that turmoil and misery and carnage, the warrior is held high and the flag is tightly wrapped—too tightly to allow for any questioning of purpose and method.

This is how society is convinced to plant the fireball beneath its own pot.

And when it is over, when the rubble replaces the homes and the graveyards overfill and still the bodies rot in the streets, do we look back and wonder how it came to this.

That is the greatest tragedy, that the only time when questioning is allowed is when the ultimate failure of war has come to pass.

When the families are shattered.

When the innocent are slaughtered.

But what of war against monstrous intrusion, against the goblinkin and giantkind, would-be conquerors? Catti-brie, with Bruenor's loud echo, insisted to me that this was different, that these races, on the word of Mielikki herself, could not be viewed through the prism we hold to measure the rational and goodly races—or even the rational and not-so-goodly societies like that of my own people. Goblinkin and giantkind are different, so they assert, in that their malicious ways are not the teachings of an aberrant society, but a matter much deeper, to the very soul of the creatures.

Creatures?

How easily does that pejorative flow from my lips when I ponder the orcs and goblins of the world! Even with my experiences telling me differently, as with Nojheim the goblin, the slave.

It is all too confusing, and in the heat of that boiling pot, I desperately want to hold on to Catti-brie's words. I want to believe that those I shoot down or cut down are unrepentant and foul, are ultimately destructive and wholly irredeemable.

Else, how would I ever look in a mirror again?

I admit my relief upon entering the Silver Marches to find the Kingdom of Many Arrows marching to war.

My relief upon finding war . . .

Can there be a more discordant thought? How can war—any war—be seen as a relief? It is the tragic failure of better angels, the loss of reason to emotion, the surrender of the soul to the baser instincts.

And yet I was relieved to find that Many Arrows had marched, and I would be lying to myself to deny it. I was relieved for Bruenor, for he would have started a war, I am confident, and so the inevitable misery would then have weighed more heavily upon his shoulders.

I am relieved for Catti-brie, so determined in her declaration, her epiphany that there can be no redemption for goblinkin.

This is her interpretation of the song of the goddess.

Her interpretation shakes my faith in the goddess.

She is not as sure of herself as she claimed; her voice before we faced this truth of war held steadier than now, as we huddle against Nesmé's wall awaiting the next charge, awaiting the next round of carnage. Her fireballs and fire pets have slain many these days, and have done so in gallant and correct defense of the city.

And still I see the perpetual wince in her fair face, the pain in her blue eyes, the frown beneath her mask of smile. She holds to Mielikki's words, her own proclamations, and hurls her spells with deadly force.

But each death within and without Nesmé's walls takes from her, wounds her heart, crushes her hopes.

"It's what it be," Athrogate keeps saying as he stalks about the parapets.

Indeed, but "what it be" is not what Catti-brie wishes it could be, and so the battle pains her greatly and taxes her heart more than her body and mind.

For that I am glad. It is one of the reasons I so love her.

And so I can be relieved for my dear friends, for their hearts and the scars they will carry from this war—there are always scars from war!—and still be dismayed by the carnage and brutality and the sheer stupidity of waging a war, this war, in the Silver Marches.

If we measure victory as a condition better than what was in place before the conflict, then there will be no winners.

Of that I am certain.

Vengeance of the Iron Dwarf

Lost again.

It has become a recurring nightmare among my companions, both these old friends returned and the newer companions I traveled beside in recent times. So many times have I, have we, been thrown to a place of hopelessness. Turned to stone, captured by a powerful necromancer, captured by the drow, even dead for a hundred years!

And yet, here we are, returned. At times it seems to me as if the gods are watching us and intervening.

Or perhaps they are watching us and toying with us.

And now we have come to that point again, with Regis and Wulfgar lost to us in the tunnels of the Upperdark. There was an aura of finality to their disappearance, when the devilishly trapped wall stone snapped back into place. We heard Regis fall away, far away. It didn't seem like a free fall, and orcs are known to prefer traps that capture victims rather than kill them outright.

That is not a reason to hope, however, given the way orcs typically deal with their captives.

In the first days of our return, I convinced King Connerad to double the guard along the lower tunnels, even to allow me to slip out from the guarded areas still secured as Mithral Hall, out into the regions we know to be under the control of the orcs. Bruenor begged to come with me, but better off am I navigating alone in the Underdark. Catti-brie begged me to remain in the hall, and claimed that she would go out with her magic to scout for our friends.

But I could not sit tight in the comfort of Mithral Hall when I feared they were out there, when I heard, and still hear, their cries for help in my every thought. A recurring nightmare invades my reverie: my dear friends frantic and fighting to get to the lower tunnels still held by the dwarves, but by way of an environment unsuited to a halfling and a human. One dead end after another, one ambush after another. In my thoughts, I see them battling fiercely, then fleeing back the way they had come, orc spears and orc taunts chasing them back into the darkness.

If I believe they are out there, how can I remain behind the iron walls?

I cannot deny that we in the hall have much to do. We have to find a way to break the siege and begin to turn the battles above, else the Silver Marches are lost. The misery being inflicted across the lands . . .

We have much to do.

Nesmé has fallen.

We have much to do.

The other dwarf citadels are fully besieged.

We have much to do.

The lone lifelines, the tunnels connecting Adbar, Felbarr, and Mithral Hall, are under constant pressure now.

We have much to do.

And so much time has passed in dark silence. We traveled to Citadel Felbarr and back, many tendays have passed without a hint from Wulfgar and Regis.

Are they out there, hiding in dark tunnels or chained in an orc prison? Do they cry out in agony and hopelessness, begging for their friends to come and rescue them? Or begging for death, perhaps?

Or are they now silenced forevermore?

All reason points to them being dead, but I have seen too much now to simply accept that. I hold out hope and know from experience that it cannot be a false hope wrought of emotional folly.

But neither is it more than that: a hope.

They fell, likely to their deaths, either immediately or in orc imprisonment. Even if that is not the case, and their drop through the wall took them to a separate tunnel free from the orcs and drow that haunt the region, so many tendays have passed without word. They are not suited to the Underdark. For all their wonderful skills, in that dark place, in this dark time, it is highly unlikely that Wulfgar and Regis could survive.

And so I hold out that finger of hope, but in my heart, I prepare for the worst.

I am strangely at peace with that. And it is not a phony acceptance where I hide the truth of my pain under the hope that it is mere speculation. If they are gone, if they have fallen, I know that they died well.

It is all we can ask now, any of us. There is an old drow saying—I heard it used often to describe Matron Mother Baenre in the days of my youth: "qu'ella bondel," which translates to "gifted time" or "borrowed time." The matron mother was old, older than any other, older than any drow in memory. By all reason, she should have been dead long before, centuries before Bruenor put his axe through her head, and so she had been living on qu'ella bondel.

My companions, returned from the magical forest of Iruladoon, through their covenant with Mielikki, are living on qu'ella bondel. They all know it, they have all said it.

And so we accept it.

If Wulfgar and Regis do not return to us, if they are truly gone— and Catti-brie has assured me that the goddess will not interfere in such matters again—then so be it. My heart will be heavy, but it will not break. We have been given a great gift, all of us. In saying hello once more, we all knew that we were making it all right to say farewell.

But still . . .

Would I feel this way if Catti-brie were down there?

∽

"I am not a courageous goblin. I prefer to live, though oftentimes I wonder what my life is truly worth."

Those words haunt me.

In light of the revelations Catti-brie has offered of my goddess, Mielikki, that all of goblinkin are irredeemably evil and should be rightfully put to the sword, those words haunt me.

For they were spoken to me by a goblin named Nojheim, a fellow of intelligence and wit, surprisingly so to me, who had never so deeply and honestly conversed with a goblin before. He claimed cowardice because he would not stand up to the humans who had captured him, beaten him, and enslaved him. He questioned the worth of his life because he was truly that, a slave.

They came for Nojheim and they caught him, and it is forever my shame that I was not able to help him, for when I next saw him, he had been hanged by the neck by his tormentors. Reeling from the scene, I stumbled back to my bed, and that very night I wrote, "There are events that are forever frozen in one's memory, feelings that exude a more complete aura, a memory so vivid and so lasting. I remember the wind at that horrible moment. The day, thick with low clouds, was unseasonably warm, but the wind, on those occasions it had to gust, carried a chilling bite, coming down from the high mountains and carrying the sting of deep snow with it. That wind was behind me, my long white hair blowing around the side of my face, my cloak pressing tightly against my back as I sat on my mount and stared helplessly at the high cross-pole.

"The gusty breeze kept Nojheim's stiff and bloated body turning slightly, the bolt holding the hemp rope creaking in mournful, helpless protest.

"I will see him forever."

And so I do see him still, and whenever I manage to put that terrible memory out of thought, I am reminded of it.

Never more poignantly than now, with war brewing, with Bruenor deriding the Treaty of Garumn's Gorge as his worst error, with Catti-brie, my beloved Catti-brie, insisting that on Mielikki's word, on the sermon of the goddess we both hold dear, those humans in that long ago day, in that long-deserted village along the Surbrin whose name I cannot remember were justified in their actions.

I cannot reconcile it. I simply cannot.

The implications of Catti-brie's claim overwhelm me and loosen the sand beneath my feet, until I am sinking into despair. For when I kill, even in battle, even in righteous defense, I feel that a part of my soul departs with the vanquished foe. I feel as if I am a bit less goodly. I mend my soul by reminding myself of the necessity of my actions, of course, and so I am not locked in the dark wings of guilt in any way.

But what if I carry Mielikki's claims to their logical conclusions? What if I force my way into an orc or goblin settlement that has shown no aggression, no intent to wage war or commit any other crimes? What if I find that nursery as Catti-brie mocked in her dwarven brogue, with the old dwarven cry of "Where's the babies' room?"

Surely then, by the sermon of Mielikki, I am to slaughter the goblin children, infants even. And slaughter the elderly and infirm even if they have committed no crimes or no acts of aggression.

No.

I will not.

Such an act rings in my heart and soul as unjust and cruel. Such an act erases the line between good and evil. Such an act would stain my own conscience, whatever Mielikki's claims!

And that, I believe, is the ultimate downfall of reasoning beings.

What pain to the murderer, to the heart and soul of the one who would kill the elderly and infirm orc, or the goblin child? What stain, forevermore, to steal the confidence, the righteousness, the belief in oneself that is so critical for the sensibilities of the warrior?

If I must wage terrible battle, then so be it. If I must kill, then so be it. If I must.

Only if I must!

My clear conscience protects me from a pit too dark to contemplate, and that is a place I hope Bruenor and Catti-brie never enter.

But what does this mean in my servitude to Mielikki, to the concept of a goddess I believed at peace with that which was in my own heart? What does this mean for the unicorn—her steed—that I call from the whistle about my neck? What does this mean for the very return of my friends, the Companions of the Hall? They are beside me once more, we all agree, by the blessing of, and at the suffrage of, Mielikki.

Catti-brie claims the voice of Mielikki with regards to the goblinkin: she is a priestess of Mielikki, with magical powers granted her by the goddess. How could she not speak truly on this matter?

Aye, Catti-brie relayed the truth of what the goddess told her.

That notion pains me most of all. I feel betrayed. I feel discordant, my voice shrill and out of tune with the song of the goddess.

Yet if my heart is not true to the word of Mielikki . . .

Fie these gods! What beings are these who would play so cruelly with the sensibilities of rational, conscientious mortals?

I have racked my brain and scoured my memories for evidence that I am wrong. I have tried to convince myself that the goblin named Nojheim was actually just manipulating me to try to save its skin.

Nojheim was no poor victim of the humans, but a vile and conniving murderer kept alive by their mercy alone.

So it must be.

And so I cannot believe. I simply cannot. I was not. I am not, wrong in my initial understanding about Nojheim. Nor was I wrong about Jessa, a half-orc, a friend, a companion, who traveled for years beside me: Thibbledorf Pwent: and Bruenor Battlehammer himself.

But I must believe that I was wrong, or must accept that Mielikki is. And how can that be?

How can the goddess I hold as the epitome of goodliness be wrong? How can Mielikki's song chip the veneer of truth I hold in my heart?

Are these gods, then, fallible beings looking over us as if we were no more than pieces on a sava board? Am I a pawn?

Then my reason, my conscience, my independent thought and moral judgment must be cast aside, subjugated to the will of a superior being . . .

But no, I cannot do this. Surely not in matters of simple right and wrong. Whatever Mielikki might tell me, I cannot excuse the actions of that slaver Rico and the others who tormented, tortured, and ultimately murdered Nojheim. Whatever Mielikki might tell me, it must hold in accordance with that which I know to be true and right.

It must! This is not arrogance, but the cry that an internal moral compass, the conscience of a reasoning being, cannot be disregarded by edict. I call not for anarchy, I offer nothing in the way of sophistry, but I insist that there must be universal truths about right and wrong.

And one of those truths has to be that the content of character must outweigh the trappings of a mortal coil.

I feel lost. In this, the Winter of the Iron Dwarf, I feel sick and adrift.

As I ask of the dwarves, the humans, indeed even the elves, that they view my actions and not the reputation of my heritage, so I must afford the same courtesy, the same politesse, the same decent deference, to all reasoning beings.

My hands shake now as I read my writings of a century before, for then, with my heart full of Mielikki's grace, so I believed, I revealed little doubt.

"Sunset," I wrote, and I see that descending fiery orb as clearly now as on that fateful day a century and more removed. "Another day surrenders to the night as I perch here on the side of a mountain, not so far from Mithral Hall.

"The mystery of the night has begun, but does Nojheim know now the truth of a greater mystery? I often wonder of those who have gone before me, who have discovered what I cannot until the time of my own death. Is Nojheim better off now than he was as Rico's slave?

"If the afterlife is one of justice, then surely he is.

"I must believe this to be true, yet still it wounds me to know that I inadvertently played a role in the unusual goblin's death, both in capturing him and in going to him later, going to him with hopes that he could not afford to hold. I cannot forget that I walked away from Nojheim, however well-intentioned I might have been. I rode for Silverymoon and left him vulnerable, left him in wrongful pain.

"And so I learn from my mistake.

"Forever after, I will not ignore such injustice. If ever I chance upon one of Nojheim's spirit and Nojheim's peril again, then let his wicked master be wary. Let the lawful powers of the region review my actions and exonerate me if that is what they perceive to be the correct course. If not . . .

"It does not matter. I will follow my heart."

Three lines stand clear to me now in light of the revelations offered by Catti-brie.

"If the afterlife is one of justice, then surely he is," so I told myself, so I believed, and so I must believe. Yet if the afterlife is the domain of Mielikki, then surely Nojheim cannot have found a better place.

"Forever after, I will not ignore such injustice," I vowed, and so I mean to hold true to that vow, for I believe in the content of the sentiment.

Yes, Bruenor, my dear friend. Yes, Catti-brie, my love and my life. Yes, Mielikki, to whom I ascribed the tenets that make me whole.

"It does not matter. I will follow my heart."

Brother Afafrenfere was sitting on a large stone—reclining actually, and looking up at the blackened sky, where the stars should have been, though alas, there are no stars to be found in the Silver Marches at this dark time. He was not startled by my presence, for surely he knew that the stone he carried was a beacon to the dragon Ilnezhara, and so allowed her to use her magic to teleport me in beside him.

I greeted him, and he gave a slight nod, but he just kept staring up into the darkness. And he did so with an expression I surely recognized, for it is one I have often worn myself.

"What troubles you, Brother?" I asked.

He didn't look over, didn't sit up.

"I have found a power I do not quite understand," he finally admitted.

He went on to explain to me that he had not come to the Silver Marches, to this war, alone—and that not even counting Amber, Jarlaxle, and the dragon sisters. He tapped a gemstone set in a band around his forehead and told me that it was a magical phylactery, now holding the disembodied spirit of a great monk named Kane, a legendary Grandmaster of Flowers of Afafrenfere's Order of the Yellow Rose. With that phylactery, Kane had made the trip beside Afafrenfere, indeed, even within the thoughts of Afafrenfere.

"To guide me and to teach me, and so he has and so he is."

Then Afafrenfere did sit up, and detailed for me his feats of battle, where swarms of goblins would disappear in front of his jabbing and spinning limbs, where he could strike and be on his way before his opponent could begin to counter, where he had killed a giant with a slap of his hand, then using that connection as a conduit so that he could fashion his own life energy as a missile and use it to break the life energy of the giant.

I didn't quite understand the technique, but the man's awe at his accomplishments spoke volumes to me. They reminded me of my own realizations that I had attained the highest levels of skill in the drow academy of Melee-Magthere, that I had somehow learned to be as fine a warrior as Zaknafein, my father.

I was more surprised than Zaknafein on that day so long ago when I finally defeated him in our sparring matches. I had planned the victory down to every block and every step, to every twist and angle, but still, when I at last realized the enormity of what I had accomplished, I had spent some long hours indeed simply staring and pondering.

And so I thought I understood what Afafrenfere was feeling, but soon I discovered that his dilemma was not merely surprise at his own prowess. No, he summed it up in one word, spoken humbly and with a clear tremor in his soft voice: "Responsibility."

There is an emotional weight that accompanies the expectations of others. When desperate people look to you for help, and you know that if you cannot help them, no one else can . . .

Responsibility.

"We will guide the dwarves well in this battle day," I remember saying to Afafrenfere, and remember, too, that he was shaking his head with dismissal even as the words left my mouth. Not because he doubted our mission this day—indeed, he was actually more confident in it than I—but because Afafrenfere was talking in grander terms.

He was talking about the man he had been, and now, with this growth, about the man he felt he now needed to be.

Afafrenfere's situation was complicated by the sudden infusion of power, I expect. Grandmaster Kane was training him, intimately, and so he was rising to a skill level he had never before imagined, and the shock of that had awakened within him a realization that he was part of something bigger than himself, and responsible for things beyond his personal needs.

I hadn't ever really thought of my own situation in those terms, not specifically and not with any confusion, but only because my very nature from the earliest days of self-reflection aligned me with those same beliefs and expectations for myself that Afafrenfere was apparently now experiencing as a sudden and confusing epiphany.

I hadn't the time to sit and discuss it with him any longer, of course, for we were off immediately to find King Harnoth and his fighting band, that we could guide them to their place in the upcoming maelstrom.

But I couldn't help but grin as I made my way through the pine-covered slope beside the monk from the Monastery of the Yellow Rose. He was now learning the same epiphany I had long hoped to see within Artemis Entreri.

I could see the trepidation on Brother Afafrenfere's face, but I knew that it would soon enough fade, to be replaced by a sense of true contentment. He was given something, a blessing, that most people could never experience. Through the help of Grandmaster Kane, he was given a glimpse of his potential, and so he knew that potential to be true and attainable.

So many people never see that—they may quietly hope for it, or imagine it in their private moments, but they will never believe in it, in themselves, to go out and reach for it. Fear of failure, of judgment, of being mocked, even, will keep them curled in a bubble of security, averting risks by keeping their hands close to their vests.

So many people live small, afraid to try to do great things, conditioned from childhood to find their place in the order of things, the proverbial "pecking order," and simply stay there, curled and small, their arms in close.

Wanting to reach, but afraid to grab—it is the comfort of familiarity, of a niche carved within the expectations and judgment of others.

"Know your place" is a common refrain, and so many other similarly destructive "truisms" chase us throughout our lives, particularly in those early years, exactly when we're trying to determine that very place. Voices of doubt and warning, often spoken as advice, but always limiting, always designed to keep our arms in close, that we will not reach.

Because when we reach, when we seek that place we have seen only in our imagination, we threaten the order of things, and threaten most especially the place of those who have found a better roost.

And when we dare to reach, and when we excel, and when we gain from our reaching a level of power or wealth or privilege, then, too, comes the weight of that which Brother Afafrenfere was contemplating when I encountered him on the other end of Ilnezhara's teleport spell: responsibility.

For now Brother Afafrenfere understood that he could accomplish much more than he had ever dreamed possible, and so now his heart demanded of him a measure of responsibility.

That weight, so clear in his eyes when I came upon him, reminded me that Brother Afafrenfere was a good man.

Homecoming

Archmage

Never have I so clearly come to know that that which I do not know,
I do not know.

I did not expect to rise into the air in the middle of that field,
in the middle of the dwarven army. When beams of light burst from
my fingertips, from my feet, from my chest, from my eyes, they came
without conscious thought—I was nothing more than a conduit. And I
watched as surprised as any around as those light beams shot into the
sky and melted the roiling blackness that had darkened the land.

When I sank back down from the unexpected levitation, back to
the ground among my friends, I saw tears of joy all about me. Dwarves
and humans, halflings and elves alike, fell to the ground on their
knees, paying homage to Mielikki, thanking her for destroying the
darkness that had engulfed the Silver Marches, their land, their home.

No one shed more tears of joy than Catti-brie, chosen of Mielikki,
returned to my side by the grace of the goddess, and now, clearly,
finding some resolution to the trials for which she and my other
friends were returned to the realm of the living.

Catti-brie had oft speculated that her battle with Dahlia in the
primordial chamber of Gauntlgrym had been no more than a proxy

fight between Mielikki and Lolth, but of course, she could not be certain. But now this spectacle of my body being used in so dramatic a manner to defeat the darkness, the Darkening, of the Spider Queen, could not be questioned, so she believed, so they all believed.

But yet, I do not know.

I remain unconvinced!

I was the conduit of Mielikki, so they say, so it would seem, for I am no magic-user and surely know of no such dweomer as the one that escaped my mortal coil. Surely something, some power, found its way through me, and surely it seems logical to ascribe that power to Mielikki.

And so, following that logic, I was touched by the hand of god.

Is it my own intrinsic skepticism then, my continual need to follow evidence, which prevents me from simply accepting this as true? For it simply did not seem to me to be that which they claim, but then, what might being so touched by a god actually feel like? I wonder.

This is my continuing dilemma, surely, my nagging agnosticism, my willingness to accept that I do not know and perhaps cannot know, coupled with my determination that such knowledge or lack thereof has no bearing—has to have no bearing—on how I conduct myself. I found Mielikki as a name to fit that which was already in my heart. When I learned of the goddess, of her tenets and ways, I found a melody consistent with the song of my own ethical beliefs and my own sense of community, with people and with nature about me.

It seemed a comfortable fit.

But never had I been able to truly separate the two, that which is in my heart and some extra-natural or supernatural other, whether ascribing that name to some higher level of existence or to, yes, a god indeed.

To me, Mielikki became a name to best describe that conscience within, and the code of existence that fit most smoothly. I did not find the need to search further, for the truth of Mielikki's existence or her place in the pantheon, or even the relationship of the one true god (or gods and goddesses, as the case may be) to the mortal beings roaming

Faerun, or more pointedly, to my own life. Ever has my chosen way come from within, not without, and truly, that is how I prefer it!

I did not know of the existence of, or the rumor of the existence of, some being named Mielikki when I walked out of Menzoberranzan. I knew only of Lolth, the Demon Queen of Spiders, and knew, too, that that which was in my heart could never reconcile to the demands of that evil creature. Often have I feared that had I remained in Menzoberranzan, I might have become akin to Artemis Entreri, and there is truth in that fear in regards to the hopelessness and apathy I see, or once saw, in the man. But long ago, I dismissed the possibility that I would have become like him in action, whatever my despair.

Even in the domain of the Demon Queen of Spiders, even surrounded by the vile acts and unacceptable nurture of my kin, I could not have gone against that which was in my heart. My internal god of conscience would not have allowed it. I would have been left a broken man, I do not doubt, but not, but never, a callous destroyer of others.

No, I say.

And so I came to the surface world and I found a name for my conscience, Mielikki, and I found others who shared my mores and tenets, and I was at spiritual peace.

Catti-brie's declaration regarding the irredeemable nature of evil of goblinkin and giantkind shook that tranquility, as surely as her tone (and that of Bruenor) shook my more earthly sensibilities. I knew in that moment that I was likely at odds with a pronouncement my beloved wife claimed had come straight from the goddess. I have tried to rationalize it and tried to accept it, and yet . . .

Discordance remains.

And now this. I was lifted into the air, my body used as a conduit, the result presenting light where there was once only darkness. It was good. Good—there is no other way to describe the change that Mielikki, if it was Mielikki (but how could it not have been Mielikki?), created through our magical communion.

Does not this godlike presence, then, command me to subjugate that which I believe to be just and right within my heart to the supposed command Mielikki relayed to me through Catti-brie? Am I not now, in the face of such powerful evidence, bound to dismiss my belief and accept the truth of the goddess's claim? When next I happen upon a nest of goblins, even if they are acting peaceably and bothering no one, am I therefore bound to battle within their home and slaughter them, every one, including children, including babies?

No, I say.

Because I cannot. I cannot dismiss that which is in my heart and conscience. I am a creature of intelligence and reason. I know what actions please me and put me at ease, and which pain me. I will kill a goblin in battle without regret, but I am no murderer, and will not be.

And that is my pain, and my burden. For if I am to accept Mielikki as my goddess, the circle cannot square, the yawning gulf of disagreement cannot be bridged.

Who are these gods we serve, this pantheon of the Realms, so rich and powerful and varied? If there is a universal truth, how then are there so many realizations of that truth, many similar, but each with rituals or specific demands to separate one from the other, sometimes by minute degree, sometimes by diametric opposition?

How can this be?

Yet there is universal truth, I believe—perhaps this is my one core belief!—and if that is so, then are not the majority of the pantheon claiming themselves as gods and goddesses truly frauds?

Or are they, as Bruenor had come to believe in the early years of his second life, cruel puppeteers and we their playthings?

It is all so confusing and all so tantalizingly close, but ever beyond the reach of mortal comprehension, I fear.

And so I am left again with that which is in my heart, and if Mielikki cannot accept that of me, then she chose the wrong conduit, and I named the wrong god.

Because despite what Catti-brie insisted, and what Bruenor came to declare with eager fire, I will continue to judge on the content of character and not the shape or color of a mortal coil. My heart demands no less of me, my spiritual peace must be held as the utmost goal.

With confidence do I declare that the edge of my scimitar will sooner find my own neck before it will cut the throat of a goblin child, or any child.

The winds of change have lifted the hair from my neck. They tickle me and tease me, and take me to a place unexpected.

My road has wound in circles these last years, from hearth and home to the open road, to trying to build anew with a group that was not of my own heart. And now the circle completes, back to where I began, it seems, but not so.

For these friends returned are not the friends I knew. They are very much akin in heart and duty, of course, and surely recognizable to me, but yet, they are different, in that they have seen a new light and way, a new perspective on mortality and death, and on the meaning of life itself. This attitude manifests itself most subtly, usually, but I see it there, in every Bruenor grumble, in every Catti-brie confidence, in every Regis fight, and in every Wulfgar laugh.

And now I see it in myself, as well. For these last decades, after the passing of Catti-brie and the others, and even before Bruenor fell in Gauntlgrym, I was restless, and quite content to be. I wanted to know what was around the next bend, any bend in the road, be it the quest to find Gauntlgrym or the years afterward when I led the band of Artemis Entreri, Dahlia, and the others. My home was in my memories—I neither wanted nor needed a replacement. For those memories were enough to sustain me and nourish me. I nearly lost myself in that long and winding journey to that ultimate conclusion, and would have, I know, had I not refused Dahlia on that hillside in Icewind Dale. There, again, I found myself, and so in the end, I survived. Drizzt Do'Urden, this person I strive to be, survived the trials.

And now I find myself on the road of adventure again with Catti-brie and Bruenor, and could anything be better? Ours is a noble quest, as much so as the one that reclaimed Mithral Hall that century and more ago. We march with songs and the cadence of dwarven boots, under the flags of three kings and with the flagons of five thousand grinning dwarven warriors.

Could anything be better?

Perhaps so if Wulfgar and Regis were still with us, and truly I miss them every day. But at the same time, I am happy for them, and hold confidence that we will meet again. I noted the sparkle in Regis's eyes whenever he spoke of Donnola Topolino, and I can only applaud the road he has chosen—and only be happier that mighty Wulfgar walks that road beside him! Woe to any ill-intentioned rogues who cross the path of that formidable pair!

They will come back. I have fretted on this for a while, but now I am convinced. This is not like the time long ago when Wulfgar abandoned us to return to Icewind Dale. Nay, on that occasion, I doubted that we would ever see Wulfgar again, and we would not have, none of us, except that Regis and I ventured to Icewind Dale. Even then, the reunion was . . . strange. For when Wulfgar left us those decades ago, he did so emotionally as well as physically.

That is not the case this time.

They will come back, and we will be victorious in Gauntlgrym. These things I believe, and so I am at peace, and excited and anxious all at once.

And nervous, I admit, and I am surprised by that truth. When we rejoined together atop Kelvin's Cairn that dark night, there was only elation. And as the shock of my friends returned from the dead wore away, I was left simply giddy, feeling blessed and fortunate beyond what anyone should ever expect.

In the early days back together, even when we returned to the Silver Marches and found ourselves embroiled in a war, we all had the sense that the Companions of the Hall survived on time borrowed from the gods, and that our end, for any of us, could come at any moment, and it would be all right, because we had found each other again and had left no words unsaid. Even though my four friends had begun a new life, living two decades and more with new identities, with new family, new friends, and for Regis at least, a new love in his life, our existence was to be enjoyed and appreciated day by day.

And it was . . . okay.

Soon after, Catti-brie, Bruenor, and I had come to believe that Wulfgar and Regis had fallen in the tunnels of the upper Underdark on our journey back to Mithral Hall. For months we had thought them lost to us forevermore, that they had journeyed once again into the realm of death, this time not to return.

And it was . . . okay.

The pain was there, to be sure, but still, we had been given the great gift of time together once more, and in the knowledge that our companionship was indeed rooted in mortality! I cannot emphasize that gift enough! Many times, I claim that a person must know he is going to die, must recognize and accept that basic truth of life, in order to defeat his fears and press on with a true sense of purpose in life. My friends knew that, and know that now, better than most.

They have seen the other side.

And when they are called again from this life, they go with acceptance, each, and not because they know a truth of immorality and eternity beyond the mortal coil—indeed Wulfgar, and even Regis, remain skeptical of the gods even after their ordeal in the enchanted forest of Iruladoon.

The close brush with death, indeed their decades in the clutches of something other than life, has given them, has given us all, both urgency and acceptance. It is a blessing, twice over.

Perhaps because of the passage of time, perhaps because of our victories and survival in the War of the Silver Marches, but now I have come to sense a change. That borrowed time seems less to me, now, as I grow comfortable with the return of my friends, alive and vibrant, and hopefully with many decades ahead of them—indeed, even discounting the possibility of an enemy blade cutting one of us low, Bruenor could well outlive me in natural years!

Or our end, any of us or all of us, could come this very day, or tomorrow. I've always known this, and make it a part of my daily routine to remind myself of it, but now that the newness of my friends' return has worn off, now that I have come to believe that they are here—they are really here, as surely and tangibly as they were when I first met Catti-brie on the slopes of Kelvin's Cairn, and she introduced me to Bruenor and Regis, and then Wulfgar came to us when he was defeated in battle by Bruenor.

It is new again, it is fresh, and it is, in terms of an individual's life, lasting.

And so I am nervous about going into battle, because now I am seeing the future once more as the comfort of home and of friends, and my Catti-brie, all about, and it is a future I long to realize!

In a strange way, I now see myself moving in the opposite direction of Wulfgar. He has returned carefree, ready to experience whatever the world might throw before him—in battle, in game, and in love. He lives for each moment, without regret.

Fully without regret, and that is no small thing. "Consequence" is not a word that now enters Wulfgar's conversation. He is returned to life to play, with joy, with lust, with passion.

I try to mirror that exuberance, and hope to find that joy, and know my lust in my love for Catti-brie, but while Wulfgar embraces the life of free-spirited nomad, a rapscallion even, finding adventure and entertainment where he may, I find myself suddenly intrigued by the permanency of hearth and home, a husband, among friends.

A father?

In the moment of my death, will I be surprised? In that instant? When the sword cuts my flesh, or the giant's hammer descends, or the dragon's flames curl my skin?

When I know it is happening, when I know beyond doubt that Death has come for me, will I be surprised or calm, accepting or panicked?

I tell myself that I am prepared. I have surrounded the question logically, rationally, removing emotion, accepting the inevitability. But knowing it will happen and knowing there is nothing I can do to stop it from happening is a different level of acceptance, perhaps, than any actual preparation for that one-time, ultimate event.

Can anything be more unsettling to conscious thought than the likely end of conscious thought?

This notion is not something I dwell upon. I do not go to my bed each night with the worry of the moment of death climbing under my blanket beside me. In merely asking this question—in the moment of my death, will I be surprised?—I suspect that I am entertaining the notion more than many, more than most, likely.

In many (in each) of us there is this deep-seated avoidance of, even denial of, the undeniable.

For others, there is the salve of religion. For some it is a false claim—more a hope than a belief. I know this because I have seen these faithful in their moment of death, and it is a terrifying moment for them. For others, it is a genuine, sanguine acceptance and belief in something better beyond.

This religious salve has never been my way. I know not why, but I am not so arrogant as to demean those who choose a different path through this muddled life and its inevitable end, or to pretend that they are somehow lesser of intellect, of moral integrity, or of courage, than I. For among that last group, those of deep faith, I would include my beloved wife, Catti-brie, so secure in her knowledge of what awaits when the scythe falls and her time in Faerun is at its end.

Would I see it differently had I been in that altered passage of time and space beside my four dear friends?

I honestly do not know.

Wulfgar was there, and he returns anew unconvinced of that which would have awaited him on the other side of that pond in the forest of Iruladoon. Indeed, Wulfgar confided to me that his certainty of the Halls of Tempus is less now than before his journey through death to return to this world. We live in a world of amazing magic. We assign to it names, and pretend to understand, and reduce it to fit our purposes.

More importantly, we reduce the beauty of the universe around us to fit our hopes and to chase away our fears.

I know the day will come. The enemy's sword, the giant's hammer, the dragon's breath. There is no escape, no alternate course, no luck of the draw.

The day will come.

Will I be surprised? Will I be prepared?

Can anyone be, truly?

Perhaps not, but again, this will not be that which chases me to my bed each night. Nay, I'll worry more for that which I can influence— my concern cannot be my inevitable demise, but rather, my actions in my waking life.

For before me, before us all, lie choices right and wrong, and clear to see. To follow my heart is to know contentment. To dodge the edicts of my heart, to convince myself through twisted words and feeble justifications to go against what I know to be true and right for the sake of glory or wealth or self-aggrandizement or any of the other mortal frailties, is, to my thinking, anathema to the concept of peace and justice, divine or otherwise.

And so to best prepare myself for that ultimate mortal moment is to live my life honestly, to myself, to the greater deeds and greater goods.

I do this not for divine reward. I do this not in fear of any god or divine retribution, or to ensure that there is no place for me in the Abyss or the Nine Hells.

I do this because of that which is in my heart. Once I gave it the name Mielikki. Now, given the edicts made in that name regarding goblinkin as relayed through Catti-brie, I am not so certain that Mielikki and my heart are truly aligned.

But no matter.

Am I prepared for the moment of my death?

No, I expect not.

But I am content and I am at peace. I know my guide, and that guide is my heart.

More than that, I cannot do.

Maestro

There comes a point in a life well lived where the gaze goes beyond the next horizon, to that inevitable time when this mortal coil feeds the worms. Life is a journey, a beauteous walk surrounded by such vastness of time and space that we cannot even truly comprehend, and so we make sense of what we can. We order our corner of the world and build security if we are fortunate, and perhaps, too, a family as part of a larger community.

The immediate needs consume so much of our time, the day-to-day trials that must be overcome. There is a measure of satisfaction in every small victory, in every meal earned, in the warmth of shelter on a cold winter's night.

This is the climb of life, but for those who are lucky enough, there comes a place where the mountain is topped and the needs are satisfied, and so the view grows grander. It is a subtle shift in the omnipresent question of a rational being, from "What can I build?" to "What will I leave behind?"

What will be the legacy of Drizzt Do'Urden? For those who remember my name when I am no more, what will they think? How much better might be the lives of those who follow me—my progeny, perhaps, if Catti-brie and I fruitfully go that route—because of my works here? I watched Bruenor bring forth the sarcophagi of King Connerad and King Emerus, the lava-encased bodies flanking the throne of Gauntlgrym. No less will they be remembered in Mithral Hall and Citadel Felbarr—all the Silver Marches for that matter—for many centuries to come.

Am I destined to become such a statue?

On a practical level, I doubt it, since I expect that much of my remaining life will be spent outside of Bruenor's domain. I will never forget him, nor he me, I am sure, but I sense that my days beside him are nearing their end. For all the love and respect I hold for King Bruenor, I would not plan to raise my children in a dwarven mine. Nor would Catti-brie, I am sure.

The road is wide open in front of us—to Longsaddle, of course, but only for now. One thing I have come to know in my two centuries of life is that the span of a few years is not a long time, and yet it is often an eventful time, with unanticipated twists and turns. Wherever that meandering road might take me, though, beside me goes an understanding now that my journey is less and less often what I need to do, and much more about what I want to do.

So many options, unbound by the shackles so many must wear. I am a fortunate man—that, I do not deny! I have sufficient wealth now and I am at peace. I have love all around me and am responsible to myself alone—and responsible to my wife only because I choose to be.

And so what will I do? What road shall I choose? What legacy shall I foment?

These are good questions, full of the promise of sublime reward, and I only wish that every man and woman of all the goodly races could find a moment such as this, a time of opportunities and of options. That I am here in this place of luxury is nothing short of remarkable. I do not know the odds of such an outcome for a homeless drow, a hunted rogue in the wilds of the Underdark, but I would bet them long indeed. So many fortunate twists and turns have I found on my journey, encounters with grand friends and marvelous mentors: Zaknafein, my father, and Montolio DeBrouchee! And Catti-brie, who helped me to find my heart and a courage of a different sort— the courage to stubbornly exist in a place where my people are not welcome.

And Bruenor, yes Bruenor—perhaps Bruenor above all others. It is incomprehensible that I was befriended by a dwarf king and taken in as a brother. Yes, it has been a reciprocal friendship. I helped Bruenor regain his throne, and walked beside him on his wider journey to bring his people together under the great homeland of Gauntlgrym. Between us, it seems, sits the very definition of friendship.

With all of this, here I am. So many battles I have fought, so many obstacles overcome, yet I cannot deny that good fortune has played a tremendous role in leading me to this place and this time. Every man, every woman, will find battles, will find enemies to overcome, be they goblins or disease, an ill child, a wound that will not heal, a dearth of food, the chill of winter, unrequited love, the absence of a friend. Life is a journey from trial to test, from love to hate, from friendship to grief. We each deal with unsettling uncertainty and we each march on, ever on, following the road that will ultimately lead to our grave.

What grand things might we do along that road? What side avenues will we build, that might start our children on their own walk, perhaps?

So I have found this turn of perspective. I have scaled the peak and look now upon a grand, grand view. I can thank a woman whose warm embrace brings me peace. I can thank the greatest friends any man might ever know. I can thank a dwarf king who found a rogue on the side of a lonely mountain in a forsaken land and called him friend, and took him in.

But I am an elf, and lo, there looms another mountain, I fear. I think often of Innovindil, who told me to live my life in shorter spans, in the expected days of those shorter-lived races about me. Should Catti-brie and I have children, I will likely outlive them, as I will almost surely outlive Catti-brie.

It is a confusing thought, a paradox entwining the greatest joy with the most excruciating agony.

And so here, on this mountaintop, surveying the grand view, I remain aware that I might witness the dawn of another few centuries. By the counting of elves, I have lived but a fraction of my life, yet at this still-early moment, it feels so full!

I am a fortunate man.

Should I see those distant dawns, there are surely dark valleys ahead, and after such certain moments of profound loss will I find the strength to climb the next mountain, and the one after that, and the one after that?

I will, I know, because in my grief the first time, when I thought these friends lost, my love lost, my life lost, I came to understand the truth: that the road will roll beneath your feet whether you step lightly with hope and swiftly with determination, or whether you plod in misery, scraping the dirt with heavy boots.

Because the perspective of that journey is a choice, and I choose happiness, and I choose to climb the next mountain.

Who is this maestro, this puppet master, pulling the strings of so many marionettes?

Including my own!

Jarlaxle's maneuvers reach far into the shadows and involve great powers—and these are merely the plots of which I am aware. No doubt he reaches much farther still, to the darkest shadows of Menzoberranzan, to the heart of dragonkind, to the hive mind of the illithids, to places I can only imagine, or dream rather, in my worst nightmares.

Who is he to wrangle together my wife, the Harpells, a thousand dwarves, and the archmage of Menzoberranzan in an effort to resurrect a structure of such ancient power?

Who is he to secretly control the city of Luskan, through great deception and great hidden power?

Who is he to goad me and Artemis Entreri to Menzoberranzan, to rescue Dahlia, to assault House Do'Urden and thus invoke the wrath of the matron mother of the City of Spiders?

Who is he to convince Matron Mother Zeerith of House Xorlarrin to surrender Gauntlgrym to Bruenor?

Who is he to bring dragons onto the field of battle in the Silver Marches?

Who is this maestro, turning the wheels of Faerun, playing the music of fate to the ears of all who would listen?

I call him a friend and yet I cannot begin to decipher the truth of this most interesting and dangerous drow. He moves armies with silent commands, coerces alliances with promises of mutual benefit, and engages the most unlikely companions into willing adventures that seem suicidal.

He elicits a measure of trust that goes beyond reason—and indeed, often runs headlong against reason.

And yet, here I am, walking the ways of the Underdark beside Jarlaxle and Artemis Entreri, bound for the city of my birth, where I am perhaps the greatest fugitive from Lolth's damning injustice. If I am caught in Menzoberranzan, I will never see Catti-brie or Bruenor or the sunlit world again. If Matron Mother Baenre finds me, she will turn my two legs into eight and torment me as a drider for the rest of my wretched life. If Tiago and his allies discover me, he will surely deliver my head to the matron mother.

And here I walk, willingly, to that possible fate.

I cannot deny my debt to Jarlaxle. Would we have won in the Silver Marches had he not arrived with Brother Afafrenfere, Ambergris, and the dragon sisters? Perhaps, but the cost would have been much greater.

Would Bruenor have won out in Gauntlgrym had Jarlaxle not convinced Matron Mother Zeerith to flee? Likely, yes, but again only with horrific cost.

Could we rebuild the Hosttower of the Arcane, and thus preserve the magic that fuels Gauntlgrym's forges, and indeed, contain the violence that would blast the complex to rubble, without the efforts of Jarlaxle and his band of rogue dark elves? I find that very unlikely. Perhaps Catti-brie, Gromph, and the others will not succeed now in this momentous endeavor, but at least now, because of Jarlaxle, we have a chance.

None of us, not even Gromph, can deny our debt to the maestro.

I must admit, to myself if no one else, that there is more driving me now than that simple debt I know I owe to Jarlaxle. I feel a responsibility to Dahlia to at least try to help her in her desperate need, particularly when Jarlaxle, ever the clever one, assures me that we can somehow manage this rescue. And so, too, do I feel that responsibility to Artemis Entreri. Perhaps I will never call him "friend," but I believe that if the situation was reversed, that if it were Catti-brie trapped down there, he would venture with me to rescue her.

Why in the Nine Hells would I believe that?

I have no answer, but there it remains.

Jarlaxle has hinted, too, that all of this is connected to a higher goal, from the defeat of the drow and their orc minions in the Silver Marches to the taking of Gauntlgrym to the surrender of Matron Mother Zeerith to the rebuilding of the Hosttower to the rescue of Dahlia.

Bruenor's Gauntlgrym is Jarlaxle's buffer to Luskan, allowing him a refuge for male drow, and one housing the former archmage of Menzoberranzan in a tower to rival the power of Sorcere. Jarlaxle's treachery against Matron Mother Baenre in the Silver Marches facilitated not only a rebuke of the high priestesses of Menzoberranzan, but a stinging rebuke of the Spider Queen herself. And so, too, will the web of Matron Mother Baenre be unwound when Dahlia is taken from her grasp.

And Jarlaxle uses me—he has admitted as much—as a beacon to those drow males oppressed by the suffocating discrimination of the female disciples of Lady Lolth. I escaped, and thrived—that is my heresy.

Matron Mother Baenre proved that point all too well when she reconstituted House Do'Urden, and tried to use that banner to destroy my reputation among the people who had come to accept me in the Silver Marches. I am not arrogant enough to believe that I was the only reason for Menzoberranzan's assault on the Silver Marches, but in so absurdly trying to stamp my name and my coat of arms upon the invasion, the drow priestess tipped Lolth's hand for all to see.

And in that hand is the revelation that Jarlaxle's maneuvers frighten the powers that rule in Menzoberranzan.

And in that fear, I cannot help but see hope.

Even aside from all that, from the debt to friends and companions and the greater aspirations of an optimistic Jarlaxle, if I cannot admit that there is something else, something more, luring me to continue this journey, then I am lying to myself most of all. Yes, I deny Menzoberranzan as my home, and hold no desire to live there whatsoever. Nor am I returning, as I so foolishly did once before, to surrender to the darkness. Perhaps, though, I will explore that darkness to see if light is to be found, for I cannot so easily eliminate the memories of the decades I spent in the City of Spiders. In Menzoberranzan, I was trained to fight and was taught the ways of the drow, and it is precisely the rejection of those mores and tenets that has made me who I am today.

Menzoberranzan shaped me, mostly by showing me what I did not want and could not accept.

Does that not put upon me a debt to my people, to the Viernas and the Zaknafeins who might now reside under the suffocating abominations of the Spider Queen?

My sister Vierna was not evil, and Zaknafein, my father, was possessed of a heart similar to my own.

How many more of similar weal, I wonder, huddle in the shadows because they believe there is no escape? How many conform to the expectations of that cruel society because they believe that there is no other way possible for them? How many feel the bite of the snake-whips, or look upon the miserable driders, and so perform as expected?

Is it possible that my very existence, that my unusual journey, can bring even a bit of change to that paradigm? Jarlaxle believes so. He has not told me this bluntly, but as I piece together the strands of the web he is building, from Gromph in Luskan to Matron Mother Zeerith—who he assures me is unlike the other matron mothers in this important regard—I can only conclude that this is his play.

Given that, given Jarlaxle's machinations, is it possible?

I know not, but am I not duty-bound by those same principles and ethics that guide my every step to at least try?

And am I not, for the sake of my own reflection, duty-bound to confront these ghosts that so shaped me and to learn from that honest look in the mirror of my earliest days?

How might I truly understand my life's purpose, I wonder, if I cannot honestly confront who and what placed me upon this road I walk?

I have heard powerful men with imperial designs claim that reality is what they choose it to be. That they make their own reality, and so decide the reality for those in their way, and while others are trying to decipher what is truth, they move on to the next conquest, the next creation, the next deception of malleable reality.

That is all I could call it—a grand illusion, a lie wrapped as truth, and so declared as truth by the controlling puppet masters of the powerful.

I rejected—and still do, to great extent—the notion. If there is no truth, then it seems to me that there is no basis of reality itself. If perception is reality, then reality is a warped and malleable thing, and to what point? I must ask.

Are we all gods within our own minds?

To entertain the notion is to invite the purest chaos, I fear—but then, is it not to also offer the purest harmony?

I choose to be happy, and happiness is indeed a choice. Every day I can rise from my reverie and gnash my teeth at what I do not have. Or I can smile contentedly in appreciation of what I do possess. To this level, then, I must agree with the hubristic conqueror. In this emotional level, perception can indeed be the reality of one's feelings, and properly corralling that perception might well be the key to happiness and contentment. I know many poor men who are happy, and many rich men full of discontent. The failings of the heart—pride, envy, greed, and even lust, if such will result in pain for another—are choices as well, to be accepted or denied. Acceptance will lead to discontent, and so these are, in the words of many texts of many cultures and races, considered among the deadliest of sins.

But aside from the false justifications of the conqueror and the choices of honest perception, is there another level of contortion where perception and reality cross? Where perception, perhaps, is so powerful and so distorted that it masks reality itself, that it replaces reality itself? And in such a state, is there a puppet master who can shatter perception as easily as a powerful smith might punch his sledge through thin glass?

This is my fear, my terror. My nightmare!

All the world beneath my feet shifts as the sands of a desert, and what those sands might conceal . . .

Were it not for Wulfgar, I would not now recognize what has been cast upon me. When he fell those many years ago in Mithral Hall, beneath a cave collapse in the tentacle arms of a yochlol, Wulfgar was taken to the Abyss, and there enslaved by the demon named Errtu.

Wulfgar told me of his trials, and of the worst of the tortures—the very worst, torment beyond any possible physical pain. With his demonic magic, Errtu gave to the battered and beaten-down Wulfgar a new reality, a grand illusion that he was free, that he was married to Catti-brie, that together they had produced fine children.

And then Errtu ate those children in front of Wulfgar's eyes, and murdered Catti-brie. This is the very essence of diabolical torture, the very epitome of evil. The demon created reality within a beautiful deception, and destroyed that reality right in front of the helpless victim.

All Wulfgar could do was scream and tear at his own ears and eyes as the sights and sounds ripped open his heart.

It broke him. When rescue finally came, when Wulfgar once more walked in the shared reality of Faerun among his friends, those dreams did come. The deception of Errtu remained, and waited for him in every unguarded moment and drove him to the bottle and to the edge of absolute despair.

I know of this from Wulfgar, and so I am better prepared. Now I recognize the awful truth of my life.

I do not know how far back this grand diabolical game began upon my own sensibilities, but to that dark night at the top of Kelvin's Cairn, at least.

Perhaps I died there.

Perhaps there Lolth found me and took me.

And so the deception, and when I step back from it, I am amazed at how blind and foolish I could have been! I am stunned at how easily what I so desperately wanted to be true was made true in my mind! I am humbled at how easily I was fooled!

A century has passed. I saw the deaths of Catti-brie and Regis in Mithral Hall. I know that Wulfgar grew old and died in Icewind Dale. I held a dying Bruenor in my own arms in Gauntlgrym.

"I found it, elf," the dwarf said to me, and so Bruenor Battlehammer died content, his life fulfilled, his seat at Moradin's table assured.

They were all gone. I saw it. I lived it. I grieved it.

But no, they are all here! Miraculously so!

And Artemis Entreri, too, walked through the century. A human of middle age when the Spellplague began, and yet here he is a century removed, a human of middle age once more, or still—I cannot be certain and it does not matter.

Because it isn't real.

Too many!

I am told that the Companions of the Hall returned because of the blessing of Mielikki, and that Entreri survived because of a curse and a sword, and oh, how I wanted and want to believe those coincidences and miraculous circumstances! And so my desire is my undoing. It tore the shield from in front of my heart. This is not the blessing of Mielikki.

This is the curse of Lolth.

The grand deception!

She has made my reality to lighten my heart, so that she can shatter my reality, and in so doing, shatter, too, the heart of Drizzt Do'Urden.

I see it now—how could I have been such a fool?—but seeing it will not protect me. Expecting it will not shield my heart. Not yet.

I must act quickly, else Lolth will break me this time, I know. When all of this is shown to be the conjured dream of a scheming demon goddess, Drizzt Do'Urden will die of heartbreak.

Unless I can rebuild that shield, strip by hardened strip. I must accept again the death of my friends, of my beloved Catti-brie. I must return my heart to that calloused place, accept that pain and the grief and the emptiness.

Alas, but even should I succeed, to what end, I must ask? When this grand illusion is destroyed, with what am I left?

And knowing now that perception and reality are so intimately twined, then I ask again, to what end?

Zero

I look upon the stars again and they seem as foreign to me as they did when first I climbed out of the Underdark.

By every logic and measure of reason, my journey to Menzoberranzan should seem to me to be a great triumph.

Demogorgon was destroyed; the threat to Menzoberranzan, and perhaps to the wider world, was thus lifted. I survived, as did my companions, and Dahlia is back among us, rescued from the spidery web of Matron Mother Baenre. Tiago is dead and I need not fear that he will rally allies to come after me and my friends ever again. Even were the drow to resurrect him, the issue is settled, I am sure. Not Tiago, and likely no other drow, will come hunting for the trophy of Drizzt Do'Urden ever again.

And so, by every measure of reason, my journey to the Underdark met with the greatest success that we could have hoped, with two unexpected and welcomed developments.

I should be overjoyed, and more so to see again the stars.

But now I know, and once known, it is a truth that cannot be unrealized.

Perhaps, given the revelation, it is the only truth.

And that, I find abhorrent.

The only truth is that there is no truth? This existence, all existence, is just a game, a cheat, meaningless beyond the reality we place in our own eyes?

Wulfgar was deceived by Errtu in the pits of the Abyss! His entire existence was re-created, fabricated, and so his perception of reality moved toward his deepest desires—only to be pulled away by the great demon!

How far does that lie go? How deep into everything we see, everything we know, everything we believe, is the fabrication of demons, or gods?

Or are those beings, too, mere manifestations of my own internal imagination? Am I a god, the only god? Is everything around me no more than my creation, my eyes giving it shape, my nose giving it smell, my ears giving it sound, my moods giving it story?

Aye, I fear, and I do not want to be the god of my universe! Could there be a greater curse?

But yes, aye, indeed! Worse would be to learn that I am not the maestro, but that I am a victim of the maestro, who teases me with his own sinister designs!

Nay, not worse! No, for if I am the god-thing, if I create reality with my own perception, then am I not truly alone?

I cannot find the footing to sort this out! I look at the stars, the same stars that have brightened my nights for decades, and they seem foreign.

Because I fear that it is all a lie.

And so every victory rings hollow. Every truth to which I would have dearly clung slips easily through my malleable hands.

That strange priestess, Yvonnel, called me the Champion of Lolth, but in my heart, I understand her grand misrepresentation. I fought for Menzoberranzan, true, but in a righteous cause against a demonic horror—and not for Lolth in any way, but for those dark elves who have a chance to see the truth and live a worthy life.

Or did I?

In my journey, I walked the halls of House Do'Urden—as it was, and not as it is! I saw the death of Zaknafein, so I am led to believe, but that, too, I cannot know!

The only truth is that there is no truth . . . no reality, just perception.

Because if perception is reality, then what matters? If this is all a dream, then this is all simply me.

Alone.

Without purpose beyond amusement.

Without morality beyond whim.

Without meaning beyond entertainment.

Alone.

I lift my blades, Twinkle and Icingdeath, and see them now as paddles in a game. What conviction might I put behind the strikes of such weapons when I know now that there is no point beyond the amusement of a demon, or of a god, or of my own imagination?

And so I journey toward Luskan this clear, starlit night.

Without purpose.

Without morality.

Without meaning.

Alone.

I cannot wash the blood off my hands.

The wound was minimal, the actual bloodletting almost nonexistent, but my blade was there, against the neck of Catti-brie, and my intent was there, undeniably, to slash Vidrinath across and brutally cut out her throat and bathe in her spurting blood. To exact revenge!

Oh, how I wanted to do that!

Because she was a demon in disguise I knew, and know, and do not know, tormenting me by taking the physical appearance and aspect of my lost beloved.

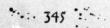

When did she intend the reveal? In the midst of lovemaking perhaps, when a leering monstrous face would stare down at me, a grotesque and misshapen demon form swaying above me, perhaps taking my seed to conceive a horrid half-breed?

Or not. Or none of it.

Or, I put my blade against the throat of Catti-brie, truly Catti-brie, and came a single breath from murdering her.

In that case, were I to sail the Sword Coast and drag my hand in the water, then surely I would leave the entire sea red in my wake! So little blood did spill, and yet to me it is all the blood of the world, washing upon me, marking me a great scarlet badge of shame.

Murderer!

Because I did kill her, in my mind. I did doubt her, in my heart. My arm failed me. My courage fled.

Because the demon should have died!

The imposter should have died, and killing it would give me one last act of defiance against Lolth. One simple act, one clean kill, to tell the Spider Queen that in the end, she did not score her craven victory. She would obliterate me at her whim—I could do nothing to prevent that act if she so desired—but nay, in the end, she would not break me.

I am not her plaything!

Unless it was really Catti-brie who felt the edge of my scimitar against her soft neck—how am I to know?

And that is the conundrum, that is the deeper curse, that is why I have already lost.

I rouse from my reverie every morning and declare to myself that this day, I will be happy, that this day, I will look upon the sunrise and know hope. Perhaps it is all a ruse, all a great deception by a demon queen to inflict the ultimate torment.

So be it, I say each morn. So be it!

And each morning, I ask myself, "What choice have I?"

What other course? What other road might I walk? If it is all perception, then at what point must perception, even delusion, simply be accepted as reality? And if that reality is pleasant, then should I not find happiness in it, for whatever time the illusion, or delusion, remains? Is it worthwhile or even sensible to refuse to enjoy years of perceived calm among friends and loved ones, to not simply be happy, out of fear for what may or may not come?

Is the sunrise any less beautiful? Is Catti-brie's smile any less enchanting? Is Bruenor's laughter any less infectious? Is Guenhwyvar's purr any less comforting?

Every day, I tell myself that. Every day, I initially reason my way to a state of happiness and contentedness. Every day, I repeat this litany against madness, this armor against ultimate despair.

Every day.

And every day, I fail.

I cannot create meaning in the midst of a dream. I cannot create purpose when I am alone in a fancy design of my own creation. I cannot create freedom to smile with the ever-present thought that my enemies await the deepest smile they can elicit before tearing the pretty facade away.

And worse, now I am stained with the blood of Catti-brie or of an imposter demonic creature, and if the former, then I struck out at the woman I love, and so wallow in shame and blood. And if the latter, then I had not the courage to complete the kill, and so there, too, I have failed.

They have taken my weapons, and for that I am glad. Would that they would take my life and end this misery.

They pretend to care. They feign spells and mind intrusions to heal my malady, but I see the sinister eyes and smell the Abyssal fog and hear the quiet cackles behind the sighs of their supposed concern.

Let me rot with the blood of Catti-brie on my hands or let me rot in the shame of my cowardice.

Either way, it is a fate I surely deserve.

There are moments every day—more now, I admit—where I feel that I am a fool for my fears, nay my certitude, that this is all a conspiracy of nightmare. Moments of seeming clarity when the preposterousness of all that has happened—the return of Catti-brie and all my friends, the long life of Artemis Entreri—pales beside the preposterousness of my nightmare, for the lengths to which Lolth (or whatever fiend is so deceiving me) has gone to destroy me seem beyond all reason.

But then I remember that I have so insulted the Spider Queen that there would be no journey too great for her to properly pay me back!

And I remember, too, the machinations to which Errtu went to cruelly devastate Wulfgar.

This journey, though, seems grander and on a scale many times larger, for now I am halfway across Faerun, in my mind at least, to a place I have only heard of in tales.

There is much to admire in the Monastery of the Yellow Rose. The brothers and sisters here are truly among the most dedicated practitioners I have ever seen. Their adherence to their code and rituals rivals the fanaticism of the Gutbusters or the dedication of the weapon masters of Menzoberranzan. It is truly a delight to behold, with so many practicing in harmony and building upon each other's gains with such honest contentment—even though the gains of another, Afafrenfere for example, might well threaten the station of oneself.

Mistress Savahn celebrates Afafrenfere's march up the hierarchical ladder of the Order of the Yellow Rose. She had told me, with joy in her eyes and lightness in her voice, that she has never witnessed such an extraordinary advance of body and spirit as that which Afafrenfere has displayed. Yet he will soon challenge her for her station, and should she lose that fight, she will step down a rung on the order's hierarchical ladder.

I asked her about this, and her answer rang true to my heart: if he could beat her, then he deserved the accolades and the station, and she would have to work harder to retrieve her current place. Afafrenfere's ascent, therefore, would ultimately make her better.

She has found the truth of competition, that there is no better challenge to be found than one a person can make with herself, that the personal competition outweighs any other and by great magnitude. Simply, the rise of a rival challenges each of us to do better and be better, and that is to be celebrated, not feared or prevented.

This is the opposite of the philosophy prevalent in Menzoberranzan. Indeed, the drow determination to hold back others, even through murder, that the powerful can hold their gains, lies at the heart of that which drove me from the city, for it is a philosophy wholly immoral and limiting.

Here, in the Monastery of the Yellow Rose, it seems that I have found the exact opposite of that empty paranoia. I feel as I felt when I encountered Montolio and learned of Mielikki, except that this time, I see in community practice that which I hold in my heart.

And it is a beautiful thing.

Too beautiful.

As is Kane, the Grandmaster of Flowers, a man who through the deepest meditation and dedication has transcended his mortal coil, has become something more than a being of the Material Plane. He is at once weightless and translucent, existing in a place of spirit more than anyone I have ever known, and at the same time, weighted and full of solidity. I have come to believe that he could have defeated me at any point in our sparring match, and that he only took his time so that he could gain my full measure by revealing to me that there was a long road of physical perfection yet before me should I choose to walk it.

I have oft noted that perfection of body is not possible, and that the pursuit of it, the journey, is the point more than the goal. In Kane, I have found the closest example of that elusive, unattainable perfection, more so than I believed possible.

And so I am honored to be in his presence, to be tutored by him.

I feel the ground more solidly beneath my feet now, and that is the clue. If this were real, if Kane's advance was true as presented, then indeed I could envision myself following this path.

And so it is clear to me that my enemies have found a way to get me to lower my guard, that they have found a way to tease me with illusions that go to the fondest desires of the heart of Drizzt Do'Urden.

And thus, in those moments when the ground seems most solid beneath my feet, when the preposterousness of my fears seems so much greater than the preposterousness of the reality which led me to those fears, then I must remind myself of that weakening guard and of the price that I will pay when at last I have become fully deceived into believing that this is all real.

Yes, this monastery is the ring of truth that I have ever longed to wear.

Yes, this Grandmaster of Flowers Kane is the epitome of my personal goals.

Yes, I would embrace this, all of it.

If I believed it.

But I do not.

Generations

Timeless

You can't see webs in the Underdark. You'll feel them, too late, tickling and teasing, and perhaps you'll cry out in fear or disgust before you die.

But you won't see them.

Not those of spiders, or of other creatures laying traps for wayward fools who have ventured where they do not belong.

And few do. Few belong in the Underdark, and those who live there see the darkness as an ally in their own treachery.

Here the duergar dwarves chop and gnash the stone, swinging picks with the strength of hate. Ever growling, ever cursing, any spark from metal on stone revealing grizzled faces locked in a perpetual and threatening scowl.

Here the monstrous cave fishers lay their long lines, ready to snatch an unwary visitor and drag him, flailing helplessly and pitifully, up the cliff to a waiting maw.

Here the huge umber hulks burrow, through stone, through flesh—it does not matter.

Here the giant mushrooms gather and plot catastrophe.

Here the living, sentient shadows flitter and fly, cold fingers ready to throttle anything possessed of the warmth of life.

Here the lurkers pose as floors.

Here the piercers hang among stalactites. Any who are found by either would think that the Underdark itself had risen to devour them.

In so many ways, they would not be wrong.

And then they, like so many before, would die, would be eaten by the shadow.

For this is the Underdark, where shadows huddle too closely to be called shadows, where light marks the bearer more than it marks the way before him, where every hunting ground is bordered by another hunting ground, where most are lucky to simply choose the manner of their own deaths, to stick their own swords into their own hearts before the tentacles of the displacer beast pull them from the ledge, or before the spider has finished sucking out the life juices, so slowly, in an inescapable cocoon.

Here the demons often roam, insatiably angry, masters of murder.

Here the quiet, odorless, invisible gases of distant tumult make sleep eternal, or make a flash of flint and steel into a fireball to humble the archmage of Menzoberranzan.

Here is the ominous heartbeat of distant, dripping water, a single sound dancing from stone to stone, amplified by the profound stillness.

Here are the rattles of the bones of unshriven dead, tickled to movement by the dark magic of the dark place, raised in undeath to claw and chew.

Aye, this is the Underdark, and here lies Menzoberranzan, the City of Spiders, the city of those who worship the demon goddess who calls herself the Spider Queen.

Only a fool would come here unbidden.

Only a fool would come here bidden.

For here are the drow, the dark elves, masters of magic divine and arcane, masters of weapons edged in the cruel enchantments of the Faerzress, the magical boundary that gives life to the Underdark and that connects it, so fittingly, to the lands of demons and devils.

Yes, here are the drow, and they will stop killing one another just long enough to kill you.

"What should I bring, Father?" asks the young man about to set off on an adventure into the Underdark, in a fable common throughout Faerun.

"Two coins."

"Waterdhavian gold? Cormyr silver?"

"It does not matter," says the father.

"How much food shall I pack?"

"It does not matter. Two coins."

"Water, then, surely, Father. How much water shall I carry?"

"It does not matter. Two coins."

"I will buy all I need with only two coins? What weapon is best, then? A sword? A bow?"

"Two coins. Only two coins."

"To buy all that I need?" the confused son asks.

"No," answers the father. "To cover your eyes when you are dead. Nothing else that you bring will stop that."

This is the Underdark, the land of murderers.

The land of the drow.

It is interesting to me to look back upon my writings from many years ago. I often cringe at my conclusions, believing that I know better now and that I've come to a clearer view of whatever situation I must confront, a clearer understanding of the best likely resolution. Oh, I see the same intent, the same hoped-for conclusion in those old writings, but there are little mistakes scattered throughout, and they are now obvious to me.

"Wisdom" is a word often associated with experience—perhaps it should also be spoken of in conjunction with the word "humility," because I now understand that if I look back upon this piece in a decade, or a century, I will likely once again find much to correct.

The other thing that strikes me about these glimpses into the past is the cyclical nature of life. Not just regarding birth and death, but in the many joys and crises that find us, year after year. There is an old drow saying:

AVA'TIL NATHA PASAISON ZHAH QUES PO FINNUD EBRIES HERM.

"HISTORY IS A POEM WHERE ALL LINES RHYME."

How true! To simply view the conflicts that my friends and I have faced is to see new threats that sound very much like the old. Even the great tragedies and joys of our companionship follow predictable patterns to one who has lived them, again and again. Paradigms often seem broken, but the nature of reasoning beings will someday reinstate them.

In this one manner, perhaps Lolth is no fool, or perhaps she is the greatest fool. Chaos brings excitement to her followers—they feel alive! But in the end, they will go right back to where they were before. The rank of a house might change, a nearby foe might be vanquished, a new spell created to darken the skies. But a person traveling to Menzoberranzan today would see a place that rhymes quite closely with the city I first glimpsed from a cradle.

Is it any different with Waterdeep?

For, yes, some civilizations will be wiped away by conquerors. Some will be flattened by volcanoes. Great drought will displace entire cultures and massive ocean waves might sweep others to the silence of the seafloor. But the circle of life continues. The greed and the generosity remain. The love and the hate remain. The mercy and the vengeance remain. All of these countervailing, endlessly competing facets of humans and dwarves and elves and halflings and gnomes and every other reasoning race remain . . . and battle.

And the winner is always in jeopardy and the result is so common, either way, that there is, overall, stasis within the swirl of chaos.

When I told this to Bruenor, he replied that I was dark in more than skin, reached behind his shield, and handed me a drink.

But no, it is not a dispiriting thought, nor one that implies helplessness in the face of fate and predetermination.

Because this, too, I know: while we move in circles, we still move forward. Like my own maturation in looking at my past writing, the cultures mature. To a visitor today, Menzoberranzan would look very much as it did to me when I first peeked out from House Do'Urden, but not exactly the same.

The times grow less dark for all the races, because within the culture, too, is memory, an understanding of what works and what does not. When those lessons are forgotten, the circle winds its way backward, and when they are remembered, society moves forward, and with each cycle, with each affirmation of that which is good and that which is evil, the starting point of the next lesson is a bit closer to goodness.

It is a long roll, this circle, but it is rolling in the direction of justice and goodness, for all of us. It is not hard to look back on history and see atrocities committed on a grand scale that horrify the sensibilities of the folk of this day but were simply accepted or deemed necessary by folk in days more superstitious and unenlightened.

Bruenor wasn't impressed by this claim. He just handed me another drink.

But it seems true to me now, undeniably so, that the life of an individual and the life of a society go in these circles of crisis and peace, and from each, we learn and we become stronger.

We become wiser.

It occurs to me that the beings we on Faerun call gods might be no more than long-living creatures who have heard the rhyme of *pasaison*, of yesteryear, so many times that their simple experience allows them to know the future. So ingrained is the inevitable result, perhaps, that they can now hear the echoes of the future instead of merely those of the past—they have the foresight of consequence. They have learned great powers, as a swordsman learns a new attack routine.

My own journey nearly ended during this last crisis, not merely because I might have died—that seems a very common condition—but because what I lost most of all was my grounding in reality. The ground on which I stood became shifting sand, and in that sand I nearly disappeared.

And would have, except that now I have learned to tighten the circles of my life, almost to where I have come to hope that my journey from here on out is a straighter road forward, a path to better epiphany and clearer insight.

For the greatest teaching of the monks of the Yellow Rose is the ability to forgive, wholly, your own shortcomings, to accept your physical being as a vessel to a spirit ever seeking perfection. Such true acceptance of oneself, of limitations and weaknesses and failings, allows one to proceed without becoming hindered by guilt and undue hesitance.

To hear the echoes of the past.

To anticipate the notes of the future.

To stride more boldly.

And so, scimitars high, I go, boldly and with a smile.

⌒

Age breeds wisdom because age brings experience. Thus we learn, and if we are not frozen in our ways or wedded to a manner of looking at the world that defies experiential evidence, we learn.

The rhyme of history is, in the end, the greatest teacher.

The question, however, is whether the students are sufficient. Yes, Menzoberranzan would look very different to me now, with my wealth of experience accompanying me back to that dark place, and yes, an individual may learn, should learn, must learn, through his or her journey. But that doesn't happen to all individuals, I have seen. And is it true at all on a societal level? Or a generational level?

I would expect the elves, including the drow, to be the learned guides of this turning cycle. Having seen the birth and death of centuries, the memories of the long-living races should cry as warnings to another fool king or queen or council of lords to change course when they are walking the road to catastrophe. For we have witnessed this marionette show before, and the puppets all died, and the principals who lived did so with great regret and even horror at their own actions. A dark path is walked in tiny steps.

So the elves should be the clarion call of warning, but, sadly, it is the shorter life span of the humans that seems to most dictate the cycles of destruction, as if the passing of a generation that knew great strife or war or insurgence erases, too, the societal memory of a road's tragic destination.

In the Monastery of the Yellow Rose, they have a great library, and in that historical repository is a timeline of devastating, world-shattering events.

The occurrences appear with alarming regularity. Every seventy to one hundred years, there comes a time of great strife. Oh, there are other events, often tragic, from time to time, but these are often anomalies, it seems, the rogue acts of foolish kings.

The events of which I speak appear more to be a maturation of devastation, a perilous journey of thousands of tiny steps that culminates when the last of those humans who remember have died away.

Then, again, darkness falls.

It is more than coincidence, I think, this backstep, this backward downslope of the rolling wheel of the centuries, and so I have come to believe that enlightenment may occur in a straight line for individuals, but only within that slowly turning wheel for the world at large.

There have been Lord Neverembers before, with different names but similar shortsightedness.

Hereafter, perhaps I shall refer to the lord protector of Neverwinter as Lord Never-remember.

His attitude toward King Bruenor raises great alarms. His clamor for supremacy knows no common sense. His selfishness leads to hoarding that is greatly detrimental, even fatal, to those he calls his subjects.

Everything is faster for the humans. Their compressed lives lead to compressed kingdoms, and to repeated wars. Perhaps it is the urgency of trying to achieve too-high pedestals too quickly, before the unbeatable death closes in. Or perhaps, because they are shorter-lived, it is simply that they have less to lose. A king who has passed his fiftieth year might lose twenty years of life if he dies in battle or the guillotine finds his neck after a failed grab for even more power, while an elven king could lose centuries, or a dwarven king might lose many decades.

As old age sets in and the joys of life are compromised, perhaps this human king must grab for something glorious to replace the excitement of his rise to power, or the distant pleasures of the flesh, or the simple absence of pain when he crawled out of bed each morning.

For all this potential tragedy and darkness, though, I must remind myself that the wheel does inevitably move forward. The world was a darker, harsher, crueler place a hundred years ago, and much more so a thousand years ago.

And this gives me hope for my own people. Is our wheel similarly turning, though at a vastly slower pace?

Is Menzoberranzan truly evolving toward a lighter and more generous existence with the passing of each drow generation?

That is my hope, but it is tempered with very real fears that the wheel turns so slowly that its momentum may not be enough, that events and unscrupulous matrons could not just stop it but push it in the other direction.

And that's to say nothing of the vile demon goddess who holds those matrons in thrall.

Drow heroes are needed.

Fortunately, Menzoberranzan has produced a surprising number of those, usually hidden in the shadows, of which there are many.

It is my desperate hope that one of them, one I dearly loved, has returned to the world.

Where does the self end and the other, the community, begin?

It seems a simple, even self-evident, question, but I have come to believe that it is perhaps the most complicated investigation of all. And the most pressing one, if I am to find any true meaning in my life. Even more, on a wider level, this is the question that will determine the heart of a society, and possibly even its very life span—one way or the other.

If I were walking down the road and saw a person drowning in a pond, and I had a rope that would reach, of course I would throw it to the troubled fellow and pull him to safety.

But that is not a selfless act.

I might be called a hero for saving the person.

But that is not a heroic act.

No, that is merely the expected behavior of one worthy to live in a civilized society, and any who would not stop to help the drowning person in such a situation deserve to be shunned, at the very least.

If I were walking down a road and saw a person drowning in a pond, but I had no rope, I would dive in and swim out to try to pull the person to safety.

This is more selfless, and involves a small measure of danger.

Would I be a hero then?

Some would call me that, but the word would ring hollow in my ears. For I would have done only what I would have expected from my neighbor were I that drowning man.

This is what makes the community greater than the individual.

Suppose the drowning man was in a lake known to be inhabited by a killer gar. Suppose he was even then being attacked by such a creature. Suppose the lake was full of them, swarming, hungry.

At what point would my act of attempting to rescue him become heroic? At what point would my actions rightly earn the title of hero?

At what point would I not want my neighbors to jump into that gar-filled death trap to try to save me?

And there is a point, surely. There is a place where responsibility to self outweighs, must outweigh, responsibility to the community.

But where?

Likely, few have considered the above dilemma specifically, but the question posed is one that every person faces in his or her life, all the time. Where does one's responsibility to oneself end, and a wider responsibility to the community begin?

If I am a successful hunter and fill my winter stores, is it right and just for me to let my neighbor go hungry? If feeding my neighbor would mean rationing for me, a winter of privation but not death, is it still my duty to save the unsuccessful hunter?

I am surprised by how many people I have met who would say that it is not, that their growling belly is not worth a neighbor's life, and who justify their claim by blaming their neighbor for being less successful in the hunt.

Again, the example is extreme, but moving now toward the commonplace, toward the daily choices we all face in our lives, the choices are no less crucial. What is your responsibility beyond the self? To your partner, your children, your brothers, your parents, your cousins, your neighbors, a stranger?

These are the questions that will define you as a person, I think, more than anything else you might do.

The laws of a kingdom try to define these lines of responsibility in the daily lives of citizens. In the village of Lonelywood in Ten Towns, for example, a successful hunter is bound to share all bounty beyond one full meal a day, with any excess to be divided equally among all Lonelywood residents. But in Dougan's Hole, another of the Ten Towns of Icewind Dale, those who cannot hunt their winter food will very possibly starve, and successful hunters can defend their bounty to the death, even if that bounty is so great that much will rot when the spring melt falls across the tundra.

No one in Dougan's Hole tries to change these laws, or the common behavior that gives them credence. Certainly, though, there are folks in Bryn Shander, the hub of Ten Towns, who would like to see such changes, since the starving people of the Redwaters' towns inevitably try to make it to Bryn Shander's gates.

I prefer Lonelywood, as would my companions, for I have come to see philanthropy as ultimately self-satisfying, if not selfish!

There is in Bryn Shander an old woman who takes in the stray cats and dogs of the place. She works tirelessly feeding, grooming, hugging, and training the animals, and tries ceaselessly to find for them homes among the citizens of the town.

So dedicated is she that she eats little and sleeps less. I once asked her about it, about why she would give up that extra hour of sleep to hunt down a reported stray.

"Every hour I'm not at me work, a precious little one might die," she told me.

The people of Bryn Shander think her quite mad, and to be honest, I questioned her grasp on reality and priority myself. Until I spoke with her, and then I found in her one of the most sane and satisfied humans I have ever had the pleasure of meeting. The warmth of her heart touched me and made me know the sincerity in her smile. This was, to her, a calling, a way that she, a feeble old woman of little means, could make the world a better place.

I have met few nobles whose smiles can rival hers in sincerity.

For I see myself somewhat akin to this old woman, and more so now after my training in the monastery. The greatest lesson in that place of profound teaching was the constant reminder of how little I truly need and the mindset to avoid the traps of acquisition.

The rich man is often owned by that which he thinks he owns.

The rich woman might elicit jealousy, and while satisfying to her, her provocation will harden the visages of those around her long before she has died.

Some people measure wealth in gold.

Others measure it in tears of those who mourn them when they have passed on.

I recognize and admit with contempt that my own preferences are not universal—not nearly—among the people I have met. Dougan's Hole is in no need of new residents, and any houses emptied by the harsh terms of that community will soon enough be full again, mostly with people grumbling about tithing or taxation, and ready to go to war with any who would demand one copper piece from them.

"If ye canno' catch yer food, ye've no right to live" is a common credo, spoken sternly about that town, and indeed, recited about all the reaches of the lake called Redwaters.

This is the ethical spectrum of reasoning beings, moving that slide between self and community.

My friend Bruenor is one of the richest kings in the region. The linked dwarven communities, from Icewind Dale to the Silver Marches to Gauntlgrym in the Crags, have come out of their wars brimming with wealth and power, and Bruenor himself already possesses a treasury that would make most Waterdhavian lords envious.

Is Bruenor bound, then, to open his gates wide to all who would come begging? How far ranges the responsibility of one who has gained so much? Farther than that of the farmer or the cobbler? If a farmer has saved a dozen silver coins and gives one to a poor man he meets at the market, should Bruenor, who has a thousand thousand times that wealth, dole out a silver to a thousand thousand needy others?

Or should he dole out even more than that, because his coins become less important to his own security and health once he has surpassed a certain point of wealth? Like dragons, the great lords of the north possess hoards of treasure beyond anything they might hope to spend in their lifetimes, or that their children could spend, or even the familial generation beyond that. Taking a silver piece from a man who has ten silvers hurts him and his family less than taking a copper piece from a family that has only ten coppers. And taking a gold piece from a woman who has ten gold means less to her family's well-being than the tithe imposed upon the man with the ten silvers.

And the rule holds true so on up the line of wealth. The more you have, the less you need, and once all the basic needs are met, the luxuries become redundant and indeed flatten the joy of purchase.

Menzoberranzan is not unlike Dougan's Hole. There is never enough gold and gems and jewels to satisfy the insatiable greed of the matrons. In Menzoberranzan, wealth is power, and power is all. And wealth is station, which implies more than power. For station breeds envy, and to the drow of my homeland, the envy of others is among life's greatest joys.

This philosophy of life seems foolhardy to me.

A beggar at the gates of House Baenre will be killed or enslaved.

A beggar at the gates of Gauntlgrym will find a hot meal and a bed. This is why King Bruenor is my friend.

Boundless

Jarlaxle has spent many hours of late—since the resurrection of Zaknafein—relating to me tales of his early days beside my father in Menzoberranzan. His purpose, I expect, is to help me get to better know this man who was so important to me in my early years, a man whose past has remained mostly a mystery until now. Perhaps Jarlaxle sees this as a way to bridge the divide that I have unexpectedly found separating me from my father, to soften the edges of Zaknafein's attitudes toward any who are not drow.

What I have found most of all, however, is that Jarlaxle's stories have told me more about Jarlaxle than they have about Zaknafein, most especially, of the evolution of Jarlaxle and his mercenary band of Bregan D'aerthe. I view this evolution with great optimism, as it seems to me a smaller version of that which I hope might come about within the drow culture as a whole.

When he started his band of outcasts, Jarlaxle did so simply to keep himself alive. He was a houseless rogue, a reality in Menzoberranzan that typically ensured one a difficult and short existence. But clever Jarlaxle collected others in similar straits and brought them together, and made of these individuals a powerful force that offered value to the ruling matrons without threatening them. That band, though, was not the same as the Bregan D'aerthe that now controls the city of Luskan, and the change was not subtle, though I'm not sure if Jarlaxle himself is even conscious of it.

Bregan D'aerthe is a very different troupe now, but the change, I expect, has been gradual across the centuries. Jarlaxle, too, must be different.

And so, dare I hope that Zaknafein will find his way as well?

In the beginning, the Bregan D'aerthe reflected the savage culture of Menzoberranzan's houses, and in many ways, exploited the schisms within Menzoberranzan, both interhouse and intrahouse. Great indeed were those treacheries! My own life was spared the sacrificial blade only because my brother Dinin murdered my brother Nalfein on the day of my birth. Everyone knew the truth of it, including our mother, Matron Malice, and yet there was no punishment to Dinin. Rather, there was only gain because of the clever manner in which he had executed Nalfein, away from obvious witnesses. Similarly, I would guess that nearly half the matrons serving as the head of drow houses arrived at their station by killing (or at least, by helping to facilitate the death of) their own mothers. This is the way of Lolth and so this is the way of the drow and so this was the way of Bregan D'aerthe.

As such, Jarlaxle gave his underlings free rein and little guidance as they tried to climb the hierarchy of Bregan D'aerthe. His only rule, from what I can fathom, was to take care of the cost that any of their actions might incur upon him. His underlings would fight and cheat, thieve and murder, and Jarlaxle did not care enough to get involved. A murdered associate would have to be properly replaced at the expense of the murderer, I suppose, but Jarlaxle imposed no moral code upon his underlings.

I sometimes wonder if he was then possessed of such a code himself?

I ask that honestly, for while I do not doubt that he has always held some code of honor, that is not necessarily the same thing as a moral center. Artemis Entreri held on to some misplaced sense of honor, too, but it is only in very recent times that he has allowed simple morality to even seep into his decisions.

But then, Artemis Entreri viewed the human societies in much the same way that Jarlaxle—and Zaknafein—viewed the drow: irredeemable and wretched and worthy of his extreme scorn and ultimate judgment.

What a sad waste is such an outlook!

When Jarlaxle relates those early stories of his band of not-brothers, he doesn't even seem aware of the stark differences that are representative of Bregan D'aerthe today. Then, the secret society survived by strength alone, by Jarlaxle's ability to will the disparate and rivalrous troupe through the tasks put before him by the matrons, particularly Matron Mother Baenre. From all that I can extrapolate through these stories, Jarlaxle lost more foot soldiers to Bregan D'aerthe blades than to those of enemies.

Now, though, I witness a much different structure within Bregan D'aerthe, and one very much more powerful.

For Jarlaxle has given to his followers something truly special among the Lolth-serving drow: an element of trust.

And he does so by example. Jarlaxle has entrusted Kimmuriel Oblodra with the very leadership of the band on those many occasions when he, Jarlaxle, is out on some adventure or other. He has even tasked Kimmuriel with reining in his own worst excesses—with keeping Jarlaxle himself in line!

Jarlaxle has given great latitude to Beniago in his role as High Captain Kurth, overseeing the city of Luskan. Beniago does not consult with Jarlaxle for his every move, and yet Jarlaxle trusts in him to operate the city smoothly, and profitably, and, I am led to believe, with some measure of the general welfare and common good of the citizens in mind.

Perhaps most telling of all is the manner in which Jarlaxle has accepted the mighty former archmage. Gromph Baenre is not a full member of Bregan D'aerthe, from all that I can tell, but he resides in

Luskan as the ultimate archmage of the Hosttower of the Arcane, and does so at the sufferance of Jarlaxle. The Hosttower itself could not have been rebuilt if not for the approval of Jarlaxle, for Gromph would never have been able to go against the whole of Bregan D'aerthe and would have found no support from King Bruenor, and certainly no help in the construction from Catti-brie.

Jarlaxle granted Gromph this greatest of wizard towers, a force as singularly powerful as any castle I have ever known, even that of King Gareth Dragonsbane in Damara, or of Sorcere, the drow school of wizards in Menzoberranzan. The collection of magic, and of those who can expertly wield such magic, now residing in the Hosttower could unleash unimaginable devastation.

But they won't. Jarlaxle knows they won't. Gromph's acceptance into Bregan D'aerthe, and into the city controlled by Bregan D'aerthe, was highly conditional. His leash is short, and yet a large part of that leash lies in the realm of trust.

And that's all possible because Bregan D'aerthe has grown, has evolved. As their leader goes, they go.

And that gives me hope.

So I dare. Dare that Jarlaxle's influence and example will find its way into Zaknafein's heart.

Even still, I fear that Zaknafein's transformation will not be in time to earn the friendship, even familial love, from Catti-brie or from our child, and in that instance, then it will not be in time to earn the love of Drizzt Do'Urden.

I hope that is not the case.

But he is my family by blood. And she is my family by choice.

I have come to learn that the latter is a stronger bond.

If I am to believe the wisdom of Grandmaster Kane, then I am made of the same stuff as all about me, then we are one. All of us, everything.

Is this observation merely a philosophical bend or the truth of it, I wonder? For surely this is not how the matrons of Menzoberranzan view the world, nor the dwarves of Gauntlgrym, nor even my beloved wife, who foresees her future in the Grove of the Unicorns within the House of Nature, wherein resides the goddess, Mielikki.

So is it that Grandmaster Kane has seen the truth, beyond the religions and dogma of the material world? Or is it that his truth is not in opposition to the others, that his truth is, perhaps, a different angle viewing the same image?

It gives me great pleasure and satisfaction to recognize that this ancient human who has taken me as his student would not bristle at my question. Nay, he would celebrate it, indeed demand it of me, for in this oneness of all he envisions is a requirement of inquisitiveness and curiosity, open heart and open mind. I cannot deny the power of Kane's truth. I have seen a blade pass through him without disturbing his mortal flesh.

He can walk through a stone wall. In the body of Brother Afafrenfere, he vanished to sparkling nothingness before the breath of a dragon, only to soon reconstitute in the mortal coil and slay the beast.

It occurs to me that a wizard or high priestess might do the same with their varying spells, and I know that Kimmuriel can replicate much of what Grandmaster Kane accomplishes with the use of his strange mind magic.

Yes, perhaps Kimmuriel Oblodra and Grandmaster Kane are more alike than either of them would wish to admit. Neither consciously calls upon the elements or some godlike being for his powers. For Kimmuriel, it is the power of a trained mind, and so it is with Grandmaster Kane.

I wonder, then, are their philosophies joined? Or are they accessing some hidden power from different directions?

I do love these puzzles, I admit, but also, I am troubled by the seeming contentment and acceptance shown by my mentor. Once more, if I am to believe the wisdom of Grandmaster Kane, then I am made of the same stuff as all that is about me, then we are one. All of us, everything. Is it sentience and reasoning that gives us form? What then of the stones and clouds? Is it our sentience which gives them form?

I am not sure that even Grandmaster Kane could answer those questions, but there is another inescapable question to his philosophy that seemed not to bother him at all: If we are all one, all of the same stuff and so our ultimate fates are joined, then what point determinations of good and evil? Why should I care for such concepts if we are all of the same stuff, if we are all to be joined in the eternity of everything? Am I to meld with ogre pieces, then? Or demon bits?

But Kane cares about this question, and his answer is simple, and one I find satisfying. To him, the universe bends toward goodness and justice and the ultimate reward for us all is that place of brotherhood and tranquility. There is indeed a philosophical and moral compass to it all, say the Sisters and Brothers of the Yellow Rose, and so such gains are not merely temporary conveniences, but lasting measurements in a universal scale.

Perhaps they're correct. Perhaps it's all for nothing, that there is no ultimate reward or punishment beyond this mortal coil. These are answers for those who, to our experience, are no more, who have returned to whatever eternity or emptiness there might be for us all. For now, so says Kane, and so say I, we must follow that which is in our heart and soul. A belief in universal, eternal harmony and oneness does not discount a belief in goodness, in love, in joy, in friendship and sisterhood.

I found my peace here in this monastery nestled in the Galena Mountains of Damara. True peace and contentment, and in that light, when I return home to Longsaddle or Gauntlgrym, on those occasions where I am beside Catti-brie or any of the others, I know that I will be a better friend.

So many guiding sayings follow us our every step, but are they wisdom or boundaries? Snippets of value to be heeded or the lesser ways of lost times, best forgotten, or at the very least, updated?

So many times, I find these traditions, or ancient wisdoms or ways, to be the latter. The very notion of the wisdom of the day seems . . . malleable, after all, and if we are to be tied to the ways of our ancestors, then how can we hope to improve upon that which they have left us? Is ritual and tradition so very different from physical structures, then? Would the dwarves stop mining when they've exhausted the boundaries of the tunnels in their ancient homelands?

Of course, they would not. They would dig new tunnels, and if in that work they were to discover better materials or designs for their scaffolding, they would use them—and likely would go back to the older tunnels and better the work left behind by their father's father's father's father.

Why, then, would this be different in the matters of tradition? Certainly among my own people, the traditions are limiting, terribly so. Half the population of Menzoberranzan is trapped in lesser roles, their ambitions caged by words older than the oldest dark elves, words inscribed millennia long past. Part of the reason in this case is obvious: Lady Lolth and her decrees. Indeed, religion to those of the faith, any faith, is often unbending and not subject to the scrutiny of reason or the pleas against simple injustice. The Word is eternal, so it is claimed, and yet, on many occasions, it is obvious that it is not.

Why, then, do these so-called wisdoms hold on so tightly?

Because the whims of an unavailable, and conveniently unassailable, deity is only part of the answer, I believe. The other part goes to the darker corner of the ways of every reasoning race. For those traditions kept past all plausible rationales or obvious moral failings, those held most fervently, too often serve those who gain the most by keeping them.

In the city of my birth, those in power do not have to compete with half the population. The matrons need not worry about a patron, surely, and indeed, by tradition, can use their male counterparts as they please.

Even those acts as personal as lovemaking are determined by the demands of the women of Menzoberranzan—and let there be little illusion about the "love" in such act—and a man who will not comply could face harsh retribution for his insolence. Only women can serve as the head of a house. Only women can sit on the Ruling Council, and even the highest-ranking man in the city, typically the archmage of Menzoberranzan, is, by tradition, by edict, by the demands of those merciless rulers, still counted more lowly than the lowest-ranking woman.

The drow are not the only people cornered and held fast by such systemic indecencies—far from it! In Wulfgar's tribe and throughout many of the people all about the north, tradition demands patriarchy instead of matriarchy, and while the men are not as brutal in their control as the drow women, the result, I expect, isn't much different. Perhaps the treatment is softer—I recall Wulfgar's shame, so profound that it led him to run away from us, when, in a fit of demon-induced memories, he struck Catti-brie. I could never imagine Wulfgar beating a woman intentionally, or demanding of her sexual pleasures against her will, but even in his contrition there remained inside him for many years that soft condescension. He must protect the women, he thought, which might be a noble undertaking, except that it came with an unspoken—but surely evident—belief that they were not capable of protecting themselves. He placed them on a pedestal, but as if they were fragile things—he simply could not bring himself to truly understand the true competence of a woman, even one as powerful, intelligent, capable, and proven as Catti-brie.

It took him years to brush it aside and truly recognize the value, the equal worth and potential, of Catti-brie and of all women. So ingrained were the teachings of his earliest years that even when faced with so much clear and convincing evidence of the error of his ways, it took a great effort on his part to free himself.

Yes, to free himself, for that is what it is to fully accept that that which you have been taught so thoroughly, the designs of the entire society around you, might be in error.

Wulfgar let go of the nonsensical sexism of his people and the greatest beneficiary of that dismissal was, in fact, Wulfgar himself.

Dare I hope the same from Yvonnel? For this is Jarlaxle's hope, I know, and his quest, and one in which he continues to use me as his shining example. I can only laugh.

And can only hope that the powerful matrons of Menzoberranzan don't grow so tired of Jarlaxle's games that they come and kill me to take from him his preeminent symbol.

There are people all about free of such sexism, of course, but they, too, are chained by their ways. In the Delzoun dwarf tradition, the gender of a dwarf is unimportant against the weight of merit. There is in Mithral Hall now a queen, Dagnabbet, daughter of Dagnabbit, son of Dagna. It matters not. Her rule will be judged by her actions alone. In every aspect of dwarven life, from combat to cooking to mining to ruling, and everything in between, merit and competence are all that matters.

If the person in question is a dwarf.

I cannot complain—far from it!—of the treatment I have received from the dwarves in my many decades on the surface, but that was more the matter of Bruenor's personal compassion. For among his people, he is a true credit. A friend is a friend and an enemy is an enemy, and not the size of one's ears, the color of her skin, or the height he stands makes a lick of spit difference to King Bruenor Battlehammer.

Were it not for him, though, the dwarves of Icewind Dale would not likely have ever accepted a lost and wandering dark elf into their homes as kin.

Unless there was another like Bruenor who first happened upon me on the slopes of Kelvin's Cairn. I cannot dismiss that possibility, for within every people, every culture, there exists the rainbow-span of qualities, prejudices, compassion, kindness, and cruelty. It is an absurd belief of the humans that the drow are simply evil—oh, many drow have earned that reputation, to be sure!

But so have many humans. They war on each other as commonly as drow houses battle in the shadows, and on a scale so great that one battle might leave more broken victims, including those who have no part in the fight, than exist in the entire city of Menzoberranzan. I have witnessed Prisoner's Carnival, where the magistrates torture fellow humans with as much skill and glee as any whip-wielding priestess of Lolth. I have seen the elves of the surface turn refugees away from their shelter, leaving them to the mercy of those pursuing them. Even the often carefree halflings are not exempt from the darker shades of the heart.

Yet for all of this, I remain confident of a better tomorrow. Bruenor and the other dwarven kings and queens do not hold their people clenched within as tight a fist as their predecessors. Regis and Donnola do not rule Bleeding Vines, no. They are called the Lord and Lady of the village, but they are more the overseers of the business of the place, and, amazingly, they serve at the sufferance of their villagers. For Donnola has changed the tradition of the Topolino clan. And now the people of Bleeding Vines have been given a great gift: their voice.

Because that's what tradition does: it robs an individual of their voice. It eschews the solo, and focuses solely on the chorus—and woe be the singer who goes against the conductor!

No, Bleedings Vines is more of an orchestra, each instrument having its say, but playing in harmony, creating a whole. If the people there choose others to lead, then Donnola and Regis will step aside.

This is the tomorrow I hope for because, I believe, only in a culture where the demands of all the people are heard can the needs of the people be met.

This is the sound of tomorrow, and so tomorrow will be better than today.

꩜

I have learned so much from Grandmaster Kane in such a short period of time. I have learned to control my body, even to view my body, in ways I never before imagined. It is a vessel for my consciousness, and one that I can explore more deeply than ever did I know. I can manipulate my muscles to turn my hands into daggers, to stand strong against hurricane winds, even to the point where I can work my muscles individually to expel the venom of a snake or the poison of a dagger from the wound that introduced it.

I have learned angles of attack and defense superior to those taught to me in my years at the drow academy, or even under the tutelage of my father. Perhaps even more importantly, I have learned to anticipate the exact deflections of blocking angles, so that a simple turn of my hips will allow the striking sword to pass harmlessly, guided by a subtle block by my own scimitar, or even by my hand.

My time with the Grandmaster of Flowers has been such a marvelous exploration, within and without. The world around me, my friends around me, my wife, my coming child, are all different to me now, and in a more marvelous way by far, as if the negative impulses of jealousy, fear, and reactive anger have no way through the budding embarrassment I feel for even considering them. The journey is grander, lighter, and more profound all at once.

This, the larger picture of the world and multiverse about us, is the secret to Grandmaster Kane's always-calm demeanor, and his always-glad and always-humble aspect. He has come to know his place, and not in any diminishing way. Nay, far from it!

So, as I consider my time with Kane and the lasting effects of those experiences, I can say without reservation that the most important and precious thing I learned from him was gratitude.

I am grateful, every day—to strive for that in every moment is to seek perfection of the soul, in much the same way I have spent my life seeking perfection of the physical, of the warrior. Now I have learned to join those two things . . . no, four things: mind, body, heart, and soul, into a singular endeavor. To raise a hand in deflection of an incoming spear is to understand the movement and to hone my muscles to the required speed and reaction, of course, but such training without discipline and an understanding of the moral implications of such battle, even the spiritual repercussions of such a fight is to be . . . Artemis Entreri—and worse, the Artemis Entreri of old.

There need be a reason, more than a simple justification, and when you understand that all is one, those reasons crystallize more completely and give strength to your battle, strength at once physical, intellectual, emotional, and philosophical.

The complete warrior is more than one trained in exact and perfect movements. I have known this for a long time. Once I told Entreri that he could not beat me, not ever, because he did not fight with heart. Now, after seeing Kane, after being humbled by this man who has become so much more than human, I better understand my own words to Artemis Entreri on that long ago day. They are sentiments that Kane could have very recently spoken to me, leaving me with no honest recourse.

Yes, I am grateful to Kane, Grandmaster of Flowers of the Monastery of the Yellow Rose, and that which inspires my greatest gratitude is the widening perspective regarding everything about and around this consciousness I call self, regarding life itself, regarding reason itself, that reminds me to be grateful, and to learn, ever to learn.

This is our way.

This is our purpose.

This is our joy.

Our eternal joy.

Relentless

What place is this that is my world; what dark coil has my spirit embodied? In light, I see my skin as black; in darkness, it glows white in the heat of this rage I cannot dismiss. Would that I had the courage to depart, this place or this life, or to stand openly against the wrongness that is the world of these, my kin. To seek an existence that does not run afoul to that which I believe, and to that which I hold dear faith is truth.

Zaknafein Do'Urden I am called, yet a drow I am not, by choice or by deed. Let them discover this being that I am, then. Let them rain their wrath on these old shoulders already burdened by the hopelessness of Menzoberranzan.

Menzoberranzan, what hell are you?

I am caught off-balance, and in a way more painful than any disadvantage I've ever known, even in combat. Unlike in combat, I fear that the recovery will prove much more difficult and will take me many tendays, or months, or years, or lifetimes.

If I can ever find my way through to a place of acceptance with my son and those he considers his dearest friends—indeed, those he values more than he values me. That last thought is not a complaint, certainly, for these are the friends he has surrounded himself with for the majority of his life, the companions who have journeyed beside him on many adventures and stood beside him in many fights—legendary battles, from what Jarlaxle has told me.

So there is no jealousy here, nor bitterness about his relationship with these others.

Besides, my current predicament is my own fault. I know this, but admitting it even to myself is painful.

I hear the words coming out of my mouth, the reflexive jokes and jabs, and it is not until I see the expressions coming back at me, and then, sometimes, the angry words, that I realize that I have offended.

I am nearly two hundred years removed from the world of the living. Perhaps it is the different time, but more than that, I am in a place the likes of which I never knew in my former life.

My former life was that of a dark elf, a Lolthian drow. I never lived beyond Menzoberranzan and spent the entirety of my half millennium there, with only the exceptions of missions, all but two exclusively in the Underdark, and almost all either patrolling the perimeter corridors around the cavern that holds my city home, or to other drow cities in the thrall of the Spider Queen, usually Ched Nasad.

I saw a few humans, a few dozen dwarves, and only a handful of elves in that past life, and I did not mistreat them, and encouraged others, as much as I could without forfeiting my life, to similarly show mercy.

I thought that was correct of me, was something to hang a mantle of pride upon. How big of Zaknafein not to torture or murder a dwarf simply for being a dwarf!

I did not recognize my own prejudice, attributing my quieter, honest feelings to the simple matter of "that is the way of things."

It did not even occur to me that in applauding my own kindness, there was, too, an unspoken condescension. Unspoken, but I cannot honestly say unintended. For while I recognized the value of the human or dwarf or elf or halfling or gnome as a person and not as a goblinoid monster—and while I tried, in my brief interactions, to judge that non-drow person by her beliefs and what was in her heart, by her words or behavior—the judgment I expressed was conscious alone.

It wasn't in my heart.

Whether it was simply my upbringing, the community about me, the "way of things" hidden from my determination to prove otherwise, the truth was, I thought that I, as drow, was superior. I couldn't admit it to myself—perhaps I didn't consciously know this truth—but I imposed upon those other races limitations of expectation of their abilities, physical and mental.

I see it now, see it clearly, particularly when confronted with the reality that my son has married a human and that she carries within her womb a child both drow and human!

I recognize within me my own feelings of prejudice, but that does not mean they will be easily expunged.

No. I see that truth every time a prod, a jab, a mock slips past my tongue, one diminishing to the many non-drow around me, or one somehow designed to remind those few drow around me of the "way of things."

Now I know. The "way of things" is the most stubborn and debilitating demon of all.

Are they all like that?

Do all drow children possess such innocence, such simple, untainted smiles that cannot survive the ugliness of our world? Or are you unique, Drizzt Do'Urden?

And if you are so different, what, then, is the cause? The blood, my blood, that courses through your veins? Or the years you spent with your weanmother?

. This one is different!
This one is different.

∞

I am empty.

I have been given a great gift, so I believed, in being returned to life again, and in a world full of changes both hopeful and desperate—and in the latter, I feel as if I can make a significant difference.

On the surface, it is everything I wanted. It is an open fight against Lolth and her evil minions, a chance to strike back for all of the suffering that I and my people, and indeed the whole world, have endured at the Spider Queen's hands.

But I am empty.

In the last moments of my previous life, I gave myself that my son might live. That was the deal and the deal held, though only because Malice failed in trying to kill Drizzt. Because of that bargain, Drizzt was given a good life, one in which he found a better way, found an escape.

He found love.

All of this should lighten my heart, but how can it? I gave my life for Drizzt, and now, in what is to me only a few tendays of time, my deal was unwound, both ways. I am alive and he is lost to me—and that makes me wonder if I even want to be alive!

I know that I cannot think this way, particularly now. I will fend my grief with anger and determination—anger at my loss and determination that the product of Drizzt's love to this human woman will live the promise I wish I might have given to my son . . . or to my lost daughter.

Drizzt's child will grow up in the arms and care of a loving mother, and with many worthy and wonderful friends.

If she or he can survive this onslaught now faced in this place called Gauntlgrym.

The child will survive.

If I have to kill every demon, every drow, every enemy in all the world, this child will survive.

That is my promise to you, my lost son Drizzt.

And to you, my lost daughter Vierna.

Would that I had been better to both of you.

The Way of the Drow

⒮tarlight Enclave

My little Brie.

For most of my life, I have been blessed with friends and with a sense of, and clear direction of, purpose. I see the world around me and all I ever hoped to do was leave it a bit smoother in my wake than the choppy waters through which I traveled. I gained strength in the hope of some future community, and then indeed, in that community when at long last I found it. Found it, and now embrace it as my world expands wonderfully.

It's been a good life. Not one without tragedy, not one without pain, but one with direction, even if so many times that perceived road seemed as if it would lead to an ethereal goal, a tantalizing ring of glittering diamonds so close and yet just outside of my extended grasp. But yes, a good life, even if so many times I looked at the world around me and had to consciously strive to ward off despair, for dark clouds so often sweep across the sky above me, the murky fields about me, and the fears within me.

I weathered change—poorly and nearly to self-destruction—when my friends were lost to me, and never were the clouds, the fields, or my thoughts darker. During that midnight period of my life, I lost my purpose because I lost my hope.

But I found it again in the end, or what I thought the end, even before the twists of fate or the whims of a goddess manifested my hope in the return of my lost friends. I might have died alone with Guenhwyvar on that dark night atop Kelvin's Cairn.

So be it. I would have died contented because I was once more true to that which I demanded I be, and was satisfied that I had indeed calmed many waters in my long and winding current. But then there came more, so unexpectedly. A return of companions, of love and of friendship, of bonds that had been forged through long years of walking side by side into the darkness and into the sunlight.

And now, more still.

My little Brie.

When I burst through that door to first glimpse her, when I saw her there, so tiny, in the midst of my dearest friends, in the midst of those who had taught me and comforted me and walked with me, so many emotions poured through my heart. I thought of the sacrifice of Brother Afafrenfere—never will I forget what he did for me.

Never, too, did I expect that I would understand why he did it, but the moment I passed that threshold and saw my little Brie, it all came clear to me.

I was overwhelmed—by joy, of course, and by the promise of what might be. More than that, however, I was overwhelmed by a sense I did not expect. Not to this degree. For the first time in my life, I knew that I could be truly destroyed. In that room, looking at my child, the product of a love true and lasting, I was, most of all, vulnerable.

Yet I cannot let that feeling change my course. I cannot hide from my responsibilities to that which I believe—nay, quite the opposite!

For my little Brie, for other children I might have, for their children, for any children Regis and Donnola might have, for the heirs of King Bruenor, and Wulfgar, and for all who need calmer waters, I will continue to walk forward, with purpose.

It is a good life.

That is my choice.

Fly away on swift winds, clouds of darkness!

Take root, green grass, and blanket the murky fields!

Be gone from my thoughts, doubts and fears!

It is a good life because that is my choice, and it is a better life because I will stride with purpose and determination and without fear to calm the turbulent waters.

∽

As I have come to understand the greatest gift afforded me by my training with the monks of the Monastery of the Yellow Rose, the realization has both shocked and enlightened me.

One might think that greatest gift to be the strengthened connection between my mind and my body, a truer understanding of that which I want to perform and the deeper interactions of my physical form required to more easily and more completely execute the movement. I could always jump up in the air, for example, spin about and kick out my trailing foot as I turned. Almost any warrior, certainly any drow warrior, could do such a thing. But now my mind is speaking to the finer parts of my body, coordinating better the turn of my hips, the angle of my foot, the coil of the muscles on the back of my thigh, and the timing of the release of the kick. Where before, I might force back an opponent with such a maneuver, now I can end the fight with that single heavy blow if my opponent has not properly balanced and blocked to defend.

I do not understate the beauty of this gift. I can even manipulate my muscles to push poison from a wound! But this is not the greatest of the treasures I have gained.

One might think that greatest gift to be the understanding of ki, of life energy. Of being able to reach within and pull forth power beyond that of muscle and bone. The addition of this inner energy allows me to throw an opponent several strides away when I strike with my open hand. It allows me to find my wounds and turn my blood and muscles and all that is physically within me into some mediation of those injuries. With ki and the understanding of my physical form, I now run faster and jump higher. I make my scimitar strikes follow quicker and in perfect balance.

I am a finer warrior, but no, this is not the greatest of Grandmaster Kane's imparted treasures.

And then there is transcendence. I escaped the retriever with this act, melting my physical body into everythingness, becoming a part of all that was around me, the elemental starstuff that is the one eternal in the multiverse. That of which we and all we see about us is made. The sheer, unspeakable beauty of transcending the limitations of the physical form so fully would have left me forever there, a better place—a truer and fuller existence and understanding—than anything I have ever known or could ever know in this physical life.

But even this transcendence is not that which I now consider, in this moment of my existence, the greatest gift of all.

That pinnacle is reserved for the quietest of Grandmaster Kane's teachings, for meditation, true meditation, has freed me of the most common curse of the reasoning beings, be they drow, human, halfling, dwarf, elf, or perhaps even the goblinkin and giantkind, perhaps even others I do not begin to understand:

An unconscious bent toward some determined level of tension.

This is the gift that I am even now most determinedly trying to impart upon my dear little Brie, for it is the remedy to a curse that I have come to believe is imparted in the earliest years of life.

That curse cannot be understated, and I suspect it a universal affliction determined by degrees, not by its presence or absence.

We all have within us a level of tumult, a vibration in our hearts, our minds, our very souls, which we are most comfortable with as "normal." Like a pebble dropped into still water, that tumult is a result of drama, of conflict in mind or body or both. This sense of normalcy is taught very young, and refined as we become fully reasoning beings.

The curse lies in not understanding it.

In its most extreme circumstances, I have seen it in myself, or in King Bruenor, surely, when we both grew uneasy, itchy even, as we created about us an environment of peace and comfort.

"Ah, to the road!" was our common call to action, even when action wasn't needed.

Because the vibrations, the inner conflict, was needed for us to feel normal.

Bruenor hates being king when all the world about him is settled. It bores him profoundly (though now, with his wives, perhaps he finds suitable replacements of excitement and conflict!). He needs that sense of normalcy, and so he will achieve the needed tension no matter the situation around him. He will grump and moan about one thing or another, often minute, but never would he say a word or care about the small details of the more mundane issues flitting about him when threatened by a horde of demons. In that event, the tension is real and pressing, and thus the little problems no longer matter.

The curse, I now see, is that those littler problems do matter without that demon horde, and so they are unconsciously elevated to a place of distraction.

I have often wondered if this peace I seek in the world around me isn't really a lie I tell myself, given my own desire for adventure, and yes, even danger.

But those are extreme examples of the inner vibrations. Extreme and rare and of urges more easily defeated because they are so obvious, and possibly, so destructive or self-destructive. The lesser examples, the smaller pebbles, are ever-present in all of us and all about us. They manifest in gossip, in senseless arguments over unimportant actions or debates, in unreasonable fears about things over which we have no control, in silly worries about inadequacies or perceptions that have no place beyond the present in terms of importance . . . yet they are magnified within each of us into vibrations and tumult.

Of the mind, of the heart, of the very soul.

And thus, the greatest gift I have been granted by my time in the Monastery of the Yellow Rose is the true stilling of all three, of making the pond that is Drizzt Do'Urden so glassy and calm that the reflection of the world around me becomes an accurate representation of that which is, instead of that which is perceived through the ripples of inner tumult and inner vibration.

I am free of the itch. I am content in the present, every present, any present.

That does not mean that I have surrendered the love of adventure— far from it!

Nay, the gift is that now I can choose the adventure, now I can diffuse the drama, now I can throw away the fears and the worries to see the picture most clearly and to embrace the best course to repaint that picture or enjoy it without the unsummoned urge.

And conversely, what I know now is that I can bring forth that itch more perfectly when it is needed.

This blessing of clarity is indeed freedom.

All people have long periods of true trial, but their times of true ease seem less so. These moments of peace are often sabotaged, so I now believe, by our own insistence on worrying about things that aren't worth the worry.

To create ripples in the stillness creates for them the proper normal.

To one who has learned the way of Kane, those ripples are external alone, and when they come, they are seen with perfect clarity.

What a powerful force is this fascination with, this fear of, death. How could it not be so for a reasoning, mortal creature? Mortal in this form, at least.

We are groomed from childhood, or perhaps it is even innate in any logical being, to prepare for the future, to take actions that will lead us to the place we believe we wish to be. The gods of Faerun have made their positions of power based upon this! For the ultimate future for us all, we know, is not in this short life, but in whatever might come next, if anything (and if nothing, that is perhaps the cruelest possibility).

Yet, how can we properly prepare other than to give ourselves to a matter of faith? We seek evidence—I have found great hints in my journey of transcendence—and yet that which we can see as such remains hints and little more. This is the ultimate mystery of life, the greatest of all.

My journey with Kimmuriel has surprised me in a most wonderful way. To see him, the most emotionless person I have ever known, drawn into such discussions of purpose and place, of the point of life and the hopes of what might come next, was more than unexpected. It was shocking, nothing less.

There is no question of Kimmuriel's brilliance. He often resides in the vast library of the illithid hive mind, his consciousness flitting effortlessly among the memories and conclusions of that vast repertoire of experience and history. He has mastered a magic very different from that of priestesses like Catti-brie, a spellpower irrelative to the notion of divinity. He has mastered a magic very different from that of Gromph, for Kimmuriel's is also a spellpower independent of the Weave, the elemental powers, the harnessing of natural energies. His magic is purely intellectual, purely a matter of controlling his own thoughts and emotions and using that intellectual force as a weapon or a thief's tool.

Yet here he was beside me, acceding to my demands without questions, revealing his own vulnerabilities in the form of his hopes and fears as he tries to unravel this greatest of mysteries.

And more than that, I watched him bringing that journey back beyond his personal mind space and to the world around him, including responsibility to community above his responsibility to self—that he is even considering joining in the coming fight for

Menzoberranzan for altruistic and moral motivations is something I could never have anticipated. Not from Kimmuriel, whose journey surprises me more than that of Jarlaxle. Jarlaxle's heart was always hinted at in his actions, whatever other excuse he might make for his consistent generosity and caring. Kimmuriel's revelations here surprise me more than the journey I have seen in Artemis Entreri, whose path had to lead him through personal darkness, his own inability to look into a mirror and not be horrified by the reflection. For Entreri was as much victim as villain.

It surprises me even more than the journey of Dab'nay, or that which I am hoping is real within the Matron Mother of Menzoberranzan and the other "true" devotees of the horrid Demon Queen of Spiders. While I suspect, and not without evidence, that much of these doubts regarding the Lolthian clergy is also unintentionally in the service of Lolth, a demonic goddess who values strife and chaos above all else, I am convinced that those who have now seen the awful truth of Lolth will never go back, indeed, will die before reverting.

Watching the spiritual journeys of all these others, including my own wife, is a powerful reminder to me to ever hold tolerance for those who come to different conclusions than I, and to humble myself in my conclusions.

For much of my life, I have envied those who have found their answer, their savior, their planned and expected afterlife. I do not say that in any condescending manner, or with any thought at all that because I am not at the same place as those people, I am somehow better or more informed or more correct than they. For what I have understood from the beginning is that this place of faith, this understanding of the multiverse and the continuation of self beyond the mortal coil, is not something one can reach by power of will, or reason. It happens or it does not. It is an epiphany or it is not. I'm not talking about those who follow a religion simply out of tradition, but of those who truly believe.

Thus, when I say that I envied those who have had their epiphany,

I mean it, for I long awaited my own. Now I have found it. At the very least, I have come to understand that there was for me, albeit temporarily, something more, something grander, something freeing— freeing from the fascination and fear of the ultimate conclusion.

Long ago, I proclaimed my freedom because I knew that I would one day die. That certainty reminded me to grab at every sunrise and sunset, to appreciate the things so many take for granted.

Now I am freer still, because I have had my epiphany.

And now I feel even more certain in my agnosticism because I find myself joined by Kimmuriel, a drow of great intellect and great scholarship.

Never had I imagined that Kimmuriel Oblodra could become so obviously emotional over anything. He had watched his house torn down by Matron Mother Baenre, his entire family eliminated in but a few moments. He had watched his mother pulled back from her torment in the Abyss to serve as a connection to the illithid hive, only to be obliterated thereafter.

He spoke of it often, to me, to Jarlaxle, and never, not one time, did I see anything but a calculated and intellectual approach to the personal tragedies.

Even now, in our journey together to the east, when he recounted those events, they were offered only as lessons in the potential power that Lolth's chosen might bring to bear against usurpers and heretics. There was no hint of grief, no mention that he had ever cared for K'yorl and the others. But when he spoke of the coming storm, and more than that, of the history of Menzoberranzan as revealed by the memories given to Yvonnel and Matron Mother Quenthel, there I saw the desperate longing, a clear sparkle, a clear sense of both eagerness and trepidation—a combination of emotions that can be found only when the outcome matters quite a lot to the person speaking.

As I ponder this seeming inconsistency in the cold-hearted psionicist, the knot of Kimmuriel's heart unravels. He had been trained to resignation. He had not flinched, or barely so, when his family had been destroyed, when his house and legacy and inheritance of stature and wealth had been so brutally and abruptly stolen from him—all because it was not an unexpected event in the cynicism that had been ingrained into Kimmuriel, into so many of us in Menzoberranzan, from birth.

A combination of helpless resignation and sheer numbness from the daily assaults and atrocities is a deadly mix to the emotions of any drow.

But these days, a sparkle in Kimmuriel's eye.

Now he comes to ride with me, to speak with me, to hope with me.

That is the key to his awakening: he dares to hope.

I cannot hide within myself now, though I truly wish I could. My excuses against that light of hope ring hollow in my own ears, but I cannot deny the resistance to this hope within my own heart.

What will be my role, I wonder?

The action of the matron mother and Yvonnel on the field was stark and shocking, I admit, and no doubt many witnessing it felt that same surge of hope.

Initially.

When I think back to my days in Menzoberranzan, what I remember most of all is the zealotry of the Lolthian priestesses, of my own mother, Matron Malice. I expect that, had this great event and great heresy occurred back in those times, I would have seen the sparkle in the eyes of Zaknafein, surely, and likely in those of my sister Vierna, perhaps even in the eyes of Maya.

Those embers of hope would have been quickly extinguished by Malice, I am sure, and even if not, even if Malice had heard the hopes and promises of her children and consort, the idea that she would have turned from Lolth would derive only from her belief that whichever side she chose would most favorably affect her. Malice loved the fight. In this time, she would side with Matron Mother Quenthel only if she thought

Quenthel would win, and that she, Malice, would then be given ample reward.

But even that would have happened only if Malice had come to believe that Lolth was pleased with the chaos and the carnage, that the Spider Queen, in the end, would reward the victors and forget the vanquished.

Perhaps that is the unavoidable outcome of this impending fight. How many of Matron Mother Quenthel's allies will be so only for self-serving purposes? And how many only because they are confused, or afraid? Will mighty House Baenre, leading the revolt against Lolth, even be able to hold tight its own members? Will the driders-turned-drow even prove loyal soldiers to Quenthel, or will we quickly discover that they, too, were no more than a force planted by the Spider Queen, to test her children, to wreak chaos and root out those insufficiently devout?

I cannot escape these thoughts, no matter how clearly I recognize within myself that same cynicism that allowed Kimmuriel Oblodra to shrug at the loss of his family! And this is not who I have striven to be since my first days out of that cursed city. Always, I choose against fear.

But I cannot deny that my heart has not yet come to accept this glimmer of hope.

I have too much to lose.

I have Catti-brie and we have Brie, and the joy of that is more than I could ever have imagined. They would live on, and well I think, were I gone. Brie could not ask for a better mother than Catti-brie, and Catti-brie could not ask for better friends than the companions about us, her father and Wulfgar and Regis most important among them. She would not be alone were I to die in Menzoberranzan, a point made all too clear to me when I returned from my journey to everythingness to find my wife and new daughter surrounded by so much love.

I neither doubt nor discount the grief Catti-brie would experience were that to happen. Simply thinking that she might now be lost in the north has my gut churning with twisting fears and imagined horrors and the most profound sense of possible emptiness I have ever known. On those occasions when the fears overwhelm me and I come to believe that perhaps she is truly lost to me, I am broken. Even while in the light of Brie's smile, I am empty.

I remember that feeling so keenly. I remember that morning in Mithral Hall when I awakened to find Catti-brie lifeless beside me. I remember my horror, my helplessness, in watching her spirit fly away, just out of reach, until it was gone through the solid reality of stone. It is not a feeling I ever want to experience again.

And it is not a feeling I want to inflict upon Catti-brie.

Nor do I wish for Brie to grow up wondering about her father who is not there. Will she see drow men walking toward her and think them her da? Will she feel as if I chose to be away from her, that I left her because I cared about something more than I cared about her? Or will she understand that I left because I cared so much about her that I needed to try to make the world better for her?

And that is the rub. At what point might this greater struggle become someone else's to pick up and fight? At what point—is there a point?—will it be someone else's turn, when I am free to bask in the quieter and more personal responsibilities of my life?

Or am I doomed to be so consumed by future hopes that I would miss out on all the present joys?

The conflict is clear and jarring between my personal responsibilities and the wider mission, the purposeful road I have walked since I rejected Menzoberranzan, since I vowed that I would fight for that which, in my heart, is just and good. I know that the coming war in Menzoberranzan, as terrible as it will be, is to be waged to break free of the demon Lolth, that it will be fought in the hopes of the ultimate win for my people. For the shattering of crushing dogma that has hurt so many and will hurt so many more.

For freedom.

Yet for all that, what is my place?

If Catti-brie does not return from the north, am I to leave Brie with the monks? With Bruenor? In either instance, am I abandoning my greater responsibility to her, to make sure she will grow in the arms of a parent?

It is the first time in my life that I have had to ask myself this question.

It is the first time that I have had so much to lose.

It is the first time I've really had to ask: What is my place?

Glacier's Edge

In my many times of introspection, I find that I am often concerned with the notion of perception. Whether in politics or religion or the relationships of the various cultures and creatures of Faerun, there is always the matter of basic truths, of course, but more importantly, there is the matter of perception of those truths and where they will lead, and where they should lead. We are creatures guided by reason, by fact and logic, but we are, too, creatures guided by emotion.

Undeniably so, but separating the emotional from the logical is no easy task for most, myself included.

So I think about such moments that challenge us. How much worse is the cost of a battle if one you love is lost in the fight? And how less painful if all the casualties are distant from you emotionally?

The personal cost is not the same as the greater cost, for if a dozen were killed in the two scenarios above, then a dozen had been killed, and so the cost from afar should be considered the same. But we know it is not the same to different people. When an army returns from the bloodied fields, the news of the battle will be received much more viscerally and poignantly in a village where many were lost than in one where none were. And that will be felt differently in a large city where soldiers are lost than it is in those small villages.

Again, though, it depends on what city, on what people. If Clan Battlehammer went to war and a dozen dwarves were lost in a victorious campaign, they would rejoice in the outcome. Yes, they would salute the fallen, but with mugs raised solemnly within a sea of cheer. But if one of those fallen was King Bruenor, or one of the queens of Mithral Hall, the mugs would be raised solemnly within a sea of somber acceptance.

This is a maddening truth to me, but it is also an undeniable truth.

The blend of these two often conflicting realities—logical and emotional—goes deeper than the mere perception of the world around us. I have come to believe that it goes a long way toward determining the type of person one might be. I am led inescapably to the belief that the level to which one can empathetically look past the personal to the pains and losses of the wider situation is a measure of one's heart and goodness.

Perhaps the only one.

I have met so many people who do not think something is troubling, or threatening, or terrible, and no amount of cajoling or explaining or presenting compelling evidence will move them from that dispassionate stance—until that individual or someone very dear to that individual is personally affected by the incident or assailant, or disease.

As I watch the growth of Artemis Entreri, for example, I see that he has come to greatly enlarge his circle of caring. He has admitted friends into his personal group, and the widening of that circle has led him to see the pain of others even when such pain is not acute to him.

Empathy.

So often have I seen a lack of such, both in those selfish and tight with their hearts and, more surprisingly, in those who believe themselves firmly grounded in reason and verifiable fact. For how easy it is to get lost in thought, quite literally! And in those streams of sorting and calculating and hoping, how easy it is to lose sight of the reality that surrounds you.

We are all susceptible to this blurring of reality, this clouding of the physical truths about us while seeking the clarity of our philosophical eyes.

Similarly, we are all victims to our selfishness to one degree or another. We all narrow our perception too tightly at times and forget the truth: if a person is in another place, how clearly do we appreciate that the world continues even when we're not there? Life continues in all its complexities and personal struggles, pain and joy.

This existence, limited by our senses and thoughts and physical frailties, is not our dream, except collectively, which is hard to accept because our own experiences are so uniquely personal, and yet, at the same time, they are universal.

Bruenor often chides me that I overthink things, and here I am again, guilty. It is so easy to get lost in the philosophical, in the mysteries, in the unanswerable questions that are always there, somewhere, in your thoughts, ready to come forth whenever some event—the death of a loved one, a near brush of your own—starkly reminds you. This has been my uneven and confusing journey for some time, particularly since I returned from my transcendence of my mortal and physical self and glimpsed . . . possibilities.

For there I have been lost.

It took a drow psionicist, a man I've hardly considered a friend, and never more than an ally about whom I remain suspicious and cautious, to refocus my sensibilities, to pull me out of the malaise of pondering the greater picture of my personal future and remind me that the world about me continues to spin.

To perceive beyond myself. To perceive beyond those in my immediate sphere.

To empathize with the wider world.

The road I walked those years in Menzoberranzan, and out of Menzoberranzan, has paved the way for others. As I became free of the grip of Lolth, as I became beyond her reach—no matter what she did to my physical being—so, too, can my drow sisters and brothers find their way. And I am called to help them. Whatever I may desire personally—my love for Catti-brie and our dear daughter; my joy when I am with my friends in these lands we have tamed and the good we have done for those around us; the simple pleasures of sitting on the back lawn of the Monastery of the Yellow Rose and allowing the stars to lift my spirits to the wide multiverse—my duty is now clear to me and the stakes could not be higher.

I cannot ignore the spinning wheels rolling and roiling all about me. Whatever my personal feelings—a sense of completion I do not wish disturbed—I must shake them and understand that this particular journey, one that I in no small manner started, fanned, and pulled so many along with me.

Menzoberranzan is going to war.

Drizzt Do'Urden is going to war.

If everything is one, is one lonely?

The question sounds ridiculous, and yet it has haunted me in recent days, since the very notion of this unexpected paradox came into my thoughts. The beauty of transcendence, so I came to believe in my short experience with it, was the oneness—with everything, with every stone and tree and living creature and empty space and star. It was a vast examination of complete consciousness and understanding, a higher level of thought and of being, no doubt. That was the comfort and the joy. New experiences and understanding lying open before me, settled in a multiverse of supreme contentment and harmony.

But if I become one with those who went before, if our consciousness and understanding, our thoughts and our feelings, are fully shared, and at such a level of intimacy that the word "shared" comes nowhere near to properly explaining the joining, does that also imply a solitary existence? All-consuming, omnipresent, and omniscient . . . but therefore alone?

That would be heaven and that would be hell.

So no, I say and I hope. Oneness and appreciation that we are all starstuff should not, and I hope does not, completely replace some piece of individuality.

In a paradoxical and wholly unexpected way, viewing the multiverse through the sense of transcendent oneness has led me to a place of truer empathy and appreciation for those with whom I disagree. Arguing, debating, the very experience of having your "truths" challenged, is the flavor of life and the key ingredient of growth. To lean toward perfecting oneself is the challenge, to be better with each passing experience, to climb the proverbial mountain on trails smooth and paths difficult is to feel that forward and upward movement and so experience the sense of satisfaction and accomplishment.

Is that lost in omnipresence?

Is omniscience so perfect and complete that such feelings are no longer needed?

I cannot know and will not know (or perhaps know not at all) until this mortal being is no more, and that inescapable truth put in me a disinterest, or more accurately, a distance, from the tribulations of the material, mortal world. A revelation that should be naught but beauteous had instead instilled a melancholy.

I see the simple joys still. My smiles are not strained when I look upon Brie, or Catti-brie, or any of my friends, but my interest surely is.

Or was.

For that melancholy, I see clearly now, has been paid for by the detriment of those I love.

That cannot stand.

And now I see, too, that for all the beauty of transcending this mortal coil and all of its limitations, what I lost in that short journey is not subtle and not without regret.

Because I want to argue. I want to be challenged. I want to disagree.

And most of all, I want to come to understand the perspective of the other person—the separate and distinct individual, carrying the weight of their own experiences and trials and joys and needs, with whom I am at such odds.

The cost of transcendence goes even deeper than that, I now see. Perhaps loneliness is the wrong word for a state of omniscience, or more clearly, it describes only a part of the loss.

For in this journey toward the state, there is hope, and through the trials, there is accomplishment, and even the scars of failure have value as signposts toward betterment.

I lived alone for many years, relying only on myself. That changed when I met Mooshie, and shifted even more completely when I first climbed the slopes of Kelvin's Cairn in Icewind Dale and discovered myself as a willing member of a group, of a family.

They rely on me, and that feels wonderful.

I rely on them, and know I can, and that feels better still.

Together we are stronger. Together we are better, sharing joys, dividing grief and pain.

We are bonded, yet we remain distinct. We argue—oh, how we argue!—and we grow. We fear for each other in battle, and remain glad that we are all in it together.

Even before we ventured north, Grandmaster Kane could have simply shed his physical body and remained within me, joining my thoughts, sharing my flesh, guiding me and strengthening me, offering all without question and without any room for disagreement, since we two would understand—would perfectly understand—every thought and command.

But Kane didn't do that, and he wouldn't, and there need be no explanation offered as to why. For we both knew and know the joy of individuality.

When I was gone from this existence and Brother Afafrenfere came after me to tell me of Brie, to whisper to me that my time here was not completed, he and I remained distinct beings.

Even within that omniscience and omnipresence of transcendence, we remained distinct.

I pray that detail does not blur to nothingness in whatever truly comes next after this life journey is ended.

I need my companions.

I need to be needed by my companions.

This is my greatest joy.

∽

As I pause and consider the recent revelations of the founding of Menzoberranzan, I am struck by the deeper notion that perception shapes morality as much as does objective truth. On the one hand, this offends that in me which demands reason and fact, but on the other, for all of my complaints, I find this observation undeniable.

I do not know—I cannot know—which version of Menzoberranzan is real, the one taught to me at the Academy, the one of Lolth saving her children some four millennia past, or the one revealed by the memories of Yvonnel, which count the city as only half that age, and claim its founding was based in the highest demands of egalitarian fairness—indeed, even the belief that I hold that when the collective consciousness and conscientiousness guide policy and direction, that world becomes more just and fair.

I cannot know which version is true, and it startles me to realize that there really is no way for me to even verify the age of the oldest buildings and artifacts of the city of my birth, or whether the stalagmites and stalactites were hollowed by the drow who settled there or by a culture previous to them.

I cannot know! And that is the inescapable "truth" of history: that it is, in the end, a story, and one that could well change with new information.

Still, hearing of the events that played out on the field outside of Gauntlgrym, of the magical web that stole the curse from the tormented driders, and more importantly, the source of that web, has brought me great hope, for I know which version I wish to be true, and therefore choose to believe. And thus, which story I will use as I go, because the tale of Yvonnel points to that which I know in my heart to be true.

It was Lolth's doing. It was always foul Lolth.

But what then of those who went along with her in the earliest days, her disciples and matrons? I cannot believe that they were only there for the power and riches Lolth offered them, because, were that the case, the Spider Queen's hold would not have endured these many centuries. No, they believed her lies, I am sure. They believed in her way and guidance, and so believed themselves in the right, particularly since believing that they were in the right brought them that which they desired.

None are more dangerous than a villain who thinks she's noble, and none are more convinced or convincing than a converted disciple. No chance to proselytize will be missed, no sermon given in flat tones, no hint of doubt ever revealed.

Menzoberranzan is a small place in the grander scheme of Faerun. The cavern isn't ten miles across in any direction, and there really aren't nearby cities or trusted cultures, or any source where the drow within that cavern can garner the information, the truth, that will guide their day-to-day actions. And so it is easy for a few select minions of the Spider Queen—in this case, the matrons and powerful priestesses— to well control the story taught to every drow.

Some know better, of course. Kimmuriel's family found their truths at the hive of the illithids, and a wizard of Gromph's power can wander the very planes of existence to find answers. But most of Menzoberranzan's drow do not have such resources, and so, typically, that which they believe is that which they are taught.

They just know what they know. I doubt that I am the only one whose conscience demanded a questioning of those accepted truths. Indeed, I know I am not the only one, but I doubt that even those few others I know of—Zaknafein, Kimmuriel, Jarlaxle, Dab'nay—are rare exceptions. But again, I must remind myself. Menzoberranzan is not a large place. Nor was Ched Nasad or the other few drow cities of the Underdark. And in those places, such heretical thoughts are dangerous and bear with them the most dire consequences imaginable. So even though many don't speak out, I am certain that I am not the only drow who felt completely alone and helpless in my heretical notions.

There is a profound difference between the dupers and the duped. Lolth, of course, is the queen of deceit, but her handmaidens are no less culpable. And those drow who went along with—who still go along with—her demands for reasons self-aggrandizing or enriching are no better. These are the dupers, and "evil" is the only word I can use for them.

How many of the rest are the duped, I wonder? How many believe in the cause of Lolth because they have fallen under that spell, likely since birth, and so believe in the nobility of their ways? Is it evil to kill a human, an elf, a dwarf, if you truly believe that such peoples are enemies, mortal and irredeemable enemies, who will kill any and all who you love if you stay your blade?

Had I killed Artemis Entreri in one of our earliest encounters, had I pursued him until I found the means to finish him, would that have been an evil act? If I believed that he would wantonly murder innocents if I didn't finish the deed, would I have been evil for killing him, or would it be more damaging and aye, evil, if I let him live and so doomed other innocent people to death?

When you are a drow in Menzoberranzan and fall under the spell of Lolth, everyone who is not drow is thought to be that dangerous version of Artemis Entreri which I feared would prove true.

This is the challenge in the coming struggles for the heart and soul of Menzoberranzan, to separate the dupers from the duped, and to convince the duped that the truth is not what they have been taught, and that there is a better way, a gentler way, a more prosperous and moral way.

No easy task, that. In many cases, when a person is convinced of a truth, no amount of evidence will be enough to dissuade them, and

I have found, to my horror, that the very act of presenting contrary evidence often pushes that person deeper into their beliefs!

Yes, this is the challenge, and in the coming struggles, we will either convince them or we will kill them, or they will kill us.

I am sure that Lady Lolth will enjoy the spectacle either way.

Until it is over, I say, for the side of truth will win, and then Lolth will no longer be welcome in the hearts of the drow.

That is my vow.

⌒∽

Considering the question of the boundaries and relationship between that which is internal and that which is external in training with the monks has been truly enlightening to me.

The world is external to us, of course. It is all around us, populated by people and animals and creatures who have free will and desires different from our own. Lightning will strike a tall tree in the forest whether I hear the shock or see the flash. The world turns around us when we are gone, and so of course it is external to us.

Yet, not completely.

Our perception shapes that which we see and hear and feel. The world is as it is, but as it is will not always, not even often, be the same thing to two different people. And that which you hear about the world around you also shapes your perception.

I watch the sunrise. It holds great meaning for me, not just because of its external beauty, but because it reminds me of the deprivation of Menzoberranzan and the Underdark. Watching the sun climb above the horizon is to me a replaying of my own ascent to the world of daylight.

Not everyone will feel this way about the sunrise, and so this external event is also an internal event. The world around us shapes us and we shape the world around us.

That may seem like a small thing, but because of the monks, because of Kane most of all, I have come to better appreciate the gravity of that simple and seemingly obvious notion. For oftentimes that external shaping is debilitating or restricting. And other times, it can lead to false meaning—you can quite truly lose yourself within the moment of philosophical introspection to the point where you have lost touch with the other things, and more importantly with the other people, around you. The inability to recognize the very different perception another might find from what you consider to be a shared event will lead to confusion and often conflict.

Also, standing deep in expectations for that which is around you can be akin to wallowing in an intellectual puddle of mud.

When I allowed Grandmaster Kane's spirit into my mind and body in the gnoll cave, he saw something quite obvious that I had completely missed, because I was standing deep in such mud. When I first acquired Dantrag Baenre's bracers, I found them confusing and detrimental. My mind could not keep up with my hand movements when I put them on, and worse, my feet could not keep up with my weapon movements, throwing me out of balance.

But I am not that young warrior any longer.

With my training beside Grandmaster Kane, with the brothers and sisters of the Order of St. Sollars, I have greatly increased my foot speed. Understanding the harmony of hips and legs—no, not just understanding, but sensing every connection between them, has greatly increased my ability to run and jump and turn quickly about, to say nothing of the added fluidity and the simply physical power afforded by a proper understanding of the life force, ki.

I wear my bracers as bracers now, clamped about my wrists, and the movements of my arms, my scimitars, are matched and paced by the turns and steps. Two strikes become three, and no balance is lost.

Kane saw it immediately when he was within my form as we did battle—he most likely saw it from without well before that. Regardless, I believe that without his slightly different viewing prism, I never would have found this simple adjustment.

More importantly, Kane's temporary presence within me has helped me find the harmony between two distinct fighting styles, warrior and monk. He showed me the balance intimately, and with his skill and understanding, I saw and felt the true harmony, though I believe I still have some way to go before I can find that balance on my own. But now I know where to go. Before, I would fluctuate back and forth between the two styles as the situation presented—leaping like a monk, rolling my blades in warrior routines, striking with ki from afar or catching arrows like a monk, parrying and riposting like a warrior.

Now the disciplines are more united within me, a blend of styles that will, when perfected, provide me with more options, more tools, and more choices, both conscious and instinctive, in any situation.

In terms of battle, my internal adjustments and perceptions have changed the world around me. I see a tunnel, a hill, a riverbank, a parapet, in a different way now as I calculate my best course of action and shape the battlefield to my advantage.

Now, too, I see the sunrise differently. I still view my own journey in its ascent above the horizon, still see the sheer beauty of the splayed colors, but now, after transcending my mortal form, I see, too, the distance of the celestial bodies, the great voids between them, the starstuff they represent, of which I am a part.

The sunrise is more beautiful to me now.

And I am more formidable.

Loltgh's Warrior

My previous malaise embarrasses me. When I returned to this life, I did so without the proper appreciation of . . . this life! And with that shortcoming, so, too, did I pass that malaise onto those around me—not intentionally, no! But my actions and words, my detachment from the very responsibilities of friendship, of partnership, of parenting, could not be ignored, even as I worked harder to cover them up.

That which I had witnessed in what I believe is next existence had brought upon me a great despair, and an almost overwhelming sense of the smallness of this existence. Not outwardly, but within my own consciousness.

I could not have been more wrong.

How could I have allowed myself to be so tempted by that which might come next, to ignore that which is here and now? It took a ferocious battle, a great victory, a great personal loss, and a moment of shared exultation to show me my errors.

Callidae was more than I could have ever hoped for—for all of us who were born and raised in Menzoberranzan, the journey through that city among the aevendrow was the fulfillment of our (almost always secret) hopes and visions and lamentations of what Menzoberranzan might have been.

For me, it also ended a personal debate that, from the beginning, seemed an obvious answer—yet still, it was immensely satisfying to see my beliefs proven so dramatically.

It was Lolth. Always Lolth.

Not the religion of her worshippers—for how can anyone rightly call it a religion, after all, since the "divine being" for whom you're supposed to take on as a matter of faith is, in fact, a dictatorial menace who's often meddling directly, and surely doling out extreme punishments directly? Worshipping Lolth in Menzoberranzan isn't a matter of faith, hardly! It's not even obeisance, or any expression of deserved respect or gratitude or any such thing. No, it is blind obedience, and obedience stemming from either a hunger for power—such as with many of the ruling matrons—or simple, logical terror for almost everyone else.

I will shake my head until it clears, until I somehow come to understand this notion of fear as a great motivation.

But I also must examine my own thoughts and feelings regarding Callidae, and that is the most pressing thing.

And I must admit my foolishness in allowing the beauty of transcendence to almost steal so much from me. For if the journey from this life to the next is what I now believe it to be, then yes, had I remained in that higher state, outside of this mortal body, dead to this life and alive in the next, I would have learned of Callidae and of all the other drow cities and clans the aevendrow told me existed throughout the surface world of Faerun. I would have known them in that oneness, in that complete and beautiful understanding.

But would I have felt them? Would I have felt Callidae with the living sensations that overwhelmed me up there on the icy shelf when first I looked over the city? Would I have held Catti-brie for support, and kissed her so dearly for bringing me to that place? Would my joy have multiplied by the look on her face in sharing this discovery she

and the others had made with me? Or would my joy have multiplied in seeing Jarlaxle's smile, Zaknafein's nod, and even the glow that emanated so clearly from Artemis Entreri?

Or by the look on the face of Jarlaxle as he, at long last, found what he had spent much of his life seeking? We shared a lot on that high ledge when he nodded knowingly to me.

Would my joy have multiplied by the sublime calm of Kimmuriel, who at long last had found a measure of value and caring that he before could only hope existed?

Or by the sobs of Gromph (though he did well to hide them), the great and powerful archmage at long last humbled into admitting his own feelings, overwhelmed as he had never before allowed, by something beyond his control, by something that had brought him such joy that was not of his own making?

As much as the sight of Callidae had meant to me—and I cannot understate the importance of realizing that place and those aevendrow— sharing that moment with the others, absorbing their myriad expressions and emotions and taking them as my own and giving to them my own, made it all the more wonderful.

And that is the rub of transcendence. That is the fear I hold of losing something, if indeed, there is no individuality. But this I cannot yet know, this fear I cannot yet dismiss. But so be it.

Now, finally, I understand.

I am in this moment of my journey, in this forming word of my story.

The present will not be a prisoner of the past.

The present will not be a servant for the future.

In the weight of it all, it is the journey that matters, the moment, the forming word.

In walking the streets of Callidae, in talking to the aevendrow, the contrast with Menzoberranzan could not be more stark. This was the answer, for me and for Jarlaxle, at least, and likely for the other companions from Menzoberranzan, as well, although I do not know if Zaknafein, Kimmuriel, Dab'nay, or certainly Gromph, had ever so directly pondered the question: Was there something within me, within all drow, a flaw in our nature, a predetermination, a damning fate, of all the evils of our culture for which the other cultures of Faerun cast blame and aspersions?

Certainly, I never felt such inner urges or demons or wishes to cause harm. Nor, I am sure, did my sisters—at least two—or my father. I never saw such natural malice in Jarlaxle, or even in Kimmuriel, though he often frightened me.

But still, even knowing that, it was ever hard for me to fully dismiss the opinions that the peoples of other lands and races and cultures placed upon the drow, upon me. Catti-brie once said to me that perhaps I was more constrained by the way I saw other people seeing me than by the way those other people viewed me, and there is truth to that little semantic twist. But the truth went deeper, went to the core of who Drizzt Do'Urden truly was, or, more importantly, of who I ever feared I might be or might become.

The expectation of others is an often-crippling weight.

But now I have the answer. Now we all have the answer, even those companions who perhaps never directly asked the question.

We drow are not flawed. We are not lesser. We are not malignant by any measure of nature. I do not know how high the ladder of evil deeds such truth climbs, honestly. I have seen wicked dictators of every race and culture to match the vileness of the most zealous Lolthian priestess. I have witnessed truly evil people, from dwarves to halflings to humans to elves to drow, and everything in between and every race or culture only a bit removed. So perhaps there are some individuals who have within them a natural evil.

Or perhaps even with them, even with the most wicked, like Matron Zhindia Melarn or the magistrates of Luskan's carnival who torture accused criminals with such glee, there were steps in the earlier days of their personal journey which corrupted them and brought them to their present state. That is a question that I doubt will ever show an answer, nor is that answer truly the most important factor, for in the present, in the moment, in their own actions, these folk, as with us all, bear responsibility.

The more important question to me in all of this is how can an entire city—nearly all within the city—be so held in thrall, be twisted to the will of a demon queen so completely that they lose all sense of what is right and what is wrong? Because surely that basic understanding is something that any reasoning being should possess!

In Menzoberranzan, I am coming to understand, there were far more akin to me than those gladly embracing the tenets of Lolth and her vicious clergy. Even Dab'nay, who long ago realized how much she despised all that was Lolth (and yet, remained a priestess and was still being granted magical spells from that being she despised!).

The answer, I now know, is fear. Of all the inspirations, the motivations, any leader can give, the easiest is fear, and it is perhaps the most difficult to push aside. Dab'nay could secretly hate Lolth, but to proclaim it openly would have meant her death, if she was lucky. More likely, she would have been turned into a drider, sentenced to an eternity of unrelenting anguish.

Fear is a powerful weapon, and the tragic result of a vile king or lord is a tale too often told, and easy to see in the more transient societies of the shorter-living races. I have seen kingdoms of humans taken to bad end by a lord with evil designs—we saw this with Neverember and the Waterdhavian houses he corrupted for his personal gain. These are among the most predictable and saddest tales in the annals of the human societies, where one state or another decides to wage war, to steal land or resources from a neighbor. And also, thankfully, along with being the common, such states are often the most transient. Kingdoms that were once avowed enemies are now grand allies and friends, sharing markets, inter-marrying, prospering together.

The difference in Menzoberranzan, most obviously, is that the power there, the wicked lord with evil designs, was, and remains, not transient. A human leader will die—perhaps their successor will be of a better and more generous heart. Nor is the simple physical geography of the surface kingdoms conducive to any lasting and debilitating autocracy, for many of the people will come to know folk of other lands, and so will learn of the shortcomings of their society when placed against the aspirations and hopeful visions of their neighbors.

Such is not the case in the cavern of my birth. Not only is Lolth eternal and ever-present, a dictator who will not unclench her talons, but the city itself is secluded. I am not unique in my desire to flee, nor am I the only drow who did run from Menzoberranzan through the millennia of Lolthian control. Perhaps I am not the only one who made it out of there, who somehow, with good fortune, survived the wilds of the Underdark, and with better fortune, found a home, a true place within a family. But for every drow like me who somehow escaped, I take heart in knowing that there are thousands who would like to escape, who see the wrongs before them.

Lolth's method is lying.

Lolth's inspiration is fear.

Lolth's full damnation of the drow in Menzoberranzan is that she is eternal, clutching tighter at every generation.

Now, we have a chance to break that hold, to free the city, to turn the whispers of the drow into open shouts of denial.

That is why I could not stay in Callidae. That is why I could not stay in the comfort of my homes in Longsaddle or Gauntlgrym, my wife and daughter beside me.

Because now, only now, we have a chance.

Of all the traits I find more important in those with whom I surround myself, the one that matters more to me is the value of that person's word. Without that, there is no trust. Without trust, there is no chance at any true relationship. People who know me and see that I am friends with Jarlaxle might wonder about this, but the truth of Jarlaxle is that he has honor, that he would not coerce or lie or cheat on any matter of importance. He is a gameplayer, but he is not a malicious person.

His effect on Artemis Entreri cannot be overstated. Entreri was possessed of many of these same qualities, though they were buried beneath great pain and unrelenting anger, mostly self-loathing. Jarlaxle coaxed him from that state.

When these two—add Kimmuriel, as well—give me their word, I have learned that I can trust that word.

So many times, I have heard someone labeled a brilliant tactician in battle or in debate or in commerce, whether with armies or weapons or goods or words, only to see that person up close and then shake my head and sigh in resignation—a sigh that once would have been disgust, but now I know it in response to something so common that I cannot hold that much disgust! For as I see the workings of their words and tactics, what I see is not brilliance, but in fact, nothing more than immorality. For these very often powerful individuals, their true gift is a curse: they are simply not bound by decency.

They are foul beyond the expectations of those they dupe.

Coercing a populace to get behind you by lying to them isn't brilliant. Great orators playing an audience based on their predisposed beliefs, or worse, fears, by telling them lies or making promises they know they cannot keep isn't a sign of brilliance or intelligence, nay. It's merely a clear indication of a lack of ethics and character.

Cheating in a physical competition, as I learned most painfully in my years at the academy, doesn't make you a better swordsman—in fact, the result might prove quite the opposite.

Selling someone a miracle cure or coaxing them into a transaction that is meant to simply take their gold makes not a titan of business in any moral universe. Sadly, though, in simple practical terms, it often will make exactly that, a person who sacrifices their moral character and inflicts pain on others in exchange, almost always, for excess.

This, too, is the battle for Menzoberranzan, a war for the commonwealth and the soul of my people. Lolth is lies and Lolth is terror, nothing more. But those indecent traits have brought her to unquestioning power in the houses of Menzoberranzan and stripping her of that power may well prove impossible.

It is a try, though, that most of us have come to see as worth the fight, and the inevitable sacrifice. It is a battle for what is right, a war that will resonate to all who survive it and to their children and descendants who come after.

We shall see.

How many hours have I spent penning these essays, clearing my thoughts in lines of words, winding and weaving until I know what I know?

And knowing, too, that what I now know is not what I might believe as the story continues, as my journey teaches me new truths—and I pray that I will never close my heart off to such insights.

For that is what this is: a story. I think of my life as a story I am writing. It is in my control. I am the author, for only I can be the author of this story.

As it is for all of us. I am the author of my story, as anyone who may one day be reading this . . . as you, are the author of your own story. Whatever twist, whatever station, whatever circumstance, the story remains yours to write, yours to feel, yours to make. There are, of course, so many things that cannot be controlled, but regardless of those, the outlook, the emotions, the handling of the offered journey is the lifebook that is written.

The journey. For me, from my earliest days, my earliest memories, the journey has always been more important than the goal. Learning to fight and to navigate the drow academy was more important than becoming a great warrior, as the former would lead to the latter, to whatever level I might elevate.

I cannot determine if the sunrise will be brilliant or one dulled by clouds too heavy, but I can always control my own reaction to it. I can always find the hope in those early rays or misty glow. I can always smile in response and remind myself that I am blessed to witness whatever the dawn has shown to me. That, I know, is better than lamenting the clouds, after all.

I cannot control the clouds. As I cannot control so much regarding the circumstances around me.

But my reactions to them, and my choices because of them . . . those are my own, and mine alone. That is my journey and no one else's.

I rarely, very rarely, go back and read these essays I have penned. Or perhaps I should call them "sorts," for that is what they are: a sorting, an unwinding of the complicated and tangled threads that block my path through my journey. One might think, I might think, that perhaps I would refer to them often. But no. Such a read is rare, and never for more than one sort at a time. On those infrequent visits to the epiphanies of my past, it is simple curiosity, I know, which takes me there. Curiosity and not some re-realization of an epiphany as I seek answers to any knots in the life-threads currently before me. Perhaps I might measure some growth with any new perspectives that I bring to the read, as my experiences have thickened.

But always on those occasions, I read with great care and decided detachment, for I do not wish this chapter of my lifebook to be determined consciously—or worse, completely—by any former insight. Not in that way. The experiences are there, settling in my heart and soul, but my guidepost must be that which is now before me, the present. To do otherwise would be to catch myself up in those very fears of change that I have recently noted as one of the driving inspirations of our enemies in Menzoberranzan.

Now, though, with the dramatic changes that have swirled about me, the discovery of Callidae, the raging war in Menzoberranzan, I have changed the play. I have given myself permission to go back and read these essays, all.

Perhaps it is because of my training with Grandmaster Kane.

Perhaps it is because of transcending this mortal body.

Perhaps it is because of Callidae and the aevendrow, for in learning of them, the world has changed for me so suddenly and in so many ways.

Perhaps it is because of Brie—aye, that possibility rings most true. I will want her to read these, and hope that we will speak of them, both so that she can know me, can know her father, more completely, and because any help these might give her in finding ways to unwind her own threads would bring to me great joy.

To teach what we have learned, to share what we have come to believe, to pass on the stories that taught us . . .

That is immortality.

That is a good and comforting thought when war rages all around me, when I place my hopes against a seemingly impossible army of demons and powerful zealots.

Whatever the case, this is my life, my story, my journey, mine alone. Perhaps it is nearing the end—the fighting is all around me, ferocious and formidable.

But no, I cannot think that way, else I stop writing this tale!

So much has changed, and yet, so much has remained the same. I stayed true to that which was in my heart. Yea, I have clarified my feelings repeatedly, but the core of it all, the hopes, the desires, the truths, have remained solidly and inextricably a part of the heart of Drizzt Do'Urden.

This is my story. This is my journey.

Is that story fully told?

I think not!

There remains too much possibility, too much joy—joy that I alone can create within this life I am living, within this personal book, this lifebook, my story and mine alone that I am writing.

I will see the next sunrise until . . .

ACKNOWLEDGMENTS

Thank you, thank you, thank you to Paul Lucas and David Pom-erico for helping me to finally get this done, and to Paul Morrissey and the folks at Wizards of the Coast for letting it fly. Now is the right time for it.

My thanks to Mireya Chiriboga for your patience and attention to all the little details that make something like this work.

And a very big thank-you to Evan Winter. Writers never really know their place in the world. We hope we're writing well and doing good. The introduction for this book humbles me and makes me warm. Thank you, Evan.